SKIN DEEP

SKIN DEEP

Volume One

Eric Trujillo

To order additional copies of this book, contact:
Xlibris
844-714-8691
www.Xlibris.com
Orders@Xlibris.com
818035

SKIN DEEP

Volume One

Eric Trujillo

To order additional copies of this book, contact:
Xlibris
844-714-8691
www.Xlibris.com
Orders@Xlibris.com
818035

ABOUT THE AUTHOR

With his first novel, **JOY BOY**, Mr. Trujillo became a pioneer in a heretofore untapped literary genre, that of the gay, black, male detective. **SKIN DEEP** will not be the last.

Writer/photographer, Eric Trujillo, was born in southern Louisiana and educated in Louisiana and Mexico City. He speaks English and Spanish fluently and three other languages with varying degrees of fluency.

He worked for thirty years in various investigative positions, including twenty-two years with the Illinois Department of Children and Family Services (DCFS), several of which were in the Uptown area of Chicago, where *JOY BOY,* his first novel, took place.

After retirement, he returned to, and currently lives, in swampy southern Louisiana, where this novel, *SKIN DEEP*, takes place.

Mr. Trujillo is the father of Jared, an attorney, his pride and joy.

Mr. Trujillo is also a fine arts photographer, specializing in flower portraits, landscapes, and the nude male.

A canophile, Mr. Trujillo has never met a dog he did not love but his special love is for standard poodles, which he has owned, bred, and shown.

Throughout his life, he has had seventeen (and counting), of which, Leo, a black male, is currently his only roommate. The others are always in my heart.

DEDICATION

This book is dedicated to the victims of hate and of the Middle Passage; both those who made it across and those who did not. To the victims of slavery, Jim Crow, and the everyday racism that still persists in present-day America.

To the victims of homo-odio who have been persecuted from time immemorial in almost every country on the planet for being who they are and loving whom they were designed by Nature to love.

To the Black Bourgeoisie as it existed in 1950s and '60s Louisiana, when I was growing up. They lined the barbed wire of segregation and restriction with velvet and circled around us like a herd of musk oxen with horns down and pointing outward to protect us youngsters from the ugly realities of the world around us.

They helped us understand that, despite the restrictions we faced, there was nothing we could not accomplish. They taught us to believe in ourselves and to strive to reach the top.

To my son, Jared. I did the best I could for you, and my sister, Iris S. who takes my ribbing in stride and gives as well as she gets.

To my oldest unbroken friendship, Carol Simmons, a honky-tonk girl in spirit if not in practice. True friendship does not know color.

In loving memory of my parents, the two tigers who protected and shielded me from all of the dangers that could befall a gay black, boy in 1950s Louisiana.

It is also dedicated to my two good friends who entered the year 2021 in good health but did not exit it alive, Mr. Christopher Todd Trant, and Mr. Russell Joseph Crochet, for whom race, color, class, age, and sexual orientation did not exist. *Requiescat in pace.*

ALSO BY THIS AUTHOR:

ACKNOWLEDGEMENTS

My heartfelt thanks to two of the world's true living angels, Mrs. Bonnie B. Martiny for her insightful suggestions regarding the course of my novel and for all of her help and support, and Ms. Eileen Augustine, who gave up many of her nights and weekends to sit with a dying friend without complaint when his own family could not be bothered. Greater love hath no woman (or man)!

I'm a Luddite. I'd still be writing with pen and paper, were not for Bonnie's computer help. Or maybe on an old Underwood.

I owe a huge debt of gratitude to Mr. Russell Crochet for his help with Cajun French and rural Louisiana Cajun life but he died too soon. I would especially thank him for suggesting the name of the settlement, *"Toe-Toe Town,"* which really exists in unincorporated Assumption Parish, Louisiana. Sleep on, my brother. May you rest in peace!

Mrs. Murielle Pierre-Louis also helped me with some of my French language quandaries. *Merci, beaucoup, Madame la Comtesse!*

Mr. Milton Wayne Franklin provided me with honest critiques of the excerpts I sent him. His opinions helped me keep my perspective. His insights helped me understand that the poor come in all races and colors and that poor whites are in the same predicament as poor blacks.

Also by Eric Trujillo

JOY BOY

Alex Ashby, a drop-dead gorgeous 22-year old male prostitute, incarcerated In Chicago's Cook County Jail accused of three murders he did not commit, tells his life story to an African-American investigative reporter at one of Chicago's three major newspapers.

The reporter is the only person who believes that Alex did not commit the murders and sets out to find the real killer, who is known by the other hustlers as THE NIGHT CRAWLER.

Alex Ashby tells a horrendous story of a childhood of severe physical and sexual abuse by his father and uncle while the reporter, with the help of Alex's friend, Tom Pappas, trolls the depth of Chicago's seedy Uptown neighborhood where many white Southerners have settled, trying to find, not only the killer, but the only witness to the crime, a 12-year old male hustler, and is quickly drawn into a nether world of murder and child-selling, and taken on the ride of his life in the infamous Uptown street known as Blood Alley, where even angels fear to tread.

COMING SOON

EXCERPTS OF REVIEW OF

JOY BOY

A NOVEL BY ERIC TRUJILLO
By
Bertha Jackson, Bookshelves Moderator, Online Book Club
(18, Sept., 2021)

JOY BOY by Eric Trujillo has many positives and negative aspects. Eric Trujillo did an excellent job with character development....Many of the characters are hillbillies and the author uses that dialect throughout the book.

The book is written in the first tense from the investigative reporter's perspective and flows smoothly between the investigation and his interviews with Alex (the Mississippi hustler accused of killing three people, two prominent Chicagoans and a pizza boy). I liked that the author used italics and bold print to emphasize some of the events in the book...

I was emotionally affected by the debauchery, physical and sexual abuse, murder, drug abuse, bigotry, discrimination, and racism in this book....I would have preferred that he (author) had left something to the reader's imagination.

The scenes where young boys are raped or willingly participated in sexual activities were disturbing because they were graphic. This criticism is subjective because it is my personal preference for books. Having said this, I do believe readers need to be aware of this content.

To be objective and fair, I rate this book 4 out of 4 stars because the positive aspects outweigh the negative.

I recommend this book to mature adult readers who want to understand more about sex trafficking or sexual abuse of young boys. I recommend that sensitive readers not read this book because there is gory content involving murders and rape....

{NOTE: The author worked for 22 years as a sex abuse investigator for the Illinois Department of Children and Family Services and 8 years as an investigator of discrimination for the Illinois Department of Human Rights. Most of what he wrote is based on first or second-hand knowledge}

OTHER REVIEWS

"I was attracted by the cover and title of the book and after reading and I'm not disappointed at all. The book discussed many important issues which should be addressed in this world."
By Rishi, 23 Nov 2021

"I appreciate the author's bringing up the issues which mostly get (over) shadowed or suppressed."
By Priya Singh 24 Sep, 2021.

I loved read(ing) this book...to know more about how the author tackled the issue."
By Elisa Joy Ocasla, 25 Sep, 2021

"The book is a good one."
By Nazzy, 02 Oct 2021

"Your review made me ask a whole lot of questions about the book. I can't wait to satisfy my curiosity. I'm reading this book next."
By Elendu Ekechukwu, 19 Oct 2021

"From the cover, it's a colorful book written in a great descriptive style. Awesome."
By Humera955, 07 Oct 2021

"Fantastic book. Written about something most of us know nothing about and don't want to know anything about. These themes the author writes about are universal and right under our noses like rats and roaches. They only come out in the dark of night."
By R. C448, 01, 2020

FOREWORD

It's my turn to hurl yet another brick at the wall of American racism/classism/ homo-odio/colorism, and all of the other *"isms"* that make up this land of ours.

Ideally, I'd like to hurl the brick and hide my hand because I have never been very confrontational. At this stage of my life, I feel completely inadequate to confront this giant but the older I am, the more I feel compelled to try. I am alone, old, and relatively defenseless. Vulnerable.

Hell, I don't even know if I am up against one giant with many heads or many giants, each carrying a huge cudgel with which it can smash me to bits, as it has so many others.

The Bible would have us believe that when David confronted Goliath, he felt completely qualified; completely adequate, and completely competent in the battle. But I'll bet that that boy was shaking in his sandals!

The entire Israelite army was standing there in battle gear, ready for a fight. How did they choose a mere boy, a shepherd, not even a soldier, to go up against the entire Philistine army and its secret weapon, a giant named Goliath?

Did he lose at Rock-Paper-Scissors or did someone really*, really* hate David and pushed him forward with a simple challenge: *"I'll bet you can't fell that giant, David!"*

All David had was a slingshot and a pile of stones against one of the dominant forces of his time.

All I have is a pile of words. Stories that I can tell to try to get my point across.

I attempted to do this in my first novel, *JOY BOY*, but I was preaching to the choir. The message was lost on those who refused to read it because it contained such issues as rape, lynching, child physical and sexual abuse, murder, male prostitution, human trafficking, and gay characters.

One CIS ("straight," for us old-timers) male I know told me he would not read *JOY BOY* because of the title and because there was a picture of a handsome, shirtless young man on the cover. He said he would be embarrassed to be seen reading a book with that picture and title. Still, those were the only "stones" I had to hurl and that was the only story I had to tell.

I am up at bat again with *SKIN DEEP* and although the message is the same, it is more in-depth. I think it will be well-received by those who actually read it but it, too, will probably also be lost on those too timid to pick it up.

As Popeye used to say, ***"I AM WHO I AM AND THAT'S ALL WHO I AM!"*** And the stories I write are my only weapons against injustice and small-mindedness while simultaneously trying to entertain. I don't want to preach to anyone or become too didactic.

This country needs to realize that not all eyes are blue, not all hair is blond, not all skin is white, and not all love is heterosexual and that those of us who do not fit those criteria also have value, relevant stories to tell, and full lives to live.

Those of the racial, religious, and gender majorities should revel in the opportunity to see the world through different eyes, to *"take a walk on the wild side,"* so to speak, and live vicariously in someone else's skin for a few hundred pages. Maybe they will learn empathy for others.

Isn't that the primary purpose of reading?

CHAPTER ONE

The Story Ends

Skylarville, LA.
Summer, 1978

"Listen you faggots, I'll tell you-all for the last time. We. Are. *Not.* Niggers!" he growled through clenched teeth, tossing the bound document and the draft of the magazine I had given to him onto the coffee table that separated us from him.

He pointed the gun at me. "He's a nigger! I'm not, and neither is my family. I'm tired of people saying that about us! We're as *white* as…." He looked around, trying to find a comparison. His eyes were slits with the "come-hither" looks of a king cobra's. I was already ruled out. Andy was as dark as he was, and he considered the other two "white trash," which, in his mind, was as bad, if not worse than being black. There was no worthy comparison he could come up with.

"*George Washington!*" he finally said. "*Burn that!*" he growled, pointing to the portfolio.

He emphasized each word as if it were a complete sentence and glared at us as if we were vermin. His ruddy face had turned puce. His nostrils flared out like those of a fighting bull. His mouth hung open like a broken screen door with spittle spraying from it like the spray from Old Faithful. His beautiful green eyes, now red and half-lidded, had darkened to resemble twin turds in a dirty toilet.

He paused for a second, looked us over like used cars he had no intention of buying, and aimed it at us.

"I'm sick of this shit! Sick of you two," he said, *pointing at Andy and me,* *"making unannounced visits, accusing me and my family of being niggers, and my son of being not only a faggot, but a rapist!"* He looked again at Andy, snorted, and continued, *"as if he'd lower himself to rape the likes of you!*

*"I'm tired of being accused of doing something I have no knowledge of or interest in; and these **other** two dropping by as if we were old friends, bringing their porgy stink and swamp weeds into my house!*

*"**Somebody's** gonna die tonight!"* He now spoke calmly but emphatically. He looked us over carefully, as if choosing vegetables for tonight's salad.

*"Eenie, meenie, miney, **Moe!***
*Catch... **a nigger....**by the **toe!***
*When he hollers, let him **go!***
Eenie.........Meeeenie..............Miiiiiney......... Moe!
Die, Nigger!"

Just my luck!!

The vicious orange, yellow, and crimson sparks spewed forth from the barrel of the gun like curses from a madman's mouth.

I didn't even have time to blink before the bullet tore into me but in my mind, everything slowed almost to a standstill.

I heard the ear-splitting report and I smelled the acrid odor of the cordite as it issued forth into the room. I could "see" the bullet as it flew toward me. Although it traveled at terminal velocity, I felt as though I could have plucked it out of the air as it inched its way toward me.

I was so surprised he had actually pulled the trigger that even if it were not traveling at warp speed, I would have been too stunned to move. And who has ever dodged a speeding bullet besides Superman? And he ain't real!

I watched it in horror and fascination as it spiraled closer and closer like a tiny football. Things like that just don't happen to people like me.

I remember thinking of the *Superman* television series my brothers and I used to watch when we were kids. *"Faster than a speeding bullet,"* the announcer always said. *Is this as fast as he actually flew?* I asked myself. *If this is it, the only person he's fooling is himself. My granddad can move faster than that!!*

I felt the bullet's hot tip as it seared my clothing and punctured skin, bone, and internal organs. It felt as if someone had stabbed me in the chest with a hot poker! I remember falling forward. I dropped down to the floor like a hard-working piece of lint. I felt my body thud against the huge brass and glass coffee table on the way down, scattering the magnificent, hand-carved gold and lacquer chess pieces that sat untouched atop it on a board made of semi-precious stones, but it was just the dull recognition that living flesh had hit a breakable, stationary object.

I also felt the shards of thick glass as they entered my body in about a hundred places, tearing my new linen shirt to shreds, but instead of pain, I only felt a cool, crispness as I slid toward the parquet floor and I thought to myself, *I'm going to bleed all over his expensive Aubusson rug. It serves him right!* The lights went out. All sounds ended. I was at peace.

I asked myself, *am I dead?*

I felt myself lift up out of my body and float away. I was exhausted. I was more tired than I had ever been in my life. This fatigue was because I had spent what felt like an eternity struggling to shed my outer shell; my body. My old self.

I now knew how a newly-emerged butterfly feels when it sheds the cocoon or a newly-hatched chick when it finally pecks its way out of its shell. I was so very tired, with no more will to struggle left. I only wanted to rest.

I looked around but I could not, or did not want to see if my other self, my original shell, was lying on Senator Catash's floor as I headed toward wherever souls go after departing the only world they knew. As for the proverbial White Light everybody talks about, I missed it. I felt, rather than saw, everything around me.

When I did look down to where my temporal shell lay like a discarded tampon, my only thoughts were: *"this is really wild! I just shed my body like a snake sheds its skin. That's not me lying there.* ***I'm too young to die!!!!***

I was tired so I closed my eyes…and rested.

***

When I opened them again, I was on the deck of an old-fashioned wooden ship in the middle of a great body of water. There was no sign of land.

I had no idea of how I had gotten there or where I had been before popping up on the ship. It was disorienting, to say the least. Sort of like waking up in a different bed from the one in which you had gone to sleep.

The ship looked like one of Columbus' ships, the *Niña, the Pinta,* or the *Santa María,* or maybe the *Mayflower,* the *Golden Hind*, the *Bounty,* or any number of other ships that had been launched from seaports throughout Europe over a two or three hundred year period.

As a kid, I loved to read about the ships used by the early invaders of the Americas, Africa, Asia, and all of the islands between them. The history books called that era the Age of Discovery. I called it the Age of Invasion. While I was no fan of Pizarro, Cook, Columbus, Cortez, Hudson, or any of the other money-hungry bastards who left Europe for unknown worlds, I was definitely a fan of the fantastic sailing vessels they built in order to accomplish the task.

I was not sure if I was standing on the deck of a carrack or a caravel and it really didn't matter. What mattered was the fact that I was the only one there. There was no one at the helm or in the crow's nest, and no one manning the riggings or the cannons that lined the ship's sides. Their tompions were still in place.

Where was I, and how did I get to …wherever this was? My senses told me that wherever I was, it was a real place, not a dream. I could hear the riggings as they groaned in the wind.

I could see the gigantic main mast made from one solid spruce tree as big around as six of me, and its smaller sister masts, the foremast and the mizzen mast. The first two carried one large sail, two smaller ones, and one pennant each. The mizzen carried a lateen sail. In addition, there was a small sail, the sprit sail, attached to the bowsprit. It was furled but the others were open and full.

I could feel the ship as it dipped and plowed its way through the crests and troughs of the rough sea, yet it was completely yare, and I could taste the ocean spray it spit up and over the deck.

From my history books and in the authentic replicas I had made, I remembered seeing large crosses or other decorations on the sails of ships from the Age of Invasion but these sails were pristine.

Also missing were the colorful flags and pennants that proclaimed the country or ruler under whose auspices they sailed. It was as if this particular ship was announcing that it was owned by no one and owed allegiance to no one.

Directly above me, I could see the crow's nest, surrounded by the braided rope ladders crew members would have used to reach it. It now sat abandoned. Empty. As if the baby birds had fledged and their parents had moved on.

I could hear the groaning of the thick hemp ropes that lashed the sails to the riggings as they struggled to keep the wind from tearing the sails from their grasp, and I could hear the creaking of the wide oaken planks as they played their part in the intricate ballet of wind and water; dry and wet; life and death.

I could also hear the sea gulls cawing and see them flapping their wings as they landed or took to the air from the yardarms, and their larger cousins, the giant albatrosses, who floated lazily nearby but never seemed to land.

And I could smell the salty sea air and feel the fine brass fittings and the square-headed iron nails that held everything together. The brass had been polished to a high shine and gleamed in the early morning sunlight.

Cannons lined each side of the deck with their cannonballs stacked in neat black pyramids alongside, held in by low wooden corrals. Attending them were untapped powder kegs and lengths of corded fuse line, coiled like a Wyoming cowboy's lariat.

Barrels of fruit, salted fish, rum, and fresh water also lined the deck, lashed together like sacrificial virgins to prevent their being washed overboard by a large wave or the rolling of the ship. A heavy iron anchor lay nearby, attended by its neatly coiled rope. Everything was shipshape, *but there was no crew!*

I felt as if I had stepped into a stranger's unlocked home while the owner was away, as in the story of *"Goldilocks and the Three Bears,"* but unlike Goldilocks, I did not want to disturb anything or leave any trace of my ever having been there. I needed help. I needed answers but there was no one to provide them.

I looked toward the helm, one deck above me. It held steady, guided by some unseen hand. It was amazingly yare for a ship without a helmsman.

I took a seat on the steps of one of the twin "Jacob's ladders" that climbed from the main deck to the bridge of the ship on both sides. This seat gave me a direct view of the ship from all angles; bow to stern and from port to starboard.

I kept a close eye on the ship from the fo'c's'le to the aftcastle and I was determined to sit there and wait until someone appeared or the ship ran aground.

Fifteen or so minutes later, a door opened directly below the bridge, near where I sat. From it, a solemn procession of ten or so shabbily-dressed men appeared from below deck, led by a bell-ringer who shouted something in a loud voice in a language I could not understand.

Behind him, black-clad mourners cried loudly and rent their garments. Following them was a handsome young man with coal-black ringlets that hung to just above his shoulders and came down to just over his eyes. The curls danced and jounced around in the heavy sea wind. This man appeared to have been freshly scrubbed and neatly clothed, in sharp contrast to the other crew members.

The young man was dressed entirely in black. He was athletically built, darkly tanned, and had the most beautiful eyes, the color of amethysts. He appeared to look directly at me but did not take notice of my presence.

Behind him, a larger group of approximately twenty men appeared, led by a rag-tag crew of six, who carried on a makeshift litter what appeared to be a human form wrapped from head to toe in canvas and bound tightly by heavy cord.

The last man in this larger procession was maybe a priest or some other type officiant- but not of any religion with which I was familiar. He was dressed in a black surplice with three broad white vertical stripes down the front, giving him the appearance of a gigantic magpie.

On his head, he wore a high black miter trimmed in gold that kept blowing away in the strong winds that buffeted the ship. In the hand not used for keeping the miter on his head, he carried a thick black book. On the forefinger of each pudgy hand, he wore large red-stoned gold rings.

The men laid the litter next to an anchor and backed respectfully away, bowing their heads and forming a semi-circle around the priest, the cadaver, and the young man in black.

The priest finally gave up keeping the miter on his head and handed it to one of the pallbearers to hold for him. He read from the book he carried, anointing the canvas covering the body with oils from small vials he fished from his large appliquéd pockets while the young man in black looked stoically on.

The last item he took from his pocket was a large, crudely-made wooden square that was diagonally intersected by a thin piece of wood that, in effect, divided the square into two right triangles.

He broke the square at the intersecting line and gave one of the two resulting triangles to the young man in black. He placed the other atop the cadaver and then handed the young man in black a piece of what appeared to me to be leather cord. The young man accepted the cord and attached it to the triangle he had inherited, tied the ends together, and looped it around his neck.

He then bent down to where the corpse lay and did the same, attaching the triangle that had been placed there by the priest to the corpse's chest.

That done, the other crew members moved forward to bid farewell to their departed friend. All shed copious tears as they paid their respects. Some laid flowers on the shroud while others pinned money to it, but the majority appeared to attach personal items or notes and letters to the canvas covering.

Most kissed their fingertips and placed a kiss on the shroud after leaving their offering. A final prayer was said and when that was over, two of the crewmen weighed down the body with iron chains and gently pushed it into the sea.

Most of the men wiped away tears from their eyes. Some cried silently while others wailed loudly, blowing their noses noisily on their sleeves or on dirty handkerchiefs they fished from their pockets.

The man with the violet eyes said nothing the entire time. He stood and watched the ceremony, the final farewells, and the disposal of the body over the side of the ship, into the sea.

When all was done, most of the crewmen hugged him in tight, sincere embraces while others shook his hand or patted him on the back in sympathy. He received their words of comfort with a pained expression. Tears flooded down his cheeks. He made no effort to hide them or to wipe them away.

Eventually the other men drifted away, returning below deck through the same door from which they had come, leaving the young man and the priest alone on the deck.

I was too far away to hear any of the words they had uttered but the young man knelt before the older man, bowing his head respectfully.

The officiant placed his left hand on the young man's bowed head and, with his right, scooped another vial from his pocket, uncorked it with his teeth, and poured a tiny amount of the neon-green liquid within onto the young man's head, making what appeared to be signs of faith.

That finished, the younger man stood and they embraced. The younger man returned to the rail where the body had been pushed into the sea.

In one fluid, elegant motion, he picked up a nearby cannonball for ballast, jumped the rail, and threw himself into the sea, leaving the officiant stunned, his thin lips making a great "O."

***

Apparently I blinked again, though I did not remember doing so, for I now found myself on a narrow dirt trail. There were no footprints to tell me if it had been made by humans or animals. The air was cool and still. There was no sound of birds or insects. By the position of the pale twin suns and the still-evident moon, I reckoned it to be early morning.

Tall grass surrounded me on all sides for as far as I could see. The grass was taller than me by several feet. I stand over six-and-a-half feet tall and this grass was way over my head. It reached maybe ten or fifteen feet in height and was topped by blond tassels that looked like the tails of palomino ponies. The stalks looked strange, too. They were frilly, soft, and dark, dark green like giant carrot tops.

Up until now, the tallest grass I had ever seen was the sugar cane of my native Louisiana, and that of coastal Mexico, but this was much taller.

I started down the trail, to my left. I walked for a bit and found nothing but more grass and the trail continuing off to who-knows-where but getting smaller and narrower as I went. I came across several intersecting trails and pathways but they were smaller and looked seldom-used.

I walked for a while and returned to the spot where I first "appeared" in this place. I decided to sit and make a plan.

I recognized the spot where I had first appeared because the grass along the side of the pathway had been flattened by the weight of my body. It was incredibly soft and pliable. I decided to make this my starting point for any future expeditions. If need be, I could plait the grass into any number of things, ranging from a rug to a hammock. I decided I would now walk toward the right for five or ten minutes and see if I could find anybody or anything.

Before I could carry out this plan, however, I heard something or someone thrashing through the grass, coming from my right in the distance down the path.

At first I was elated. People! Maybe they could tell me where I was and explain how I'd gotten here. Maybe they could help get me back to someplace familiar-- but if I was starting from a place with twin suns, I doubted it.

They walked swiftly and in tandem, talking in low voices and only occasionally.

I could not make out the language but I knew that there were at least two, and possibly three of them. Or one crazy person with several personalities talking to himself. I always try to keep a sense of humor regardless of the situation. It helps.

One had a high-pitched laugh. All of them were male. I decided to wait for them along the side of the trail.

I tried to use the time prior to their arrival at my resting place to make myself presentable to them. I dusted off my clothes, buttoned buttons, and tucked in my shirt tail.

They rounded a bend in the path and I saw them for the first time. **PILGRIMS!!!** Or somebody dressed like America's Puritan forefathers with the dark clothing, wide, white collars, funny hats, and buckles on their shoes. One carried what appeared to be a wooden shovel about three feet tall. The others carried blunderbusses and stout walking sticks.

They moved along the path at a fast clip. I still could not make out the language but when they got to within two or three yards of me, I stepped out onto the path and said in a loud, commanding voice, "Excuse me, gentlemen, could you help me…."

They took no notice of me, continuing on their way like a fast-moving passenger train. Had I not jumped off to one side of the path, they would have plowed right into me.

I followed them, beating with fists on the last man's shoulder, but got no response. To them, I did not exist.

My first thought was that they were re-enactors like the kind one sees in Colonial Williamsburg or Plimoth Plantation, where the actors remain in character but interact with the paying public. These people, however, took no notice of me at all.

They continued on for a few hundred yards and then turned off the main trail to one of the smaller, intersecting trails, and to a copse of tall, old trees. These trees were even taller than the grass, reaching up as high as six or seven story buildings. The ground around the copse had been cleared except for some stumps of felled trees.

One man stood guard while the other two found private spots, laid their blunderbusses and walking sticks against a tree or stump, pulled down their pantaloons and copious undergarments, and proceeded to squat and defecate.

The numerous flies and other shit-eating bugs told me that this place was dedicated to that purpose. I stepped upwind a few yards and waited for them to finish.

When the two were finished, they changed positions. Two stood guard while the third man completed his "business." That finished, they stepped out into the clearing and away from the smell. They gathered in a circle and played a quick game of *Rock, Paper, Scissors.* The loser frowned, lowered his head, and whined something in their language that indicated to me that he was not happy about the outcome.

The lead man handed him the wooden shovel. He returned to the copse, dug three holes, and shoveled spades-full of dirt over their leavings, then returned a few minutes later, wiping his hands on his pantaloons.

When they had finished, they bowed their heads, folded their hands, and prayed together. At the finish of the prayer, each said something that sounded like "Go men!"

I was close enough to them to notice that they still reeked from their morning evacuations. I don't know what they had used to wipe themselves but it certainly wasn't Charmin.

Upon finishing their morning prayer, each pulled out a long-stemmed clay pipe, stuffed them with greenish-brown leaves from pouches they carried on their belts, and sat down under one of the enormous trees for a smoke.

I cleared my throat. "Excuse me, gentlemen," I began, most civilly. "I'm lost. Could you tell me where I am and direct me to a phone?"

No one moved. They took no notice of me and continued smoking their pipes, as peaceful as recently-fed felines. They seemed content to be there, smoking their pipes, their bowels and bladders relieved.

I approached to within feet, then inches of their unseeing eyes, touched each of them on the shoulder, face, or back. When that did not work, I touched each in that most private area. None even flinched. I then slapped one of them across the face and again, got no reaction whatsoever.

There was only one possible answer. *I really was dead!!* What other answer could there be?

The men finished their smoke, stood, and readied themselves for the return trip to wherever they'd come from. *I'll follow them,* I thought. *At least I won't be out here alone.*

The oldest man, a redhead with very pale skin, freckles, chicken lips, and pale blue eyes; who appeared to be in his early 30's, said something to them in a language that was close enough to English that I could *almost* understand it—but not quite.

The others nodded their heads, stood, and stretched their lean bodies like cats in the sunshine. One by one, in the same order in which they had arrived, they headed back up the path, never acknowledging me or my plea for help.

I followed them closely at first. Despite their clumsy footwear, these fellows moved fast, taking the long strides of those accustomed to walking great distances.

Before long, I was falling back, getting winded, as they continued on. Do dead people need oxygen?

I had always considered myself in excellent shape. There was not an ounce of fat on me. I swam daily, worked out on a regular basis at the health club in my condo complex, and I played racquetball at least twice a week but these men were pulling away from me fast. I needed to speed walk to catch up while they, on the other hand, hardly seemed winded.

By and by, we entered the gate of a high palisade surrounding a settlement that included about a dozen houses, a church, and several other buildings whose uses I was not able to discern. Almost everything was tree-bark brown and colorless. No one noticed me and surely, if I were visible, they would have said something. I was a tall black petunia in a field of white calla lilies.

If this was a re-enactment, I thought, it was extremely authentic, right down to the smells of infrequently washed bodies and the stench of domestic animals living a bit too closely to humans. Mud and slop clogged the walkways and thoroughfares. Only a few homes had stone pathways leading up to them. Only a few had flowers or other signs of human beautification attempts.

Barnyard and household animals ran untended behind the stockade. Other, larger animals that looked like yak but with the tough gray skin of elephants that hung almost down to the ground in deep leathery folds, were tethered behind some of the houses or corralled behind neat fences in other houses, or hobbled behind broken-down or non-existent fences in still others.

In the center of the compound, near the church and beneath a lovely elm tree, the only tree I could recognize, a haggard woman stood pilloried and miserable while a group of four or five boys of various ages stood nearby, taunting her and throwing rocks and vegetables at her head.

A small chestnut-colored ram with long, spiral-shaped horns, golden eyes, and a big black spot on its back, chewed on the hem of her dress where she had soiled herself. A pre-pubescent girl attempted to shoo it away to no avail and to the girl's consternation. I assumed the girl and a tow-headed boy, around four or five, were her children. They looked almost as miserable as she did.

There was a wooden bucket half full of tea-colored water on the ground in front of the infernal contraption and a boldly-lettered sign around the woman's neck in a language I could not decipher.

The whole scene was surreal and much too authentic to be a re-enactment.

The men took leave of one another, using brief nods and short, clipped waves of their hands. Each started off in a different direction.

I followed the last man in the procession, who appeared to be the youngest, to a low, thatch-roofed hut, made of wattle and daub, at the intersection of what appeared to be the main street and a smaller cobbled courtyard.

The man took off his heavy wooden shoes before he entered the main room of the hut, leaving them on the stoop. Upon entering, he hung his large Pilgrim-style hat with its brass buckle, on a peg next to the door.

He then took from his pocket some unused dried corn cobs of the type he had used to wipe himself after toileting. *That must hurt,* I thought.

The man put them into a wooden pail that contained approximately two dozen similar cobs in a corner near the room's front window. He used a large flat rock that looked like a piece of slate except for its bright orange color, to serve as a top to the pail, effectively covering the pile.

A large rat ran from behind the pail where the corn cobs had been stored. But for the bright neon-blue colored feathers on the tail and the emerald color of its naked body, it looked exactly like its brothers back on earth. The man picked up the flat orange slate-like rock he had used to cover the corn cobs and threw it at the animal. He missed and the animal stood on its two hind legs, hissed, and bared its long, sharp yellow teeth before it dashed through a hole in the side of the hut to the adjacent courtyard.

Through the open window, I could see several shaggy animals of various sizes and colors that barked like dogs but skittered along on a multitude of legs like giant millipedes, give chase to the rat as it made a mad dash for the palisade and the safety beyond.

The man looked at the hole through which the rat-like animal had escaped, muttered something in his native tongue, kicked at the hole, and then turned his attention to the spectacle of rat-like animal versus whatever the hell those other things were.

He smiled, yelled something that sounded like words of encouragement to the multi-pedes and then turned to a stoneware wash basin on a spindly-legged wooden washstand below the room's side window.

From a matching pitcher cradled in the basin, he poured lime-colored water into the basin. Here, he washed his face and hands and dried them on a coarse white cloth towel on the stand's towel rack.

He then took off his outer shirt, revealing a smooth, well-muscled, nearly hairless, pasty-white chest beneath a course, off-white linen undershirt. The trail of hair that began sparsely just above the belly-button and thickened below it, was the color of copper.

He chose a well-worn black book from a high wooden shelf on the wall. The word *"SAMKTUM BYBL"* was written in large gold Gothic letters on its cover and spine.

The gold leafing that had once limned the pages was now faint from years of handling by coarse, damp hands. He seated himself in a straight-backed wooden chair painted a muddy brown near the window and bowed his head to read.

I sat on the bed in the opposite corner of the room, trying to figure out where I was and what I needed to do to get back to somewhere familiar to me.

I must have dozed off while sitting on the bed, my back against the wall, because when I awoke, the twin suns were casting long shadows against the wall and into the room.

"Welcome, Traveler," said a deep, male voice that sounded soothing, sensuous and friendly. A man had appeared at a side window that looked out onto the courtyard. He beckoned me out of the hut.

The homeowner appeared to be reading, unperturbed, but he had dozed off in his chair. The book he had been reading now lay sprawled on the floor in front of him.

Leaving the hut through the open Dutch door, I was only too happy to greet the handsome, tawny-skinned young man about my own age, who had beckoned to me. He was one of the sexiest men I had ever met.

The man stood in the courtyard smiling, arms akimbo, giving me the once-over while I eyed him back. *This place might not be so bad after all*, I thought.

He wore an embroidered cotton tunic open at the throat from which tumbled a copious amount of black, curly chest hair. Over it, he wore a black leather jerkin. Black leather pants, black leather boots that folded down in a large cuff just below the knee. A small golden loop in his left ear completed the outfit. The whole ensemble was reminiscent of an eighteenth century pirate. The only items missing were the eye patch, the wooden leg, and the parrot on his shoulder.

His heavy curls were capped off by the tooled leather skullcap he sported and a Van Dyke beard and mustache through which even white teeth shone. He had the most beguiling violet eyes.

"I spotted you when you came into the village with some of the men," he smiled, looking at me the way a fat man eyes a Snickers bar. "I've been waiting for you. Who are you? Where did you come from?"

"You've been waiting for me yet you don't know who I am or where I'm from?"

The man smiled that beguiling smile of his and nodded. "I don't know how I know that you're who I've been waiting for but I know," he continued.

My name's Steve," I answered, extending my hand and advancing toward the ersatz pirate. "Stephen Wayne Mallory," I continued, returning the lustful gaze and not trying too hard to disguise my full-fledged excitement, which was pulling me toward him like an unruly dog straining on a very short leash. "Am I dead?"

"You look *very* much alive to me," he said, eyeing my crotch. "No one is going to convince that monster that you're dead. Pretty impressive."

I moved closer toward him with both my hand and my cock outstretched toward him.

The man jumped back as if poked by a cattle prod. "You're a newbie," he smiled, wagging his forefinger at me. "Rule Number One: Never, *EVER* touch any other Voyager."

"What's a Voyager?" I inquired,

"That's my name for people who suddenly pop up here every now and then," he replied. "I don't know where they come from or where they go when they leave here but I assume that they came from somewhere and that they go on to somewhere else. That's why I call them 'voyagers.' Travelers. Transients. It's all the same. They come and they go. Some stay for a while and others come and go immediately."

I shook my head, confused. "How can you see me when nobody else around here can?" I lowered my hand but my cock remained at full staff, bulging against my underpants like a rodeo bull in the chute, ready to be released from its tight confinement. "Am I dead?" I asked again. "This can't possibly be real."

"I'm Simon," the man said, nodding his head toward me in lieu of a handshake. This Gypsy-dark man was half a head shorter than me and very squarely built, like a wrestler. He was broad of shoulder and narrow at the waist. Every inch of his body was muscle.

"To answer your question about being dead or not," Simon said simply, "I don't know, but I don't think so. When I get too cold, I shiver. When I get too warm, I sweat. When I get hungry, I eat. I drink when I get thirsty and when it's time to eliminate, I do that, too." He paused for a beat or two and then said, "And I'm always horny so when I have to…take care of that, I do, too. Alone, if you know what I mean."

I nodded and smiled knowingly. "How'd I get here?" I asked instead of inquiring about his sex life.

"I don't even know how *I* got here," Simon replied. "One minute, I was playing basketball with a group of friends and then I was here. I call us 'Voyagers,'" he said, "because we come and we go.

"I guess I've been here about a year and in that time, I've seen a lot of us lost souls—Voyagers—come and go. Some have stayed for weeks or even months. Others have been here for a few hours or less. It's not so bad but it's lonely. I know all of the people here. They can't see me but they're like old friends now.

"Where'd you meet Johannes, Brutus, and Pieter? Do you know where you came from?"

"I was born on earth. In Louisiana, but I know we're not on earth now, are we?"

The man smiled. "I was born in Louisiana, too. Where in Louisiana were you born? North or south Louisiana?"

"South," I said, "Near New Orleans. This is a nightmare," I continued, "To wake up and find you're way, way out of your element and far, far away from home with no idea as to how you got here or why."

He nodded sympathetically but said nothing as I continued.

"It was like you said, first I was 'somewhere else' and then I was here. I was on an old Spanish galleon. At least, I *think* it was Spanish. It looked like the ones I used to have to draw and color around Columbus Day when I was in grade school. You know, with the big sails, the high fore- and after decks, cannons, and stuff like that.

"I guess it also could've been English, like the Mayflower, or Dutch or Portuguese but it's from around that time period, anyway. All I know is there was a funeral in progress when I got there. At the end of the funeral, after they'd prayed and consigned the body to the sea, this guy…" I started to say, *who looked a lot like you* but changed my mind, "jumped overboard after the body."

Simon winced but, again, said nothing.

"I didn't try to talk to anybody but I was seated on a ladder that went from the main deck to a higher deck, watching the proceedings and although several of the men appeared to be looking right at me, none seemed to *see* me.

"I guess they were below deck getting ready for the funeral when I first appeared. Before I could even try to communicate with them, this guy jumped overboard. I had no idea of how I got there, and then I was *here* without the faintest clue as to how I got here!

"I just popped up on the trail. I heard those guys coming and I tried to introduce myself and ask for help but they didn't hear or see me. I could see and hear them though. I take it they don't believe in circumcision here," I smiled.

He smiled back but did not answer.

"They did their morning business, had a smoke, said a prayer, and when they started back up the trail, I followed them here. Why can't they see us?"

"I wish I had some answers for you but I don't know," Simon answered. "When I got here, I looked around for some sort of Operation Manual for life on this planet but there was nothing." I didn't know if he was being sarcastic or whether this was his attempt at humor. "I've been here for what seems like ages and I don't have any more answers than you have. All I know is that you should never touch anybody."

"I touched the three guys I followed here," I said." Nothing happened then. Who's the guy in the house?"

"That was Pieter," Simon answered. "They're the Van Vlessing brothers. He's the youngest of the three. Horny little bastard, that one," Simon smiled. "He spends all of his free time either reading the Bible or choking the chicken. And the chicken gets choked a lot more often than the Bible gets read, believe me.

"I meant never touch people like us," he continued. "Other Voyagers. I once saw two Voyagers touch and they just kind of... 'exploded,'" he continued

"Exploded?" I wanted to know. "**Ka-BOOM?**"

"No," Simon said. "Not like that. More like, *'POOF!!! Twinkle-twinkle-twinkle.'* A lot of sparks and dust and pretty colors, and then they disappeared."

"So how do I know who to touch and who not to touch? All of these people seem to be blonds or red-heads and they all look Northern European," I observed. "You look Mediterranean or maybe Latino, or maybe even mulatto. Is it that: darker coloring and different style clothing?"

Simon stood back about six feet. "Look at me closely," he said. "Look closely. Then tell me what's different about me."

I definitely enjoyed the views, both front and rear. Those tight breeches left little to the imagination and that definitely wasn't a codpiece he was wearing. But, damn it! I can't touch him, anyway!

I looked at my new companion very closely, trying to raise my eyes above his waist, when suddenly I noticed it. There was a soft glow around him. Like a full-body halo, but not bright enough to really be noticeable except when one looked carefully.

"A halo?" I said. "You have a halo!"

"You have one too. I call it an aura, for lack of a better word," Simon corrected. "After you've been here a while, you'll know a Voyager when you see one."

"Maybe we *are* dead," I said.

"Maybe," Simon acceded. "Maybe we are, but this *sure* ain't heaven!"

"What about hell?" I wanted to know.

"I haven't seen any fire and brimstone," Simon smiled.

"Does this place have a name?" Steve inquired.

"Welcome to the planet Ronak in the Eleegian constellation of the Scutum Crux arm of the Milky Way galaxy.

I held up my hand for him to stop a minute to allow me to take in all of this. "What the hell is all that you said?"

He smiled patiently. "You know anything about astronomy?"

I shook my head. "Not really," I finally said. "I can find the Big Dipper, the Little Dipper, some of the easier constellations, and the North Star, though. That's about it."

"I don't have a map of the galaxy to show you what I'm talking about but picture a pinwheel. The Milky Way galaxy is like a pinwheel. It has four arms that trail out from the central body like four spokes off the main body of the pinwheel. They're actually called arms.

"One of them is called Norma, and the others are Perseus, Sagittarius, and Scutum Crux.

"That's where *we* are now, in the Scutum Crux arm. Ronak and earth seem to be twins. Earth is just a little more advanced than Ronak in some ways. A lot less advanced in others. That's the easiest way I can describe it.

"There are millions of other planets out there. Some are more advanced than earth and some less advanced than Ronak. They're at all stages of development with new ones being born all the time. I don't know how many there are but it's probably thousands in this galaxy alone. All have carbon-based life forms. Other galaxies have their own life forms. Some may be carbon-based but who knows?

"Earth, by the way, is in the Sagittarius arm, in a little backwater called the Orion Spur. About as far away from the center of the galaxy as we are now. We're in the Wild, Wild West of the Milky Way Galaxy, where anything can and does happen," he said.

"I still can't make out their language but I'm beginning to get the hang of it. It's a lot like German or Dutch.

"This is actually one of Ronak's moons called Priapus. It's a mining, fishing, and exploration colony," he continued. "They're here to colonize this place and exploit its resources. It reminds me of the Hudson Bay Colony, the Plimouth Colony, or Jamestown.

"In this settlement, they're trying to find rare *jappelweiss* and *handack trees* and a mineral called *kroydenfelder.*

Kroydenfelder's used in expensive jewelry. Ornamentation of the ultra-rich. The *jappelweiss* is used in medicine, from what I can garner, and it's the most valuable because it's the rarest, but nobody'd throw away a handack for a jappelweiss.

"Other colonies are trying to find creatures called *hixabrodds* in the seas around here. I've seen a few of them. They look like clams or oysters, only a little bigger, and they excrete something like semen, but it's sparkly like diamonds, phosphorescent, and as fluid as mercury. The super-rich back on Ronak serve it up one drop at a time, usually in a drink. From what I've been able to gather, it's the ultimate aphrodisiac there.

"The handack tree is also *very* rare. Its fruit are about as big as kumquats and has psychedelic properties. Its bark slows down the ageing process by half, and the wood itself is beautiful and highly sought after in furnishing rich peoples' houses—like mahogany or rosewood. And the root keeps old men's dicks hard.

"It pops up fully grown overnight, lives about a week, and then it dies, leaving a sickly useless skeleton where it was once a beautiful, flourishing tree, similar to a southern magnolia but not as tall.

"It's about maybe ten feet high and about ten feet around the crown, with thick red leaves. They're beautiful. If they had the large, fragrant flowers that magnolias have, they'd be perfect.

'I guess the closest thing to it in terms of value and rarity on earth would be ginseng but only ginseng's root is valuable on earth whereas the entire handack tree is valuable here.

"The jappelweiss is sparkly silver and almost transparent. It's purely medicinal. Its bark, fruit, berries, and roots all have medicinal value. Some of the people here take tiny pieces of bark and hold it under their tongues if they're sick.

Sort of like aspirin, I guess. The berries are used to cure some illness the inhabitants of Ronak have. I guess it's like cancer on earth. The root cures mental illnesses."

"How do you know all this?" I asked.

"Observation," he smiled. "There's almost nowhere you can't go if you're invisible. I've noticed that the crews that arrive to pick up and transport the goods back to Ronak will always find room for jappelweiss. Even over handack.

"There's only one company on Ronak that handles everything on this moon. It sponsors this colony and rules with an iron fist. There are people—very rich people--who will pay fortunes for jappelweiss and handack tree products. That company is richer than General Motors, Ford, and Chrysler put together. Their profits are in the trillions of *tolern*."

I was genuinely impressed by how much he had learned since he arrived, considering he doesn't speak the language. "What's a '*tolern*'?" I wanted to know.

"It's their currency. One unit is a *toler* and more than one are *tolern*. The colonists here have wars over the jappelweiss and handack trees-- and more than a few murders. All of these colonists are out for themselves. They work alone or in teams and keep their movements and their finds closely guarded secrets. The Van Vlessing brothers are a team. They trust no one outside their family. They watch one another's backs.

"If these people can find a handack tree and cut it down before it dies—and get it to the dealer, they're instant millionaires and then they'll want to go home and spend all of that new money, but if dies before they can fell it, it's no good at all to them," he continued.

"Neither the handack nor the jappelweiss can be cultivated like pine trees, mahogany, or sugar cane on earth. The root, or whatever they grow from, is in the soil here. They just spring up whenever and wherever conditions are right. This is the only place they grow.

"Shortly after I got here, a handack sprang up right in the center of the settlement. You should've seen the mayhem as everybody tried to be the first to cut it down. Four people were killed in the fight. Man, they were hacking each other up like something out of the Middle Ages! They were using axes, hatchets, lances, swords, sticks, brooms, knives, and anything else that could draw blood. It's a good thing guns aren't allowed on Priapus or they probably would've shot one another like the Earps and the Clantons at the O.K. Corral. There was blood everywhere.

"The team of brothers and cousins named Meyerling actually got it by default. They waited until the major fighting was over and the participants were either dead, wounded, or exhausted then, when the Heidels, who won the fight were about to cut the handack down, they stepped in, beat up the Heidels, and harvested it for themselves.

"The Heidels were on the warpath after that so after the Meyerlings took it, they had to hold it. They squirreled it away somewhere and didn't bring it out again until the supply ship returned.

"It took about six months before the supply ship came back. The Meyerlings started out as a team of eleven but by the time the supply ship returned, they were down to five. The Heidels started out as eight and ended up with only two left by the time the supply ship returned.

Coincidentally, all of the Meyerling cousins were killed off and only the brothers remained alive to sell their prize to the company, make their fortune, and get the hell out of here.

"I suspect the dealer and the governor moved them to another colony, not back to Ronak because they still had some more of their contract to run before they could go back home. I don't know how long they still had but I do know that neither the company nor the governor were about to let them out of it just because of a few deaths.

"So there are other settlements on this moon," I stated more as a fact than as a question.

Simon nodded his lovely head. The big ringlets that framed his angelic face danced up and down like slow motion ballet dancers. "Priapus has about fourteen other settlements like this one scattered about its surface," he continued like an ersatz tour guide.

"Some hunt for handack trees, some dive for hixabrodds, and others mine for kroydenfelder crystals. Rich people back on Ronak will pay practically anything for any of them.

"Handack is the major export for this settlement," he continued. "I mean, they pop up anywhere and all over the surface of this moon so anybody in one of the other colonies could find a handack tree, cut it down, and sell it when the supply ship arrives and receive just as much as these people here, and these people here could possibly find kroydenfelder crystals in the hills around here but hixabrodds exist only under water so they're a specialty item.

"The people who come up here have to sign up for three-year stints. They come here, try to make a lot of money, and then return to Ronak millionaires or even *billionaires*. It's a really hard three years but if they manage to stay alive, they'll be very rich when they return to Ronak.

"Why wouldn't they stay alive for three years?" I wanted to know.

"Life's tough here. The governor and a small police force try to keep order but this is like the Wild West back home. People make their own law, despite the laws the company sets down. It's sort of like the California Gold Rush. Claim jumpers, killers, thieves, et cetera.

"People stab others in the back or poison them, or cheat them or bully them into giving up what they've worked so hard to find. The first part is to find a handack tree and the second part is keeping it safe until the ship comes.

"It's not like they can take it to the bank and deposit it. *It's a fucking tree!* A relatively big tree at that, so somebody's always looking to take advantage of someone else in any way possible.

"In addition to the competition from their fellow settlers, they have to go places that are really dangerous. The terrain is rugged so deaths from falls, explosions, being crushed in landslides or mudslides, or falling into one of the deep crevasses that scar this moon are just a few of the thousand ways to die here.

"Besides that, the bark of the handack seems to be addictive. Some people up here start using it to help them relax then they simply give up on their quest, preferring to stay inside the compound and eat or smoke it. They get these tremendous erections, and become like heroin or opium junkies back home. They can't get enough sex. Instead of searching for handack, they start searching for sexual partners. That's their quest.

"The ship from Ronak comes twice a year to supply them with the things they don't have and they send back what they've been able to find. And keep.

"There's mostly men up here but recently, they've been sending a few women and some families with children. All those erections have to go somewhere," he laughed. "They've only begun sending some of their own domestic animals, too.

"By the way, you should see the natives of this moon," he said with a wry smile. I knew something was up with that but I let it ride. He was dying to tell me about them. When I said nothing, he said, "They certainly *don't* look like anybody on earth."

"What century are we in?" I asked, waiting for him to tell me about the natives.

"Do you mean back on earth or here on Ronak?"

"Here," I replied, looking around. It looked to me like maybe the sixteenth or seventeenth century on earth but then, they were advanced enough on Ronak to be able to fly from their mother planet to their moons, something earthlings didn't accomplish until the mid-twentieth century.

"I've never been on Ronak so I can't tell you," Simon said. "I don't think you can judge by this place. I think they made it rustic for a reason and they want to keep it that way. Nobody here has photos, only drawings.

"They apparently haven't discovered the art of photography, still or motion picture, and the printing press is a recent invention, from what I can see, because books are very rare. I've only seen their Bible in printed form. Most people can't afford to own one. All other reading material, except official mandates from the company, is hand-written.

"For entertainment, when they're not in church or out hunting handack trees, they meet at the local pub and either eat handack bark in very limited quantities or drink something like beer but stronger, like ale or maybe mead.

"They also have poetry readings, plays, and concerts and they go to church *a lot*. I mean three times a week, four hours each time, from 6 p.m. to ten, and all day on their Sabbath, which is mid-week, like Wednesday, but their week has ten days, not seven.

"On Sabbath Day, they have a morning service that lasts from 9 until noon and then an afternoon service that lasts from about 2 til 5 p.m. On Sabbath Day night, they have Bible study. All are mandatory. One of the deacons goes from house to house with a roster of all inhabitants of each house before each service to ensure that *everybody* attends services. If you miss any service, you'd better have a damned good reason. Like a life-threatening illness. Otherwise, you'd end up in the stocks for a few days. Usually two for the first offense and then it's incremental after that."

"All I know," I said, "is we're certainly not in Louisiana anymore. Two pale suns that give off about as much light and heat as earth's single sun, a ten-day week, and two moons! That's all too weird for me.

"I noticed the high stockade fence and the blunderbusses. What are they defending themselves from?"

Simon shook his head and smiled. *This was what he had been dying to tell me*, I thought. "You've heard of the centaurs in Greek mythology, right? Part man, part horse?"

I nodded. "They have *centaurs* here?"

Simon smiled and nodded. "They're called *trembolites*. Randiest beings I've ever seen. The front half is human-looking and the rest is equine. I wouldn't say that it's exactly a horse but it appears to be some local version of one. For lack of a better word, let's just say they're part man and part horse. They're beautiful animals. Gorgeous.

"They're definitely not dangerous but they're extremely seductive. And they have dicks for days!" he continued, drawing his hands apart and marking off approximately eighteen inches.

"They are very proudly homo-sexual except for one month a year, when they breed with the females and produce little trembolites. After that, the males revert to male-male sex and the females go back into the mountains with their youngsters, where, I assume, they have their all-female love nests.

"The young males are brought down to the plains where the males live when they're about two or three months old. Just after they're weaned, and their fathers take care of them from then on.

"During the time the young are growing up, the fathers are celebate but as soon as the juniors are on their own, the seniors make up for lost time.

"What I love about them is that they're so graceful and they come in some of the most beautiful colors! Colors I've never seen before on earth. How do you describe a color? Try describing ultra-violet, ultra-gold, or infrared! I guess those twin suns allow for a wider color spectrum than on earth," he said.

"These colonists are very, very religious. They believe anything pleasureable's a sin. I guess they're very much like the Puritans back on earth. If not, they certainly are *puritanical*," he smiled.

"The trembolites used to come into the village to help the settlers get accustomed to life here. Then they'd seduce a man or two as payment for their services and leave.

"At first, nobody minded. The colonists were practically starving until the trembolites taught them how to live here. How to grow and store their food, where to find handack and the other treasures they were seeking, and how to survive the sunlight. It can give them cancer or something similar.

"As soon as they began to prosper, however, the company sent up a preacher to save their immortal souls. That guy started giving sermons against cross-species relationships, calling them an abomination. Then they banned the trembolites from coming into the settlement and built the stockade. I guess the next step will be to kill them off, now that they don't need them anymore."

"Everything's an abomination in the eyes of preachers everywhere," I said. "I just stay away from them and their churches."

"Me too," Simon agreed. "When they didn't have women, sex with trembolites was considered preferable to having it with one of their own. It was considered 'necessary' but now, since some women have been arriving, it's not only a sin, but a crime. But if a person uses handack bark, there's no stopping him from seeking out a trembolite for maximum pleasure.

"To show you what a hypocrite the preacher is, he began seeking out the trembolites almost as soon as he got here. He still does. All of the Van Vlessing brothers say they've sworn off sex with trembolites but they all still participate in it, especially Pieter. He just doesn't tell his brothers what he does. Little does he know that both of his brothers still participate. They just don't tell him or even one another, what they do.

"It's even harder on the women, since there are so few of them and so many eligible men for them to choose from, so it's not even tolerated from women. Ask the poor widow Northfax. She's the one at the pillory."

"I've gotta see a trembolite before I leave this place," I said.

I noticed my companion's erection had gotten more pronounced in his skin-tight trousers, as had mine.

"Aw, hell," I shrugged. "We're probably dead anyway. Come hither, my comely lad," I smiled. Simon rushed forth toward me. Our hands met. Our lips touched....

***

With no advance warning, I was now in a Gothic-style building. The dark-stained oak floors and high transom windows along the right side and the nearly floor-to- ceiling windows along the left side looked familiar but it was the smell of Pine Sol and Murphy's Oil Soap that told me beyond certainty that I had been there before. Still, I could not immediately recognize the facility.

A door from the street opened and a tall, skinny, bespectacled, chocolate-colored boy of about 15 cautiously ascended the four or five marble steps that connected the street-level vestibule with the hallway in which I now stood.

The boy was all arms and legs. He wore heavy Clark Kent-style eyeglasses with rose-colored lenses, blue jeans, a Walsingham International School tee-shirt, and tan Hush-Puppy loafers.

The boy approached cautiously, apparently unfamiliar with the place and not feeling very safe in it. In the gloom of the large, silent building, the boy's movements appeared tentative and unusually cautious. He looked at every recessed doorway, apparently searching for one in particular.

As he approached the place where I stood, I got a good look at his face and let out a stifled gasp, *"Oh my Goddd!"* I said to no one in particular. The boy was *me*--at an earlier age.

Now I remembered the place and the incident. The place was St. William of Blade Academy in Skylarville, La. It was my 15th birthday, May 9, 1963.

Knowing the outcome, I followed Young Me as he continued down the hallway until, tucked away in a dark corner, he found the door marked "**BOYS.**"

Young Me entered and I followed. I had played out this scenario in my head a million times. Maybe even more.

I watched as Young Me found a urinal at the front end of the long, narrow washroom, and urinated.

When he was through, he turned, washed and dried his hands, and was about to leave when he heard a muffled noise in one of the cubicles. He stopped and listened again for the noise. All was quiet.

He knelt and looked for feet under the marble partitions that separated the toilets one from another but the marble reached from floor to well above my head. There were four stalls in all. Instinct told him that someone was there and that the person had simply lifted his feet above the bottom edge of the cubicle doors.

The Young Me washed and dried his hands and hummed a tune and made noises as if he were combing his hair and adjusting his clothing before leaving the room. He then opened the door as if he had finished and left the room.

He then tiptoed to a position behind the first partition, whose marble wall extended to the floor and separated the first toilet from the urinals. The soles of his Hush Puppies were made for sneaking around.

Quietly, he stood on the ceramic tile floor, listening and waiting until the person in the stall felt comfortable enough to continue his private activity. Fully twelve minutes passed before he heard one of the toilet doors open *ever so slightly*, then close again, *ever so softly.*

Someone had peeked out of one of the cubicles to ensure that all was clear and safe to continue whatever nefarious activity he had begun.

The high gray and black-veined white marble wainscoting that wrapped the room extended well over ten feet high, to the transom windows. The tin ceiling, which was approximately four feet above the wainscoting, and the black and white octagonal mosaic ceramic floor tiles, all combined to bounce even the slightest sound around the room as if it were a ping pong ball.

Four stalls with well-used wooden doors and marble partitions lined the right side of the room. All of the stalls' doors were closed. The Young Me cautiously opened each door, starting from the first and working his way back.

The muffled, rhythmic, slapping sounds combined with heavy breathing, commenced shortly after the occupant felt that all was clear.

As a boarding student at Walsingham International School near London, I was very familiar with it. Someone in one of the cubicles was spanking the monkey.

Young Me surreptitiously opened and closed each stall's door, holding the old-fashioned brass latches to prevent them from jostling against the doors and giving away his presence in the room.

The first two stalls were vacant. He advanced to the third stall and opened that stall's door as carefully and silently as he had opened the others.

There, leaning against the toilet's industrial-strength flushing mechanism was the most beautiful boy he had ever seen.

Young Me had caught him in mid stroke. So intent upon the task at hand was he that he had not noticed Young Me watching him.

He had unbuttoned his shirt half-way down his chest and thrown his red and blue rep necktie across his left shoulder. His left hand was thrust inside his shirt, crossing his bare chest and caressing a puce-colored right nipple.

His blue blazer with a St. William's crest was hung on a brass hook on the back of the stall's door and his books were piled above him on a tubular metal rack on the stall's rear wall.

Long, dark lashes limned his closed eyelids. His lower legs were lightly furred with dark hair while his thighs were bare. While his face was gypsy-dark, his upper body was the color of crème-bruleé.

His upper lip showed only the faintest trace of the beginning of a mustache but his cheeks, flushed, were as smooth as the proverbial baby's bottom. His features were perfect.

Young Me had been there a minute or two taking in the sight of this beautiful boy beating his meat in this marble-lined throne room when the boy opened his eyes and looked up, first in surprise and then, horror.

"You really should lock the door if you wanna spank the monkey," Young Me smiled, giving the brass latch a spin. "You're gonna have to say a *bunch* of Hail Marys for what you're doing in here."

The boy in the stall looked up through frightened violet eyes. "You gon' tell Brother Anselm?" he wanted to know. His Cajun accent was very thick.

Young Me smiled a lascivious smile, shook his head, and rubbed his own bulging crotch. "Want some help?"

Young Me lifted the boy's chin with his left hand, and pulled him even closer.

Their lips met and a surge of something unlike anything I had ever felt, ran through him. It was more than electric!! It was the wildest feeling I had ever known. *"WHAM!!!"* It left Young Me weak in the knees. The boy shivered, as if he had also experienced this wild sensation. My mouth had never left the boy's luscious lips.

The excitement of lips and tongues and hands and arms touching was enough to bring both of us to a quick conclusion.

This was the one by which all of my subsequent orgasms were measured.

Three orgasms later, we emerged from the cubicle, cleaned each other up, and kissed again and again. It was magic. There was no other way to describe it.

"I suppose we should introduce ourselves," Young Me said, passing the boy a paper towel from the wall dispenser near the door, as he turned from the sink with wet hands held forward and upward like a surgeon's.

"I'm Steven Wayne Mallory, and you?"

Until that moment, the boy had said nothing since inquiring if Young Me would tell Brother Anselm, whoever that might be. Neither had said very much. Our tongues were much too busy with other things to hold a conversation.

"I'm André François Bourgeois," he finally uttered. "Everybody calls me Andy, though. You shouldn't be here, you know. They don't let colored people go to school here."

"I'm not a student. I had to use the washroom and what better place to find one than in a boys' school? I didn't want to pee on somebody's bushes," Young Me replied. "You're some kisser!" he continued.

Andy blushed. "So are you. I guess you have a lot of experience, huh?"

"Not really," Young Steve blushed. "You're the first person I've ever kissed with an open mouth—and a tongue. You're the only person I've ever wanted to kiss. I saw you sitting there and I just couldn't help myself. You looked like you needed to be kissed so I did it."

"I love your lips," Andy smiled. "If there was a Lips Hall of Fame, I'd nominate yours. They're soft-soft. Like two fluffy pillows. My lips touched yours an' som'pn ran through me like electricity. I've never felt anything like that before. It was like a lightnin' bolt."

"You felt it, too?"

Andy nodded.

"I thought it was just me," Young Steve said.

He reached forward, pulling Young Steve downward to his height and kissed him again. "I never kissed anybody before an' I don' believe I'll ever find anybody who c'n kiss better than you."

When they finished, Young Steve said, "You know, if anybody comes through that door, you won't have to worry about who's going to tell Brother What's-His Name. We're goners. The first thing they'd see would be us snogging."

"Doing what?" Andy frowned. "You're not from here, are you? You talk funny."

"I go to school in England. Snogging is kissing."

"Sometimes you've jus' gotta take your chances," Andy smiled. "Nobody ever comes here at this time of the day. Today's the last day of school. Report card day for the underclassmen. We only had about an hour of school today. Seniors graduated two nights ago so they didn't have to show up at all. Most of the underclassmen have gone home already. Couldn't wait to get outta' here."

"Did you say your last name is Mallory?" he asked, leaning his skinny butt against the one of the four sinks.

Young Steve nodded.

"As in the colored doctors?"

Young Steve nodded and smiled.

"You mean Mallory, as in the Good Friends Clinics, Mallory Medical Center, and La Belle Terre Reserve?" he continued.

Young Steve nodded again.

"And Mallo-Mart stores?" Andy continued. "*Everything for Everybody?*'" That was the chain's motto.

Mallo-Mart was a British company my family owned. They operated throughout the UK and were hugely successful. They were just beginning to enter the American market and they were already successful in the northeast.

"I see you've been doing your reading," I said. "There aren't any Mallo-Marts in this area."

Andy smiled and nodded.

Young Steve continued. "My granddad founded it. The five-and-dimes didn't want competition from a chain of black-owned stores so they fought hard to keep us out of the American market. Now that things are getting better for black businesses, my family thought now would be the time to bring them to America."

"What about the cosmetics company?"

Steve nodded a third time. "That's my grandma's," Steve said.

"Mallo-Rex?"

"Pharmaceutical company. It's a family business. My granddad founded it as part of the Mallo-Marts. My uncle runs it, but it's a family-owned company."

Wow!" Andy said. "That's impressive. We used to go miles outta our way just to pass by y'all's house every time we went to Houma.

"Mama would make my daddy drive past y'all's house just to gawk and point it out. She would always say, 'that's where the colored doctors live' but now that y'all formed the Village of New Canaan, she says 'that's where the richest Negroes in the whole world live.'"

"Well, I don't know about that," I said, but magazines like *Forbes, Ebony,* and *Fortune* bore him out, in a way. They point out that La Belle Terre Reserve is the largest concentration of black wealth in the country. There are more black millionaires there than anywhere in the world."

The estates in New Canaan, Louisiana are every bit as grand as some of those in Lake Forest, Illinois or Greenwich, Connecticut, or Philadelphia's Main Line. My parents' idea was just to make ourselves as comfortable as possible in a land that offered us so little.

"When y'all's house was the only one there," he continued, "my daddy couldn't believe that there was such a thing as a colored doctor, let alone, two of 'em, and that they were married and built such a big, fancy house.

"Now he can't believe that your parents took a small clinic and made it into a world- class medical center, and that now there's *a lot* of black doctors and lawyers and other professionals living in such big, beautiful houses."

He referred to the huge Georgian mansion my parents named *Creswic House*. It sat on thirty-five acres; the fourteen nearest the house and fronting the road were walled and gated. The rest, on a peninsula, are open to Lake Laura, an artificial lake my parents built.

At one time the whole thing was way off the beaten track. Later, the village of New Canaan grew up around it, and then the rest of The Reserve came about. It is nineteen miles from Skylarville, equidistant from Houma, and ten from Thibodaux. Fifty miles from New Orleans but a world away.

"Not everybody who lives in The Reserve is black, you know," I said.

Andy started to say something when the door burst open. A short, swarthy boy with the compact body of power lifter entered briskly, already starting to lower the waistband of the gym shorts he wore, baring the white jock strap that held his "business" in check, as he headed toward the nearest urinal.

He was just shy of doing the Pee-Pee Dance. He looked older than we were. Eighteen or nineteen, maybe.

He was a great-looking boy. His olive skin was only a shade or two lighter than his short-cropped hair. He had a handsome, almost perfect face with wide-set emerald-green eyes, shaded by long sable-colored lashes, a perky nose, and a wide mouth with full, pink lips, not unlike those I had just kissed.

Gold hairs framed his face at the hairline, giving way to closely-cropped honey-colored hair farther back on his large, round head. The symmetry of a large head on a short, compact, perfectly-proportioned body was not unpleasant to look at. The boy was broad of chest and shoulders, tapering nicely down to a small waist above muscular thighs and the hairy, well-formed calves of a tennis player.

This boy reminded me of Spike, a character that sometimes appeared in Bugs Bunny cartoons. He is a bulldog who wears derby hat and a turtle-neck jersey, and is the leader of a street gang that taunted Bugs on every possible occasion.

"Noly!" Andy cried out in surprise, jumping back to put some space between the two of us.

"It's *Noel* to you, Swamp Boy! It's Noly to my friends, and you and I are definitely *not* friends," the boy answered, jabbing his stubby forefinger toward Andy. There was such arrogance in his tone. He acted like Spike the bulldog, too.

"I've been looking all over this campus for you!" he snapped. "I owe you something and this is as good a place to give it to you as anywhere else! He balled his fists and puffed out his chest, and barged his way toward my cowering friend, preparing to pummel the stripling into the floor.

Andy went into a crouch and closed his eyes, awaiting the inevitable pummeling.

"You're gonna hav'ta go through me first," Young Steve said, stepping between them and removing his eyeglasses and handing them to Andy, in preparation for the fight he was anticipating. The new boy halted his forward march and looked quizzically at the scene before him. "Bourgeois, what the fuck are you doing in here with this n....?"

Young Steve cut him off before he could complete the offensive epithet. "You're going to leave here without that finger if you don't put it away," he said calmly. "And if you call me what I think you're about to say, I'm going to kick your arse," he said in a pleasant but ominous tone.

"The word's '*ass,*' Choc'lit Boy! *A-S-S*! You've been hangin' around with this Swamp Thing, here, too long!" His voice was calm and his attitude belligerent. Young Steve was prepared for a fight.

Young Steve looked at Andy and smiled. "I'd say I haven't hung out with him long enough. Now get the fuck out of here before I keep my promise."

"You're not even supposed to be here," the new boy said, his voice rising. "We don't admit *your kind!"* His face was scrunched up into an ugly moue. Fire shot from his eyes. He looked Young Steve up and down, assessing his chances of winning a fistfight and then he turned and walked away, flinging open the heavy wooden door so hard its brass handle hit the marble wall behind it. "You don't belong here! Why are you in here with that Swamp Creature, anyway? No *choc'lits* allowed!!" he shouted.

"I'll catch you later, Bourgeois, when you don't have your black bodyguard with you! You wait and see!"

The echo nearly shattered our eardrums. "I'm going to tell Brother Anselm," he continued. "Bourgeois, you're in trouble and so are you, *Choc'lit Boy!* You'd better be gone by the time I get back here with Brother Anselm," he sneered as the pneumatic door closer finally did its job, cutting off his tirade.

Young Steve and Andy stood looking at each other. The only sound in the room was the gentle hiss of the pneumatic door closer and the even gentler sound of one long, lingering kiss Young Steve planted on Andy's grateful lips.

"That's Noel Catash. He's the school's bully," Andy explained when the kiss ended. "I didn't think he could even spell 'ass,'" he laughed. "He finally graduated last week. He's almost twenty years old. He's got the IQ of a crawfish! In a graduating class of thirty-five, guess who graduated Number Thirty-Five!"

"Boy," Young Steve said, "there must be some real wimps around here if he's the school's bully. Present company excepted, of course."

Andy nodded. "I'm a wimp. I'm scared to death of him. I was hiding out in here until my mama comes to pick me up. She's about a half an hour late. He's been threatening me all year. I'm glad you were here and that you weren't scared of him. He's a sadistic son-of-a-bitch.

"If you'd showed the slightest hint of fear, you'd have seen an entirely different person. He'd have been pushing both of us around. He's scared of black people."

"That's what bullies always do," Young Steve said. "First they intimidate their victim and then they attack. Rattlesnakes do the same thing with their rattles but they're mostly defensive. But at least, they have something to back up their threat. That guy had nothing despite his muscles."

"His daddy's the state senator from Bellefleur Parish. His grandpa was state senator before him," Andy said. "He'll prob'ly be the state senator after his daddy gives it up. The Catashes are prob'ly the richest family in this parish. He's an ass, jus' like his daddy."

"Nobody ever comes here, huh?" Young Steve mocked, hugging Andy around the neck and playfully ruffling his curls. "It's okay to kiss, huh?" In the short time they had been together, they had developed an easiness that appeared to be natural; as if they had known each other their entire lives. Andy smiled, apparently relishing the physical proximity and familiarity.

"You know," Young Steve observed, "He looks a lot like you. I don't mean facially, but you two blokes have the same coloring, same hair and all. He's like a stupider, older version of you. Are you two related?"

Andy shook his head vigorously. "My mama says *real* Cajuns are dark-skinned people. We're a mixture of African, American Indian, an' European; jus' like our food.

"We might'a been white Europeans when we came here from Nova Scotia two hundred an' fifty-some years ago, but a *lot'a* things can happen in that length of time.

People 'round here say the Catashes are 'passants-blancs' or 'sang mêlées.'"

"You mean they're black, passing for white?"

"That's what the ol' folks say." Andy replied, nodding. "They say his ancestors were the house slaves of one of the rich French planter families along the river in the 1700's and 1800's. They 'intermarried' for lack of a better term, with whites so often that eventually they just passed over into the white race."

Young Steve was fully aware of the premium some of Louisiana's black citizens placed on light skin, light eyes, straight hair, European facial features, and French or Spanish surnames.

Although a first-generation Louisianan, he knew all about the clandestine race-mixing that had gone on for centuries; the slave women who *had to* acquiesce to the demands of their masters or *voluntarily* chose to do so in order to give their families more status and better treatment; resulting ultimately in the

Free People of Color, the progeny of such unions who, in many cases, chose to separate themselves from their darker brethren; the famous, or infamous, octoroon balls in New Orleans during antebellum times, and the strange institution called *plaçage* in Louisiana.

In the Spanish-speaking world with which Young Steve was more familiar, it was called *"la casa chica (the little house)"* in which a man did not marry his concubine but obligated himself to care for her and any children they might produce just as if they were married. Often, the man spent more time with his concubine and her family than he did with his legal wife and children.

In Louisiana, especially in and around New Orleans, a light complexion opened doors that even tons of money and education could not open for a darker-complexioned person. Color discrimination was almost as prevalent there as racial discrimination.

Because of this, his parents wisely decided to send him and his siblings to England for their educations (not that England was a bastion of racial tolerance, either) and to Bermuda or Mexico as often as possible to avoid the blatant discrimination that chocolate-colored children would, could, or might suffer in Louisiana.

"But you're the same color as he," Young Steve said. "Is your family also *'passant- blanc' or sang melée?*" Young Steve asked, genuinely interested in the contradiction.

Andy shrugged his shoulders. "I don't know. You know how the old saying goes: *One can see the snot in somebody else's nose but not the booger in his own.'*

Young Steve laughed at the vulgar analogy. "I don't believe that was the original saying."

"That might be the case. It wouldn't bother me none but it would *definitely* bother my daddy if he thought he had black ancestors or that he'd married a black woman.

"My coloring comes from my mama's side," he explained. "They say she was the most beautiful girl on the bayou when she met an' married my daddy. From what I hear, he wasn't too ugly, either, but Daddy's kinda' racist. It would serve him right if my mama's people were 'passant-blancs.'"

"A 'sang melée' is a mixed race person, right?" Young Steve asked. He was proficient in French but Louisiana's Cajun French left him unsure of terminology.

"Mixed blood," Andy said offhandedly. "After *'octoroon'*, they ran outta names for 'em so they just called 'em sang melée. Some of those people are only 1/64th or 1/132nd black but according to the One Drop Rule, they're still considered black. You know anybody who's 1/64th anything?

"They say the Catashes came from lower Bellefleur Parish. My mama's family, the Bonvillains, came from lower Terrebonne Parish. Both are near the mouth of the River and right next to each other. We could be kin. There's a lot of *'half-n-halfs'* down there.

"Lower Bellefleur, lower Terrebonne, lower Plaquemines, and lower Lafourche parishes are all in the swampland. You ever been down there?"

Young Steve shook his head, no.

"I did a report on it. Got an *'A,'* too," Andy said proudly. "Louisiana's shaped like a big, ugly, worn-out boot with half the sole missing and dirty toes stickin' out, into the Gulf of Mexico.

"It has a worn-down heel. That's Cameron Parish in western Louisiana, a hole in the sole, right in the arch. That's St. Mary Parish. St. Bernard, Plaquemines and Jefferson Parishes form the first three toes and Terrebonne, Lafourche, and Bellefleur Parishes form the others."

"So, in addition to all of its other faults, Louisiana is polydactyl?" Steve wanted to know.

Andy nodded. "I guess so."

"All of 'em have a lot'a' mixed race people who left New Orleans, moved to the swamps, and changed their names, their race, and their lives. Could be that the Catashes did it, that the Bonvillains did it," he said philosophically. "And could be that the Bourgeois' did it, too. Who knows?

"My mama says her family is part Indian an' the dark skin came from them. Could be," he said again. "There are a lot of Indians still livin' in the swamps. Tchitimatcha, Attakapas, Houma, Tchopitoulas, and a few other tribes not even recognized by the government, so that story is just as possible as the one about them being sangs melées."

"I don't know if you know that many tribes adopted runaway slaves into their tribes so they wouldn't be able to be sold. Those that were adopted had all of the rights as the native-born tribe members and they intermarried freely so although they were Native American, they had a lot of African genetic material behind them," Young Steve said.

Andy shook his head. "I didn't know that, but that would explain why some Indians around here are so dark that you can't tell them from regular blacks."

"Even so," Young Steve said, "wouldn't they still be *sangs melées* if they were Indians who intermarried with whites?" Young Steve asked.

Andy smiled and plunked his knuckle on Young Steve's forehead. "You should be a lawyer when you grow up. They would be but for some reason, to have Indian blood is acceptable here if it's way, way back in your family's history, but to have African blood, no matter how far back, isn't.

"I don' know an' I don't spend nights tryin' to figure out where my dark skin came from, but I'll tell you one thing: If I even *thought* I was kin to Noly Catash, I'd cut my wrists and drain out every drop of blood I have. You better leave before Brother comes?" he asked.

"No," Young Steve said. "I'd like to meet him."

The door opened again just then. A tall, burly man wearing the dark gray robes of a Philippian Brother entered. He was followed closely by the swarthy, chunky kid who had denounced them.

"Where's the emergency, Noel?" he asked.

The boy pointed to Young Steve.

"Hello, young man," the Brother said, smiling. The accent was one hundred percent Old Sod. He extended a baseball mitt-sized hand to Young Steve. "I'm Brother Anselm. I'm the Prefect here."

"Young Steve took the proffered hand. "Steven Wayne Mallory," he said. "I needed to use a washroom so I came in and found one. I met Andy here and we started talking. The boy behind you came in and started raving that I was trespassing."

"When you've gotta go, you've gotta go," Brother Anselm said philosophically. "It's perfectly alright. I see you're wearing a Walsingham International School tee shirt. That's near London, isn't it?"

Steve nodded.

"There's not a whole lot of Mallorys around here. And all those that are, are related to the Negro doctors. Am I correct?"

"Yes," Young Steve smiled. "My mom's at a meeting across the street at the hospital. She said she'd only be a few minutes but it's been over an hour. I got bored and started wandering around the neighborhood looking at the houses. I needed to use the washroom so I came in here. I didn't think it would cause an international incident."

"You may not know it but it's really not safe for a young black boy to wander around this neighborhood," Brother Anselm warned. "There are a lot of knuckleheads like the one behind me, who seem to believe that they own the very ground on which we walk.

"Your parents are fine doctors. They've been extraordinarily successful in starting a hospital where colored people can be treated with dignity and respect. They've set up scholarships for needy students, vocational training schools, founded La Belle Terre Reserve. They've accomplished more for black people in less than thirty years than has been accomplished here in the last two hundred.

"I've heard through the grapevine that that's what this morning's meeting was about cooperation between St. William's Hospital and Mallory Medical. That would be wonderful if they can pull it off.

"I've never had the pleasure of meeting them, though. They're from The Bahamas, right?"

"Bermuda," Steve corrected.

"It's a shame you couldn't have gone to school here instead of being shipped off to England. I'm familiar with the International Schools and I know that they're wonderful schools and provide an unparalleled education but we do our best here, too.

"In some cases, like Bourgeois here, we've been very successful. He's one of our brightest students, but sorrowfully, we have our failures, like young Catash behind me. Were it not for his family's money and social position, I doubt he'd be good for anything. I'm ashamed to say that he is a graduate of our illustrious school."

"You'll be interested to know that I attended your school's bitter rival when I was a lad," he continued.

"Diss?" Young Steve said.

Brother Anselm smiled a wide smile. "I left to enter the monastery when I was about your age."

Diss and Walsingham were bitter rivals in everything from rugby to rhetoric.

"I'm new here. This is my first year but I can assure you that next year, St. William will be integrated," Brother Anselm continued. "I've already started the process.

"Those stupid segregation laws are coming down all around us," he continued. "It's only a matter of time before Louisiana has to integrate its schools like any civilized place. With young Kennedy in office, I know it'll happen soon."

"Not if my daddy has anything to say about it," the chunky boy said. "He's a state senator and he's willing to fight Kennedy an' anybody else to keep this state segregated."

"The Supreme Court has already spoken on that matter but the South is finding ways to stall the inevitable. It's like trying to hold back a tidal wave by keeping your finger stuck in the hole in the dike, Boy-o," Brother Anselm sniffed. "Go home, Noel Catash!! Now!! You're no longer a student here and you have no business on campus!" he barked. "If anybody's trespassing, it's you, m'boy!"

"I'll *never* go to school with a… *choc' lit*," the boy sneered as he turned, huffed, and left.

"You will and so will your children. Frankly, Boy-o, I hope one of your offspring falls in love with a …*choc 'lit*, as you call them, and marries one. It would serve you right, though personally, I don't know who, in his or her right mind, would want to marry anyone you've spawned," Brother Anselm said.

He turned to the two boys who remained in the washroom and proffered the huge hand to Young Steve again. "A nasty piece of work, that one," he said. "I've got some pressing business to take care of. Young man, it was a pleasure meeting you. Mr. Bourgeois, why don't you show him around the campus?"

To Young Steve, he said, "Stay as long as you like. You're always welcome here."

He turned to leave, filling the open door frame. "Mr. Bourgeois," he said as an after-thought, "Have you been peeling shrimp?"

Andy shook his head, having no idea of what Brother Anselm was talking about. "No, Brother. Why?"

Brother Anselm smiled a wicked smile and pointed down to Andy's pants leg. "You dropped one!"

After cleaning up the large gob of jizz from Andy's pant leg, they left the washroom and entered the school's quadrangle. A tall, skinny boy with shoulder-length, neatly parted sand-colored hair and a touch of acne ran up to them.

"T-Beau," he boy said, "Your mama's waitin'. We gotta go!" His Cajun accent was even heavier, than Andy's.

"This is my cousin, Kevin," Andy said to Steve. Young Steve shook hands with the new boy, who was dressed in regular street clothes, not the St. William's uniform.

"Tell her I'll be there soon but Brother Anselm asked me to show my new friend around the school," he said. "He's a student ambassador from a school in England. He threatened to kick Noly Catash's ass."

"Right on," Kevin said, fist-pumping the air. "Somebody needs to do it."

***

ZAP!! I was at the place from which all souls emanate, and to which all souls return. I was with many other injured and battered souls.

"Your mission is not finished. Go back and complete it," a sweet, warm voice said to me.

***

I'm in a heavy fog. I can hear someone calling to me and telling me to wake up but I couldn't locate the source of the sound. I can't follow it because I can't tell which direction it's coming from.

"Wayne, wake up!" a brisk, authoritative female voice called, in a crisp English accent. "Wake up! Wake up, Wayne!" The voice came from far away and was distracting me from the most pleasant dream I had had in a long time. The voice insisted I wake up. I didn't want to wake up. Not now, not ever. All I wanted was to stay in 1963 with young Andy Bourgeois.

The female voice stopped and a soothing, familiar male voice took over, coaxing me into consciousness. "Wayne!! It's me, Andy. Wake up. Please." I wanted to run toward that voice but I did not know where it was coming from, either. It seemed to come from everywhere but nowhere in particular.

I then heard the same sweet, warm voice that said, *"Your mission is not yet completed. Go back!"* It was a command, not a request.

I opened my eyes, blinking at the harsh, white ambient lighting, and looked around, trying to get my bearings. I was in a bed in a totally unfamiliar place with no idea of where I was or how I had gotten there.

The walls were white ceramic tile in a running bond pattern that reached the ceiling. The ceiling was white. My bedding was white. I couldn't see the floor but I assumed that it was white too. Everything I could see, except the people, was white.

I was in a room that was smaller than the walk-in closet in my old bedroom at *Creswic House*, my parents' mansion. The two walls that I could see, to my left and right, were solid but the one in front of me, which looked out onto a larger room, was glass from floor to ceiling. An open sliding glass patio door gave passage to the larger room. The curtains had been pulled back as far as they would go. Like everything else in the place, they were white.

Individuals or small groups of people moved briskly about in the larger room. Some manned a bank of flashing lights and small television screens in the center of the room while others conversed in hushed tones.

A group of three persons consulted long reams of paper which were spread out along a high counter. Others talked softly on telephones that had soft, nearly-silent ringers.

The place did not look at all familiar to me—and neither did some of the people who were standing there smiling at me. Two people I did not recognize stood at the foot of my bed, partially obstructing my view of the larger room beyond the glass wall. The woman was tall, dark, well-built, and big-breasted. She radiated strength and health like an Olympian. I thought first of the goddess Juno, and then, of Harriet Tubman.

She was older, maybe late 30's or early 40's. She wore no make-up, allowing her natural beauty to burst forth on her face like sunshine. *This is what all black women should look like,* I thought to myself.

Her hair was styled in a short Afro beginning to go gray. Her teeth looked strong and healthy. Well-cared for. Her skin was a rich, dark chocolate color like mine. Her face looked familiar but I could not place it. There was something in her face, her smile, which inspired instant trust.

A short, mousy-looking young man the color of beer, with a huge Afro stood next to her. Beside her, he looked insignificant. He had the body of a really strong twelve-year old but he appeared to be about my age. When he smiled, a gold incisor shone from the top left side of his mouth.

I had no idea of who he was or why he was here but he appeared to know me and appeared to be happy to see me awake. He playfully jiggled my right toe.

My sister-in-law, Dr. Philippa "Pippa" Mallory, stood at the bed's right corner. Her stethoscope, white lab coat with her name embroidered in red on her breast pocket, and the Mallory Medical Center logo just below it, told me where I was.

It was her authoritative voice that had slapped me back to consciousness. Andy's seduced me back.

My parents were at knee-and waist level on my right side. My mother, looking regal, as always, beamed, while my dad, looking taciturn, held my right hand in his. He seemed relieved. Closer to my right shoulder and head, contraptions buzzed, beeped, and dripped fluids into me.

My grandma, for whatever reason, was not present. I looked around, almost in a panic, when I realized that Andy was not there, either.

I lay there confused, wondering if something had happened to him.

I had no recollection of what had happened to me to cause me to be in the ICU of Mallory Medical Center but I wondered if he lay in the walk-in closet sized cubicle next door, when someone snapped his fingers near my left ear.

"Hey," he said, almost whispering, "You're not gon' say hello to me?" He kissed my forehead. Chucked my chin.

Andy sat at my bedside to my left, holding my hand and smiling. The pressure was so constant that I initially thought it was another machine holding me down, pumping fluids into or draining them out of me.

His normally bright eyes were half-lidded. They looked tired, red, and worried. His four-o'clock shadow had gone well past eight o'clock and a dark, luxurious beard now covered his cheeks and chin. He looked sexy as hell... despite looking haggard!!

"Welcome back to the world of the living," Pippa said. "I knew you weren't ready to leave us quite yet. And I just knew you weren't about to leave this gorgeous hunk behind."

Everybody else smiled. I hate to be condescended to, even if it was by family members. Andy bent over and kissed my forehead again as he squeezed my hand even more tightly.

The tube down my throat prevented me from asking a gazillion questions. I asked them with my eyes.

"You died four times on the operatin' table," Andy said. "Pippa brought you back each time. She's a hell of a surgeon!"

I raised my eyebrows in confusion.

"You don' remember?" Andy continued.

I shook my head.

"Senator Catash shot you," Andy said. "Just missed your heart. When we brought you in here, you weren't breathing. Pippa worked on you an' wouldn't give up. She brought you back but you kep' slippin' away again. You were unconscious for six days."

I furrowed my brow.

"Don't worry, Cher, I took care of him for you," Andy continued. "He's dead. I made sure of that."

"And Andy's been here constantly," Pippa said. "Grandma, Mom, Dad, Jeremy and Daniel," she continued, referring to my brothers, "have all stayed with you, left, and returned, but this man has not budged since they brought you in here.

"I had a cot brought in for him but it doesn't look like he has used it at all."

I just lay there, confused. I had no recollection of the incident that almost ended my life.

"Let's give him a chance to rest," Pippa said, taking my wrist from Andy's hand while she wrapped a bag around my bicep, pumped it up, and checked my blood pressure.

"He'll be all right," she said. "He's passed the crisis stage but we don't want to tire him out. Go home and get some rest, everybody. Dr. Foster-Truehill will most likely take out the tube and he'll be able to talk—for a short time, anyway."

She injected something into a plastic tube that ran from a fluid-filled bag hanging on a metal skeleton above my right arm down to me and I began to slip away again. "Andy," she said on her way out, "He's OK now. Get some rest."

Family and friends began to kiss me or touch my hand and file out. I waved good-bye to them. Only Andy remained. He seated himself near the head of my bed.

I made the sign for a pen and something to write with.

Andy retrieved a small pad and a pencil from the night stand's drawer.

I wrote: "Do you believe in reincarnation?"

"Never thought about it," Andy said into my ear. "But I don't see why not. It's just as plausible as heaven or hell. Why?"

I wrote, *I think I revisited some of our past lives. We've been together a long, long time. You had different names and I suppose I did too. We lived in different time periods, and even on at least one planet that wasn't earth. Possibly two, but in one life, we were on a ship. An old sailing ship like Columbus'. I don't know where that was but I don't think it was earth.*

I wanted to write this down before I forgot it.

Andy looked dubious. "Those drugs they gave you can make you have weird dreams," he said.

I don't think they were dreams, I wrote. *You know where Scutum Crux is, or what it is?*

"No, what is it?" he wanted to know.

I wrote as fast but legibly as I could under the circumstances. *It's in this galaxy. The Milky Way galaxy. But according to your reincarnation there,*

Scutum Crux is the name of one of the arms of the Milky Way. Earth is in the Perseus arm. I told him the story just as sexy Simon on Ronak had told me.

I didn't know any of that before now. I never even thought about the arms of the galaxy or whether the galaxy even had arms. When I get out of here, I have some research to do.

We were on the planet Ronak in the Eweegian constellation in the Scutum Crux arm," I continued. Andy smiled indulgently. Like an over-indulgent parent hearing their only child tell about a visit from the tooth fairy. *Your reincarnation there was named Simon. He told me that the Milky Way galaxy has four arms: Perseus, Norma, Sagittarius, and Scutum Crux. He said earth is in the Perseus arm, in a little cul-de-sac called the Orion Spur.*

How the hell would I know that? I wanted to know. *I've never taken a class in astronomy. I've never owned a telescope and I've only been to the planetarium a few times. Astronomy has never interested me except during the solar eclipses.*

I have no idea whether this is true or not but I want to find out. I've never heard of the planet Ronak and if we can even see Ronak through telescopes on earth, it's possible that the planet and the constellation may have different names but the arms of the galaxy may be the same.

Creswic House has a huge library. There's at least one book on every conceivable subject. Can you call there and ask one of the librarians to check out the names of the arms of the galaxy for me? Or better still, give it to one of my parents and have them tell the librarians what I need.

"Okay," Andy said. "Now I'll tell *you* som'pn," he said in a low, confidential voice. "If Pippa hadn't been able to revive you, I'd already made plans to put a bullet through my head an' join you," he confided. "I lost you once for fourteen years. I'm not about to lose you again forever. Without you, I have no life."

No. Don't do that. Please. If something else were to happen to me, I want you to live out your own natural lifetime. You have a mission to complete. So do I.

I told him about the place I had been, where the Voice told me to return to my current life because I hadn't completed the mission I had been sent here to do.

I continued writing, using up many of the note pad's pages, then turning them over and using the reverse sides: *On that sailing ship, I was already dead,* I wrote. *I assume that that was me that they had gotten ready for burial at sea. You were there and I could see what was going on but nobody could see me. After the funeral and my body had been pushed overboard, you were talking to the priest and all of a sudden, you picked up one of the cannonballs on the deck and jumped overboard. It's happened before,* I continued. *But I don't want you to ever do that again!*

You don't have to worry. We've been together through many lifetimes. We'll be together in the next one. And the one after that. And the one after that. You waited for me on Ronak. Maybe I'll wait for you in the next one.

He squeezed my hand tightly, more as reassurance for himself than for me, and then he kissed me on the cheek. I wiped away his tears before I slipped back into oblivion.

***

The next day, Judy Bedell, appeared at my bedside with a smile and a sheaf of papers. Judy is the head librarian and chief documentarian of *Creswic House's* vast library,

"I'm glad to see that you're better, Wayne," she said in the manner of one accustomed to speaking in a lowered voice. Everyone in the household was worried that you wouldn't make it. It was like existing in a tomb!"

She plopped the sheaf of papers on my bedside. "I did a lot of work on what you asked for. The Milky Way galaxy. I've bookmarked the information you wanted about the arms of this galaxy. I never knew they had names or even particularly cared about our place in it. You've given me a whole new area to study.

"I'm old-school, I guess," she continued. "I always thought we were at the center of it or at least, somewhere *near* the center, but in doing your research, I found out that we're way on the outskirts of the galaxy and in a backwater of the Perseus arm, is it? I can't remember." She looked frustrated.

"I can't stay long. I have a lot of cataloging to do but I want to find out some more about our place in the universe."

"Thanks, Judy," I said. "I'll have something to read while I recover."

"Have they told you when you can come home?"

I nodded. "Pippa said I should be able to go home in a few days. She's just keeping me here for observation. I had a pretty close call."

She nodded. "Those Catashes are dangerous people." She turned her face to Andy, who stood holding my hand, and smiled. "But I guess you're even more dangerous, huh, Quick Draw McGraw?"

She turned and headed for the door. As she grabbed the handle, she turned back toward me, allowing her long brown hair to swing free, and asked me one final question, "How'd you ever come up with that request? About the arms of this galaxy, I mean?"

"I dreamed about it while I was in the coma. Weird, huh?"

She smiled, nodded, "Toodle-oo," she said softly as she disappeared through the door, leaving only the papers and the aroma of her signature fragrance in her wake.

THE MATANGALAND SAGA
The Story of Three Families

The Three Sisters

July, 1687
Pinehurst Plantation
Near Charleston, South Carolina

The old woman lay on a low bed made of scrap lumber her friends and family had scavenged from various places around the farm. Her son, Abraham, had hammered the pieces together and covered them with a mattress made of Spanish moss and chicken feathers to make her a little more comfortable.

Her body, now old and frail, was covered by a length of muslin that one day would be her shroud. Beneath it, she wore a simple cotton tunic.

Her frail body bore the scars of her many years of involuntary servitude. Keloids, skin thickened by lashes she had received for being "lazy," "uncooperative," or "obstinate," covered her back and sides while her wrists and ankles bore the scars of the manacles and hobbles she wore as she was being transferred from one place to another, from one owner to another, or from one continent to another.

When she was more valuable to the plantation's owners, she had lived inside the Big House, providing her precious milk to the master's sickly children while her own children went without. In the end, she had lost three of her thirteen children to malnutrition while the master's children grew strong and healthy on her milk.

As she became less valuable to the master and as she lost status; with the signs of old age and hard physical labor imprinted her body, she was her moved into a hut close to the Big House but her hut was moved farther and farther from the Big House and the master's family as she became older and of less value. Now it sat farthest from the front of the slave quarter, at the head of a row of cotton. Her next stop would be the slaves' graveyard, which sat a few yards east of her place.

A patchwork quilt she had begun many years before was nailed to the wall opposite her cot. It was her pride and joy. It depicted her life from her birth up to the time her arthritic fingers became so gnarled and painful she could no longer sew the panels that recorded the first four score and seven years of her existence in this world.

The final score and two would have to be recorded by someone else, most likely her daughter, Temerity, her granddaughter, Lucretzia Borgia, and her great-great granddaughter, Akiva, to whom she had willed the quilt.

Although her body had shriveled up like a strip of bacon on a hot griddle, her mind remained alert. Despite her years, her face, though aged, was hardly touched by time.

Insects zipped around her tiny room, bumping into one another and buzzing in and out of the uncovered windows. Mosquitoes hummed nearby, disappointed that there was not enough blood in that old, frail body for a good meal.

Her sky-blue curtains, made of the remnants of a bolt of muslin the mistress of the manor had given her more than a score of years prior, hung limp on the open window that offered her a view of the fields of cotton but denied her a breeze to cool her ravaged body.

In a far corner of the room, a long, black rat snake lay undetected in the shadows, waiting for its next meal to enter through the open doorway. It had come every evening at dusk and left at dawn every day for the past week, always choosing that same spot, undetected except by the old woman, growing fat on the ground squirrels, field mice, and other vermin that dared to enter the hovel, seeking to scavenge the bits of human food and grain that lay strewn about the dirt floor, or to feast upon the body of the ancient one who lay helpless on the makeshift bed.

"Tell me again, Baba, about Matangaland and how you came to America," Akiva requested.

"I will tell you," the old woman replied in a strong voice, "but first..."

The child sighed. The old woman chuckled softly, for she was old but not mentally infirm and this was a ritual familiar to both of them. First she drilled the child in the Matanga tongue, correcting her now and then and adding a new word or phrase from the few she still remembered.

"Why do you want me to learn the Matanga language, Baba?" the child inquired. She had used the informal term for "grandmother" today. "Na-Ema" was the formal term, used at court and in formal settings. "We ain't never going back to Africa."

The old woman corrected the girl's English and continued, shaking her head sadly. "It's not for that reason, but because I don't want you to forget who you are and where you come from.

"We are forbidden to learn to read and write or even to speak our native tongue or to practice our native religion but no one can forbid us to remember. Keep your mind active. Learn all you can from nature. If the opportunity comes to learn to read or write, snatch it up and hold it dear, but for now, you have the best book of all to help you, your mind.

"Your mind is quick to grasp and hold whatever it comes across. Never reveal this to the whites because we were brought here to work, to toil like beasts in the fields, not to learn, not to better ourselves.

"They are afraid of us. Afraid that if we had even a little knowledge, we will conquer them and take over their land as they took this land from the Indians, and our lands in Africa. We are a strong but degraded People. We must never forget who we are or we will truly become like the beasts of the fields.

"The rich white man has the gift of reading and writing. The poor ones are no better than we are but they believe their white skin gives them entrée to a world in which they will one day be allowed to participate. Their only advantage is that although most of them can neither read nor write, those who are not indentured are free to come and go as they will and those who are still indentured will eventually obtain their freedom.

"Most poor whites toil the fields beside us. But books are their real key to freedom, for the rich ones, who know how to read and write can transfer their remembering to paper and keep it safe for all time.

"If a book is destroyed, the knowledge is lost. If an African dies without passing on his or her knowledge, the knowledge is lost. Books can live forever but humans cannot. It is important that you pass on the knowledge that I give you for you are my book, as were your mama and your grandma, your uncles, aunts, and cousins. That is the way knowledge was passed down from generation to generation in Africa for thousands of years. That oral tradition must not be lost.

"You all are the receptacles of my knowledge," she smiled with teeth that resembled old ivory. When she was young, they were like pearls. She had been a great beauty. Like Sheba, she had been black and beautiful.

She began her oft-told tale:

"My name is now Faith. Before that, it was Esperanza, before that, Saffronia. Before that, Eulalia. And in between, many other names that I no longer remember. In Matangaland, West Africa, it was Efula. It means *"rainbow"* in the Matanga language.

"My sisters were Ula and Be-ula. Ula—she pronounced it "Oo-la-- means *"sky"* and Be-ula means *"cloud."*

The child, now ten years old, tall, strong, and black as onyx, as the old woman had been at that time in her life, sat in rapt attention, though she had heard the narrative hundreds of times before.

The old woman had told her it was vital that she learn this saga by rote. Word for word. Only the gender or the person should change. She had taught it to her children and their children, and their children's children.

Akiva had a quick mind and often mouthed the words as the old woman spoke.

"Our people were attacked by the neighboring tribe, the Malangani, bearing the firearms supplied to them by white men. We were put aboard ships and taken away from our homeland forever."

"Tell me about the Passage, Baba," the girl asked.

"In order," the old woman responded. "Always in order."

"Do you remember the Matanga words for father and mother?" the old woman asked.

The child nodded. "'*Edo*' is father and '*Ema*' is mother."

The old woman smiled again. "My father's name was *Omano* and it means what in English?" the old woman inquired.

"Mountain," the girl replied proudly.

The old woman smiled and squeezed the child's hand softly in approval for she was too weak and frail to reach up and pat the child's head from her low bed.

She realized that her days on this earth were numbered and she wanted to ensure that her message was passed down to future generations. "Do you remember my 'Ema's' name?"

The child again nodded and replied. *"Ajanuwe."* She said it slowly to get the syllabication right: A-JAHN-u-way. "And it means 'flower,'" she said before she could be asked.

She continued. "We were members of the royal household." This was the part of the narrative the child liked best. "Our tribe was broken down into many clans. We are the Clan of the Lion Cub, we are of royal blood. We were separate and apart from the others of our tribe.

"All of the villages of Matangaland were subjects of *Na-Ema*, my grandmother. Maybe ten thousand people in all. Maybe more.

"Na-Ema's consort, my *Na-Ma-Edo*, my maternal grandfather, had died before I was born.

"I loved it when we accompanied Na-Ema to the seashore during the very hot, sticky weather. We lived with Na-Ema in a large walled compound within the walled city of Dondi, the capital, with my other mothers and fathers.

"In western society, they are called aunts and uncles. In our culture, they were all called 'Ema' with no distinction between those who brought us into the world and her sisters. The men, whether the sons of Na-Ema or the husbands of Na-Ema's daughters, were all my fathers.

"All of their children were my *'zinas,'* sisters, and *'manus'*, brothers.

"I was five years old when the white men came. They said they wanted to share with us the knowledge of their god and goddess. They had no guns at that time. Their teachers were called *"padres,"* in Portuguese, their language.

"They left two priests with us to live among us, pouring water on our heads and pronouncing our souls as saved. The priests remained with us for three years, trying as they might, to convert our people, especially Na-Ema, to their religion but Na-Ema would have none of it. She allowed those of her people who wanted to listen to them and be splashed with water to do so if they so chose. Most did not.

"Na-Ema also allowed them to build a special hut with a wooden cross atop to serve as a worship center. A church. In it, they installed a large cross with the image of a dead and very bloody white man on it, to which all must kneel and pray. They said this dead man was their god and that despite having been killed by soldiers over a thousand, five hundred years before, he arose from the dead and lives now in a place in the sky, beyond the clouds, called heaven. They told even more fantastic stories about his conception and birth and his life on earth.

"They claimed that his mother was a human virgin before, during and after her son's conception and also worthy of being worshipped. His father was one of three invisible beings, one of which was a white bird. There was a human man who was his and his mother's earthly caretaker but he and the mother lived like brother and sister, not as husband and wife, and did not procreate. The tales went on and on.

"On the other hand, this Jesus whom they worshipped had many good qualities. He preached love and humility. Inclusion and love of all living things. Of all people, regardless of their station in life or their color, but even his acolytes, the priests themselves, did not practice this, for they were vain and arrogant and believed that although it was their duty to convert us to their religion, we were not truly their brothers in Christ, for our dark skin made us inferior to them; they who could not even stay outside in the African sun for more than a few minutes without fainting.

"They believed that although this Jesus came from the same place as we, he was wan and pale with white skin, blue eyes, and light-colored, lank hair that would not have protected him from the harsh African sun. They did not understand that the land of Israel was multi-racial. Many people from many lands were there but they were mostly dark-skinned people. They laughed when we told them that we had originated in that part of the world more than a millennium ago, that our forefathers had come from the same Jerusalem that Jesus had entered on the back of an ass, and that the kingdoms of Egypt and Nubia were rich black kingdoms.

"Our people found the stories the priests told about their god as ludicrous as the priests found our stories of our origin. When they saw the sacred writings our priests had brought all the way from Jerusalem, they accused of having waylaid a 'real Jew' and taken his possessions.

"When, after two years, they had attained almost no converts, the soldiers returned and the priests left with them, eager to be free of such 'hard-headed savages,' as one priest told a soldier in my earshot. They boarded their ships after ceremoniously removing the dead white man on the cross and the image of his mother from the church they had built and then burning the church.

"Two years later, the soldiers returned but as slave hunters this time. Because we refused to convert to Christianity and our neighbors to the south, the Malangani, had, the white me incited the Malangani to become slave hunters, supplied them with guns and alcohol and sent them to Matangaland to rape, rob, and plunder.

"The Malangani had always coveted our land and our wealth. There had been many wars in the distant past, as the Malangani considered the land on which the Matanga settled, to be part of their kingdom and they wanted it back. After a while, they gave up their quest to conquer the Matanga and lived peaceably near us.

"Our people, the Matanga were excellent metal workers. We shaped the finest, sharpest spearheads, shields, axes, adzes, arrows, swords, and machetes to defend ourselves and to harvest our crops.

"Our craftsmen also made beautiful jewelry of gold, silver, and iron with or without precious stones. Our woodcarvers and weavers were famous throughout the region for the fine quality of their work. In addition, we were fine poets, singers, dancers, and artists but most of all, our people were great healers. People from all of the neighboring tribes, including the Malangani, came to us for healing."

The old woman herself, had been a great healer, using knowledge of herbs and potions, salves and creams, passed down from mother to daughter, from father to son, to cure ailments western doctors had no clue how to treat.

"It was not until the white men came and provided our enemies with rifles, bullets, and alcohol did the balance of power change," she continued.

"But Baba, why did we not convert to Christianity at that time? We are now Christians. We go to church on Sunday and we are baptized by the preachers every Easter Sunday. What's the difference?" the girl wanted to know.

The old woman shook her head again. "A forced conversion is not a true conversion. It is a conversion of the body but not of the soul. Not of the spirit, and that's what counts. Do you believe the things the preachers tell you?" she asked.

The little girl shook her head. "No, Baba," she said, almost in a whisper for there were many eyes and ears on the plantation, waiting to hear and report to the master through the overseer.

"Our people are special people. We are believers in the One God and exiles from a far away land called Israel whose capital city was Jerusalem. We are the people of the Book.

"When Jerusalem was destroyed many hundreds of years ago, our clan and several other clans joined together and trekked southward and westward for almost a thousand years, stopping in many places, staying a while— sometimes for generations, then moving on, always trekking westward, until we came to an uninhabited land and established our own kingdom by the sea.

"By that time, we had forgotten most of our original language except for those the priests of our religion continued to recite day after day and taught us. We formed our own language made up of some of our remembered Hebrew words and words from the many languages we encountered in our journey. We called our language and ourselves the Matanga, meaning "blessed." We lived at peace with our neighbors for many years until the white men came and sowed dissention among our neighbors.

"Never, ever forget that."

"I won't, Baba, and I will teach it to my children and tell them to teach it to their children."

The old woman smiled a weak smile. "Some will forget and some will discard it as nonsense, fable, or invention but there will always be those who will remember what you have taught them and teach it to their children.

"The priests brought swine and sea turtles and other bottom dwellers and filth-eaters from their ship for us to eat. The Matanga consider those animals unclean and we did not eat them; nor would we allow them to contaminate our land so that presented a huge problem.

"Even now, our diet consists mostly of grains, fruits, vegetables, and barn fowls while other slaves here on the plantation eat the unclean animals. We are baptized because we are as chattel. We must obey our master and the master has deemed that all of his slaves be baptized and given Christian names. Your Christian name is Georgia but your Matanga and Hebrew name is Akiva."

The old woman held up one bony finger before she continued her saga as if to make a point. "*But...*" she stressed. "Even though we are considered the white man's chattel, we must never, *ever* give up our fight to be free, be it peacefully or by subterfuge or force.

"We are too few and the whites are too many for us to ever win an armed rebellion but there are other ways. One day I will tell you how but not now. You must never, ever stop trying to obtain your own freedom and that of your people."

"I won't, Baba," the girl said. "Even for the Malangani who live among us? Even though they conquered us and sold us into slavery?"

The old woman nodded. "In Africa, we were different tribes. As different one from the other as day is from night, but in this land, we are all considered one. We must unite if we are ever going to be free but that's for another day."

The old woman continued her tale: "The white men continued down the coast until they came to the land of the Malangani, who were less civilized, less cultured, and less formal than the Matanga but more gullible and more willing to believe the tales the white priests told them. The white men preferred this because the Malangani had few, if any, ceremonies and almost no traditions to speak of. All of the other kingdoms in the area, the Obi, the Kurk, the Nafuti, and the smaller kingdoms, looked down on the Malangani.

"As with the Matanga, the priests stayed among the Malangani and attempted to convert them. With the Malangani, they had much more success. They baptized the Malangani rulers and their court and from there, their entire kingdom.

"The whites, still upset that we would not convert, started the rumor that we were cannibals and that we should be wiped off the face of the earth or, worse still, be sent to the New World as slaves, so they taught the Malangani to use rifles and guns and incited them to go to war against the Matanga one last time by providing them with alcohol in large quantities.

"Both the Malangani and the Matanga only used alcohol for religious purposes and on festive occasions but the white men drank it for no particular reason other than that it felt good going down and that they were bored aboard ship.

'The war lasted three weeks. At the end, half the Matanga were killed and the rest were captured and sent into exile as slaves in the Americas."

Although she already knew the answer, the child asked the question anyway. "Did the Malangani take our land and our beautiful capital of Dondi?"

"No, child," the old woman said. "After the war was over and the Matanga were being kept in holding pens near the shore, the Malangani and the white men held a great victory feast. The white men had been instructed to pretend to drink and to act as though they were intoxicated. When the Malangani warriors were drunk and passed out from too much food and drink, the white men confiscated the weapons they had given to them to use against the Matanga and chained them with the same heavy chains they had used to chain the Matanga. They had already raped and enslaved the Malangani women and children.

"When the Malangani warriors awoke, still drowsy from the drink, they found themselves also in chains. They were herded into the same prison cells we, the Matanga were in. When the ship sailed, the Malangani and the Matanga were all prisoners of the white devils.

"To this day, I spit whenever I hear the names of Portugal and Malangani. There are many Malangani right here at Pinehurst so be careful whom you choose to love. The master can make you breed but only you can give your heart.

"I am now getting sleepy, my dearest," she said. "Look in my cupboard. There's a gift for you."

The girl stood and went to the cupboard two or three feet away from the bed in which her great-grandmother reclined and inches from where the snake lay in wait for its next meal.

"Take care not to step on N'goka," she warned. *N'goka* was the Matanga word for "snake."

Startled, the girl jumped back and let out a scream. *"Where?"* she wanted to know.

"There, by the cupboard," her grandmother laughed. "By your right foot. In the corner."

"He is not venomous," the old woman said. "He keeps out the vermin."

"The girl peered into the dark recess between the cupboard and the wall. There, she saw the snake. N'goka. Jet black, sleek and beautiful, as it lay coiled and apparently ready for its next meal. In the low light, its scales appeared almost iridescent, capturing and casting off the low light in the cottage. He was black as night with muted undertones of aubergine, burgundy, emerald, and sapphire. Only the black beady eyes and its bifurcated tongue could readily be distinguished.

She had no idea of its length as it was coiled into a neat ball but since the snake did not constitute a threat either to her or the old woman, the girl did nothing to further disturb it as she reached into the cupboard for her treat.

Wrapped in a cotton cloth, she found two small gingerbread women, given to her great-grandmother by Maggie, the cook, but saved for Akiva as a reward for knowing and remembering her lesson.

The girl rewrapped one of the cookies and placed it in her smock's only pocket. She then broke the other one in half, knelt next to the bed, and fed it slowly to her grandmother.

The old woman always gave her something. Sometimes it was a sweet, other times, it was other things: a needle, some thread, a piece of cloth, or rarely, a coin. If there was nothing to give, the old woman gave her the only thing she had, a Matanga blessing called The Blessing for God's Favored, with which she always ended their sessions.

After that, the girl went next door to her own home, leaving the old woman alone with her friend, N'goka, the snake.

The old woman waited for death. Ngoka, for his next meal.

***

Charlottesville, VA.
July 4th weekend, 1973

The handsome Federalist mansion was almost two hundred years old. It had been visited by several Presidents, past and recent. Its large, handsome white-columned portico and octagonal marble-floored rotunda were reminiscent of *Monticello,* Thomas Jefferson's home, nearby.

The men visiting the house had been called upon on this day in this place to take back the United States from the "Forces of Darkness" that had gained strength since the founding of the United States of America.

The attendees were from every region of the country. There were fifty-two of them excluding the host. One representative from each state plus two others, the son-in-law of the host and the representatives from Kansas, the Kroll brothers, who acted and voted as one, but they were as different from one another as night and day in some cases but what had united them was their common background as "Old Money" and their single-minded dedication to the eradication of "dark forces" from Government and from the country.

They were all white. All were Protestant, and all were male. All were influential in their own spheres of operation. All were wealthy, and all but a couple were over forty years old. No women were invited.

They moved with the casual elegance of the monied classes. Many spoke with the clinched jaws of the Eastern elite, regardless of where they had been reared. Others spoke with a western twang or a southern drawl.

In fact, they even looked alike: most were blue-eyed with what many called the New England Squint, obtained from staring at the open seas across the bows of their yachts; steel-jawed, and with silver or salt-and-pepper hair, casually tousled like the Kennedys or neatly parted on the left like the actor, Robert Redford's.

Most represented the Old Money class, having ancestors who arrived on these shores on the *Mayflower* in 1620 or in those that followed it, the *Fortune,* the

Little James, or the *Anne*. Some were descended from the Robber Barons, as the early U.S. Industrialists were called. Some were of the southern "planter" class and still others were investors in land. Real estate, as they preferred, stripping the earth of its resources or of charging renters and buyers exorbitant prices for cracker-box houses or shoe box apartments.

In crowds, they stood out like well-manicured thumbs. Others, not of their ilk, instantly deferred to them. They were privileged. Entitled, and well aware of that fact. They bore surnames like Sloane, Endicott, Blair, Blake, and Whitney. They represented the most exclusive neighborhoods, boarding schools, country, and yachting clubs. They were the country's top echelon. The One Percent of *The One Percent*. A few were "New Money," in awe at being invited into such august company.

George Washington's and Thomas Jefferson's bewigged countenances looked down upon the small, self-righteous group from larger-than life portraits on opposite sides of the rotunda. Nearby, on a walnut-paneled wall in the mansion's smallest sitting room, was a large portrait of a handsome, dark-haired man with a sinister countenance and a dark mustache, John Wilkes Booth by name. And below his portrait, were the words, *"Sic Simper Tyrannis," (Thus always to tyrants),* which, not coincidentally is the Commonwealth of Virginia's motto.

Outside *Radley House*, as the mansion was called, spring colts frolicked and kicked up their heels in verdant pastures in the warm summer breeze. Grooms and attendants moved about and among them, their ebony brows and backs covered with perspiration. Their ebony bodies sculpted as if by Michelangelo himself.

Lest they overhear the purpose of the meeting, the house servants were given the weekend off to celebrate the nation's independence. Only the family's butler and the cook, his wife, were retained to attend to the needs of the guests. The host of the gathering and master of *Radley House* judged them too feather-brained, too child-like, to fathom what was being said.

They could be trusted if they were to overhear any part of the conversations that were about to be embarked upon, the owner thought. After all, they were illiterate and would not have the mental wherewithal to grasp the concepts that were about to be shared.

Most of the positions in The Big House had been handed down from mother to daughter; from father to son, for many generations. "Where else can you get job security like that these days?" the home's owner frequently joked.

Those who cared to move on, who chose not to become part of the fabric of *Radley Farm,* as the horse farm was called, usually did so after high school. Some later returned but most did not except on holidays and special occasions such as for weddings and funerals.

The men gathered there this were carefully screened for their "attitudes," their backgrounds, their political leanings, their wealth, power, and their willingness to contribute to "The Cause."

Because of the gravity of their undertaking, Senator J. Covington Dayel, the owner of *Radley Farm*, had to be sure that those invited today could be trusted. After years of observing and testing the men before him, he was absolutely sure they were trustworthy.

They represented all branches of the United States military, the clergy, the judiciary, law enforcement, the media, both Houses of Congress, and the private sector.

After their sumptuous buffet meal in the cherry-paneled dining room, the men settled themselves around the large mahogany-paneled drawing room smoking cigars, drinking expensive liquor, making small talk while introducing themselves to one another and waiting anxiously for the meeting to start. Although all had an idea of why they were there, few actually knew what the meeting involved.

"Gentlemen," Senator Dayel said, ringing a small crystal bell, "please take your seats. I'd like to begin the meeting now." His rich baritone filled the luxurious room and those still standing found seating nearby. All eyes focused on the front of the room, below Thomas Jefferson's portrait.

"I am familiar with each and every one of you," Senator Dayel said, "but not everyone here knows everyone else.

"That, Gentlemen, will change over the coming years. Our association will be long and intimate. You men were chosen with even more care than I would choose a stud for my breeding mares or mates for my foxhounds." Everyone chuckled, knowing the pride with which the senator managed his horses and his fox hunting packs.

"Gentlemen, you are The Chosen. You were specially selected for your own pedigrees just as I choose the horses I select for breeding. Those horses are the *'crème de la crème,'* the very best there is, and so are all of you. Aristocrats!

"Pure Aryan!"

"For our undertaking, we will need only the best, but before I go any further, I would like to know if there is anyone here who is *not* willing to risk his life, his fortune, his good name, and reputation for the betterment of the United States of America?"

No one came forth.

After a short wait, the senator, surveying the room, said, "Good. Good," and smiled a reptilian smile.

"Gentlemen, I must warn you that the mission which you are about to undertake may be considered treason by some, genocide by others, and Hitleresque by still others. In the end, all of the above may be true but it will make this country again what the Founding Fathers intended it to be."

There was a small murmur or two but the senator knew that his audience was still with him.

"To better explain why we are here and what we must do to save our great country, I would like to present to you one of this country's most distinguished military men, Colonel Terry Wycliff of the United States Marine Corps, Retired."

A loud round of applause went up from the group as the square-jawed, silver-haired colonel with the boyish good looks and cornflower blue eyes entered through one of the paneled doors that led into the rotunda and made his way toward the podium near the double entry doors.

The colonel had just recently been implicated in a political scandal that had tarnished his name and image to the point where he felt his best course of action was to resign his commission. Had it not been for his and the senator's political clout, he would probably be in the brig instead of addressing some of the nation's most influential citizens.

"Gentlemen," he said in his northern Virginia accent, "you all know what I recently endured. Days, weeks, even months of interrogation before congressional committee after committee. One after the other. After a while, I didn't even know which committee I was addressing."

A smattering of laughter erupted from the men seated around the room. The solder continued. "But I endured. I have to admit there were times when I felt like I wanted to take my pistol and put it to my head rather than go back to Capitol Hill and face the same questions from the same lizard-lipped liberals but I did what I had to do because I knew it would be better for the country.

"Worst of all was being quizzed by that baboon who calls himself the chairman of the Joint Chiefs of Staff. But I did what I had to do. And that's why we're here today.

"Gentlemen," he said with the "honest, down-home" inflection he had practiced for hours before the cheval mirror of the master bedroom of his palatial home nearby, "first of all, I want you to know that assemblies such as this one have been going on since before the War Between the States. This is not the first of these assemblies and it won't be the last. Some of your grandfathers or great grandfathers may have attended some of them but that's not important. The important thing is that now, it's our turn to do what must be done; to carry forward the mission with which we are charged. We pull the strings and control the votes. We run this country! And we must do what we must do to save it.

"Sometimes, to prevent the spread of cancer, it is necessary to cut out organs, tissue, and bone. To amputate, if necessary. Other times, it is only necessary to remove fatty tissue and expurgate the offending black cells.

"It's important that you gentlemen understand that this country is founded upon the principles of 'Divide *and Conquer*' and *'One Step Forward, Two Steps Backward,'* and not *'all men are created equal'* despite what ol' Tom Jefferson wrote. What he should've said is *'all men of quality are created equal.'*

"This has been going on since the founding of our great country. We did it with the Indians. We signed three hundred and eighty-eight treaties with them, promising them one thing or another and each time, reneging on them and claiming whatever we swore we would honor.

"And we call *them* Indian Givers," a voice from the back of the room said. This caused a spate of laughs and guffaws. The colonel ignored it and continued speaking.

"We did it again after the War Between the States," the colonel continued after the laughter subsided. "I think it was a little deal called '*Reconstruction.*' Was this great land of ours ever… 'reconstructed?' he used air quotes.

Before anyone could answer his rhetorical question, he continued. "Children cry and whine when they don't get what they want. We had to give the coloreds something they could call 'reparations' for slavery. The Indians want "compensation" for taking '*their*' land.

"The coloreds are like little children, gentlemen," he said soberly. "So what do we do with a crying, whiny child?" He looked around. When no one volunteered an answer, he continued. "We can either swat the shit out of 'em or give 'em something to shut 'em up!

"The first 'solution' just makes the kid cry louder, so the *smart* parent gives him something to pacify him for a while. Either something sweet to eat or something shiny to play with. *That* shuts 'em up! And then, when they're asleep or otherwise distracted, we take it back.

"That's the way it is with the coloreds and the Indians, among others. They cry and we give 'em something to shut 'em the fuck up!" He smiled at his use of the *"F"* word. "Right?" he asked, again, rhetorically.

"They felt that they were owed something for two hundred years of slavery and Andrew Johnson devised the scheme to keep 'em quiet.

"It lasted less than twenty years and then it was pulled out from under them." And, with the help of our hooded brethren, they were forced back onto the plantations and into the same conditions they had left. But now it was called '*share-cropping.*'

"Gentlemen, that was no accident. Many of our ancestors sat right here in this room in 1865 and formulated plans for the take-back. And it worked. Worked beautifully for over a hundred years. In fact, it's still working in one form or another. Look out the windows, Gentlemen, and tell me if those old men didn't know what they were doing!

He paused for twelve seconds to allow that to sink in and then continued. "When they got uppity again and wanted to sit with us on public transportation and send their little pickaninnies to school with our sons and daughters, we slapped 'em down again, this time under the guise of the doctrine of *'Separate-But-Equal.'*

"Imagine how much *true* equality would've cost the states! They were *separate* but they certainly were *not* equal!" He smiled a diabolical smile, arched his eyebrows, and twisted his non-existent *Oil Can Harry* mustache.

"This country was founded for and by *landed white men*. Men of substance. Men of property. Every single one of you--with an exception or two--" He looked directly at Reverend Billy Curry, whom he looked down upon, "came from illustrious old monied families.

"*Almost* everyone in this room is a member of *First Families;* families who were sent here by Almighty God, from Europe long before the American Revolution to colonize and civilize this savage land. Anyone else who washed up on these shores was an interloper. They were brought here or allowed to remain here to serve us. Simple as that!"

He paused for effect. He had timed the pause to last exactly twenty-four seconds. When he had counted off those pregnant seconds, he continued. "What we propose today is to remove the fatty tissue, the cancer-ridden fatty tissue, from the United States of America and take back our country.

"I'll try to be brief," Wycliff continued, "so I draw your minds to the Presidential elections of 1896. Yet another instance of 'take-back.' A group of like-minded aristocrats, men like yourselves, did something to save the country. Does anyone know what I'm talking about?"

He looked around for hands. None was raised so he continued. "In that election, gentlemen, J.P. Morgan, Andrew Carnegie, John D. Rockefeller, and a few others of similar ilk, decided to commandeer the Republican Party for the good of the nation and, naturally, for their own good. These were the men who built America. They were enemies. Business rivals. They *hated* each other but they came together for one solid purpose: to bring the country back to what the Founding Fathers wanted it to be.

"This nation was founded on the principles of capitalism, gentlemen. Free enterprise and not Socialism. This is not a society where we *share and share alike.*' It's more like King of the Hill or even Dog-Eat-Dog. To the *winner* go the spoils. But lately, the country is leaning more and more to the Left.

"Gradually, the country is becoming more and more socialistic. 'Share and share alike was *not* one of the principles of the Founding Fathers. This country was meant to be a plutocracy, where the rich rule. Poor whites, poor Negroes, and poor Indians were here only to do the physical labor.

"Well, at that time, there was this bitter little Socialist named William Jennings Bryan who proposed breaking up not only the companies that those tough old men had built, but their fortunes as well, and handing them over to the workers who manned the factories, the mines, and the fields, or those who laid tracks or drove the trains of the great Iron Horses, with no regard for the rights of the owners who had financed these ventures.

"Those illustrious gentlemen of the Gilded Age, whom many called 'Robber Barons,' hogs, and worse, were faced with the unpleasant thought of losing everything they had built because of a *populist!*" He spat out the word as if it were a bitter pill that refused to go down.

"Today we'd call Bryan a Commie. Or worst! What right does a fellow who hasn't spent *one day* in those fields, factories, or mines, or working on those railroads, have telling the owners of the companies how they should handle *their* companies?"

A loud round of applause and foot-stomping arose from the audience, peppered with *"hear-hear!"* erupted from the group as they rankled under new government restraints that had been handed down to them in regard to the conditions they could or could *not* impose upon their workers.

"Bryan was running on the Democrat ticket and spewing dribble that no one in America should be as rich as Rockefeller, Carnegie, and Morgan, or the Vanderbilts," the colonel continued.

"They were *Captains of Industry*, not Robber Barons, but that's how they were portrayed by Mr. William Jennings *'Goody-Two-Shoes'* Bryan."

More shouts of *"hear-hear!"* were heard from the audience, interspersed by a smattering of boisterous applause. Like an itinerant southern preacher, Wycliff was on a roll. He had started off slow but now he was gathering momentum.

Most of the guests had not heard the story of the 1898 Presidential elections but as they found themselves in similar situations, many being attacked by workers and beset by unions, they sat listening, all ears.

"Desperate times call for desperate measures, Gentlemen," Wycliff continued. "Those brave men banded together despite sometimes bitter rivalries, to run their own candidate, none other than Mr. William McKinley.

"McKinley may not have been the sharpest tool in the shed or the brightest bulb in the chandelier, but he was willing to play the game. He was willing to give them what they wanted. For a price, of course," he said, almost as an aside.

"It was touch and go at first but in the end, McKinley won with a little help from his 'friends' at the highest levels of society." Then he got assassinated and that Judas, Theodore Roosevelt, became President and ruined everything.

He continued. "We're not here for a history lesson and I'm not a history teacher, but in the Great Depression, a group of landed gentry joined together to form the American Liberty League and bankrolled the presidential campaign of Alf Landon, to do their bidding should he be elected.

"Unfortunately, another Roosevelt, Franklin this time, won the election by a landslide and the American Liberty League disbanded soon after.

"My point is that we, the wealthy, are being bombarded from all sides. We win a battle but never the war. It's time all of that changed, Gentlemen." And what we discuss here today will turn the tide of war forever. We are meant to rule. This land is meant for us just as the Almighty gave the Promised Land to the *Israelites—not* the Jews.

"Forgive me for interrupting you, Colonel," said a booming voice from the middle of the audience, "but are you inferring that we do the same? That we all become Republicans—I mean those of us who are not *already* Republicans—and run our own candidate?"

The speaker was the Speaker of the House of the great State of Georgia, a dyed-in-the-wool Southerner who, in 1948, left the established Democratic Party and became a member of the "Dixiecrats." Now they were suggesting that he leave again and become a Republican! The party of Lincoln, the South's most hated white man.

The colonel nodded. "Exactly," but that's only Stage One of our plan to make this country more livable.

"But the South is almost solidly Democrat. White people are *not* going to join the party of Abraham Lincoln. There's no way!"

"The Republican Party is the party of the *rich*," the colonel emphasized, slowly, deliberately, as if talking to a vegetable. "Southern whites will follow you if you play your cards right. They're sheep. They'll follow you wherever you lead them.

"We got their grandfathers to fight and die for us in the War Between The States even though most of them didn't own even *one* slave and probably never would've, didn't we?

"The sons of the wealthy didn't fight until the very end of the war, and then, it was for the glory. For the ol' South!" The colonel smiled a devilish smile. "They're already beginning to switch parties in Kansas. Ask the Kroll brothers. For those who don't know who y'all are, why don't you two gentlemen stand up?"

Two chinless men stood and held up their hands in a salute that was a cross between a Nazi *Seig Heil* salute and a British royal wave. Merswell turned clockwise while Maxwell turned counter-clockwise, each smiling, waving, and looking like figures on a German clock tower.

The brothers had come from a family that had become wealthy making brass buttons. Their surname had originally been Droll but they substituted a *"K"* for the *"D."*

"You can sit down now, Gentlemen," Wycliff said to the brothers, as they continued smiling and waving long after the applause had ceased.

"This is their idea," he said. "They brought it to Senator Holt of their home state and Senator Holt took it to Senator Dayel. We'll talk more about this later because those two have a few other ideas, but as I was saying about taking over the Republican Party, we have to look at this like a chess game." Wycliff was again on a roll. "*We* are the rulers. The back row of the board, king, the queen, the rooks, bishops, and knights, protected from harm by our money, power, position, and most of all, by our pawns.

"Your constituents are your pawns. Your employees are your pawns. Those who imitate us are your pawns. And most of all, *those who want to **be** us are our pawns*. They're easily ordered about, easily led, and *very* expendable.

"We tell them to jump and they ask, 'how high, Sir?'" Everyone there applauded and stomped their feet in agreement. They knew the truth but most had not thought of it in those terms.

The colonel droned on and on, comparing the group before him with "patriots" such as Jeffery Amherst and Benjamin Franklin, who had advocated that Native Americans be exterminated by giving them gifts of blankets infested with the smallpox virus, to which the Native Americans had no natural immunity.

"You gentlemen are this century's Amhersts and Franklins," the colonel continued. "It is up to you not to flinch when you know that there is an unpleasant job out there that has to be done and that you are the men chosen to do it."

"Just what are you proposing, Colonel?" a voice from the back of the room inquired. It was that of North Carolina televangelist, Billy Curry, the colonel's enemy.

Curry was one of the few men there whose pedigree was not as "sterling" as the other attendees. Although his ancestors had arrived on American soil long before the American Revolution, he had grown up barefoot, and dirt poor in a dog-trot log cabin way back in a holler in the Appalachians but he had a sharp, shifty mind, a strong dislike for non-whites, and a talent for getting folks to do what he wanted them to do; to give money to him even though they knew he was full of shit.

Curry had made a fortune promising the old, the poor, the infirm, and the hopeless, that if they pledged their savings to his organization, this life would be full of all of the good things the good Lord intended for them but that somehow, they had been misappropriated by others.

Curry's weekday telecasts were full of tearful mountain folk or swamp folk, or trailer park folk standing in front of multi-million dollar mansions or expensive motorcars or luxury yachts with accents so thick they sometimes needed subtitles, who told tales of not having known what a toilet was, of not having running water, or living with rats larger than Petey, their pet 'possum, until they sent their last few dollars to Brother Curry's Morality Ministry and, suddenly, everything changed for them. The Lord's blessings started rolling in on them like an endless tidal wave.

And, as one tired-looking woman from Dothan, Alabama said, "the cherry on top of the sundae was Brother Curry's love. Brother Curry *is* love." That segment was played before and after every broadcast. In reality, the tired-looking woman was Curry's wife.

Curry's organization was called The American Morality Ministry. His Sunday morning church service, called *The Sunday Morning Morality Rally,* was broadcast from his crystal cathedral and was hugely popular with the poor. Unlike most pastors, Curry preached that good things should be experienced on this earth and whatever there was forthcoming in the next world would be experienced once his followers get there.

"I'm about to get to that, Reverend," just hang in there a little longer, please," Wycliff said condescendingly. "And would you wake up the fellow next to you?

"That's Step Two of our plan but for now; let's not worry about that one. We've got to get Step One implemented first."

"You cain't tell us that you have something dastardly planned and then not tell us what it is," Rev. Curry said in his backwoods accent. The majority of the audience concurred. Wycliff looked over to Senator Dayel, who nodded, held up his hands for silence, and stepped to the podium.

"We're a little hesitant to discuss Step Two at this point," Dayel said. "Not until we have to have everyone's *sworn oath.*"

There were some gasps and murmurs from the crowd. One young man, Senator Dayel's son-in-law, said, "I'll have no part in anything that involves treason."

"Yes, you will, Michael Sennett," Senator Dayel said through clenched teeth. "You're married to my daughter and, as such, you're part of my family. You'll do as I tell you. Now sit down and shut up!"

"You and your cabal want to get rid of blacks, Jews, Asians, homosexuals, and Hispanics. What have those people done to you?" Michael Sennett asked in a loud, tough voice. "Who do you think will do the work you don't want to do? And don't want your wives or children to do?

"You don't want to get off your asses to hit a lick at a snake," he challenged, using an old Southern expression. "Who's gonna do that? Who's gonna wipe your children's asses, cook and serve your food, mow your grass, or tend your horses and other farm animals, the Irish? The Dagoes?

"That's who we white people used to turn to when we didn't want black or brown people in our houses but now the Irish are 'like us.' They *are* us. They were the niggers of Europe but since Kennedy won the presidency, they've come a long way! They've been Anglicized. Americanized.

"How many of you are Irish?" Michael Sennett asked, looking around the room. When no one raised their hand, he pointed to a man sitting near him. "Mr. O'Connor, *you're not Irish?* What about you, Rev. Curry? Mr. Brehenny? Mr. Adair? If you're guys aren't Irish, you're certainly carrying Irish surnames!

"There was a time when my father-in-law up there wouldn't have even wasted spit on an Irishman. To him, an Irishman is just a European nigger. I've heard him say it a thousand times!

"I guess the Italians are still not good enough to grace the gracious Senator's table or drawing room, since there aren't any here.... I knew there'd be no Jews here but I don't know why you want to get rid of them, too."

"But I know for sure that Congressman Luckey here marched in Chicago's South Side Irish parade last St. Patrick's Day. Didn't you, Congressman?" Jimmy Luckey lowered his head and turned beet red and said, "Try to get votes in Chicago without acknowledging the Irish! See how far you get! Besides, on St. Paddy's Day, *everybody's* Irish!

"Sit down, Michael!" Senator Dayel demanded.

"No, sir, Senator... *Horowitz!*" Michael Sennett said, smiling a knowing smile. "You think I'm your puppet just because I married your precious daughter? I want answers! I want to know why you're attempting to bring these men-and me-into something that might get us all shot as traitors. Benedict Arnolds?

"You might get us shot but you think I'm gonna be quiet and not question your sanity? Before I put my name on any agreement, I want to know why you're doing this and what you, the Kroll brothers, and the colonel are *really* getting us into! We have a right to know."

When things had calmed down, Michael Sennett had one final quip. He stood as if he were leaving the assembly and quietly said, "Senator, let's start with the truth. Tell them that you were Little Heshie Horowitz, a violin prodigy, *before* you became Senator J. Covington Dayel!

The senator turned scarlet. "*I'm not a Jew!* I've always been who I say I am, Michael, and you know it! You're a lying little back-stabber! Get out of here!" Dayel said. "*Now!*"

"Check out his dick" Michael Sennett shouted as he was being muscled out of the room. He's circumcised!"

He sent his two "aides" to escort Michael Sennett out of the assembly.

To the others, he said, "Gentlemen, Michael Sennett is a severely troubled young man. We will get him some help. And he, from one of this country's oldest and most prestigious families!

"I don't have the slightest idea where he came up with that one! I am, and always have been, a God-fearing Presbyterian."

He used his "serious" face and voice, both of which he had practiced in his bedroom for months, for his next words, "I would like you-all to know that what we propose will *not* get you into any kind of trouble. My little introduction and the colonel's were just to test you. Added for dramatic effect.

"These meetings have been going on since Day One of this republic. I'm sure you've heard of, or been involved in 'back door politics' and the proverbial 'smoky rooms' where politics are *really* performed. Most of your fathers and grandfathers probably practiced them and participated in meetings such of this one.

"We pull the strings in this country and we control the votes. We run this country. Always have and always will.

"Your cells are already up and running. Have been for years. We will meet here for your formal initiation into the group. At that time, you will meet some of our existing members. Just remember, though, that what you have heard here tonight is not to go beyond this room. We will meet here or at some other designated location from time to time to see how things are going. Most of our communication, however, will be via mail. When you receive a communiqué from *'Headquarters,'* you are to read it and destroy it. Only your most trusted seconds need to know what was asked of you. But even your Seconds-In-Charge are not to be told anything about Headquarters. If he is not in this room right now, Gentlemen, he is to be told *nothing* about these meetings. Is that understood? Nada! Zilch!'

There was a murmur of agreement. The senator looked over the room. "If my instructions are not understood by anyone here, please raise your hands."

No hands went up. The senator nodded and continued. "We will be in touch soon. Have a safe trip back to your homes."

High above them, in a small storage room that looked down upon the rotunda, Nate "Dooley" Celery, Senator Dayel's elderly black butler, sat recording everything that was being said below.

"Dooley" Celery knew the house inside and out, having had the run of it since he could crawl. All of his ancestors, enslaved and free, had worked in the house since it was built. In fact, his enslaved ancestors, both male and female, had toiled day and night, through fair weather and foul, building it nearly two hundred years prior.

Senator Dayel, its current owner, had only been the master of Radley House for only about twenty years.

***

Heshie Horowitz, Rest in Peace

Washington, D.C.
December 13, 1941

"I'll *never* go back to Brooklyn!" Herschel "Heshie" Horowitz said to his mirror image as he took the pair of scissors he had bought for the occasion and snipped off the tawny side locks he had worn all of his life. "And I'm *not* wearing these stupid clothes anymore!"

First he snipped off the left curl and tied one end with a thin blue satin ribbon. He placed it in a small robin's egg blue jewelry box and then he snipped off the right curl.

Payot, they had called them in the home of Avram and Esther Horowitz in the Borough Park section of Brooklyn.

"People spit at us," he continued. "They sic their dogs on us and call us kikes, sheenies, and Christ-killers!" A tear formed in his eyes as he remembered the abuse he and his father had taken while trying to make a living.

Unlike most other Hasidim, who stayed close to their beloved community, Avram Horowitz and his only son, Herschel, called "Heshie," roamed far and wide, to the state of Alabama. They were tinkers and their trade was one not needed in Brooklyn but in Alabama, where the people were dirt poor, to have a utensil repaired instead of replaced, was a saving they treasured.

Still, pushing their heavy wooden cart and walking around in the Deep South was not without peril for two Hasidic Jews dressed in black from head to toe as they were, and speaking heavily accented English as they did.

On more than one occasion, they were set upon by "gentlemen" mounted on horses and dressed in white robes and hoods.

Over their hearts, they wore a patch emblazoned with a cross and a drop of blood, which, they said, symbolized the death of their "Lord and Savior, Jesus Christ," caused by Jews more than two millennia ago. That their "lord and Savior, Jesus Christ," was also a Jew had never entered their minds. Or if it did, they dismissed it as a lie perpetrated by "sheenies."

After the third time their cart was overturned and burned and they were roughed up, Heshie refused to return to Alabama or to any state in what was the former Confederacy.

Only by quick action was Heshie able to save his beloved violin, a classic not quite as good as a Stradivarius or a Guarneri, or even as good as an Amati, but it was old and beautifully made, and the sounds it was capable of producing were heavenly.

She was called *"La Celestina* (the Heavenly One) because of her beautiful sounds. Although Heshie had never heard a Stradivarius or a Guarneri, or any of the others, He was positive that *La Celestina*, made by Guglielmo Lorenzetti, aka, Fra Celestino, a relatively unknown luthier, was among the finest still in the hands of the hoi polloi and not yet scooped up by the large museums and the violin cognoscenti.

"They love my music but they hate me, the maker of that music! How's that? How does that work?" he asked his mirror image.

Next, he removed the long black overcoat, the starched white shirt, and out-of-date trousers, the smaller four-cornered prayer shawl (tallit katán) with its (tzitzit) fringes on all four corners, the larger black and white striped prayer shawl (tallit gadol), and then the koppel and the larger black hat he wore over it.

Instead of reverently removing the garments, he balled them up and threw them into the large cardboard box he had bought for the express purpose of sending them back to his parents. Atop the mound of discarded clothing, he threw several books in Hebrew and Yiddish, including his Siddur (his daily prayer book), his dirty underpants, socks, and the heavy black clod-hoppers he had been forced to wear since childhood.

Before closing the nearly-full box, he threw in his t'fillin and the gold Mogan Duvvid his parents had given him for his bar mitzvah.

Last, he threw in the small blue box containing his peyot and a sealed envelope that contained a simple note:

Abba and Ema,

I have had plastic surgery to get rid of that sheenie schnozz, changed my name, and my religion. I am now Presbyterian. I have taken on a whole new identity and I have joined the U.S. Army. Please do not look for me.

Sit Shiva for me if you want, for I am dead to you and you to me.

Your former son,
Herschel

***

January, 1974
Radley House,
Charlottesville, VA.

"During the past few years scientists in Russia, South Africa, and Cuba, have made huge advances in the field of germ and viral warfare," Colonel Wycliff said at the beginning of their second meeting.

"South African and Rhodesian scientists have developed and almost perfected a virus that is completely man-made. The South Africans tried it first on their own native population and then in Angola. Then the Rhodesians tried it out on their own natives. It works, Gentlemen," he smiled.

"If Hitler had had this virus, he could've wiped out the Jews and nobody would've known what happened to them. Just one more scourge eradicated from the earth," he said, poker-faced.

"In this country, we've inherited the Jews, Niggers, Chinks, Japs who, let us not forget, bombed Pearl Harbor; fags; redskins, Mexicans, and anybody else's trash than can swim, fly, or float to these shores. What other country does that? None! Not a one! Just us! But we're going to get rid of all of that trash!

"Gentlemen, we have samples of that virus and we will be testing our modifications to it first in Africa and ultimately, we will try it here.

"In short, we will begin our own secret extermination plan, to rid the USA of its cancer. We will be hailed as heroes!" his voice rising.

"Or shot as traitors," a voice from the audience said.

"Shut up and sit down, Michael!" Senator Dayel ordered.

When the room had cleared, Senator Dayel closed the home's heavy mahogany double doors as the last limousine turned past the round-about at the end of the cobblestone driveway.

"Kill Michael Sennett," he said to Brian Ingleside, the tall blond man who was constantly at his side. "I want that idiot dead! I don't care how but do it. Just make it look like an accident!"

Brian Ingleside was Senator Dayel's *aide de camp*, his "enforcer," and his lover. They had met when Brian was the senator's Congressional page. Brian was sixteen years old at the time. The senator was fifty-two.

Only Brian Ingleside knew the senator's deepest, darkest, secrets: that the senator was indeed the former Jew, turned Presbyterian, the former child prodigy, "Heshie" Horowitz, and that the senator, despite constantly railing against homosexuals and their lifestyle, was, himself gay. He knew that the senator was a total hypocrite.

***

The Story Begins

Skylarville, La.
Summer, 1976

I'd forgotten how hot and humid Louisiana was during the summer. I had just arrived from Chicago but it didn't take me long to remember.

Sweating like a well-dressed pig, I walked into the large, open, depressing waiting room that had at one time been painted a festive lime green on its lower half and the color of heavy cream above the chair rail but it had lost its *joie-de-vivre* at least a decade ago. All that was left was the sad, chipped remnant of a paint job long lost. This was the waiting room of the Skylarville, Louisiana Police Department.

I strode up to the knee wall that grew into a five foot high counter to service the public. It was the only thing that separated the public from the officers on duty. In Chicago, they used bullet-proof acrylic to accomplish the same task.

One officer, a middle-aged, gum-chewing sort with a bad comb-over and thin, silver-framed glasses, sat at the desk doing a one-finger hunt and peck number on an old Underwood.

"Have a seat and somebody will be with you in a minute," he said to me, not taking his eyes off the paper he was murdering.

"Hey Andy," he yelled to someone in the back, "we got a visitor! Can you take care of him for me? I *gotta* finish this report. Chief wants it *now!*"

"Be right there," a voice from the rear of the building called out. The waiting area was empty except for me. I took a seat in the front row of three rows of mouse-brown metal folding chairs. Each chair had long ago been stenciled with the initials of the Skylarville Police Department on its backrest but not even one had the "SPD" still intact.

The chair I chose had only one letter partially visible. It was one of the hump-back letters but I was unsure if it was the *"P"* or the *"D."* From its position on the backrest, I assumed it was the *"P."*

Old issues of *Time, Newsweek, Red Book, Good Housekeeping,* and others that appeared to be gun and ammo magazines, whose covers had been torn off, sat on a low, round fake wood table at the end of the row. Not one of them was intact.

After a short wait, a well-built, tawny-skinned officer came from around a set of Army-green file cabinets that were taller than he, even if you didn't consider the white file boxes piled three high on top of them.

He carried four thick file folders, each approximately eight inches thick that covered his front from belt to chin.

He used his chin to steady the top of the stack. Each folder was bound shut by thick rubber bands. Ropey veins bulged as his thick, hairy forearms struggled against the weight of the files.

"Can I help you?" he asked, not looking up at me.

It had to be the same guy. Fourteen years later but Bellefleur Parish could not be so fortunate as to have two tawny-skinned white guys with a mop of jet black curls that would not be tamed. It was black as a raven's wing and wild as the wind.

I was positive this was the same kid I'd met, kissed, and fallen in love with, at St. William's School all those years ago, now grown up. I still had not seen his eyes but my dick knew and jumped to life.

I'd never have guessed that he would've become a cop. I'd never thought about what he would actually do with his life but ...a cop?

"Can I *help* you?" he said, again, jarring me from my reverie. He was still preoccupied with the file folders, trying to find a place to set them down, and did not seem to recognize me but he definitely liked what he saw.

I heard a low groan of appreciation escape from his throat as he eyed me unabashedly from head to toe as I strode up to the counter.

"You been eatin' at Dalrymple's again, Andy?" the officer at the typewriter asked. "I told you their food would give you gas but you wouldn't believe me."

His name tag read: *"Off. A. Bourgeois!"* That and those purple eyes cinched it for me. Andy Bourgeois. I'd never forgotten the name or the face that went with it.

I walked over to the knee wall to state my business. I decided to play with him for a while to see if he remembered me. My dick wasn't so willing to play the game but it has always had a mind of its own.

"I'm looking for Chief Authement," I said. "Is he in?".

He looked me up and down again, noticing my burgeoning erection. "How... big *are* you?" he said, clearly in awe. "I mean, how *tall* you are?" he said, correcting himself and turning beet-red.

"I asked you my question first," I said. I took up a modified;; "parade rest" stance, placing my cupped hands in front of my crotch instead of behind me.

"He's gone for the day," he said, still eying my middle. "Can I help you with som'pn?"

Before I could answer, he asked, "You with the Feds?"

I smiled, hoping he would remember me as I remembered him. He had filled out beautifully.

When I last saw him, although he was a beautiful schoolboy, the key word was "*boy*." He was not yet fully formed but he had major potential.

Standing here now, watching him, savoring his beauty, I saw that he had fulfilled his potential and then some.

It was as if I had seen the caterpillar, touched it, and then put it back on its leaf to mature into the beautiful butterfly I was seeing revealed before me today.

Shaded under dove's wing ebony eyebrows and protected by lashes so long they could cause windstorms when he blinked, were those gorgeous Liz Taylor eyes. His shoulders had widened, his waist had narrowed, and now he had Bluto-sized biceps on Popeye-sized forearms. I remembered everything about him: Those wild curls, the sensuous lips, and his skin, as dark as that of a Greek fisherman's. This man was too pretty to be a cop!

I remembered that his legs were lightly furred and beautifully formed. I also remembered that his calf muscles, even at that age, were works of art, and the newly-emerged jet black hair on his legs that stood out against his walnut-colored skin. I've always been a leg man.

He hadn't grown a lot, though. Vertically, I mean. He looked to me to be around 5feet, ten inches tall and maybe 180 pounds, all muscle. He was perfectly proportioned and reminded me of one of the fighting bulls of Spain, while his movements, deliberate and graceful, reminded me of a matador's.

I answered a question with a question. "Why would you think I'm with the Feds?"

"You act like you're used to giving orders, like Federal agents do," he said. "I think they call it an '*authoritarian* air.'"

"I know you!" he said when he finally decided to look above my beltline. He held his head from side to side, like a puppy-dog, thinking. "I know I know you, but I don't believe it! I've waited so long to see you again." His eyes were beginning to fill with tears. So were mine. I had to fight the overwhelming urge to grab him and kiss him right then and there. He was the answer to my prayers.

"St. William's," he said. "The last day of school in my freshman year there. 1963! Steven Wayne Mallory!" His face was lit up like the Rockefeller Center Christmas tree. He came around the knee wall through a waist-high plywood swinging door stained dark, and hugged me like an anaconda squeezing the life out of this week's dinner. He smelled of Jade East cologne. I hugged him back for all I was worth.

"What is this," the older officer said, "ol' home week?"

"Kind'a," Andy said, not letting go of me. "Man, it's *really* good to see you again! The last time I saw you, you were a gangly, gawky teenager. Now you're…" he searched for the correct word… "*Humongous!* Snogged anybody lately?" he smiled.

I was surprised that he remembered the English term for kissing. "I've been trying to find you since that day at St. William's," he continued.

"I tried to find you, too," I said. "Do you know how many Bourgeois' there are in this parish? Hundreds. *Thousands, maybe.* I called several hundred of them and none of them knew you. I finally gave up."

"My parents have an unlisted home telephone number," he replied, and so do I. "You wouldn'a been able to find it in the phone book, anyway but I gave it to you before you left."

"That's a long story but basically, it got lost in the shuffle between here and Bermuda. I was devastated when I couldn't find it so I started calling every Bourgeois in the Skylarville phone book.

"When I came back the following summer, I called St. Williams and asked for Brother Anselm to ask him to have you call me, but the person who answered said he had 'deceased.' That was his word, not mine."

"You wouldn'a found it in the Skylarville phone book, anyway," he said. "I'm from Belle Glade. Brother Anselm died during my sophomore year," Andy replied, "but he did integrate St. William's like he said he would.

"You remember Noel Catash, the boy who came into the bathroom while we were... talking?" He smiled a rakish, almost lascivious, smile.

I nodded, remembering the boy who looked enough like Andy to be his older brother. I also remembered that he was a racist.

"His family, the Catashes, protested so much that they almost got excommunicated from the Catholic Church. I say good riddance to 'em. But that shut 'em up."

"I asked for the registrar's office but the person who answered said he could neither take a message for you nor give me any information about you or any St. William's student," I added.

"I called that number you gave me," Andy said, cutting me off, as excited as a schoolboy, "an' the person who answered said, 'Mahster Steven had a death in the family and he is spending the remainder of the summer in Bermuda,'" he said, imitating Butters, our butler. "I didn' leave a message for you, though."

"I wish you had, or at least left me your number again. The maid washed the pants I was wearing that day and your phone number got washed along with them.

"My grandfather died a few days after we met," I said in the way of explanation. "I spent the rest of that summer with my grandmother helping her pack up some of his stuff and keeping her company."

"I'm sorry," he said. "I didn' know, but I *did* try to find you. Look," he said, taking out his wallet. "I still have it." Folded up on a small slip of notebook paper in one of the cellophane picture slots, was my family's phone number in my handwriting from almost fifteen years prior.

"This is a different wallet but I've always kep' it but I didn't call again," he said. He grabbed me by the waist and said, "Come on, we've got some catchin' up to do. Let's get this party *rollin'*!"

He turned to the bespectacled officer. "I'm punchin' out, Clem. You gon' be okay?"

The bespectacled officer grunted something about "long-lost love and us being like Evangeline and Gabriel and continued pecking away at the typewriter. He briefly looked up and smiled. "You finally found him, huh, Beau?" he said. "Congratulations."

"Thanks Clem," Andy said. "See you Monday."

To me, he said, "you've gotta come over to the house. We've got fourteen years, two months, and three days worth of catchin' up to do."

Louisiana's summer heat slapped me across the face like a spurned lover as we walked out of the gelid air of the police station. My glasses fogged up immediately. I reached into my left rear pocket, pulled out my handkerchief, and cleared them so I could see where I was going. I was reminded of the biblical story of the Hebrew children who were fed into a fiery furnace and I could definitely empathize with them.

What'd you want to see the Chief about?" Andy asked off-handedly.

"I came about that deputy's murder."

"Don't waste your time," he said, turning up his nose. "That one had it coming. Where'd you park?"

"Across from the newspaper office," I replied. It was two blocks away but in the blistering summer heat and drenching humidity, it could've been two miles away. Nobody in Louisiana walked around any more than they had to. They scurried from their air-conditioned homes to their air-conditioned vehicles to the air-conditioned stores, schools, or churches.

This is one place where one literally could fry eggs on the sidewalks. Sidewalks and roadways sometimes buckled under the heat. And before they found better ways of reinforcing the glass in motor vehicles left standing in full sun, the glass would routinely explode from the expanding pressure of the summer heat if windows were not left rolled down a crack to allow the built-up heat inside to escape.

Andy's car had stood all day in full sun in a shell parking lot behind the station. The sign at the lot's entry gate read,

POLICE PERSONNEL ONLY.
ALL OTHERS WILL BE TOWED
AT THE OWNER'S EXPENSE.

"I'll drive you to your car an' you can follow me over to my house," he said, taking my hand. "*Damn*, it's good to see you again!"

Andy's brand new Pontiac Firebird was parked under a tall magnolia tree near the rear of the parking lot. It roared to life when he turned the key, then purred like a well-satisfied tiger. When the infernal heat had been allowed to escape to a more agreeable temperature, he rolled up the windows, ramped up the a/c to "high," and said, "Snog me right now!! I've been waiting too long for this." He turned his handsome face up toward mine and I kissed him with all the passion I had been saving up for fourteen years. His lips and tongue tasted like mint.

When we had finished one of the best snogs I had ever had, I asked, **"**Can we go St. William's first? I want to see the place where we met,"

"Great idea," Andy smiled wickedly. "We'll take my car over there and we can pick up yours on the way back. Then you can follow me over to my house."

We drove to the campus of St. William of Blade Academy. Its imposing Gothic-style buildings had not changed in the intervening years. Only the English ivy had gotten thicker, giving it that Eastern prep school look that many private schools tried for. We walked around the administration building but all of the doors were locked tight. There was no one around. All staff appear to have had fled Louisiana's summer for cooler climes.

"I know what we can do since we're here," said Andy, disappointed as I was that we could not get into the administration building's washroom to make out for a spell.

"What?" I wanted to know, expecting him to lead me to one of the other dark, out-of-the way corners where we had made out that day.

"Let me take you to Brother Anselm's grave. I go there sometimes to leave flowers or just to sit, think, and pray. He was a good man. He helped me a lot."

We drove two blocks from the school's campus to the Catholic cemetery of St. William of Blade. The large above-ground tombs, constructed mainly of stuccoed brick and capped with large crosses, shone dazzlingly white in the late afternoon sun. A few in the front of the cemetery were made of marble instead of brick coated with stucco. They were the burial mansions of the area's movers and shakers.

Behind the huge family tombs and private mausoleums of the rich and powerful were the more modest tombs of the "ordinary people," and separated by a low white picket fence, was the section of the cemetery reserved for the priests, nuns, and religious brothers of the Order of St. Philip of Nazareth, who serviced the school, church, and hospital.

"Here it is," Andy said, pointing to a simple slab of white marble under a large live oak with gray Spanish moss trailing almost to the ground. We sat on a cement bench at the foot of the grave. I read the epitaph:

IF IGNORANCE AND PREJUDICE
WERE SO EASILY VANQUISHED,
I WOULD NOT HAVE SPENT
MY ENTIRE LIFE
WARRING AGAINST THEM.
BROTHER AETHELRED ANSELM, O.S.P. N.
(ne` Lawrence Michael O'Toole)
April 17, 1905 to Nov. 10, 1964.
REQUIESCAT IN PACE

Andy crossed himself and said a brief prayer. He crossed himself again, took my hand, and resumed our conversation.

"He knew what we'd been doing in that bathroom, yeh," Andy said. "He tol' me it was all right to be gay and that God loves the gay person just as much as he loves the straight person.

"He also tol' me God doesn't make mistakes an' if he didn't want gay people to be part of the population, he wouldn't have made 'em." He corrected himself. "I should say, made *us*."

"I thought he had some suspicion of what we'd been doing when he told you to wipe that shrimp off your pants leg," I smiled, remembering. "Or was it oysters he wanted you to wipe off? He was a wise man."

Andy continued, "He told me both St. Aethelred and St. Anselm were gay. That's why he chose those names when he entered the novitiate. He said gay love was jus' as pure as straight love but he warned me not to become promiscuous."

He changed his accent to that of the Irishman, 'Just because ye have a willie, mi boyo, doesn't mean that you have to use it on everyone you meet. Find ye'self a nice mate an' settle down with the one.'

"He tol' me about popes and kings, actors, singers, poets, artists, and generals, as well as ordinary people who were gay, but history doesn't record the lives of ordinary people. As he said, 'God doesn't make mistakes. Everyone and everything on this green earth has a purpose.'

"When he died, he left his most prized possession, an ancient icon of two early Christian martyrs, Saints Sergio and Bacchus, to me.

"He said they were Roman soldiers and early Christian converts who were married to each other and lived openly as a couple in the eyes of God and the Church. He said the early Church was much more open to that sort of thing than now and it actually sanctioned gay marriages. He said Sergio and Bacchus were martyred for their faith when they refused to serve the old Roman gods.

"He knew a lot about gay history, especially in regard to the early Christian church and said he *knows* that Jesus would'a accepted gays, if he, himself, wasn't gay."

I looked surprised. I'd never heard anyone express such a thought.

"He didn't think Jesus was gay," Andy said, "but he thought that that might've been a possibility. He was, after all, celebate, and that was unusual for that place and time. Jewish boys were expected to get married early and produce a lot of strong, healthy sons but Nature has a way of raising her sweet little head in Man's plans and saying 'not this one.'"

"I don't know what I would've done back then," I said. "I have no desire to be with a woman."

"You probably would've done what one-tenth of the male population did. You'd have a lot of *headaches*," he laughed, when it came time to please your wife. He reached over and took my hand again then continued.

"I'd imagine that if you were a flaming queen instead of the big, strong, macho man you turned out to be, they'd have been stoned you to death or maybe you would've lived out your life as a male harlot, but most gay men just got married, had a couple of kids, then went off and did what they wanted to with their 'fishin' buddies.' Sort of like they do down here now in sout' Louisiana," he smiled.

"A lot of what goes on out there in those fishin' camps *stays* in those fishin' camps."

"I have the icon of Bacchus and Sergio on my dresser in my bedroom. When we get to the house, I'll show it to you. It's my most treasured possession. If I had a fire and could save just one thing, that would be it."

I followed Andy to Skylarville's first subdivision, called Mimosa Park, on the north side of town.

Mimosa Park was comprised of small, single-family bungalows. The floor plan was exactly the same but the initial buyers had the choice of buying one made of wood on all sides, wood with a brick façade, brick veneer, or painted and stuccoed cement block. The buyers had the choice five Easter egg colors. The lots were fenced-in parcels of land a little larger in size than a postage stamp.

The term, *"ticky-tack"* stuck in my mind as I drove down Mimosa Park Avenue, the main street into and out of the subdivision, but there was also a definite pride of ownership reflected in these tiny houses. Lawns were manicured, the houses well-kept. The colors of these tiny houses were vibrant, and hardscaping was abundant and well-tended.

Although all of the houses contained every type of tree, vine, bush, and flower that the rich delta soil of southern Louisiana would grow, the one thing they all had in common was a spreading mimosa tree in their front yards. In early spring, their flowers fluttered in the sultry spring breezes like wooly pink butterflies.

They were part of the builder's incentive package to encourage people to purchase a home in *"beautiful Mimosa Park."*

At that time, the subdivision was for whites only but as I drove by, I saw several black and mixed-race families participating in the "American Dream" there.

At the time of its inception, Mimosa Park was an unincorporated entity on the northern edge of town, headed *"up the bayou,"* away from the Gulf of Mexico. Since then, it had been annexed by Skylarville as the town grew and embraced it.

The city limit had since moved further north to accommodate some of the newer, fancier subdivisions that wanted the fire and police protection that the parish either couldn't or wouldn't provide.

Andy waved to two old women across the street and a few houses down, whose conversation in Cajun French wafted over the neighborhood like the drone of a lazy hornet in the still, humid quiet. He then waved to a group of three young men who worked around and beneath the hood of a tan Chevy van in the driveway of the corner house whose front door faced Mimosa Park Avenue.

Andy's house was a tidy white stucco bungalow with forest green trim. It was the first house in, facing west on Ligustrum Street. He shared his side yard with the other house's back yard. There was no fence between them, as was the case in so many others of the neighborhood's houses. He pulled the Firebird under a one-car carport attached to the main building like a barnacle. I parked my mother's Jaguar behind the Firebird on the short cement driveway.

We walked up the short sidewalk that ran from the driveway to the house's front door, past the picture window, trimmed in forest green, which, apparently, was also requisite for Mimosa Park's houses. An air-conditioning unit painted the same forest green, stuck out of a high, specially-built opening in the side of the house, protected from weather by the roof of the carport.

"Y'all still workin' on that thing?" he called jocularly.

"Still workin,'" someone affirmed. "We've almost got it runnin,'" another, deeper voice added.

"Get a horse!" Andy kidded.

"Hol' up a minute, T-Beau," called a tall, thin, shirtless guy about our age with long, sand-colored hair and a sandy goatee, who extricated himself from the van's entrails and strode the 30 feet of open lawn between the two houses.

"Excuse us a minute," he said to me as he pulled Andy a few feet away and said something to him, sotto voce. In the stillness of the afternoon, I could still hear what he wanted to convey to his cousin. "That shit we harvested is dry enough to smoke and it's pretty good. Wanna try some later?"

Andy nodded and returned to where I stood sweltering in the late afternoon sun. "This is Wayne," Andy said, "my friend from Chicago." I shook the guy's proffered, grease-stained hand. His handshake was firm, warm, and sincere.

"*Dammnn,* you're tall," he said looking me up and down. "You gotta be either a weight lifter, a heavy-weight prize fighter, or a football player," he said, awestruck.

I shook my head and smiled. "None of the above."

"Well, you *could* be, lookin' at your build. Shit, if I had a build like that, I'd be at the Saints' training camp."

"Thanks," I muttered. I liked this man already.

He turned to Andy. "Look at the arms on him!" he said, as if Andy had failed to notice.

Turning back to me, he said, "you're bout, what, six-four?' I'm six-one and you got me beat by a good bit."

"Six-six, 250," I said, adding weight before he even asked. I get the same question all the time. They tend to go together so I just give people both height and weight and save myself some time.

"This is my cousin, Kevin," Andy said. "You prob'ly don't remember him but y'all met briefly at St. William's too."

The name hit me in the gut like a ton of bricks. I hadn't thought of "the other Kevin" since I met Andy but now all of the feelings and emotions came rushing back.

I remembered the boy with the Moe Howard bowl-style haircut who came running up to us after we left the administration building's washroom as vividly as if the whole thing had happened yesterday afternoon. I remembered everything about that day. *Everything!*

His name, however, reminded me of Kevin Kincannon, the basketball phenom/male model who had shared my life for the last three years before he unceremoniously dumped me because I was a threat to his popularity, according to his agent.

It was to escape the hurt that I had come to Louisiana, ostensibly to visit my parents. *Creswic House* was always my refuge in times of stress.

Andy turned to Kevin and said, "Come over 'bout seven. You wanna have supper with us? I'll be cookin' steaks." I noticed his Cajun accent had become even more pronounced when he talked to Kevin.

Kevin smiled and nodded then turned and loped back to the van. "See y'all later."

"*You,*" Andy emphasized, "*not* the whole gang, OK?"

Kevin waved assent as he crawled back under the van's front end.

We entered a small, cheery living room painted a creamy yellow with an ice white ceiling and crown molding. He closed the door, flicked on the window air conditioner, and B&O stereo component system. Miles Davis wafted from the stereo's speakers as cooled air poured from the window unit.

"Sit down while I change out'a this uniform," he said. "I'll be right back. If you want a drink, liquor's in the cabinet next to the ice box. Ice is in the freezer, and if you wanna mix it, there's juices an' cold-drinks in the ice box."

I had fallen out of the habit of calling soda pop cold-drinks and refrigerators 'ice boxes'. He still called them by those very typically Louisiana names.

"You need some help getting that uniform off?" I volunteered.

He gave me a quick, devilish smile and said, "Well, I *have* been having trouble getting my gun belt off. Som'pn 'bout that last notch. *Vien ici, mon amour.*"

We entered an arched, cased opening onto a short oak-floored hallway painted the same pale yellow as the living room. We turned right, toward the front of the house, and entered a large, dark bedroom. A second bedroom, its doorway open, was at the other end of the hallway. Between them, was bathroom tiled in black and white octagonal ceramic subway tiles.

The two side walls of Andy's bedroom were painted battleship gray. The near wall, which contained the entry door into the room and a closet door, was painted dove gray. The far wall, the one over the headboard with double windows to the street, was painted black.

The ceiling, curtains, and cove molding were snow white. The king-size bed was covered with a gray and black duvet with matching shams.

The wall to my left as I entered the room contained a large double window flanked by floor to ceiling wood bookcases. A window air-conditioning unit purred to life when Andy flicked the switch. Black Venetian blinds and gauzy white curtains blocked out the sun, the heat, and the prying eyes of neighbors. The main window, over the long, low headboard, facing Ligustrum Street, was similarly outfitted.

Andy stored his service revolver in a gun safe in the closet then went to the six-drawer dresser that sat between the entry door and the closet door. He removed a gabled wooden picture frame from the top of the dresser and handed it to me. It was covered over with gold leaf. It appeared to be very old.

It was a triptych, consisting of a large center icon about the size of an 8x10 photograph and two hinged 5x7 side panels that folded forward from each side of the main icon, serving as support for standing the entire shrine instead of an easel on the back, and for propaganda for the two saints to whom it was dedicated.

The icons were hand-painted in the flat style of the religious art of ancient Byzantium. The two smaller side panels consisted of an image of each of the two men depicted in the main icon. St. Sergio was to the left panel and St. Bacchus was on the right. Printed in bold uncial lettering under each saint was the Latin phrase, "**ORA PRO NOBIS.**"

In the foreground of the center panel stood the two men, both with halos around their heads and weapons in their right hands. Their faces appeared to be drawn by hand while the halos had been appliqué-ed with gold leaf and limned with silver leaf.

One man carried a sword and the other, a shield. They faced forward, their left hands clasped to each other's in a manner reminiscent of the Vermeer painting depicting a wedded straight couple. Their clothing appeared to be made of hand-applied linen while their weapons were also or gold, silver, and bronze leaf. The work was absolutely fabulous.

Around his neck, each wore what appeared to be a large solid neck piece that looked like a large brass key ring. Sergio's necklace contained one oval between two rectangles, while Bacchus' contained one rectangle between two ovals. All of the rectangles were inlaid with a diamond-shaped object. I asked Andy if he knew the significance of the neck pieces but he did not.

A bearded figure, drawn smaller to show perspective, hovered in the background above the two men, dead center. He also faced forward, full face. I assumed him to be Jesus.

He smiled and extended both of his hands outward toward the loving couple below and to either side of him, as if giving them his blessing from heaven or clasping them by the shoulders as they walked forward in some far away garden and conversed pleasantly about whatever topic they chose.

Jesus' halo and the rays he emitted were also of gold leaf, limned in silver. His bearded face was also drawn in by hand. His clothing appeared to be of appliqué-ed silk, now very old.

"It's one of my prized possessions," Andy said, kissing me as I returned it to him.

I unbuttoned and removed his shirt. Around his neck, almost unnoticeable in the thick mat of black chest hair, was a silver chain with a small oval medallion of Sts. Sergio and Bacchus. "They're my new patron saints," Andy said.

Our tongues did a long, slow dance as I attempted to inhale him into me. The laws of physics allow only one body to inhabit any particular space at a given time. I wished like hell that I could change that law because I could not get him as close to me as I wanted. I wanted him so close to me that we inhabited the same space at the same time. I wanted him so close to me that even the Jaws of Life could not separate us. I had never felt that way about anybody.

I once saw a documentary about snakes. Boa constrictors, I believe. The videographer had captured two snakes copulating. The narrator said the coupling lasted for hours. They may have slowed down the action to emphasize the snakes' graceful movements as they undulated their way toward a final orgasm. It was one of the most sensuous things I had ever witnessed. I felt like one of the boas as Andy and I writhed slowly and sensuously, attempting to become one.

I wanted to be one with Andy. I wanted to share his soul.

"We got 'bout half an hour," he half-whispered. "But if I know Kevin," he'll be here in a lot less than that. He wants to know why I got this tall, gorgeous black man in my house.

"I don't usually have *anybody* in my house except for my cousins," he replied, turning over on his side to face me.

"So they don't know you're gay, I presume."

"That might be all right for Chicago but it's not gon' fly here in south Louisiana," he said quietly. "I could lose my job for bein' gay," he continued. "A gay cop in Bellefleur Parish? *I don' think so.*"

I lay on my back studying the ceiling. "There's no sense starting something we may not be able to finish."

"I guess you're right," Andy reluctantly agreed. "I had to invite him," he said.

His four o'clock shadow tickled as he laid his head on my chest. We spent the next twenty minutes being close, attempting to defy the laws of physics.

When we had sated ourselves, I helped Andy "clean up the oysters" and change his bedding. We showered together. I then recovered my clothes, put them on, and returned to the living room.

Andy emerged from the bedroom a few minutes later wearing a yellow t-shirt with a large outline of the State of Louisiana on the front. Within the borders of the state was a stick figure reclining in a hammock tied between two cypress trees, a tall drink in one hand.

Beside the tree nearest the figure's head was a small table that contained a pitcher of something potable. In the background, an alligator slept peacefully nearby, chained to a doghouse that had the name *"Rex"* printed above the door.

Only the figure's round head, bulbous nose, drink hand, and feet were visible. The bulk of the figure's body was buried in the commodious hammock. The caption read, ***"I Luv-EZ-ANA."***

Great tee-shirt," I said.

"A friend of mine makes 'em. I'll get some in your size and give 'em to you to take back to Chicago with you," he responded.

Dark, curly hairs peeked over the rounded neckline. He was also wearing faded blue jeans tailored in the waist to fit his form, and brown huaraches which revealed short, curly black hairs on his toes and the tops of his feet. His toenails were neatly manicured.

"You're not mad that I invited Kevin, are you?" he asked, taking a seat on the couch next to me but leaving the center cushion vacant.

"No," I laughed. "Whatever gave you that idea?" I took his hand into mine and gently pulled him toward me. I kissed him long and hard when he came within reach.

When his head rested against my chest, I said, "I'm not mad at all but it's better not to start something we may not be able to finish.

"Why don't you use this time to tell me about Deputy Eck? I'm sure there's a lot I don't know."

I pulled out my wallet and took out a joint from the secret compartment. "I heard what your cousin didn't want me to overhear so let's smoke this and I'll help you make dinner. That's safe and non-sexual enough to keep me from jumping your bones," I said as I leaned over to kiss his luscious lips yet again.

"Fire it up," he said, smiling a sly half-smile. Miles Davis was replaced by John Coltrane as we got blasted.

***

Blue and white vinyl tiles in a checkerboard pattern adorned the floor of Andy's spacious kitchen. We sat in red and white metal chairs at a Coca-Cola-red metal table with tubular chrome legs and chrome accents at the corners.

This room had been extended beyond the bungalow's original footprint. A double-wide arched doorway from the wood-floored living room provided access. A smaller archway allowed access from the small hallway, adjacent to the home's second bedroom.

A black clock in the form of a cat wearing a jeweled collar, whose large eyes and swinging tail marked time, hung on the wall near the entryway to the living room.

A grouping of three 16x20 black and white photographs of Louisiana scenes, matted in white in oversize black metal frames hung on the wall behind the table.

"Eck was about forty, I guess," Andy said as he prepared for supper. "He could've been younger but his hair was thinning and it made him look older than he probably was. I don't really know how old he was."

He smiled that sly half-smile again and said, "Know what I did?" His eyes twinkled.

I shook my head, waiting for the mischief to be disclosed.

"I told him that syphilis causes baldness and that might be the reason why his hair was fallin' out!"

"How'd he take that?" I asked.

"It took him aback, that's for sure. I could tell he was worried about his rapid hair loss but he was too scared of the results of a simple blood test to have himself checked out, so I got even bolder." He was ecstatic as he explained how he prolonged Eck's agony.

"I went to the parish health unit and got a handful of pamphlets on syphilis and gave 'em to him. That's the only thing that ever shut him up.

"When he started talking about fags or niggers, I'd ask him if he'd gone to get himself tested. He'd always say yes but he wasn't a good liar. I could see the fear in his eyes. There were literally days when he'd come in, talk about whatever arrests we had had that overlapped, and move out before I could ask him about it.

"That lasted right up 'til somebody blew his brains out," he smiled.

Andy handed me a large wooden salad bowl, a chef's knife, a head of lettuce, a large yellow onion, a brown grocery bag full of home-grown cucumbers, another full of tomatoes, and still another full of carrots. Huge carrots!

"Try one of these," he said, cutting one in half and offering me the top half. He took the lower part. These were the sweetest carrots I had ever had in this country. They rivaled some I had in Mexico City. They were delicious.

"You can make the salads," he said. He then smiled deliciously and said, "I'll toss yours later," as he handed me three salad plates.

I broke the lettuce leaves off the head, washed them, placed them on a paper towel to dry, and cut up the vegetables, placing them into the salad bowl. While I was thus occupied, he had filled a small metal pot and set three eggs to boil.

"He was the public relations officer for the Bellefleur Parish Sheriff's Office and I'm the P.R. officer for the Skylarville Police Department," he said, continuing his narrative about Deputy Eck, "So we had to see each other almost daily."

He poked holes in three large potatoes with a dinner fork, getting them ready for baking.

"As I said, a lot of what they do overlaps with what we do, so we have to have some communication between departments, especially when it comes to arrests.

"He was from Muffin Tuck, Mississippi, or somp'n like that, up 'round where Elvis was born. He made no attempt to disguise his hatred for 'coons,' 'queers,' and 'coon-asses,' as he was fond of saying."

"Blacks, gays, and Cajuns?" I asked.

Andy nodded his head and smiled. "Ah, so you know what a coon-ass is!"

"I've heard both those terms used only too frequently," I replied. "I may not have spent a lot of time in Louisiana but I didn't live in a vacuum, either. The only difference is now, wherever I go, I see tee-shirts and bumper stickers that say, '**Proud Coon-ass.**' What's that all about?"

"We took ownership of the word," he said. "Outsiders like to come here, eat our food, work our oilfields, take our money, enjoy our way of life, and then call us names because they feel superior to us," he said.

"Outsiders?" I asked. "Chinese people?"

He ignored the sarcasm. "People from other parts of the country. Mostly Texas, north Louisiana, and Mississippi. They come here to work in the oilfields. They're dirty, rude, uncultured, and bigoted."

"Not that south Louisiana doesn't already have its own home-grown variety of all of the above, right?" My sarcasm was getting the better of me but my point was well-taken.

"I'd be the last one to defend south Louisiana's racism but here it's kind of a *laissez-faire* situation. Things are gettin' better all of the time. Race relations have improved dramatically since that time we met.

"Brother Anselm kept his word. St. William's started winning its football and basketball games after they integrated and recruited black players. They jus' had their first black valedictorian and its first black homecoming king a few years back. The valedictorian was a National Merit Scholar, too. His name is Victorian Washington.

"He lettered in baseball, basketball and football. He was captain of his track team, and got the Group "W" Award for Spanish.

"The Group "W" award is the highest award a student can get in any subject. They hadta flip a coin as to which one he was gon' receive the award in, because you can only get one Group "W" Award regardless of how many categories they excel in. His daddy is principal of Skylarville Middle School and his mama teaches French at the Skylarville High.

"The homecoming queen is always from St. Willie's sister school, St. Emma's; and she was white. Their coronation didn't even raise an eyebrow," he said proudly. "Remember when we met? Noly Catash was so put out that you had used the bathroom there that he never did go.

"South Louisiana is like a foreign country to the outsiders. They don't understand our language, our culture, our religion, our accent, or our background.

"They don't like or understand *us* and we don't like or understand *them*. They say the only thing worse than being a *coon* is being a *coon's ass*—a Cajun."

I worked and listened. This was obviously something that greatly interested and disturbed him.

"I call it tribal hatred," he continued. "Same as racism, just that it's only among white people.

"There's never been any love lost amongst the peoples of Europe," I interjected. "The French and English, the Protestants against the Catholics, the northern Europeans against the southern Europeans, et cetera, et cetera, et cetera! The history of Europe is mostly told in its wars."

Andy nodded. "Eck was a bully. He didn't respect jurisdiction and he certainly didn't respect authority. He felt that that li'l tin badge he got gave him the right to go anywhere an' do whatever he wanted. He wanted to be Bellefleur Parish's Joe Friday but he was really more like its Barney Fife.

"He had no jurisdiction whatsoever in Skylarville beyond detaining a suspect for the city police but we were constantly getting complaints about sump'n he did.

"Jus' last week he single-handedly stopped a peaceful protest march by about a hundred blacks and publicly humiliated 'em."

"I saw it on TV", I said. "That was him?"

Andy nodded.

"They started their march at the Mimosa Park strip mall at the intersection of St. Patrick Highway and Mimosa Park Avenue, two blocks from here, where we came into the subdivision. That's well within the town limits."

St. Patrick Highway was the main north-south thoroughfare through the City of Skylarville.

"They marched from the strip mall and had planned to take a petition to the courthouse and sheriff's office. When they got to the courthouse steps, Eck was there to meet 'em. He held his weapon in one hand and his badge in the other and told 'em that they'd better go on home.

"Somebody in the crowd pointed out that as a sheriff's deputy, he had no jurisdiction within the town limits and that they were going to present their grievance letter to the Sheriff. Know what Eck did then?"

I knew exactly what had happened and where this was going. I had seen the pictures on every television channel in Chicago and in all of the Chicago newspapers. All three of them. Ours ran the story and the accompanying pictures in large type and bold headlines?

Andy continued, obviously not remembering that I am a reporter. "He made 'em all kneel down in front of the courthouse with their butts in the air and foreheads to the ground, like prayer time in Mecca. All you could see was a sea of asses and R.C. Eck holding his gun in one hand and his badge in the other on the steps of the Bellefleur Parish Courthouse.

"A local reporter was there and so was a news crew from one of the New Orleans television stations. The TV crew caught it on film. It got picked up by stations across the state and across the nation.

"I saw it," I said. "It was embarrassing. Whenever there's something like that anywhere in Louisiana, one or another of my colleagues will point it out to me. It seems as though nothing positive about Louisiana ever makes the news in Chicago except Mardi Gras, and even that's not always positive.

"By the way, what were they protesting?"

"RC Eck," he said dryly. *"Fils p'tain!* I hope he rots in hell."

"And the sheriff just let him get away with it?"

"Not hardly!" he said. "He was suspended and on unpaid administrative leave. He was up for a disciplinary hearing the day after he was shot. I was hopin' he'd get fired for what he did but this is even better."

He walked to the rear of the kitchen, which led to a screened porch. "I gotta show you som'pn," he smiled. He opened the door and a small white bundle of fur bounded into the room.

"A miniature poodle," I said, surprised that someone as meticulous as Andy would have a dog.

"His name's Wallace and he was Eck's dog. Some people shouldn't have animals. Eck was *definitely* one of them. I've been keepin' him out on the porch when I'm not home 'cuz I didn't know if he's housebroken or not but he appears to be. He wants to please me. He probably would've gone outside if Eck had taken him out on a regular basis but he didn't.

"Eck's apartment was dark and filthy. Dirt was caked on everything; door handles, drawer pulls, the shower, the toilet lever…you name it! I was scared to sit anywhere because it was so nasty. I stood in the middle of the living room looking around and takin' it all in."

He scooped up the little bundle of fluff, held him close, and caressed him, blowing kisses to the little animal and telling him how beautiful he was and what a good dog he was, while he surveyed the porch for land mines.

Finding none, he said, "I gotta take him out so he can do his business. I'll be right back. Have some more wine."

He returned a few minutes later with the dog following him. He brought in two metal bowls, washed and dried them, and filled one with kibble and the other with water and placed them in one corner of the large kitchen, near the water heater.

"I believe I can leave him inside cuz he's not destructive and he seems to be housebroken.

"How'd you come by him?"

"Eck lived in a one-bedroom apartment over Mr. Styron's garage on President Street. Two days after Eck was killed, Mr. Styron called us and told us that Eck had a little dog, so I went over to find the dog and take him to the Pound.

"Mr. Styron gave me a key to the apartment but he refused to go in with me. He said he'd get sick if he went in there. He also said he would've kicked Eck out long ago but Eck threatened him with bodily harm if he did.

"That apartment was *awful*! Nasty and dirty! *Filthy!!* When I went in, Wallace was at the door barking his head off but when I entered the apartment and tried to pick him up, he ran and hid, barking the entire time. I didn't know where he'd gone but it was a small space so there weren't too many places he could've hid. It took me a while to catch him. He didn't wanna be touched by anybody. I'll skip the details except that the place was one of the nastiest places I've ever had the displeasure to visit. Roaches, mold...you name it."

"It took me more than an hour to catch him. I found his leash and took him out. When he finished doin' his business, I took 'im back inside and unleashed him. He ran into the bedroom and brought me this thick packet of plastic.

"He stood right in the doorway between the kitchen and the living room wagging his tail with the plastic bag in his mouth and then dropped it at my feet.

"I guess that was his way of thanking me for feeding him and giving him some water. I pocketed it when I saw what it was.

"I put him into the pet carrier I'd brought with me and took him directly to the nearest vet. They cleaned his teeth and ears, sheared him, bathed him, de-matted and de-flea'ed him, and gave him his shots. He was there for three days.

"When I retrieved him, he looked like a different dog. I took him home with me, and started showing him some love and affection and we've been friends ever since. He's a great little dog. I'm glad I didn't put him in the Pound. Anybody who had to live with Eck has suffered enough already."

"What did he bring you?" I wanted to know.

"Some *really* good-ass pot! Ditch weed! Know what else he showed me?" Andy said.

Before I could answer, he said, "He led me to where Eck kept a stack of dirty pictures and magazines! They were in the linen closet in the bathroom, underneath a pile of filthy clothes in a hamper.

"When I got home, I lit up a joint of the stuff Wallace had brought me. It was pretty good, if I do say so. Eck prob'ly got it from somebody at *Spooky's*. That place is known for drug dealing and prostitution but it was high quality, that's for sure.

"That hypercritical bastard always said he hated black people but he had a stack of Polaroids of black men and boys. Knowin' Eck, I'm pretty sure he threatened to arrest 'em if they didn't pose for him. No tellin' what else he did to those poor guys. Not one of 'em looked like he was there willingly. He liked to throw his weight around.

"He also had muscle magazines that featured black men. He'd'a *loved* you!" he smiled.

"The SO is still trying to find any of those guys. They'll prob'ly hav'ta wait until school starts to find the boys but they're pulling all of his traffic stops and his arrest records to see if any of them were molested by Eck. The problem is that most men won't admit to being raped.

"The dog's name is Wallace? As in George and Lurleen?" I inquired.

"I suppose," he said. "People like George and Lurleen Wallace were his idols, along with Governor Orval Faubus of Arkansas, Lester Maddox, and Bull Connor."

"Eck was always talking about his hatred for black people and gays," Andy said. "Meanwhile, he was at home getting his rocks off on pictures of black men and boys."

He shook his head. "It's not the size part, it's the *black* part that gets me! If you don't like black people, why would you fantasize about black men, well-hung or not?

The question was rhetorical, rather than anything I could answer. I could see what he meant. "Why do you think black people range in color from ebony to ivory?" I asked. "Some of the most ardent segregationists by day were some of the biggest chocolate-lovers by night. If you don't like people of a certain ilk, why associate with them when the sun goes down?"

"I'd never thought of it like that," Andy said.

"Yes, you did," I challenged. "I distinctly remember having this same discussion with you at St. William's when we met. Where do you think the mulattos, octoroons, et cetera, came from? How they got here.

"My old memory isn't as good as it used'ta be?" he smiled.

"Did the detectives find any evidence in the apartment?"

"I haven't been payin' much attention to what's been goin' on 'cuz I hated Eck and everything he stood for," he replied. "I hope they never find the killer. That person did the City of Skylarville and Bellefleur Parish a favor.

"That's the report my buddy was typing up when you walked in. Eck was the kind that would find a person's weakness and then start picking at it and digging at it until you wanted to strangle him."

"Or shoot him," I commented. "You *sure* you didn't kill him?" I asked, semi-seriously. He did not reply for a long time.

"I hated Eck, true enough," Andy finally said, "but I didn' kill him. I *should've* but I didn't. *I felt like it*...But I didn't. Eck was high on my list but there's people higher than him on it."

"Like who?" I wanted to know.

"One day, I'll tell you about them but not today, okay?" he finally said. "Besides, I didn't have to worry about killin' Eck. I knew that in this gun-loving part of the country, all I had to do was wait. Somebody else would do what I sincerely *wanted* to do. Now it's done and I applaud the person who did it." He was very sincere in his response.

"What's so bad about Spookie's?" I wanted to know.

"Well, first of all, they wouldn't even let you in. After all of these years of integration, they *still* refuse to serve black people there. Of course, no respectable black person wants to go there, either. They should've been shut down a long time ago but they declared themselves a private club to avoid having to serve blacks and any other 'undesirables.'

"It's the kind of place your mama warned you about," he smiled. "There's a red-neck bar on one side and a dirty pool hall on the other, separated by a wide doorway. There are Confederate flags all over the place, pictures of Lee, Jackson, Jeff Davis, and other Rebel quote-quote 'heroes.'

"There are always brawls, shootings, trashy, drunk men, and women nobody would wanna acknowledge in the light of day. Most of the locals, black or white, don't go there. Their customers are mostly oilfield trash who moved here from other parts of the country.

"It's everything I *hate* about white Southern culture. And it's everything he held dear.

"There had to be more to it than that," I said. "Do you think maybe he was attracted to you? You're a gorgeous man. I can see where a closeted man like he was, would be attracted to you but he just didn't know how to convey it to you so he did what little boys have done to little girls from time immemorial: being mean."

Andy shook his head. "Who knows what was going on in that peanut brain of his?"

"He was older than you and he wasn't married, so how could he feel so free to make comments about your sexuality when he was in the same boat?"

"He never made comments about my sexuality. He was more subtle than that. Every day it was the same thing. No matter what the subject, he'd find some way of bringing it around to being gay. If not that, it was 'niggers' or sump'n else. Seeing Eck was the worse part of my day. I'm glad his visits only lasted 'bout fifteen minutes to half an hour at the most."

"And after you started telling him about syphilis, it all stopped, right?" I asked.

Andy nodded and smiled. "He was too glad to get away from me, then. I'd found his weakness jus' like he found mine. I hammered on him jus' like he hammered on me."

***

Half an hour and three joints later, Wallace watched from a kidney bean-shaped wicker bed as we prepared three New York strip steaks and put them on the grill, made the salads, and started the potatoes baking in the oven. The wine sat chilling in a metal ice bucket Andy pulled from the hall closet. The table was set. Everything was ready for a feast. The only element missing was Kevin Blanchard, Andy's cousin.

Kevin was tall and lanky with soft brown eyes, long, sand-colored Andy Bourgeois eyelashes, a scraggly, sand-colored mustache and goatee, a very prominent Adam's apple that bobbed up and down when he talked or swallowed, and long, thick, shoulder-length, honey-colored hair that he parted down the middle. His complexion, though suntanned, was considerably lighter than Andy's.

He wore well-worn, tattered and faded bell-bottom blue jeans full of burn holes, indicative of his profession of welder in one of the local shipyards, a black tee shirt with the almost-faded logo of some long-extinct rock and roll band, and a leather headband that kept all of that hair in place. On his feet he wore white ribbed tube socks, and blue-and-white Keds, which he doffed at the door.

The lower right corner of his upper left incisor was missing and the entire tooth was dark gray. The chip formed a small, diagonal like the page of a novel that had been turned down by a careless reader too lazy to use a bookmark. *It must leave an interesting pattern when he bites an apple,* I thought.

"I got hit in the mouth by a power drill," Kevin said, noticing my stare. "I was at the bottom of a ladder steadying it for my buddy, who was makin' holes. He lost his grip and dropped the drill he was usin.' It hit me in the mouth an' chipped my tooth. Hurt like hell, too. I had a split lip for a week and I almost lost the tooth. It's still loose but I'd hate to be gap-toothed like a seven-year old!"

"I didn't mean to stare. I'm sorry," I said. "I was noticing how much you look like Andy, but with different coloring. Sort of like those black dolls they sell in the toy stores. They don't have any African features at all. They're just white dolls dipped in brown paint."

"I thought you had noticed my chipped front tooth," Kevin said.

"There's a good cosmetic dentist in New Canaan," I said. "He can fix it if you want."

He nodded and smiled. He now seemed to be a little more relaxed. "You a cop, too?" he wanted to know. When I said no, he asked if I smoked weed. When I smiled and nodded, he pulled a plastic baggie from his right sock, asked Andy for his rolling tray, and began cleaning, de-seeding, and rolling thick, healthy-looking joints.

"This here's home-grown, yeah," he bragged. "Born and bred on Bayou Mal Enfant. Just like me an' T-Beau."

Bayou Belle Fleur gave the parish its name as the parish's major waterway. Bayou Mal Enfant was but one of its many siblings. Both were offshoots of the Mississippi River, which ran languidly toward the Gulf of Mexico a hundred or so miles south. The river spawned hundreds of similar bayous and smaller waterways as spillways as the land flattened out and met the sea.

After he had rolled four or five of the monsters, he selected one and held it up for inspection. "Not bad, huh?" he said to me. "This one's perfect."

He then pulled a lighter from his left jeans pocket and lit it, passing it first to me, as the guest. I passed it to Andy, who passed it to its maker.

"What's that you call him?" I asked Kevin, as much to break the ice between us as to learn more about my friend.

"T-Beau," he replied. "Everybody 'round home calls him that, or jus' Beau. It means 'L'il Handsome One' or 'Dear L'il Handsome One.' Cajuns use *'T'* before a name to mean som'pn we hold dear. It's short for *'p'-TEE.'"*

He inhaled his product, held it inside his lungs a good long time before exhaling, and smiled agreeably. I thought maybe he had sampled some of his product with his mechanic friends before he arrived.

"You know French?" he inquired as he removed himself from the wing chair in which he had been sitting, and onto the large area rug that covered the oak floor.

"I went to high school near London and French was the second language. I've also spent a lot of time in France, Canada, Haiti, and St. Martin. Cajun French is a whole 'nother animal.

"It's a *man's* language," he boasted. "Not that frou-frou stuff they speak in France or Canada. I know words and phrases," he confessed, "but I can't hold a conversation in it."

Andy ducked into the kitchen with Wallace close behind. They returned to the living room after checking on the steaks on the grill and the potatoes baking in the oven. Wallace settled himself in his little bed and kept a close eye on the proceedings from his own little command post.

"They'll only be a few minutes more," he announced. "Wanna jus' hold the rest of this 'til after we eat?" he asked his cousin.

Kevin nodded and pinched the lit end of the joint with calloused fingers.

Andy had set the table with a white damask tablecloth, matching cloth napkins inserted into bamboo napkin rings, clear plastic place mats, and two tall lighted candles inserted into low brass candleholders. He poured plum wine into wine glasses etched with vines that wrapped around the stems and flowers that cupped the bowls.

"Dinner is served, gentlemen," he announced.

After an excellent meal of "dirty rice" and gravy, garden veggies with mushrooms, and broiled steaks, we washed, dried, and put away the dishes. That task completed, Andy rummaged under the sink, through several neatly folded brown paper grocery bags emblazoned with the names of local food stores on them.

He went to the rear screened porch to an old wooden table painted chartreuse and flecked with paint rings and dried paint specks of varying colors.

Andy busied himself filling the empty bags with beans, peas, carrots, corn, and leafy vegetables of various kinds from similar bags that were lined up on a larger table leaning against the wall that separated the kitchen from the porch.

I stood in the doorway of the kitchen watching. When the bags were full, he handed two of them to me and carried two. "Take this to your mama. Why don't you put 'em by the front door now so you don't forget 'em when you leave? Now *laissez les bon temps roulez!"*

Kevin had anticipated his cousin and was now seated on the sofa. He had divided the joints he had rolled among the three of us and placed them in plastic food storage bags. "This is for you," he said, offering me one of the bags. Put it with the veggies," he said.

"Thanks, Kevin," I smiled. The ice had been broken.

He nodded in acknowledgement, "Cajun hospitality!"

He had cleared the coffee table and a large bong stood in the space formerly occupied by his rolling tray. He had filled its protuberant middle with water. "Want a hit?" he asked me, smiling a Cheshire cat smile...

***

I awoke in a ganja- and alcohol-induced haze in a strange, darkened bedroom. The heavily curtained windows with wide-slatted Venetian blinds effectively prevented me from distinguishing many details in the room.

Sitting up for a few minutes in the chilled air and trying to gather my wits, I became aware for the first time of the covered figure that lay next to me in the large bed.

I pulled back a heavy duvet, a chenille bedspread, and then a crisp white top sheet with high thread count, and introduced myself to one of the finest sets of hairy buns I had ever had the pleasure to meet. They were hard as basketballs, perfectly round, and covered with dark, curly hair. Just the way I like 'em!

The owner's head was covered by a pillow and faced away from me so I still had no idea of to whom these delicious buns belonged.

A few muffled grunts that emitted from beneath the pillow indicated that the owner did not like the idea of his buns being left exposed to the chill.

I pulled the bedding back up to cover the sleeping one's back and he stirred no more, continuing to inhale and exhale rhythmically.

I placed my hand beneath the coverings again, touching the broad, lightly furred back. I moved my hand down to the buttocks area again. I liked the feel of those buns of steel.

This was a man who worked out!

The lighted digital clock on the night stand adjacent to the bed read "6:42." I decided to lay back and get some extra shut-eye.

I did a quick recap of my day yesterday. It seems that everything got out of hand after supper.

The sleeper next to me could be none other than the great lust of my life, Andy Bourgeois.

I remembered smoking the joints Andy's cousin offered me, then the three joints I had stashed in my wallet, finishing off the rest of the plum wine, and then moving on to some red wine; then smoking some of the stuff Andy had gotten from the poodle, drinking so many beers that I lost count, going constantly to the bathroom to piss it all out almost as fast as it went in, and then taking hit after hit from the bong.

I also vaguely remembered calling my parents to tell them that I was spending the night at a friend's house. I remembered my mother asking me if I wanted her to send Alex, their chauffeur, to Skylarville to drive me home and my very enthusiastic *"no!"*

I studied Andy's body while he slumbered. Somehow, it looked larger when he was asleep than when he was awake. His body was like some kind of stretchy material. It relaxed when not in use but was taut and compact, smaller, when in use. I turned over and snuggled close to him. We just seem to go together like a hand and glove.

Kevin Kincannon was the reason I had come to Louisiana in the first place. After a four-year on-and-off relationship, he had just walked out on me because my being gay would or could endanger his commercial endorsements. I guess I need to tell Andy that I'm damaged goods. On the rebound, so to speak.

This had been one of the most pleasant evenings I had spent in a long time. We listened to good jazz on Andy's stereo system, smoked some excellent pot, drank some good wine and too much beer and had a pleasant conversation about the "Golden Rectangle," as Kevin called the area between Assumption, Lafourche, Terrebonne, and Bellefleur Parishes, which, he said, is very fertile and perfect for growing marijuana.

The day with Andy had been so wonderful that I had not even thought of "the other Kevin" even once since I walked into the Skylarville Police Department. While I had thought that looking into the death of a sheriff's deputy would take my mind off of my reason for being in Louisiana, I had not counted on having it change my entire life.

Kevin Kincannon was the ebony demi-god/professional basketball player who had shared my life for the past two years until he walked out on me for fear that I would destroy his income potential.

I was heartbroken when I entered the police station but after meeting Andy again, it was as if Kevin Kincannon had never even existed.

I snuggled close to Andy as he breathed rhythmically in the cool, dark bedroom. I took in his sweet, manly scent. Could he be "The One?" I kissed him on the nape of his neck, where the wild curls cascaded to an abrupt end like the bottom of a waterfall.

My grandma believes that everyone has a soul-mate; a perfect match. The Other Half of his or her soul. I never believed that. I have always been a skeptic of the "Romeo and Juliet Syndrome," as I call it. I have never believed that it only takes one moment, one look, to find one's True Love until now.

At this early stage, I'm not sure whether what I have with Andy is love or lust but if I'm not in love with him, I know beyond a shadow of a doubt that I'm in lust. The man turns me on like no one else has ever been able to do.

Everything feels so "right" with Andy. Although it has only been about 18 hours, it seems as though I've known him a lifetime.

The best way to describe it is to compare it to shoes. You can walk forever in shoes that are *almost* right. Eventually, your foot conforms to the shoe or the shoe conforms to your foot, but if you step into a pair of custom-made, hand-stitched English or Italian loafers, there is no comparison at all. When it's right, you know it.

***

"Good morning, Light-Weight," Andy said, turning over and smiling. His bushy mustache served as parenthesis for his wide smile. "You passed out on me."

"I fell asleep," I smiled, bringing my nakedness closer to his. "I wanted to talk to you about something," I said.

"Sounds serious."

"Not really, but I wanted to get past it once and for all," I said, sounding a little more nervous than I thought I would."

"Go 'head," Andy said, holding my hand beneath the covers.

"Well, I came to Louisiana because I'm on the rebound. I had this lover…"

"Kevin," Andy said.

"How'd you know that?" I asked.

"You talk in your sleep.

"I do not!" I smiled.

"Oh, yes you do, Cher. At first I thought you were talkin' about my *cousin,* Kevin. I was gettin' jealous at first, but then it became obvious that you didn't mean him."

"I was talking about Kevin Kincannon."

"The basketball player?"

"Yep."

"Your lover is Kevin Kincannon of the Chicago basketball team? NEGRONICUS?"

"*You're* my lover. Kevin Kincannon was my *boyfriend.* He's only in love with himself. I was too stupid to see it until he walked out and then I realized how little it really mattered."

"But that guy's phenomenal. And he plays well, too," he smiled. "I've had many fantasies involving him. Wow!! And you mean... he's *gay?*"

"As a goose," I responded.

"You want breakfast?" he asked, trying to take in the information I had just supplied. Not many people knew about Kevin Kincannon's real proclivity but most people would react the same way Andy did if they found out that the greatest ball-handler, base stealer, golfer, or field goal kicker in the world is gay.

"We can talk about it after we've cleaned up a little, OK?" he said. "It's never a good idea to talk about serious matters on an empty stomach and before we've emptied our bladders." He leaned over and kissed me. "We got time for that."

I agreed.

"It's not even seven o'clock yet. Why don't you lay back and relax."

"I can relax for a while but I need to get back to my parents' house. I'm sure they're worried about me. I'd been home for less than two hours when I left for Skylarville to talk to the sheriff and the police chief and I haven't returned.

"You called 'em last night. Don't you remember? You gave 'em my name, address, and phone number in case I wanted to sell you into white slavery."

We showered together. It wasn't easy in that small tub with the shower at one end but it was one of the most sensual experiences I have ever had. This day was starting off full of superlatives.

Over grits, eggs, toast, orange juice for me and grits, eggs, and coffee with chicory for Andy, we discussed the situation in which we found ourselves.

We cleared away the breakfast dishes. Andy washed and I dried. We then returned to the darkened living room where, when Andy opened the heavy drapes and blinds, we found Kevin Blanchard sound asleep on the sofa, covered up from neck to toes with a blue and white blanket, with Wallace curled up into a tight little ball on his bed nearby.

"Now I know why I don't remember when he left," Andy said, closing the drapes and blinds again. "Let's go into the bedroom. We can talk there soon as I take Wallace out."

As we left the room, Andy gathered up an assortment of smoking utensils, half-empty bottles, and very full ashtrays. He distributed the clutter between us and led the way to the kitchen, where he disposed of the un-potable potables and empty bottles. Those that still contained potable liquids were either drained or placed in the refrigerator. Those that did not, were placed on a shelf in a glass-fronted liquor cabinet in one corner of the living room.

His next task was to walk Wallace, which he accomplished in only a few minutes by letting the little dog loose into the fenced-in rear yard. When they returned, the little dog was a bouncing ball of energy. Andy changed his water and gave him his breakfast in a metal dog dish in one corner of the kitchen, near the rear door.

I had to marvel at Andy's organizational skills. He was like an army general. *A place for everything and everything in its place.* His last job was to clean the ashtrays and separate the still smokeable marijuana roaches from Kevin's cigarette butts and place them for future use in a huge blue plastic jug that had once contained spring water. The jug occupied an obscure corner of the large kitchen, near the stove.

"When this thing gets full," he said, "I'm gon' have the biggest pot party Bellefleur Parish has ever seen."

"I can see it now," I said. "A cop holding a pot party in a small town. How long before that gets back to your chief? Besides, looking at the miniscule amount you have in there now, it might be a while yet," I joked, eyeing the contents of the jar, the bottom of which contained a few lonely marijuana "roaches."

"Not when you have cousins like mine. They'd never rat me out. That thing'll be full before Christmas next year. Let's go back into the bedroom."

We sat on the bed as Andy rolled joints on the small round metal tray Kevin had used the night before.

"So where does this leave you and Kevin Kincannon?" he said.

I told him the story of Kevin Kincannon and me:

Kevin Kincannon is the star player for the Chicago team. He is on everybody's "want list." Not only is he a phenomenal basketball player, but he has model-quality looks.

He just signed a three year contract that made him the highest paid athlete in history. To top that, he makes even more from product endorsements than he makes from his seven-figure basketball salary. He truly believes he is God's gift to the world. He is big, bold, brash, beautiful, and perfectly formed. And totally "Inner City." He is truly a pleasure to behold.

"I met Kevin my freshman year in college," I began. "I attended Drake University in Des Moines, Iowa. He was going to begin his senior year in high school the following September. He was at Drake for a six-week long summer basketball camp. I was either the only black male undergrad on campus that summer or one of the very few. Kevin was suffering from culture shock. He had never been in an all-white environment and he was homesick.

"When he saw me, he was like a duckling imprinting on the first object it sees when it hatches. We spent a lot of time together in my dorm room that summer. I had not played very much basketball and he had not played any tennis at all but we played a lot of one-on-one games after his day was over. It was our first shower together that led us to sex."

Andy's face fell.

"Don't worry, little Buckaroo," I said. "I never *loved* him. I was in *lust* of him but not love. I feel more for you after just one afternoon thirteen years ago and one afternoon yesterday than I ever felt for him." His face lit up again, making me happy. I would never want to do or say anything—except the truth-- that would hurt this man.

"Kevin Kincannon is beautiful," I continued. "Gorgeous! All of the other boys in the camp were gangly teenagers. Too big for their hands and feet, with acne, or braces. Most were tall, awkward, and skinny. Like I was when we met.

"Kevin was taller than all of them, at six-six, at least, and as perfectly formed as any Greek god. And he was still growing! He was absolutely perfect.

"He seemed to have this kind of inner light that set him apart from everyone else. He stood out from the others. I've never met anyone else who had that characteristic. I can't explain it but if you ever meet him, you'll see what I mean. He was the color of obsidian with a perfect smile and beautiful full lips. He was perfectly proportioned even to the smallest detail.

"He reminded me of that passage from the Bible. In the Song of Solomon, I believe, where the Queen of Sheba told the women of Jerusalem, 'I am black but comely, O' ye daughters of Jerusalem....'

"I think she should have said, 'I am black *and* comely,' not 'black *but* comely,' but that's another matter. Well, Kevin was black *and* comely. Being a photographer, I took literally hundreds of photos of him, nude, semi-nude, dressed, over-dressed, dribbling a basketball, *not* dribbling a basketball, asleep.... You name it. The camera loved him and he loved to be loved, both by the camera and lusted after by me.

"Nobody ever told me that if you're black, you're supposed to automatically know all about basketball but Kevin thought so, anyway. I knew nothing about it. Tennis, golf, swimming, rugby and cricket yes, but not basketball--or baseball, or football, for that matter.

"Kevin was a high school junior going into senior year and already famous as one of the top potential recruits. He was as good in baseball and football as he was in basketball. They were comparing him with Jim Thorpe.

"College scouts and pro-team agents were kissing his ass and he was still in high school but he and the other boys had been playing since they were in diapers."

"Kevin came from a hard-scrabble neighborhood in Baltimore. He would tell me about it at night, telling me that I had no idea of what it means to be black in America. I told him that he was right. Although I was born in this country, my parents had done their best to keep me and my siblings away from American racism by building The Reserve and keeping us out of the country as much as possible.

"He had never heard of the Mallory family and that suited me just fine. He just thought I was a kid who was richer than he was. Hell, just about everybody was richer than he was. He was everything I was not. My polar opposite, so to speak. The only things we had in common were the color of our skin and the fact that we both loved and appreciated men.

"He told me how hard it was, adjusting to life on the Drake campus, how he missed the noise and confusion of the streets of Baltimore. He had a problem with open green space because he had never grown up with it. He frequently commented on how different I was from anybody he had ever met.

"By the time the camp was over, we were inseparable. I'd learned far more about basketball than I ever cared to know. He wanted me to go into the NBA, where he was headed as soon as he became eligible because I had the height and he had taught me the skills I'd need over the course of the six weeks we were together. To him, college was just a tunnel he had to pass through on his way to the NBA. He had no interest in learning anything college could teach him. His future was already made, as far as he was concerned.

"He taught me a whole lot about basketball and about sex. I was a virgin except for that time at St. William's with you," Andy blushed and reached for my hand. I continued. "But he had girls and boys, men and women, throwing themselves at him. Kevin was still genuine at that time. Unassuming and only slightly affected by the hubbub around him. He was well on his way but he still hadn't gotten the swollen head he developed later, when he found out that he could treat people like shit and they'd allow it because he was Kevin Kincannon.

"We lost contact after a while. He graduated from high school and went to the college that promised him and his family the most bang for his buck. Under the table, of course.

"Out of college, he was drafted in the first round by Baltimore, just like the pundits predicted. He played well for Baltimore but he wanted more. He followed the money Philadelphia offered him and he played there for a few seasons, getting better, perfecting his craft as he went but they were just stepping stones. He had always said he wanted to play for Chicago and he was unhappy anywhere else until he proved to them that he was ready.

"He made some awesome last minute three pointers in crucial games that got the press on his side and got his team into the playoffs. I followed his career but not too closely. I never expected to see him again until I got a phone call at work one day. By that time, I was living in Chicago.

"I knew he was unhappy about being in Philly and that he wanted to be traded to Chicago, the top team in the NBA.

Finally, he managed to get himself traded to Chicago, his dream team, but I didn't even think he remembered me. I was pretty awkward, even in college. It wasn't until my junior year in college that things sort of fell into place and I stopped growing and started pulling everything together—body-wise, I mean." Andy rubbed my chest and placed a kiss lightly on my left nipple.

"Anyway, I got this phone call at work one day. It was from him. He had asked my editor if I could interview him for a piece the paper planned to run, since he and I were old friends. I'd never done sports before, and I didn't know how to do a successful sports article but I had little choice in the matter. Kevin wanted it and the editor agreed, since it was either me or no article at all. The *Chicago News Register* would get the pleasure of an exclusive interview with him.

I gave him the nickname that has followed him ever since, NEGRONICUS!

"You gave him that nickname?" Andy asked, both surprised and impressed. "Makes him sound like a gladiator."

"After the interview, he asked that I show him around town, being careful to avoid the gay areas. I agreed and we became friends again. He said he didn't know who he could trust besides me. The sex didn't start up again until about three or four months after our initial meeting.

"He told me that he was afraid that someone would find out about his sexuality and he'd be ostracized and lose everything he had worked so hard to gain. He was supporting his entire family and couldn't afford to lose what he had worked so hard for. He said he knew he could count on me to be discreet, so we began seeing each other on a regular basis, first as friends, then as boyfriends.

"All the time," his star was rising and he began to believe all the hype that was being written about him. It was all true. He was phenomenal in every aspect of his life.

"Modeling agencies started calling him to pitch products for them, his agent, a guy named Eli Levinson, was constantly telling him that if he wanted the big money to keep rolling in, he'd better lie really low and be seen in public with the women Eli provided for him.

"He had an apartment in a downtown highrise and I was living on Farwell in Rogers Park, on the far north side, near the Evanston border, but he spent more time at my condo than he did at his own until Eli deemed that we were spending too much time together and it wasn't good for Kevin's image, since I was "out" and proud of being gay.

"Eli wanted Kevin to marry some woman Eli found for him. After a few months, they'd pay the woman off, she and Kevin would divorce, and that would cement Kevin's image as a heterosexual stud. Believe me, though, Kevin was a total bottom! There was absolutely nothing a woman could do for him sexually.

"Kevin had women throwing themselves at him at every turn. There was nowhere he could go where there weren't women waiting for him.

"They found out where he lived and stationed themselves outside his building. Since they couldn't get into the lobby, some of them stationed themselves outside the entrance to the garage, where he would have to pass. There was a time lapse from the time he pressed the button for the garage door to go up and the time he could actually drive in so he was extremely vulnerable right there. One woman even threw herself in front of his car so he'd have to acknowledge her. "I've never seen such predatory humans in my life.

"If I wanted to see him, I had to drive into the garage, pick him up, put him on the floor of my car's back seat, cover him up with a blanket, and exit the garage in order to spend time with him. That, or stay in at his place. It was scary."

"I never read where Kevin Kincannon ever got married," Andy said. "Did I miss som'pn?"

"No, I said. "It never came to that. Kevin refused. He's still deeply in the closet but at least he wasn't stupid enough to get married."

"I'm out and proud of it," I said. "We began having problems about that. Eli had a lot to do with it, too. But you know something?" I asked Andy.

"No, what?"

"I kept remembering the day we met. Every now and then, I'd call Directory Assistance for Skylarville and ask if there was a listing for you but for a long time, there wasn't one. Once I called and there was one for you but it was unlisted."

Andy interrupted me. "I was with my parents at first, and then I joined the Marines. I didn't get a phone of my own until after I joined the P.D. All police officers' home numbers are unlisted to keep people from calling 'em at home or finding out where we live. There are a lot of vengeful people 'round here. Do som'pn they don't like an' they'd just as soon lay in wait for you an' blast you to hell."

I continued after his explanation. "I kept looking for the same connection with Kevin that I'd had that first time with you. We drifted farther and farther apart as he became more and more famous.

"Kevin snaps his fingers and the world jumps. Well, not I," I said. "He couldn't make me jump when he snapped his fingers or demanded certain outrageous things just because he was Kevin Kincannon.

"I told him more than once that I didn't need him and he didn't like that. Eli didn't like the fact that he spent most of his time at my place. We were drifting farther and farther apart until he just left me. It sat wrong with me because in my mind, I guess I didn't like the idea of being dumped. *I do the dumping,"* I said.

What had seemed to me like a major catastrophe when I boarded a plane and headed south for the warm embrace of family, now seemed like a non-issue.

"What seemed like a rebound had turned into a slam-dunk," I smiled.

Andy nodded his head, satisfied. "So where's he now?" he wanted to know.

"I have no idea. When I got home his things were gone. He'd left a note with my housekeeper saying, "I'm getting too much negative publicity with you as my 'best friend.' People are beginning to talk. *I can't afford to lose everything over you, so you gotta go, Dude. Good luck to you.*"

"I changed the locks and told my housekeeper not to let him in, should he return, and then I got on a plane headed home.

"I've been saving myself for you for thirteen years," Andy said. "I *knew* we'd hook up again someday. I jus' didn't know when or how. Let's go to New Orleans an' celebrate."

"I really want to talk to the Chief about that deputy's murder," I said.

"Cher Bay-Bay, you don't really expect to find the Chief in the office on a Saturday, do you?" he said, talking to me like one would talk to a dim-witted child. "I'll bet you even money that wherever he spends his weekends, Eck is the farthest thing from his mind right now. There's nothin' that can't wait 'til Monday," he continued. "Eck's dead and good riddance."

"You can follow me to my parents' house and I can return the car but I was thinking. Why don't we go to Avery Island instead? Have you ever been there?"

"Great idea," Andy said. "I haven't been to Avery Island since I was in seventh grade. We went on a class field trip. We should get an early start, though. It's a lot farther than New Orleans."

"What's for breakfast?" Kevin Bourgeois said, yawning and stretching his lanky frame as he entered the bedroom.

"A granola bar and a glass of milk," Andy joked as he cracked eggs into a still-hot frying pan and spooned grits into a clean plate for his cousin. "How you want your eggs?" he asked Kevin. "We were going to pin a note on your chest telling you to lock up when you left.

"Scrambled," Kevin answered. "Make sure there's nothin' runny in 'em."

Andy nodded. "Sit down and eat while I get dressed." When he returned a few minutes later, he gave Kevin some final instructions. If I'm not back by supper time, be sure to come over, walk Wallace, and feed him, OK?"

"Can I take him over to my house?" Kevin asked. "That way, he won't be alone all day."

Andy agreed.

***

The area around Skylarville had changed greatly since my last visit three years prior. Where the drive between Skylarville and The Reserve had once been nineteen boring miles, hip-roofed brick ranches had sprung up like mushrooms after a summer rainstorm.

What had once been open, vacant land, sugar cane fields, marshland, or pasture had now been filled with new subdivisions featuring the ubiquitous, ground-hugging brick rectangles with attached garages or carports.

This was due partially to Louisiana's recent oil and industrial prosperity and partially to the success of the Mallory Research and Industrial Corridor, Mallory Medical Center, Mallory Land Development Corporation, and their ancillary businesses; Queen Esther, Lady Iris, and Lord Whitfield Cosmetics, or to the overwhelming success of The La Belle Terre Reserve.

The lushness of the vegetation that abounds due to Louisiana's rich soil and sub-tropical climate never fails to impress me.

As Andy's cousin Kevin had said, this was Louisiana's Golden Rectangle. If you stuck a stick in the ground and watered it for a few days, it takes root and bares fruit. Living in Chicago, I had forgotten this.

My parents live in New Canaan nineteen miles from Skylarville. I led the way and Andy followed closely in his long, sleek black Pontiac Firebird.

We followed Bayou Belle Fleur for fifteen miles and then turned off the main highway onto C'est Vrai Road to the toney villages of New Canaan, Kingstown, and New Bern as well as newer villages and unincorporated areas in La Belle Terre Reserve.

My parents named the road *C'est Vrai* because when they settled in Louisiana many of the local white residents, some of whom spoke very little English or a mixture of French and English, would drive down the lane to observe the building of *Creswic House*, by far, the largest privately owned home in the area.

Large signs saying, "**Private Property. No trespassing**" and chain link fencing kept them at bay but rumors had circulated about what the gigantic building was going to be: a sanitarium, a reformatory, a monastery, a college for deaf mutes, a home for wayward boys or girls, to name only a few. That it might be the private residence of the new colored doctors, who had recently settled in Houma and built a clinic and hospital to treat colored patients never entered their minds.

"C'est vrai?" they would ask anyone who could provide truthful answers, "Is it true? Is this is really a house and it is being built by the colored doctors in Houma?"

The final answer was "Oui, C'est vrai." ("Yes, it's true."), hence, the name.

C'est Vrai Lane became C'est Vrai Road, when the lane was widened into a two-lane, paved thoroughfare.

Four miles later, it widens again and becomes C'est Vrai Boulevard, a four-lane, tree- and flower-lined thoroughfare and the principal east-west traffic artery between the villages that have already been developed as well as those that are still on the drawing boards.

Good Friends Clinic remained open in Terrebonne Parish as an urgent aid station and branches were established in Bellefleur, Lafourche, and Assumption Parishes. Eventually, the plan was to serve the entire bayou region, as the area between New Orleans and Baton Rouge is called. After that, who knows?

Good Friends Hospital in Houma (Terrebonne Parish) became Mallory Medical Center Complex in Kingstown, which had achieved outstanding success by providing quality medical care to any patient, regardless of race, hiring top quality staff and attracting national and international patients.

The clinic and hospital initially garnered a reputation among the black bourgeoisie along the Gulf Coast from Houston to Pensacola and as far north as Memphis, Tennessee for its excellent services and gentle, dignified treatment of all who entered its doors.

It and St. Jude Hospital in Memphis, Tennessee, were the only two hospitals in the south that were completely integrated, right down to the water fountains, though few if any, white patients sprang forth to take advantage of this blessing.

The hospital's reputation took off about five years after my parents had settled in Houma. An international flap developed after Lenora Lagarde, an internationally famous black opera star and Baton Rouge native; fell ill while visiting relatives.

She was initially transported to the nearest private hospital but the flap arose when Miss Lagarde, who divides her time between homes in New York City, London, and Basle, Switzerland, was refused an upgrade from the dingy semi-private room reserved for "colored" patients, to a spacious private suite, reserved for whites.

Dr. Jake Schneiter, the hospital's owner and spokesman, told reporters he had not even considered the woman's request because, "despite her fame and fortune, she is not entitled to anything that any other Negro would be entitled to, and that included an upgrade to a suite on the 'white' side of his hospital.

"Negroes always want what white people have," he sniffed, addressing a coterie of news people from Europe and America.

"If we had Stink-On-A-Stick, they'd want that, too," he continued. "It's not because they *like* Stink-On-A-Stick, mind you, but because *we* have it. They're just like little children and I refuse to indulge them.

"I believe that God intended for the races to remain separated at all costs," the silver-haired, florid faced Dr. Schneiter said. "I took an oath to provide the best quality medical care that I am capable of providing to all of my patients but I *didn't* take an oath saying that they had to use the same facilities or be housed together.

"Some of the other private hospitals around here don't even accept colored patients," he continued. "I accept all patients who have the means to pay but I see no reason why my colored patients and my white patients should share waiting rooms, patient rooms, bathrooms, or even the same wing of the hospital, since specific spaces have already been designated for each race."

An irate French correspondent asked why, if the good doctor practiced *Separate-But-Equal* equally, white patients had been provided with a VIP suite while black patients had not.

"How many Very Important Negroes do you know?" Dr. Schneiter replied sarcastically. "That suite would sit empty until Miss Opera Singer deigns to make her next royal visit to our fair city. For all I know, that might be never.

"Does the money your white patients pay and the money your colored patients pay go into the same cash drawer?" the French reporter inquired. "Into the same bank account?"

"Of course it does," Dr. Schneiter replied curtly.

"Well why can't the patients go into the same rooms?

The doctor ignored him. "I am told that *Mr.* Opera Singer is Swiss," he continued. "I'd be willing to bet he's not Swiss *chocolate*, if you know what I mean!" he laughed. "We're not ready for that kind of stuff here. If this were in some other parts of the South, they both might have been lynched."

Dr. Schneiter turned and walked away, leaving the press corps with a myriad of questions still unanswered. He referred the singer to Good Friends Hospital.

Good Friends Hospital graciously accepted the referral and offered Miss Lagarde their VIP suite, which was private, spacious, and worthy of a very important person of any race. No amenity was missing.

Miss Lagarde's gynecological problem was cured and the child she was carrying was not harmed.

The subsequent news articles turned the spotlight on Louisiana's overt racism yet again but it garnered favorable attention for the hospital and for Dr. Laura Mallory, a young, but very skilled, ob-gyn.

The diva and her husband became good friends of my parents, so much so that they purchased a large piece of property near *Creswic House*, built a beautiful mansion in the Beaux-Arts style, and named it *Le Baiser* (The Kiss).

The Reserve was incorporated under the name, "La Belle Terre Reserve," an acronym for "***L***" *afourche*- "***A***" *ssumption*-"***BELLE***" *fleur and* "***TERRE***" *bonne* Parishes and warning signs promptly went up shortly afterward saying,

LA BELLE TERRE RESERVE

NO TRESPASSING.

NO HUNTING, NO FISHING, NO TRAPPING.

VIOLATORS WILL BE PROSECUTED TO THE FULLEST EXTENT OF THE LAW.

La Belle Terre Land Development Corp.
Mallory Land Development Corp.

***

C'est Vrai Road, as it snakes through New Bern, Kingstown, and The Reserve's unincorporated areas, following Bayou St. Eloi until it reaches New Canaan, reminds me of Sheridan Road, north of Chicago, as it snakes along Lake Michigan's shoreline from Evanston until it reaches Lake Forest, that area's crowning jewel. They are both beautiful drives.

C'est Vrai Road becomes C'est Vrai Boulevard as it enters New Bern. Farther on, it becomes C'est Vrai Parkway as it enters Kingstown, and then, C'est Vrai Road again when it traverses New Canaan and continues south-westward toward the unincorporated areas within the Reserve.

We followed C'est Vrai Road for a few miles and turned south onto St. Eloi Road for a split second, crossed Bayou St. Eloi onto the private, gated island known as New Canaan Estates, one of seven subdivisions that, collectively, make up the Village of New Canaan, Louisiana.

We turned east again onto McGrath Road, which parallels C'est Vrai Road, but on the south side—the gated side--of Bayou St. Eloi.

We passed the palatial homes behind high brick or stone walls, hedges, or wrought iron fences, with names such as Mt. Blessed, Larchmont, Astleigh, Meadow House, and Westley Manor, until we got to McGrath Court, a shallow, cobblestone cul-de-sac where Creswic House stands, its only resident. My mother's maiden name was McGrath.

We passed through high, open, intricately-wrought iron gates onto a long cobbled drive planted down the wide median with monkey grass, blood-red day lilies, and pink-flowered crape myrtles, their cotton candy-pink flowers blowing lazily in the early morning breeze.

We parked in the family's motor court near the west side of the house instead of using the visitor's parking spots in front.

My parents' other vehicles, a midnight blue Bentley saloon car, two BMW's, a Range Rover, and an extraordinary yellow Italian sports car, were lined up on the cobblestones of the circular motor court, having just been washed and detailed. Andy was drawn to the low-slung yellow number like a filing to a magnet, drooling all the way.

I could see the awe on his face as he took it all in. "This is a palace," he said, eyeing the mansion, eyes wide and mouth agape. "When I was a kid, I used to see y'all's house from a distance, so I knew it was big and that y'all were rich but *damn*…. I think y'all have the Catashes beat by a country mile."

I pulled Andy, still drooling, away from my dad's Lamborghini.

From a double-wide porte-cochere, built along the west side of the house to allow entry and exit from vehicles during Louisiana's frequent rains, we entered the mansion through mahogany double doors and stepped into what we call "the family foyer." It measures approximately fifteen feet square.

Bisque-colored ceramic tiles form a basket-weave design on the groin vaulted ceiling and dripped down onto the upper part of the walls.

The floor is Carrara marble tiles with diamond-shaped Mexican onyx inlays of varying shades of black, dark gray, light gray, tan, and saddle brown, that form a rope design around the room's perimeter. An intricate Arabic rosette made of the marble, carnelian, and onyx tiles forms the floor's center.

The area between the high wainscoting and the ceiling was of ivory-painted pecky-cypress paneling. An octagonal cherry wood table containing cut flowers in a tall crystal vase, stood near the opposite wall of the room. A low leather banquette on each side of the room provided seating.

Soft cove lighting, paired brass wall sconces on three of the four walls, and a large brass and glass chandelier that hung from the center of the room provided illumination to this jewel box of a room.

Andy took a sharp, audible breath, in awe. He stood near the center of the room for a minute or two, smiling and taking in the scene before him. "And this is the family's everyday entry and exit?" he said. "It's like bein' inside a jewelry box."

"It's for family and friends," I said. "You fall into the latter category. We rarely use the front entry so my parents wanted it to be even more special than the main foyer, where guests enter."

"Usually it's the other way around," he said. "Most people want the *guests* to have the best part of the house and keep what the family uses really dumpy."

"Why should anybody have a better entry to the house than the family that lives there?" I questioned. "Besides, what they don't know won't hurt them."

We passed through carved mahogany doors with beveled glass insets to a large mud room.

We deposited the bags of vegetables on a small oak work table before continuing onward, passing several maids dressed in their pale yellow dresses with white aprons and white soft-sole shoes, *Creswic House's* colors. They smiled pleasantly, said good morning, and continued their various tasks.

My mom and a younger, caramel-colored woman sat chatting amiably as they counted and polished silverware before cradling them in individual cloth body bags and placing them in a large wooden box. At Mum's feet lay Leo, her white standard poodle.

To her left, the open door to the "silver room," or Fort Knox, as my siblings and I called it, gave onlookers a glimpse of my family's silver hoard: silver platters, salvers, pitchers, candelabras and picture frames; and more silver and gold serving dishes and flatware than most people see in a lifetime. Each piece was carefully cataloged and has to be accounted for before the last box of flatware is returned to the vault and the door locked once more. This is a monthly ritual.

"Hi, Mum," I said, stepping across the vast room to the small round table in the room's bay window, where they sat. "This is my mate, Andy," I said, kissing her on the cheek.

"So, my prodigal son has returned," she laughed, turning to the younger woman. She rose, lithe and graceful, and extended her hand to Andy.

She wore a white short-sleeve raw cotton blouse she had purchased on a recent visit to Mexico and black cotton slacks that flared slightly at the bottom, covering all but the soles of her saddle-colored leather sandals.

Silver strands were beginning to infiltrate her head of thick, black African hair that she had combed straight back and tied in a bun at the nape of her neck. Her only adornment was a tear drop-shaped blue topaz about the size of my thumbnail that hung from a gold chain around her neck and a large, square-cut citrine ring surrounded on all sides by square-shaped diamonds that captured light from any available source and flung it back into the room in a kaleidoscope of tiny lightning flashes.

"Welcome," she said. "I'm pleased to meet you, Andy. I'm Laura Mallory. What a handsome young man you are. You have beautiful eyes!" she exclaimed. "And that hair!"

Andy smiled widely. And blushed like a schoolgirl.

"And a dazzling smile," she chided.

"This is Rosa Braithwaite, our housekeeper," she said.

Rosa smiled and nodded her head to Andy but did not rise. Andy shook first my mother's hand and then Rosa's. Leo sniffed Andy's legs and feet.

"And that's Leo, sniffing at your feet," she said to Andy, "I hope you're not afraid of dogs."

"No, Ma'am," Andy said. "I guess he smells the scent of my dog on me."

"He has a white mini," I interjected.

"But I've just fallen in love with the standard variety," Andy said, petting Leo's head. "That's the biggest damned—I meant *darned*. Sorry," he apologized, "poodle I've ever seen. You don't see many of 'em round here. In fact, before today, I'd *never* seen one."

I told Rosa about the veggies on the table in the mud room. "I'll give them to Cook," she said, exiting the room.

"Andy gave them to you," I said to my mother. "They came from his garden."

"My *parents'* garden," Andy corrected.

"Thank you, Andy. They'll be put to good use. We eat a lot of vegetables around here," she smiled.

"Andy and I met thirteen years ago," I said.

"The boy from St. William's School??" she smiled, remembering the hissy fit I threw when a new maid had not emptied my pockets before washing them. Mostly, I blamed myself for not emptying them but I had nothing good to say to the maid, either.

I nodded and smiled. "I finally found him, Mum," I said, my eyes brimming. "We had some catching up to do. And I know you wouldn't want me driving in the condition I was in last night."

She looked at me, shook her head, but said nothing for a long time. "Your eyes tell me everything," she said. "You're old enough to know when to stop *'having fun.'"* She knew we had partaken of something other than alcohol.

I patted Leo's head and looked sheepish. The dog looked up adoringly at me. I could do no wrong in his eyes.

Andy stood looking around the enormous room. I didn't know if he was trying to avert his eyes from my mother's scrutiny, admiring the hand-painted murals or the furnishings. "Y'all eat here every day?" he finally asked. "This table has seating for twenty." He was admiring the enormous mahogany table and eighteen hand-carved side chairs that were the focal point of the room. The two end chairs were high-backed wing chairs covered in butter-yellow chintz.

"We use this room for parties, large gatherings, or for special occasions, like birthdays or Thanksgiving dinner, when the entire family gets together or when we entertain." I answered. "This is the formal dining room. My grandparents gave this dining room set to my parents when they got married. It was hand-carved in Brazil for this house."

"There's a smaller, family dining room off the kitchen, where we usually take our meals," my mother said. "Why don't you show him around, Wayne?"

"Wayne?" Andy asked, surprised.

"My whole name is Steven Wayne Adelbert David Mallory. My family calls me Wayne. Almost everybody else calls me Steve," I explained. "The first two are for my paternal grandpa and the last two are for my maternal grandpa."

"Who calls you *Adelbert*?" he smiled.

"Thankfully, nobody. And don't get any ideas!" I smiled.

Which do you want me to call you?" he asked.

"Whichever you wish, as long as it's not Adelbert."

"I don't know why he has never liked that name," Mum said to Andy. "Adelbert is an old family name. My father and grandfather were both named that. It goes back at least three generations in my family. Wayne says it's time to give it a rest," she smiled. "Maybe he's right. Do you like it, Andy?

My new mate turned several shades of red and smiled. "It's unusual," he said shyly.

"Mum, we're going to Avery Island," I said to rescue him. "May we use the Jag?"

"Yes," she said.

"Why don't we take my car?" Andy suggested.

"OK by me," I smiled

"When are you going to visit your grandmother?" my mum wanted to know. "She's been here three times looking for you."

"Soon," I said. "I promise."

***

Seen from above, *Creswic House* is shaped like a gigantic capital letter "I" with a few extra wings to spoil the letter's perfect symmetry. If the Gallery were shorter and the North and South Wings longer, it would look like a giant capital "H."

The Gallery, a long, extra-wide, promenade with sand-colored marble flooring inlaid with the same diamond-shaped onyx as in the family's entry, forms the center, or vertical, part of the "I" and is the main thoroughfare between the two crossbars (called the North and South Wings) on either end. The rooms off it, the formal living room, and the movie theater, provide thickness to the vertical part of the "I" and formal entertaining space for *Creswic House.*

The kitchen, the housekeeper's apartment, family dining room, formal dining room, butler's pantry, billiards room, music room, rear stair hall, tea room (no one calling themselves English would be without one), three powder rooms, and two parlors (called The Lady's Parlor and The Gentleman's Parlor, respectively) form the rear cross bar (or the North Wing).

The main foyer, Rotunda, butler's apartment, mud room, east and west stair halls, east and west elevator halls, family's (small) living room, two powder rooms, a huge two-story library, and a four-car attached garage form the South Wing.

There are seven kitchens in the house: The banquet (large) kitchen, the regular (small) kitchen, the *petite dejuners* in my parents' suite of rooms and in the butler's and housekeeper's private apartments, a fully-equipped kitchen in the children's activity room on the second floor, and a fully-equipped chef's kitchen on the pool deck.

The "grace notes" are comprised of the two detached garages (above which there is living space for some of the grounds crew and other employees), chauffeur's quarters, conservatory, the summer house, and two covered courtyards, called the East and West Courts, and beyond them, the East and West Guest Houses.

To round things out, between the main house and the two story pool house, there is a huge swimming pool, an enormous two-tiered, pergola'ed pool deck, a privet maze, art garden, and dog yard. The head groundskeeper and his family have a cottage near the front entry gates.

The other thirty-some acres consist of a lot of open lawn space, a boat dock onto Lake Laura, another, smaller dock on Bayou St. Eloi, and more staff housing.

"I'll go up and change and we can get started." Andy followed me as I left the room.

I started up the stairs. "Could we take the elevator up?" Andy asked. "I've never been in an elevator in a private home before."

"I'll meet you on two," I replied.

At the top of the landing, we followed the herring bone-patterned parquet flooring down a hallway toward the bedroom suites, passing framed family portraits and artwork along the walls. Tall potted palms with golden pothos at their feet, soaked up the sun from floor-to-ceiling Palladian windows on one side of the wide corridor while figurative and abstract sculptures peered down on us from their private niches on the opposite side.

We came to the four-room suite I had occupied growing up. It was, still is, and probably will always be known as Wayne's rooms. Even my nephews and nieces call it "Uncle Wayne's rooms.".

"You know you talk more British when you talk to your mama?" he asked.

"I hadn't realized it," I answered. "But I noticed last night that *you* have a more pronounced Cajun accent when you talk to your cousin than when you talk to me."

Servants had dutifully unpacked my bags and put away my luggage. I chucked my clothing from yesterday into a laundry hamper in my dressing room and went to the large walk-in closet for fresh clothing more in tune with Louisiana's fierce summer heat.

Andy kicked off his shoes and lay on my bed, a California King. "This is bigger than my whole house," he said as he fondled me through my silk boxers.

"Which, my bed, my willie, or my bedchamber?"

"All three," he replied, taking me deeply into his mouth. When he came up for air, I lay down next to him, kissed and hugged him, and looked into that adorable, trusting face and realized just how fortunate Kevin Kincannon's abrupt departure had been for me.

"I love you," Andy said. "That's the first and only time I've ever said that to anybody."

He was open and honest. I could be no less. "When I got off the plane yesterday, I was singing that song that Dionne Warwick sang in the late '60's, *"I'll Never Fall In Love Again."* I hummed a few bars for him.

"That song summed up *perfectly* how I felt about what was going on in my life. I must have sung it in my head a thousand times on the flight between Chicago and here. Then I found you and realized that Kevin Kincannon was just a short interlude in what I hope will be a long life."

Andy smiled broadly.

"I only re-met you yesterday but I feel more for you in less than twenty-four hours than I felt for Kevin Kincannon in all the time I've known him. All I can do now is wish him well, wherever he is. But don't you think it's a little early to know if we're in *love* or just in *lust?*" I wanted to know.

"It's not too early for me," he said. "I know, Cher...I know."

I wished I had the same certainty he had. "I'm sorry," I said after a fairly long pause. "I'm a little bit more cynical. I need more time before making any declarations. I hope you don't mind."

"Take all the time you want, Cher. It's not gon' change my mind."

"Well, what are we going to do if it turns out to be the real thing? I'll only be here for a week; then I'll be back in Chicago and you'll be here. Long distance romances never work."

"Things have a way of workin' themselves out," Andy replied. "What's meant to be will be. That's what I believe. You'll see.

I smiled to myself. *Qué será será!*

"By the way, do your parents know you're gay?"

It had been so long that I had been asked such a question that I hardly knew how else to answer. "Of course," I shrugged my shoulders.

"How'd they find out?" he wanted to know.

"I told them. I told them right after I met you. I told them I had met this boy in Skylarville and I was in love with him. When I never heard from the boy again, I guess they thought I'd made him up to tell them that I was gay. I really don't know what they thought but I was frantic when I couldn't find your phone number.

"How'd they take it?"

"They're doctors," I said. "They know that homosexuality's a fact of life. There's nothing else they could say but tell me to use condoms and to try to find a good man to settle down with."

"Well, they'll be happy to know that you've found one," he said happily.

"From the way you're talking, I assume your parents don't know, right?"

"Yep," he said. A few seconds of silence passed before either of us said anything.

I finally asked. "I remember from our conversation back at St. William's that you said your dad was a bit of a racist. Am I correct?"

"He's changed a lot since then but I don't know how he's gonna take all this," he said breaking a long silence and slowly shaking his head.

Andy nodded his head, looking as if the thought of how his parents would react to his new-found relationship had never before crossed his mind, and then he steeled himself. I could see it in his whole demeanor. He reminded me of St. George girding himself to slay the dragon. He had taken a long time to answer my question. "I don't know but I guess we'll find out soon enough," he finally said.

"If we're going to Avery Island, we'd better get going," I said, pulling him closer to me and kissing him yet again. This man had spunk.

***

Andy drove the Firebird around the shores of Lake Laura, over hills and dells created from the dirt unearthed when Lake Laura and several other waterways were dug, dredged, or rechanneled.

We rode through the business districts of Kingstown and New Bern, and were in Kingstown Farms, an unincorporated section of Kingstown, which consisted mostly of large estates, gentleman's farms, and working farms that offered riding lessons, dog and puppy classes, fresh milk, eggs, fruit or vegetables in season, boarding for one's horses, or kenneling and spa services for one's dogs. It was also the home of the Creswic Hunt.

Fifty feet from the intersection of Hunt Club Road and Los Moros, red lights similar to those at railroad crossings blinked on and a large orange, diamond-shaped sign displaying a mounted rider, lit up saying *Prepare to Stop.*

A few feet beyond that, a round sign with lights that looked like two red eyes blinking alternatively, lit up. It carried the warning, *Equestrian Crossing* on top of the red eyes and *Beware of Riders* below them.

Ten feet from the intersection, the yellow and black striped arms of a crossing gate lowered, stopping traffic on Los Moros.

Andy pulled to a stop and waited. We lowered our windows but kept the T-Tops in place to ward off the blazing sun. After a few minutes, a girl wearing a seal-colored suede riding helmet, a forest green polo shirt, and tan jodhpurs parked her chestnut Hanoverian in front of the gate to further ensure that no one would attempt to pass the lowered gates unless they did so over her and her horse's dead bodies.

Her hair was twisted into a single thick braid that reached past her shoulders and tied just below the helmet with a small red bow.

The horse's English saddle and blanket were custom made for her in Argentina, as were his halter, reins, and bridle. The horse's bit was hand-forged in Mexico. Her riding boots, polished to a mirror shine, were the same color as her helmet and came to just below her knees. Those boots, made by the finest boot maker in England, probably cost more than Andy's car.

They were certainly more expensive than my car, a boxy green Datsun sedan that was perfect for the city, where parking was limited and sometimes non-existent, where drivers often left the scene of an accident despite the presence of witnesses, where vandals frequently keyed expensive cars or tore off their side mirrors or radio antennas for no apparent reason, and where expensive cars are frequently stolen and sold to chop shops.

My Datsun was strictly utilitarian. It had no class at all. It did not call attention to itself or to me. Although I have assigned parking at my condominium complex, it is frequently left on the street at night while I complete assignments in some of Chicago's worst neighborhoods. Andy's flashy new Firebird wouldn't last a week on the mean streets of Chicago.

The girl sat haughtily astride the enormous gelding, her left side to us, revealing a regal profile as she beckoned to other riders still on the bridle path near Hunt Club Road.

Hidden from view by the high hedges and wrought iron fence of Mount Blessed, a luxurious estate owned by the Seligman family, they began to cross Los Moros at a diagonal, from southeast to northwest, as the red lights flashed and the bell *ting*'ed its warning to drivers that human and equine lives were at stake.

Single file or in twos or threes, they slowly filed past the intersection, led by a second teen-ager on a dapple gray Irish Thoroughbred gelding. The klip-klopping of their hooves made musical sounds on the pavement as they crossed and entered the bridle path on the other side of Hunt Club Road.

Although most of the riders were black, there were several Asians and whites in the group. Most were pre-pubescent females but both sexes were represented. They ranged in age from around sixty down to about four or five. The youngest riders were in front; the adults behind. Some of the adults, mostly mothers, accompanied the younger riders, providing encouragement. There were approximately twenty in all.

When the last rider had passed, the girl lightly tapped the big gelding on his rump with the riding crop she held in one hand, squeezed her strong thighs against the horse's sides and, with head up and heels down, she rode first to the roadside traffic light, pressed a discreetly placed button on its side that simultaneously raised the crossing gates, turned off the red warning lights, and stopped the *ting'ing* of the of bell. She then cantered off.

"Now *that* girl has class!" Andy smiled. "Everything about her exudes class: the way she holds her head, her movements. *Everything*. She reminds me of you. Must be som'pn in the water 'round here but if I had a daughter, that's the way I'd want her to be. She commands respect."

"I'll tell her," I smiled. "I'm sure she'd love to hear your compliment."

"You know her?" he asked.

"She's my niece, Laurette. She's fifteen. A real sweetheart. You'll meet her soon enough."

"Laurette," Andy said. "That's French. I thought y'all were British."

"Her first name is Laura, after my mum. To avoid having to call my mom Big Laura and her Little Laura, everybody calls her Laurette."

"I can't believe she got away with just one name when you got 'bout eighty," he smiled.

I smiled back. "Most Mallory children have at least three given names. Some have four."

"So what's her whole name?"

"Laura Philippa Beatrice Rose," I grinned.

"An' y'all couldn'a just chosen to call her one of her other million names, could you?" Andy chucked my chin. "I should've known she was a Mallory, though. That kind of *hauteur* takes generations to breed into a person."

"The younger girl on the dapple gray is her sister, Beth. She's thirteen. I won't even tell you her whole name," I smiled.

"Hit me," Andy said. "I can take it."

"Elizabeth Rosamond Cynthia Mary," I peeled off.

***

We connected with Louisiana Hwy. 90 from Insurgents Park Ave., near The Reserve's private airport, which was named for the world's first black aviatrix, Bessie Coleman.

I removed a joint from the secret compartment in my wallet and lit it, took a few hits, and passed it to Andy. We put in some jazz cassettes that Andy kept stored in a vinyl storage case in his car and chatted amiably as the music and the herb worked their magic on our minds.

I watched the Louisiana landscape change from the manicured refinement of The Reserve with its moss-draped waterways, arched stone bridges, wide-spreading live oaks and cypress-kneed marshlands to miles and miles of sugar cane fields, punctuated every now and then by the ubiquitous brick ranches, dilapidated wooden sharecroppers' shacks, mobile homes, or an occasional antebellum-style mansion, set back from the highway, their white columns glistening in the summer sun.

Andy increased the speed from sixty to ninety. "You know you're going to get a ticket if you keep this speed up," I said when the needle hit 110.

"I'm a cop, remember? Nobody's gonna give me a ticket," he replied.

We paid the man at the guard house and entered the magical wonderland that is Avery Island, Louisiana, one of my favorite places in the entire world.

Here, centuries-old live oaks, red oaks, water oaks and palms of various kinds lined up to greet the visitor while rare birds, reptiles, and insects fight for survival in Nature's continual battle of predator and prey.

We followed the map that the smiling woman in the gift shop had given us. We got out at the appropriate places and viewed the various gardens, holding hands, following the paths, and taking pictures with my Leica to remember this day forever.

We descended the stone stairs that led to a little lagoon that hosted the rookery. Egrets, herons, cranes, and other water birds nested here by the thousands.

I took Andy's hand and led him into the bamboo grove. We walked into the coolness provided by the evenly-spaced canes, out of Louisiana's savage heat and drenching humidity. Neither of us said much. We just walked, holding hands and enjoying each other's company. I put my arm around his shoulder and held him near me. Just being with this man made all the madness of the world disappear.

When we were far from the stone steps, I turned to face him, cupped his face in my hands and drew it near and kissed him on those luscious lips. The kiss was long and deep. I relished every second of it. We continued to kiss, finally breaking it off when we heard footsteps on the stone stairs that descended to the rookery.

We stood there, surrounded by bird sounds, holding hands and being close. *Life is sweet*, I thought to myself.

"Tell me about your family," I said on our way back to New Canaan after a long day.

"There's not a lot to say. I'm a mutt. I don' even know my family past my grandparents," he said.

"Most people don't." I countered. "It's rare to find someone who has a written pedigree."

"I guess I could have one if I wanted one," he said. "Most of my daddy's people are buried in St. Chris' cemetery out in Belle Glade. You saw how small my house is, right?" he said.

I said nothing and he continued. "I live better than most of my relatives. My mama had this phobia about hookworms and germs in general so I had to wear shoes and socks everywhere I went when I was growing up, even in the summer, but my two cousins, Kevin and Paul, never wore 'em except on Sundays, special occasions, and during the winter, 'til they were 'bout to enter first grade.

"My people are mostly small farmers, fishermen, shrimpers, hunters, and trappers. They make their living from the swamps. Bayou Mal Enfant is in back of my parents' property. It connects to Bayou Belle Fleur on one end and the coastal marsh, including the Atchafalaya Swamp, on the other. All the way down to Balbuena Bay an' out to the Gulf.

"My pa-paw on my daddy's side was a moss picker. A few of my relatives are truck farmers. Now that industry has come to south Louisiana, my generation works offshore or in some kind of small industry working jobs like welding or as factory workers," he said. "My daddy's a foreman at Clydesdale."

I knew the place well. The Reserve ended only a mile or so from Clydesdale Shipyard's gates. I interrupted his story. "What's a pa-paw?"

"Grandpa," he said as he smiled a crinkly smile. "I'm the first member of the family to finish college," he continued.

"Hell," he said, "I'm the only male member of the family to even *go* to college but both of my sisters went.

"We had an outhouse until I was about seven," he continued. "I slept with my two boy cousins in the garçonniere of my parents' big old house until they built a new house about a quarter of a mile away.

"You know what the garçonniere is," he asked. "Right?"

"It's the place where the unmarried males in a lot of Cajun families slept," I replied, nodding.

He nodded. "Coe-*rect*! Do you want to take the money and run, Steven Wayne Sump'n-Sump'n *Adelbert* Mallory, or do you want to go for the sixty-four dollar question?" he said, imitating a game show host.

I ignored his levity. "I thought garçonnieres had gone out with dueling under the oaks, high-button shoes, hoop skirts, and whale-bone corsets."

He switched back to his regular voice. "They did, but they still exist in some older places, 'specially where there's limited space where there's boys and girls living under the same roof.

"Hell, if not for them building the new house that had a bedroom for me downstairs, instead of a garçonniere, I'd have prob'ly stayed there 'til I moved out or died.

"My cousins would eventually get married an' I'd prob'ly be the only one left up there. I'd prob'ly die up there in the garçonniere, bein' gay an' all. Or I'd prob'ly hav'ta move to New Orleans where I'd become the 'eccentric' uncle that everyone whispers about but nobody ever discusses in front of the children."

"But you didn't, did you?" I reminded him. "You went to college, got a job, moved to Skylarville, bought your own house, and live your own life."

"I was joking," he smiled. "It's not that bad."

"How many children are in the family?" I asked. I knew nothing about his family except for his cousin Kevin and the other boy cousin with whom he spent his first years in the garçonniere. "You seem rather spoiled."

"Me? Spoiled? Why'd you say that?"

"You said they didn't have a lot of money but they sent you to an expensive private school. That seems a sacrifice they didn't have to commit to."

"I went to St. William's on a scholarship. Mama always wanted the best for her kids. She and my daddy sacrificed whatever they had to for us. They wanted us to make sump'n out of ourselves.

"They felt that public school wasn't gon' give us the education we needed to get ahead in life. Mama, especially, wanted her kids to be better than she was. My sisters an' I went to St. Christopher School, in Belle Glade.

"When I was in sixth grade, they gave us some IQ tests and I guess I got really good scores 'cuz they skipped me to seventh grade mid-year. The next year, they offered me a scholarship to St. William's.

"I didn' wanna take it an' leave, Paul an' Kevin, but Mama made me go. Kevin, an' I were in the same grade Paul was a year ahead. After I got skipped, Paul an' I were in the same grade an' poor Kevin was by himself.

"Even after I got skipped, I still spent mos' of my time with them between classes, at lunch, an' after school. We're more like my brothers than cousins. You'll meet Paul soon.

"What do you mean your mom *made* you go?"

"Yeah. She wanted me to make som'pn out'a myself. She always said if a white man couldn't make it in this country, with all the cards stacked in his favor, then there's som'pn wrong with him, and nobody she knew was makin' it.

"She wanted me to rub elbows with people like Noly Catash, Peter Klein, the Chauvin twins, an' the Trosclair brothers. They all have money. *Lots* of money! An' they didn't wanna have nothing to do with me. I was the scholarship student. The charity case. The poor kid. And they never let me forget it.

"Mama's dream for me was that I'd go on to Tulane or Loyola after St. William's, get a degree, and then, to Tulane Law School or Tulane's medical school. After that, I'd marry some pretty blonde girl and make her some rich, blond grandkids. Boy, did things turn out different," he almost laughed.

"Why didn't you go on to law school or medical school?"

"I didn't go to medical school because I hate the sight of blood, but I go to LSU School of Law in Baton Rouge three times a week. On the G.I Bill. It's takin' a bit longer than if I'd 'a gone straight through, from high school to college to law school full time but I'm in no rush."

"Where did you get your undergrad degree?"

"Nicholls State in Thibodaux." Thibodaux is a pretty little city in Lafourche Parish, one of Belle Fleur Parish's neighbors. The *"L"* in *"La* Belle Terre Reserve."

"I'm a country boy," he continued. "Always was an' always will be. I wasn't ready for life in the city. I got the job with the Police Department right after I got out of the Marines. I've been there now for three years.

"A jar-head, huh?" I said. That explained his fascination for order.

He smiled, as if thinking over what I'd said. "You know, I guess I *was* spoiled. My two sisters say I was. According to them, I got away with murder but I'm the only boy so you can imagine my status in the family. I don't usually admit it but I *was* spoiled."

We arrived at *Creswic House* at twilight. The house was lit up but the cars had been stored in their garages. Andy parked the Firebird on the rim of the circular, cobblestone motor court between the main house and one of the two detached garages, adjuncts to the four car attached garage where my parents' more expensive autos were stored.

A huge iron sugar-boiling kettle outfitted as a fountain and lit from below the water, sat spewing silver droplets and soothing sounds into the night from its nest of variegated ginger. The trickle of the water and the ever-present crickets and peepers, were the only sounds.

A pair of headlights passed through the wrought iron gates and started up the long, meandering driveway where the lamp posts along the median, equipped with motion sensors, lit up before them. They came to a stop under the porte-cochere at the family's usual entrance at the side of the house.

The liveried chauffeur emerged from the driver's seat, opened the rear passenger-side door, and my dad emerged from the wine-colored Rolls Royce long-based sedan and started for the side door of the house, not noticing the two of us in the Firebird.

"That's my dad," I said. "I want you to meet him."

***

Andy and I stood gazing at a huge maquette of the La Belle Terre Reserve in the center of *Creswic House's* enormous two-story library. It had been mostly maps and line drawings when I last saw it, but now, here it was in 3-D. The completed sections were in color and the proposed sections in white, like ghosts of things to come.

There are a total of nine proposed towns and villages with many smaller settlements and unincorporated areas. In the maquette, roads and streets were paved, neighborhoods, complete with little cars and tiny people relaxing beside miniature swimming pools or performing other quotidian activities, were built, commercial centers, parks, recreation spaces, cemeteries, schools, and places of worship were all there.

At the center of it all were the three original villages, with the huge Mallory Medical Center Complex, the multi-storied Queen Esther, Lord Whitfield, and Lady Iris Cosmetics buildings, and Creswic House in full color. So were the airport, yacht club, and the Creswic Hunt Club.

Tucked at the end of a two-lane highway on its own little peninsula, southernmost at The Reserve, was the Mallory Research and Industrial Corridor.

My dad, with his usual sense of humor, had made a small red arrow pointing to Creswic House that read, *You Are Here.*

I stood there, mouth agog, with Andy, looking at the long term plans for this region. "When do you think this'll all be finished, Dad?" I asked.

"I expect to have the last nail driven and the last ribbon cut around the year 2000. I'll be an old man by then," my dad replied.

"That's jus' twenty-three years from now," Andy said. "You'd jus' be hittin' your prime by then." He turned to me and said, "And we'll be…" he said, calculating our ages in his head, "…fifty-one an' forty-nine."

Butters, my family's majordomo, served us our drinks and silently left the room. Dad sat in his favorite chair, a deeply tufted black leather Queen Anne wing back with nail-head trim. He pulled up the matching ottoman and rested his long legs on it.

He wore a silver-colored satin dressing gown with a black silk sash, collar, and lapels over black silk pajamas. On his feet, he wore monogrammed black velvet English house shoes, exposing black silk hosiery.

"This project has been progressing at a phenomenal rate," he continued. "It may be completed before the scheduled date."

"Why here?" Andy asked, "If I may be so bold to ask. Why'd y'all choose to come here to do it?"

"Prior to the Emancipation Proclamation, this area had the highest number of slaves per capita in the nation," my dad replied. "This land was a slave-breeding plantation in addition to its other crops of sugar, cotton, and indigo. One of my ancestors was born and bred right here.

"This area is extremely fertile and made the slave-owners and their descendents very, very wealthy. They took all they could get from the land, the slaves, and their descendents but they gave nothing back to them: Inferior schools or none at all, and inadequate health care. They worked the slaves until they dropped. Or bred the women until their uteruses could bear no more. It was a human puppy mill.

"After Emancipation, when they could no longer breed human beings, they continued the growing of crops under the sharecropper system until we purchased it.

"In fact, although slavery was ended, Negroes were still treated as though that weren't the case, right up to the present day. I can take you less than five miles from here and you'd think you were still back in Antebellum days."

"You don't have to take me," Andy said, "I've seen it for myself."

I had no idea of what they were talking about.

My dad continued his narrative. "The slave owners and their descendents consider themselves 'aristocrats.' They're above doing manual labor themselves but they feel that they're entitled to deferential treatment solely by virtue of the fact that their ancestors once owned slaves. They have nothing but contempt the people who toiled in the fields or staffed their homes or nursed their children. They were all for the concept of *noblesse* but they forgot about the concept of *noblesse oblige.*

"The Negro population in this area was among the poorest and least educated in the nation. Only Mississippi has a higher illiteracy rate among blacks. But throughout the south, it was the same. They were kept ignorant and illiterate. That is a crime against nature as far as we're concerned.

"Before World War II, little Negro children were brought up to believe that the only thing they could look forward to was being someone's maid or houseman if they were "lucky" or working in the sugar industry if they were not. All hope of living a good, productive, *rich* life had been bred or beaten out of them years ago.

"Before World War II and well into the 1950s, there wasn't even a single high school for Negroes in the four-parish area. School went as far as seventh or eighth grade and most Negroes didn't even go that far. Kids were pulled out of school during the planting season and again during the harvest season, which is just before Christmas.

"Children as young as first grade were taken out of school on a regular basis to help with the planting or with the harvesting of the sugar cane. No one said a word about this atrocity. The white school board members thought there was no need for any education higher than eighth grade for Negroes because Negroes didn't need any more formal education to work in a kitchen or in the field.

"Girls were taught home economics during the last year of grade school if they made it that far, and boys were taught agriculture. Some schools included carpentry. Most didn't.

"Strangely," he continued, "the home economics course was not geared to teaching the girl how to manage *her own* kitchen but how to manage her mistress' kitchen when she went into domestic servitude and most of the boys' agricultural education was on-the-job training.

"If you were black, lived in one of the four 'La Belle Terre' parishes, and wanted to go to high school, you had to go away from here. The nearest high schools you could attend were in Baton Rouge and New Orleans. Once you went to either of those cities, you rarely returned here.

"This area, believe it or not, was not even the worst off in the state or the country, but it is very high on the list.

"My wife and I initially visited this area just before Pearl Harbor. We came with a group of medical students from Britain that was touring this country. Pearl Harbor was bombed and we couldn't get back to England.

"Being from Bermuda, my wife and I could return home but the rest of the group either went to Canada or like us, to Bermuda, the nearest English territories.

"We had been warned of what we would see in the southern United States, and what we would or could possibly experience here so we opted to skip most of what was the old Confederacy, except for Charleston, Jackson, Mississippi, and New Orleans.

"All were horrible places for Negroes. What we observed or went through is another story so I'll skip that part of it, except to say that my wife, being a quote-quote 'lady doctor,' as the locals called them, endured even more discrimination than I did.

He turned to Andy. "As you know, it was common in the south to call white adult females 'ladies' and black adult females either 'women' or 'girls,' or if she's an older lady, 'Auntie.'"

"We had to call any lady, regardless of race, '*Miz*,'" Andy said, "but I know what you mean."

"Well," Dad continued, "they didn't know what to call Laura. They had never seen a 'lady doctor,' let alone, a '*colored* lady doctor.' My dad still clung to the terms "colored" and "Negro" that were popular when he grew up, instead of using the currently accepted term of "black." His reasoning is not to be faulted. He said he knows many "black" people who are whiter than many white people. He also says he has seldom seen a truly black person. His favored term is *melano*, a person with melanin in his or her skin, but he rarely uses outside of conversations with family members.

"One of our hosts made the mistake of referring to her as a 'girl.'"

He lay back in his chair and smiled, hands behind his head, eyes closed, savoring the memory. "Now, my wife is as gentle and mild as a baby lamb unless you ruffle her feathers and, Man, does she get riled up when she's disrespected. She excoriated that man in such a dignified, professional way that was almost left physical marks on him and she never even raised her voice. After that, no one had any doubts as to whether or not she was a lady."

Reminiscence over, he continued his story. "This area was as backward as any Third World Country. We found it appalling that there had been so little progress since the end of the Civil War.

"This place reminded me of India, more than any other country. There was a caste system here, just as surely as there was one in India. There were certain jobs that only blacks were expected to do, like domestic work, garbage collection, field work, to name a few. Segregation was a way of life that everyone accepted and saw no end to. Worse still, they saw no reason to end it. As far as the whites were concerned, the system worked. There were the 'Haves and the Have-Nots.' You were born to be one or the other and seldom broke out of the role you were destined to fulfill.

"And it worked the same for whites as well as blacks. There were rich whites and poor whites. The poor whites lived in the swamps, for the most part, worked small farms, or made a living 'swamping. They were Catholic and spoke French or were the descendents of Francophones. Most of the poor WASPs lived north of Baton Rouge or in north Louisiana. The rich WASPS were mostly Episcopalians who came here before the Civil War."

"Well my fam'ly was *definitely* among the 'Have-Nots,'" Andy said. "On both sides. Most of 'em, even today, are swampers or small farmers. A few like my daddy an' my two cousins work in the shipyards or offshore now.

"What's swamping?" I asked.

"Moss-pickin', fishin', alligator huntin', trappin', shrimpin', froggin'. You name it." Andy said. "Anything you can catch or gather from the swamps.

"Around here, most of the poor whites were Cajuns and most could hardly speak English. In north Louisiana, they were the original cotton-picking red-necks."

My dad nodded and continued. "But despite their hardships and deprivation, we saw very happy people here. I guess that old adage, *'Ignorance is bliss,'* is true.

"There were only a few people who could even visualize a time when whites and blacks would be treated as equals.

"Next to the racial discrimination, the most appalling thing we saw was the *color discrimination*, where lighter-skinned Negroes held the same contemptuous attitudes toward their darker brothers and sisters as whites.

In most places in the world, being mixed race is a disgrace because of the implications of infidelity, prostitution, or rape, but in Louisiana, it's a matter of pride. It is still taken to heights I had never heard of anywhere else. Even a little bit of white blood, is looked upon with pride. The lighter one is, the haughtier. Even if they didn't have a pot to pee in.

"We were fighting a world war because one group of people wanted to exterminate another group of people based on their racial and genetic heritage, yet the U.S. had done nothing to ensure that its own Negro citizens had the basic liberties that it espouses throughout the world. Worse still, the armed forces were segregated all during the war.

"But I digress and it's getting late. To answer your question, young man, we chose south Louisiana because despite all of its blatant racism and the utter disrespect for people of color, it was the safest area for us to put into practice what we wanted to accomplish. This area is predominately French and Catholic, hence, no Ku Klux Klan to speak of. Plenty of racism, but nothing as organized and hateful as the Klan.

"The Klan looks down on Catholics and Cajuns with the same eyes it views black people," he continued.

"They call us coon-asses," Andy said. "Wayne and I were talking about that just yesterday."

My dad smiled. "Cajuns don't get a pass on racism," he said. "This area has many blatant racists and a lot of Cajuns are as mean and hateful toward Negroes as any Klansman but they're not organized, vitriolic racists like in other parts of the south and I've never heard of any lynchings in this area.

Cajuns have more of a laissez-faire mentality rather than an *'I'll go out of my way to do you harm'* mentality like in most of the south.

"We visited Charity Hospital in New Orleans one day," he continued. "It's the largest public hospital in the country. What we saw there was repulsive, to say the least, in regard to how badly the staff abused or disrespected its Negro patients and not one Negro protested or stood up for himself.

"We observed the utter disrespect, sometimes bordering on contempt, with which the staff treated the black patients, starting at the attending physicians and medical residents down to the nurses and other white personnel there. There were always exceptions but very, very few.

We never saw the nuns who ran the place interact with the Negro patients at all.

"My wife and I decided that we would come back one day and open a hospital where Negro patients could be treated with dignity and respect regardless of their own particular shade of brown, social status, or ability to pay. We realized that that was only the tip of the iceberg; that the discrimination was systemic. We knew we couldn't re-build the entire south or even Terrebonne Parish. But we could create an oasis where racism, classism, and colorism didn't exist.

"Why should it stop at medical services? We wanted a place where Negroes were welcome in stores, where we would not be followed around to ensure that we're not stealing the merchandise or where we could try on clothes and not have to take them home to do so. Those are basic human rights, not just black civil rights. We started with *Creswic House* as a safe haven for our own children and then expanded outward.

"We were more disturbed about color prejudice than we were about racial prejudice. What kind of person hates his own? In Italy, the Italians are divided into regions; the Genovesi, the Bolognesi, the Romani, the Siciliani, or whoever, but here, they're all Italians. The same for the Spaniards. They're regionalists: Asturians, Extremadurans, Catalonians, Andalusians, and all of the other regions.

"The Nazis made the Jews of Europe into a cohesive group and, as a result, the State of Israel now exists, but even there, there's a difference between Ashkenazi Jews, Oriental, and Sephardic Jews. Before that, the German Jews felt they were superior to the Polish Yiddish-speaking Jews, who may have felt they were better than the Lithuanians, or whatever.

With Negroes, it's the lighter ones against the darker ones, the educated ones against the undereducated ones. The city blacks as opposed to the country blacks. I saw the same thing in India—color discrimination.

"As long as there are two individuals, one will find some way of feeling superior to the other.

"We decided we would head back to England as soon as we could book passage after the war, and then we would come back to Louisiana to start our clinic."

"Could I ask you another personal question?" Andy asked, making his voice small.

"That hasn't stopped you 'til now, young man," Dad smiled.

"That li'l hospital in Houma didn't generate all this, did it?" Andy asked.

My dad laughed. "You don't fool around, do you? You're absolutely right. When we returned to Louisiana, we were planning a community based on merit rather than color or race long before anything was built, including this house. I don't know if you've ever thought about it but did you know that two thirds of the women in the world are women of color?"

"No," Andy admitted, shaking his head. "I hadn't given it a thought."

"Well," Dad said, "all women want to be beautiful. Up until the first Queen Esther and Lady Iris products came out, women of color needed and wanted cosmetics to complement their own shades but the major cosmetics companies were white-owned and only catered to white women. Women of color had to modify their products to make them fit their own skin tones or they just used them as is, which made for some awful-looking dark-skinned women! *That's* the niche that we filled. We gave the colored women of the world cosmetics that complimented their own color tones.

"Have you ever heard of *Phenocudine*?"

Andy shook his head.

"Almost nobody has, unless you're a chemist," my dad said. "Well, my grandfather, William Mallory, invented it back in the 1920's. It's a gasoline additive. It makes engines run faster, longer, smoother, and quieter. It's also makes the engine more efficient with a lot less pollution. Lately, they've been using it as an additive for the rockets into outer space and jet engines.

"The McGraths, my wife's family, made their fortune in vegetable oil. Cooking oil, as it were. Despite the labels they slap on the bottles, almost all of the world's cooking oil is made by McGrath Industries.

"They later ventured out into making candy. McGrath Sweets are very popular in Britain and its territories but not in the U.S. They supplied sweets to the British, Australian, and Canadian troops during both World Wars. The boys, especially the Australians, developed quite a taste for it.

"They make an English toffee, a rum-flavored peanut brittle, a chocolate drop, and a hard candy wafer that's really popular in the Caribbean. It's made of guava. Most Americans don't like guava, if they've ever tasted it at all.

"McGrath Sweets tend not to be as sweet as American sweets. Americans are sugarholics.

"Now they're diversifying again into information technology. We're building an R&D campus right here at The Reserve, in New Bern.

"*We*, meaning the Mallory and the McGrath families," my dad continued, smiling as he reminisced, "formed a corporation and started buying land as soon as we got here and continued until we had enough to start building what has become known as La Belle Terre Reserve one village at a time. There are nine proposed villages in the Reserve. All of them have at least some building activity going on in them. As you can see on the maquette, streets have been laid out for all of them, the necessary infrastructure has been put in place, and all have names," he said.

"The medical center was always our first priority, after this house, of course, because we had started a family and did not want them to grow up subjected to Louisiana's racism.

"I've seen a major shift in attitude among whites in the last few years," he said. "When we came here, no white, *anywhere*, would be treated by a black doctor, unless it was to perform an abortion or some other nefarious activity that they wanted to keep secret.

"Most white women would have rather died rather than have a black male doctor touch them. Now, it's completely the opposite. They come in to be treated by our ob-gyn and dare their husbands to say a word. Their husbands sometimes even accompany them. It's standing practice to have the husbands accompany them for the examination. That way, there's no possibility of a false accusation. Most of our ob-gyns are women and that puts all women, white or black more at ease.

"Their husbands, brothers, fathers, and sons have been coming in lately, too, especially since we completed the spinal cord injury hospital, the trauma center, and the urgent aid center. A lot of them work offshore and end up injured. They can get excellent treatment near home, rather than having to make the trip into New Orleans, Baton Rouge, or Houston.

"Gradually," he continued, "we're even getting applications from local whites who want to move into La Belle Terre. I never thought I'd see that!" he smiled.

"You treated my uncle Yogi a few years ago. He fell off a ladder on an oil rig an' hurt his back," Andy said. "He swears by you!"

"Yogi Bourgeois from Belle Glade is your uncle?" my dad smiled. "He was one of my very first white patients. What a character! How's he doing?"

"He's fine," Andy replied. "Same Yogi as always." He turned to me. "You'll meet him and my aunt Maybelline soon enough. My uncle Yogi is my cousin Paul's daddy an' my aunt Maybelline is Kevin's mama. They're triplets. Two boys an' a girl."

"Please give him my regards," Dad said to Andy. "What a character!" my dad smiled, shaking his head in private thought.

"Curiouser," Dad continued, picking up his train of thought exactly where he had left it, "is the number of whites who've come in recently to complete employment applications. I mean local whites.

"That would not have happened thirty-odd years ago but now, we regularly get applications from local whites, women mostly, who are applying for jobs as therapists, teachers, nurses, CNA's, and housekeepers, among others."

"How can you keep all this under control?" Andy asked. My dad made a moue, lifting his eyebrows, not comprehending. Andy explained further. "I mean, you have all this planned out but how can you keep it all under control. Looks to me like planting a tree and then trying to control the limbs.

My dad still did not seem to understand. "Could you be more explicit?" he finally asked.

"Ok," Andy said. "I understand how you, as the builder, can sell to whoever you want, or whoever has the money to buy a property, but what about when that person wants to move on? How can you prevent him from sellin' it to somebody you might not want livin' here?"

My dad smiled, finally understanding what Andy was trying to convey. "The Japanese do it all of the time. It's called bonsai. It's called the Right of First Refusal," he said. "All buyers must sign an agreement in which they agree to give the Corporation the right to either buy back the property they're selling or approve the sale to the new prospective buyer. That's how we control the quality of the people who live here." Did I detect a little bit of smugness in his voice?

He explained that there were very few people who have actually wanted to sell or rent their property but in the future, through attrition, that could be the case.

"The Corporation is very well funded," he said. "Even as the properties have continued to rise in value, we have been able to keep up with the market.

"Take for example, the athletes who came to this area when New Orleans got its first professional sports teams," he continued. "Many were affluent young blacks who were not welcome in most of the neighborhoods in which they wanted to purchase homes.

"As soon as they moved in, the whites moved out, causing the properties to be worth less than when the athletes purchased them. It's called 'white flight.'

"Trying to avoid that, many of them moved to the Reserve. Since then, some of them have been traded to other teams but many of their families have continued to live here year round while the athletes themselves rent apartments in the cities they were traded to. They return during the off-season, more than happy to be here in the Reserve.

"Does that answer your question, Andy?" he said before turning to me. "You've been home now for two days and you haven't even asked about your Grandma. She's getting old, you know."

"I know, Dad," I said. "I really want to see her but I also want to see the Bellefleur Parish Sheriff and the Skylarville Police Chief."

"Didn't you see them last night?" my dad asked a note of concern in his voice.

"No. They had already gone for the weekend."

"I still don't understand why you want to get involved in that murder," my dad said, shaking his head. "There are not a lot of murders in this area, especially not of lawmen," he continued, "but when there are, there is usually a good underlying reason for them."

Andy nodded agreement.

"I'm an investigative reporter," I countered. "That's what I do. I investigate."

"In Chicago. Not in Louisiana. Things work a little bit differently here than in Chicago."

Andy smiled and nodded but said nothing.

"There may be a good story here. I may be able to sell it to some of the big magazines." I replied. "Besides, who doesn't like a good *who-done-it?*"

"I've never had any run-ins with that guy," my dad said, "but Danny has."

Danny, an attorney, is my oldest brother, married to Ada, head of audiology at Mallory Medical. Jeremy, a banker and also an attorney, is my middle brother, married to Philippa ("Pippa" for short), the chief of surgery at Mallory

Medical's Trauma and Urgent Aid Center. Jeremy heads the financial wing of Mallory Properties and the Mallory Trust.

If I were ever to come back home, I'm sure they'd find something grown-up for me to do, too.

My dad continued, "Deputy Eck thought that it was his right to patrol the Reserve's streets, since New Bern and some of the unincorporated areas around it are in Belle Fleur Parish.

Dan heads La Belle Terre's Board of Regents. He told Eck that we have our own security force and La Belle Terre Reserve is private property. Just as he does not have the right to patrol the streets of Chantilly Country Club's residential areas uninvited, he does not have the right to patrol inside the Reserve. If there is an emergency or a crime, he would be called. Other than that, he was not welcome at the Reserve.

Chantilly Country Club, where Skylarville's elite play and live, is on the outskirts of Skylarville, on the route to New Orleans, and about 25 miles from the Reserve.

Its 18-hole golf course is ringed by large, expensive homes. The other area is Acadia Woods, within the Skylarville city limits. St. William's Catholic Church, school and hospital are located there. Those who live there are Skylarville's "old money" set. Chantilly's residents are mostly "new money" who made their fortunes in the booming offshore oil industry or they are the scions of Skylarville's ruling elite who chose not to live in Acadia Woods.

The Catash family lives on Arapaho Drive in a wedding cake of a house a stone's throw from St. William's campus.

"Deputy Eck didn't understand that so Danny filed an injunction against him," my dad continued. "That stopped him insisting on coming into the Reserve to flaunt his authority but he set out to harass people coming into and leaving the Reserve by giving them traffic tickets for the least little perceived infraction of the law. Again, Danny filed an injunction against him and the Belle Fleur Parish Sheriff's Office. The sheriff must have reined him in after that because we never had any more problems from him.

"One of my Belle Fleur Parish patients described him as sitting outside the Reserve's gates like a hungry crocodile, sitting in the bushes, waiting for a thirsty gazelle to come along. Most began taking alternate entrances into and out of the Reserve," he continued.

There were several ways into and out of the Reserve, none of which was gated but all clearly marked. This allowed workers, gapers, patients, and shoppers unhindered entry to and from the property without unnecessary restriction. Most of the communities and all of the larger estates in unincorporated areas are gated and have restricted entry.

"The people were getting up a petition against him, you know," he continued between sips of Tehuacán water and lime. "He seemed to be everywhere," he continued, "writing speeding tickets outside the Reserve, writing parking or too-slow tickets in Skylarville, writing jay walking tickets, starting more family arguments than he settled. He was doing the jobs of both the sheriff's office and the city police. Nobody but Daniel challenged him, it seems. Too much power in the hands of a fool is dangerous."

I deliberately avoided telling my dad Andy's occupation and former relationship with RC Eck.

After a few more drinks, Andy excused himself to the adjacent washroom. "It's obvious you're keen on that young man and he's keen on you. What's going on there?" my dad asked. "If you don't mind my asking."

I gave my dad the brief version of how we had met as teenagers years ago at St. William's school, lost touch, and re-met yesterday. I deliberately left out *exactly where* we had re-met.

"And what about Kevin Kincannon?" He knew that Kevin and I had had some problems in our relationship but I had been intentionally vague about what had happened or how deeply it had affected me when I decided to return home to mope.

"Sometimes things happen for a reason," I said, not a believer in pre-destination.

"Kevin is a showboat. He is all fluff but no substance. He was more in love with himself than he could ever be in love with you or anyone else, for that matter. Or that's my impression of him," he quickly added.

"When you told me and your mother that you were gay, do you remember what we told you?" he asked. Andy had returned from the washroom, accompanied by Leo and Tessa, his daughter, my parents' two dogs, who took places on the floor near me and my dad. Andy listened intently.

"You told me to find a good man and settle down—preferably in La Belle Terre Reserve."

This was the first time the issue of my sexual orientation had been discussed between my dad and me since that day so many years ago. There really had been nothing to say.

"Frankly, I don't even know if I know what love is," I admitted. Andy's face looked pained but he said nothing.

"You remember Leo from a few years ago, right?"

"The Kennedy kid? Of course I remember him," my dad said. Dad had always called him that because with his great head of heavy brown hair, bright blue eyes, and toothy smile, he looked like one of the younger generation of Kennedy children.

I nodded. Leo Morrissey was the center of my world before Kevin Kincannon. He was an apprentice carpenter whom I had met while having some custom millwork done in my condominium unit. During our two-year relationship, my parents had met him several times when they visited me in Chicago.

Leo and I were polar opposites. Where I was tall, Leo was a little guy, measuring no more than 5'-7" in elevator shoes. I was "out" about my sexuality while he was still very, very closeted about his.

His milk-white skin freckled easily while I was sun-tolerant. In describing himself, Leo said he was "the pastiest man on earth." My eyes were brown and my skin, the color of rich, dark chocolate, my lips are substantial, my nose, broad, and my hair, woolly.

I was "white collar' and he, "blue collar" through and through. He was a scruffy little Irishman who worked with his hands and I, a large black man who worked with my mind. He seldom read books while I read constantly. He drank prodigious quantities of Irish whiskey, beer, ale, stout, or malt liquor while I seldom drink.

I live on the north side of the city, where the Chicago Cubs play. He was from the Bridgeport neighborhood on the south side of Chicago, near Comiskey Park, where the Chicago White Sox play.

Leo liked to get pounded in our intimacies. "If they could see me now," he'd frequently say after a particularly strenuous session, "they'd shit themselves." I often wondered if his relationship with me was more to get back at his racist Irish family than it was based on love of another human being.

Not being a native Chicagoan, I failed to fully grasp the significance of the north-south divide for which the city was famous. Where North-siders are generally considered to be white collar professionals, financially better-off, better educated, and "more liberal," the south side is considered to be working class, less educated, less economically well-off, and bigoted. Personally, I find the entire city lacking in true liberal-ness.

"I'm from Mayor Daley's neighborhood," Leo liked to say. "If my family and friends even *thought* that I was gay, they'd kill me and if they had any idea that I was being boffed by an African giant, they'd kill *both* of us." Little did he know that I was not the only "African giant" out there plowing horny Bridgeport residents, nor did he know that he was not the first Bridgeport resident I had screwed.

Bridgeport was known for being unwelcoming to outsiders, especially those of us of the African persuasion.

When I moved to Chicago, Bridgeport and its neighbors, Marquette Park, where Dr. King was hit by a rock while marching through it, Brighton Park, and Gage Park, were four of the neighborhoods my black friends told me I should avoid. Leo told me the same thing, though it may have been more for his protection than mine.

I never met Leo's parents, any of his friends, or any other member of his family, though he was only too proud to tell them that he had a black friend who was a reporter at the *Chicago News Register*.

He felt family and peer pressure to find a woman with whom he could settle down and raise the next generation of Morrisseys. His idea was to continue to see me even after he had married his new girlfriend, Kathleen Kenna.

His unwillingness to come out of the closet and the fact that we had almost nothing in common beyond the fantastic sex, were the reasons we eventually split up.

"Leo most certainly was not right for you. You had no common goals," my dad said. "You obviously saw it because you constantly mentioned the differences between what you hoped to accomplish in life and what he wanted. Two people who plan to spend a life together have to establish common goals. It doesn't make a bit of difference if the couple is gay or straight, white or black, or a combination thereof.

"The couple must be like a team of horses pulling a wagon. You know that the journey will not be easy but if you pull together, the load is much lighter. If one pulls the complete load or feels that the other is not pulling his weight toward that goal, there is going to be friction. If the two are actively trying to reach different goals, it's impossible.

"Your mother and I have stayed together for just those reasons, plus the fact that we genuinely love each other. We established our goals a long time ago. We wanted to start a family, build *Creswic House*, establish Mallory Medical Center as a place where black citizens of this area could get the respect they deserved as patients, and to turn this little piece of God's green earth around from what it was to what it is now.

"Being gay," Dad continued, "it's even harder for you than for us because you have no legal sanction for your union. You don't even have much societal sanction. Besides, most people want your relationship to fail. Some "experts" (he used air quotes here) even say that love between members of the same sex is impossible but I know differently. Some of the strongest marriages I've ever seen have been between same sex couples.

"Gay partnerships are based solely on the two individuals' declared intention to live together as spouses. If things get tough, they can easily dissolve their union, as you've done in the past. There is no legal incentive to stay together, to try to work things out," my dad was saying. "So it's even more important to find the exact match before you decide to open up your heart and your home to someone.

"I never declared my intention to live as spouses with anybody," I said when he had finished. "And I never considered myself married to any of them. When I get married, it'll be a big, formal, splashy affair just like my brothers had."

I wanted to explore another idea that had been kicking around in my head for a while. "I don't know whether the male was meant to be monogamous or not but why should he limit himself to just one spouse?

"For whatever reason, Western culture has decided that the marriage bond should be between one man and one woman but in other parts of the world, a man can have more than one spouse.

"I don't know how that works out among the women but as I see it, if all parties are in agreement, why couldn't the marriage bond—and the marriage bed, for that matter, include more than one spouse?

"As gay people, we're in control of our own destinies right now. If the State gets involved with gay relationships and approves gay marriages, they're going to want us to follow the same Western mold that straight couples follow: Two men or two women.

"At this phase of our lives and of development, in which the State has not dictated how many partners we can have, we can explore all of our options instead of just blindly following straight society.

"Until I *re*-met Andy yesterday, I had never given any serious thought to finding just one partner and being faithful to that person but there's something different about this guy. I don't know where this is leading but at least I'm beginning to think in that direction.

"I was faithful to Kevin because that's the way I am, but I never considered myself married to him. I'm not a hunter. I'm not constantly on the prowl for the next great sexual fling but if I had met Andy while Kevin and I were still together, I'm pretty sure that Andy would still be the person sitting across from me talking about this now," I said.

"Why do you think that?" my dad wanted to know.

"Because everything seems right when I'm with him. It's like finding the shoe that was custom made just for you. It was that way when I met him thirteen years ago and it remains true today." I looked across the sofa where Andy sat smiling, and continued. "I'd always believed that if there's no possibility of producing children, the sex act—among two consenting adults—is just a way of relieving sexual tension and that it can be jolly good sport but now I believe that it's also a way of expressing love for the one you're with.

"Except for the legal issues that arise when children or property are involved, I never saw the importance of marriage, gay or straight, and I didn't want to complicate my life with those legalities.

"With this guy and me, it's almost like we were made for each other. Everything just seems right.

"And you know me, Dad. You know that I never, ever make snap judgments."

My dad nodded his head and smiled. He said nothing but I believe he understood what I was talking about better than he let on.

"Tell Andy how you and Mom met, Dad."

My dad shook his head. "I'm sure our guest doesn't want to hear that," he finally said.

"Come on, Dad," I chided. "It's a great story.

Andy chimed in. "I'd really like to hear it, Dr. Mallory."

"OK," Dad finally said after a long time. "It's simple," he began, looking at Andy rather than at me, since I've heard it a few thousand times.

"We met in kindergarten. Laura was born in England but her family originated in Bermuda. I was born in Bermuda and lived there until it was time for university.

"Well," Laura's parents sent her to spend the summer in Bermuda with her grandparents. We were both five years old and in kindergarten. I had been ill and missed the first week of school.

"On my first day, I thought I was ready for this but when Mum left the building; I wanted to go with her. I threw a hissy-fit like few others ever have! I wanted to go with my mum and that teacher was not going to stop me, though she tried hard to keep me there. I was screaming and crying to go with Mum when, all of a sudden, someone calmly tapped me on my shoulder while I was fighting against the teacher to be let out the door.

"I turned around and there was this beautiful little brown-skinned girl. She smiled at me and I was smitten right then and there. She said, 'don't cry, little boy. Your mum will come back for you in three hours. I'll tell you when that time is up and then, you'll see, your mum will be back for you.

"'My name is Laura. You can sit with me.'"

"I calmed down immediately. I could've asked at that point, 'Mum who?' As long as Laura was there, I really didn't care if Mum ever came for me. When it was time to go home, I wanted to stay with Laura." He concluded.

"Even when she went back to England, we kept in touch. I had no doubt in my mind that this was the girl I would marry someday and I really didn't know what it all meant. I just knew that we were in for the long haul."

Andy spoke up. "I felt the same way about Steve. I mean Wayne," he said. "I knew it the minute I looked up and saw him looking at me."

The version we told my dad was that I had gone into St. William's school looking for a washroom and that I opened the unlocked cubicle door where Andy was relieving himself. We told him that we started talking when we had finished our business and, since it was the last day of school, we had time to talk. Both of us knew that we'd be in for the long haul, too, but then we lost touch for thirteen years, only to reconnect yesterday.

At that point, Andy's occupation had to come out and did.

Andy, said, "I've always believed that the human male *is* meant to be monogamous but the human male has a sense of entitlement that he can have all he can conquer. He has no self control. Most men don't have it. They live in the here and now and don't worry about the implications of infidelity."

"You're absolutely right, Andy," my dad said. "The male has always had the freedom to travel and spread his seed as he went. Available females—or males—made it easy and fun to copulate and be on one's merry way without a thought as to what he was actually leaving in his wake."

I could not agree more. I've traveled the world and copulated in every country from Iceland to Israel and from Pakistan to Peru and enjoyed every minute of it. Luckily, I have only copulated with males so I know there are no little Waynes being left behind in those places in which I've touched down. In addition, I've always used condoms, so I neither left any infections nor took any with me.

***

Sunday morning

"Hey, Young Prince, are you awake?" Andy said. He had shaved and was wearing a short white terrycloth bathrobe with dark blue sash and dark blue piping on the collar, lapels, and pockets.

Andy kissed me lightly on the mouth and stuffed a breakfast link into my mouth when I finally opened my eyes. "One Sunday a month, I go to visit my parents in Belle Glade for lunch and today's that day. We're having a crawfish boil. Wanna come along?"

"Will I be welcome?" I inquired. Belle Glade is not known for being very welcoming to black people.

"Of course," Andy said, "as long as you remember to keep your hands off my butt."

"They won't mind your bringing a black friend to Belle Glade with you?"

Andy shook his head. "There's a black lady who used to live down the road about a quarter of a mile from us. Her name was Miz Delia but everybody called her Miz Zah. I found some rental receipts when my Nonc Ro-*bair* died. They were made out to Delia Robinson. Nobody 'round here bothered her. In fact, she was a *traiteuse.* You know what that is, right?"

"I've always understood it to be some kind of folk healer or *voodooienne*," I responded.

"Not *really* voodoo," he said. "They pray for you. They treat you wit' herbs, holy water, an' prayers. It's based on Cat'lic tradition more than anything else. A lot of people from 'round here went to her for treatment. They didn't care what color she was. Besides, that," he continued, "there will prob'ly be some more black people there. Some of my daddy's friends from work usually come when we hold crawfish boils."

Wallace's bark and then a gentle knock at the door interrupted what might have led to a second close encounter of a sexual kind. Andy scurried to the second bedroom at the opposite end of the hallway.

"What are you doing?" I asked, confused.

"I'm rumpling the bed," he replied. "It's prob'ly Kevin and he rambles. It wouldn't do for him to know that we spent the night in the same bed. Why don't you get the door and I'll pull on my clothes."

"But we slept together Friday night," I reminded him. "Kevin was here. He knows that."

"What?" Andy said. "What about it?"

"Well, we spent the first night we met in the same bed. What's the difference?"

Andy looked blank, confused, and desperate. "Haven't you ever played *'The Game?'*" he asked in a hushed voice. His whole demeanor had changed.

"What 'Game?'" I wanted to know.

"Remind me to explain it later, OK?"

There was a second, louder, more insistent, knock and louder barks from Wallace. Someone impatiently jiggled the doorknob as Wallace began to growl and bark warnings.

"Just a minute," Andy called from the guest bedroom. "Get the door, will you?" he said.

"In this robe?" I asked. "What if it's not Kevin? I'd look like a fool in this thing. It's too short."

Andy was moving swiftly between the guest bedroom, the bathroom, and his own bedroom, looking for telltale signs of last night's odyssey.

"Put your clothes on in the other bedroom," Andy said, a little calmer as he zipped up yesterday's blue jeans and throwing on a light blue crewneck tee-shirt. "*I'll* get the door."

I decided to join in on "The Game" Andy was playing. I grabbed my clothes and took them to the back bedroom and proceeded to put them on.

Satisfied that all signs of last night's love odyssey had been eradicated, Andy tousled his hair and returned to the living room to open the door, looking properly sleepy and disheveled as he did.

Through the closed bedroom door, I could hear voices but music from the stereo Andy had flicked on on his way to answer the door, blocked out the words. I emerged from the bedroom about three minutes later, giving the interloper enough time to be seated. I poked my head into the living room through the passageway, where I saw Kevin and a taller young man with shoulder-length chocolate-colored hair sitting on the sofa and talking to Andy, who had remained standing near the door, arms akimbo.

"I heard all the racket Wallace was making so I decided to get up and see what was going on," I said, faking a yawn. I shook hands with Kevin and was introduced to Paul, Andy's other cousin. I promptly excused myself on the pretext of having to take care of the morning's duties, then entered the bathroom and washed the taste of the huge breakfast from my mouth. I then returned to the living room.

"You slept in the back bedroom?" Paul wanted to know.

I smiled and nodded.

"There's no way you could fit in that li'l bed," Paul said, eyeing me up and down.

"I managed," I replied.

"You should'a jus' slept with T'Beau," he continued. "Or if y'all didn't wanna bump up together during the night, T'Beau shudda taken the small bed."

I looked at Andy and stifled a smile. "I sleep wherever the master of the house wants me to," I finally said pointedly,

"You're a really big man," Paul continued, looking me up and down like a cheap piece of meat.

I gave him my stats before he could ask.

Paul Bourgeois was taller than Andy but not quite as tall as Kevin, though he was much broader across the chest; much more muscled.

He had a handsome face; not very different from Kevin's or Andy's. Two small, flesh-colored moles, one on the upper left side of his right cheek near his nostril, and the other on his left cheek, just below the corner of his mouth, dotted his otherwise perfect features. His eyes were hazel. A dark shadow above his upper lip indicated where a mustache had been or would be.

The three of them looked more like brothers than first cousins.

Paul wore a black Stetson with a woven geometric hatband and a brown and white feather tucked in it on the right side. He also wore a dark blue chambray shirt with pearl snap buttons, the top three of which were unsnapped, exposing a dense patch of dark chest hair.

He wore heavily starched boot-cut jeans with a razor crease. On his size twelve feet, he wore highly polished black cowboy boots that reached up to the middle of his calves.

"You a foreign car salesman?" Kevin asked me.

"No, why?" I wanted to know.

"Friday, you had a dark green Jaguar and now you have that Range Rover outside.

"His parents are the colored doctors," Andy interjected blandly. That seemed to explain everything. "You should see that awesome Lamborghini his daddy's got!" A lustful look crossed his face as he remembered my dad's ultimate driving fantasy.

"Did you get a chance to drive it?" Kevin wanted to know.

"My dad won't even let *me* drive it," I said, "let alone, a total stranger."

"Your daddy operated on my old man's back," Paul said.

"How'd he get hurt?" I asked.

"He was workin' on a rig in the Gulf an' he and another guy were carryin' some heavy tool boxes down some stairs. It was a three or even a four-man job. My daddy was in front goin' down and the other guy was in back. The guy slipped. They fell down two flights of stairs. The other guy and the boxes they were carryin' fell on top of Daddy. The other guy walked away with no injuries at all but they had to helicopter Daddy to New Orleans. We're gon' be almost as rich as your old man soon as the lawsuit is settled. Your daddy has to testify about his injuries as an expert witness.

"Daddy had been to a lot of back specialists before one of his friends at work tol' him about your daddy. Your daddy operated on him and after that, he was a new man. Before the operation, all he could do was lay on a pallet on the floor poppin' pain pills and groanin' day an' night."

"My dad gets big bucks for testifying as an expert witness."

"He couldn't walk without help an' he couldn't sleep for the pain. He was takin' all kinds of pain relievers but nothin' worked. Now he can sleep at night in his own bed. He went dancing a few weeks ago. He can even prob'ly hump my mama again now," Paul smiled. "But I don' even wanna *think* about that!" he quickly added.

"Jus' what you need," Kevin laughed. "A baby brother!"

"I got enough of 'em already. You the lawyer?" Paul asked.

"No, I'm the newspaper reporter."

"You ought'ta do a story 'bout the oil companies an' how they treat their workers, especially when they get hurt. The fuckers don't want to pay 'em.

"I'm sure your old man can tell you a lot of stories about oilfield injuries. He's an expert witness so he testifies a lot. That's why my old man's friend recommended that he go see your daddy. The oil companies' lawyers haven't been able to trip him up yet. He knows his stuff," Paul said.

Kevin placed a sandwich-size plastic bag of some very green pot on the coffee table, produced some rolling papers from the rear pockets of his jeans, and rolled two joints. He then rolled a third joint and lit the first one, taking a toke and passing it to Andy, who declined the invitation saying he was headed soon to Belle Glade and that being high so early in the day was not a good idea.

Following Andy's lead, I also declined when Kevin offered it to me. Paul and Kevin passed it back and forth between themselves.

"That reminds me," Paul said, "my van's still not workin'. Can me an' Kev get a ride to Belle Glade with y'all?"

We hadn't made any formal arrangements as to who was driving which vehicle but I assumed that we were going in the Rover so I consented. Andy told them we would be ready to leave in about two hours.

The cousins took one of the remaining joints and left the other for Andy and me to smoke. Kevin folded the rolling materials and the pot into his clothing and left with Paul following closely behind.

***

I had driven away from *Creswic House* with my dad's whispered admonition still ringing in my ears, "I can see that Andy's smitten with you. I don't think he'd do anything to hurt you but still, be careful in Belle Glade," he had said. "The people back there are known racists. Not all of them, mind you, but they do have a reputation for being insular and very, very racist.

"Many a black body has turned up floating in Bayou Mal Enfant after they went fishing back there, having mysteriously 'drowned.' I've heard that some didn't even have water in their lungs but that's just hearsay. Others went fishing back there and disappeared altogether. Keep your wits about you while you're there."

I assured him that I would.

***

The French have occupied what is now Louisiana since the 1600's but the Cajuns did not arrive there until 1764. They were two separate and very different groups of people, though both spoke French, were of French ancestry, and had the Roman Catholic religion in common.

The French and the French Creoles, their American-born progeny, were early white settlers, some of whom later became plantation owners who had arrived as soldiers, fortune hunters, prisoners, prostitutes, school girls, or rapscallions more than a century earlier than the Cajuns.

They appropriated the lands owned by the local indigenous population to plant rice, sugar cane, or cotton but you can hardly call yourself a *planter* if you brought thousands of Africans to do the actual *planting* because you were too lazy to do it yourself, can you? But those who could did.

Some took advantage of the importation of African slaves, prospered, and became "aristocrats." As soon as they could, they left the land to others to manage for them and settled in or around New Orleans, where there were the accoutrements of French civilization, which they idealized.

Others, regardless of how hard they tried, never amounted to much. They, too, were mostly urban, or associated with the life in and around New Orleans and carved out niches for themselves wherever and however they could.

The Cajuns, who arrived from Nova Scotia, were refugees. The bayou region, which includes the area around Bellefleur and its neighboring parishes, was settled by Creoles but populated mostly by Cajuns.

The name Cajun is a corruption of the French word *"Acadién,"* because they came from *Acadie,* present-day, Nova Scotia.

Belle Glade is in *"The Brulé."* The term *"brulé,"* meaning "burned" in French, came about because South Louisiana was, and still is, heavily forested. Before settlements could be built, trees had to be chopped down and burned off. Usually, the first structure Cajuns built was their church. Originally, and to this day, most of the brulés are Francophone, Catholic, and are usually named after the Catholic saints for whom their local church is named.

There are too many "brulés" in south Louisiana to count. They are usually undefined, wild spaces in the woods. No one knows exactly where the brulés of Bellefleur Parish begin or end. When we outsiders speak of The Brulé, we always preface it with "*back there*," or "*in* the Brulé," or "*back in* the Brulé," indicating that they are not easily accessible.

Belle Glade is the largest and most easily accessible of Bellefleur Parish's *brulés*. In addition to Belle Glade, there are the smaller communities of Brulé Ste. Catherine, Brulé St. Elmo, and others whose names I do not know. Belle Glade has a post office and can be found on a map but most of the others cannot. Before it became officially known as Belle Glade, La., it was called Brulé St. Camille.

Bellefleur Parish's *brulé* communities are a series of settlements on bayous and smaller waterways extending southward to the Atchafalaya River Basin, the nation's largest swamp.

The people built hovels out of whatever they could find or cart in by boat. Many of the people still live full time on houseboats.

All my life, I've heard the people of "The Brulé," Belle Glade in particular, referred to as "mean people" or racists. They have often been described as people who have very little regard for the lives of outsiders, especially if that outsider happens to be of African origin. The movie, *"Deliverance"* reminded me of the stereotypes I've always carried in my mind of Belle Glade and its surrounding communities. I've always thought of the residents of Belle Glade as *"swamp-billies,"* French-speaking rednecks, as there are no hills nearby.

There has always been only one very narrow, winding two-lane road through The Brulé. It went from Skylarville to Belle Glade, and dead-ends in the settlement of Darbonneville on the Fin de Terre Peninsula, approximately fifty miles beyond Belle Glade. When I was growing up, it was gravel. Later, it was blacktopped, and remains so today.

At some point, the road branches off toward Thibodaux in Lafourche Parish. At a different point, it intersects with La. Highway One that traverses the state from north to south like a gastro-intestinal tract, much as the Mississippi River traverses the nation.

***

Andy pulled the Firebird into the driveway of a well-maintained white brick split-level on a cement slab. It was long and low-slung. The main level was white brick. The bedroom level sat atop it like the hump on Quasimodo's back. This upper level was made of wood and painted battleship gray, with white louvered shutters flanking the large windows but obviously not intended to cover them. The upper windows were shaded by black and white striped metal awnings. On the front lawn, near the front door, Our Lady of the Immaculate Conception stood protected in her sanctuary, the rear half of an old porcelain claw-foot bathtub with the feet removed. Before her, a bunch of faded plastic flowers drooped in a cement vase.

Andy parked the Firebird behind a Dodge conversion van under the double carport. I parked the Rover behind the Firebird and turned it facing the road... just in case I had to make a fast getaway.

Kevin had ridden shotgun with me, luxuriating in all of the Rover's creature comforts. He loved motor vehicles, especially big, expensive ones. He and I stepped out of the Rover's air-conditioned comfort and into Louisiana's ferocious summer heat and drenching humidity. In front of us, Andy and Paul did the same; all of us mopped our brows as the sweat popped up on our foreheads like popcorn.

"So where's the garçonniere you and your cousins slept in?" I asked, looking around and pretending to be bewildered. "I was expecting a Cajun version of *Tobacco Road.*"

All I could see was mile after mile of sugar cane, interspersed here and there by the roofs of houses every quarter mile or so. "This looks like standard-issue, mid-century modern south Louisiana architecture to me," I said. "In fact, it's larger than most south Louisiana houses because it's a split-level."

"You saw that big, wood house we passed 'bout a quarter mile back?" he asked.

I nodded. I had slowed the Rover to a stop on the seldom-traveled highway when I passed this architectural jewel.

Kevin had told me that this was where Andy had grown up. It was a lovely old cypress structure with so much paint peeled off that I had no idea what its original color had been. It had a deep front porch, called a *gallerie*, supported by six thin wooden columns, three on each side of the main entry, and topped by a large Palladian window in a gabled dormer. A smaller gabled dormer flanked the large gable on either side. A steeply-pitched tin roof with exposed rafter tails that flared out gracefully from the main roofline gave it a note of distinction.

It sat back from the roadway on brick piers over three feet high, like a southern belle raising her skirts to avoid high water while hiding from passing traffic behind a wide-branching, live oak that dripped Spanish moss onto the brick pathway that led up to it. Resurrection vine covered the tree's branches like long, elegant, verdant opera gloves.

Cast iron plants and snake plants still grew in wild abandon around the base of the oak. Poison ivy ran up and down its trunk, intertwining itself with the resurrection vine, surrounding and embracing it like a Latin lover.

Broken latticework covered the base of the porch between the brick piers.

Its central doorway was topped by a fanlight in the shape of a half-oval and flanked on either side by broken sidelights. The wide cypress door still wore its brass knocker, now tarnished to the color of the wood onto which it was affixed. Two pairs of ceiling-to-floor French doors that opened from the two front rooms onto the porch flanked the main entry, giving it balance and class. Breeze-catching transoms above the French doors allowed the heat to escape without letting insects in.

The louvered wooden shutters that had once closed off the delicate French doors in times of storms or at night were long gone. Only their outlines remained pressed against the front of the building like ghosts of Hiroshima. The wooden steps that led up to it were badly in need of repair. The front yard was knee-high in weeds.

Appended to its side like a carbuncle, behind a large flowering magnolia, was what I assumed to be the bathroom because of its high, narrow, horizontal window. In houses this age, bathrooms were always an add-on.

In front of the bathroom addition that jutted out perpendicular to the main body of the house, was a narrow-roofed side porch that was probably added at the time the bathroom was added.

In times before washing machines, a metal wash tub and washboard usually festooned the exterior bathroom wall, attached by heavy nails or pegs, near the side entry door. The family's wash was done on this porch and hung out to dry on clotheslines in the side or back yard. In the yard, a few feet away from the side door, a tall, round oak cistern usually stood like a huge oak barrel, three or four metal bands girdling it to keep it from spilling its contents out into the world.

There were three brick chimneys: One appended to each side of the house in the two front rooms, and a third that popped up from the center of the roof.

I had heard several names for this type of architecture: Low Country vernacular architecture, a Lowland Planter's Cottage, a Louisiana Coastal Cottage, or a Louisiana Vernacular Cottage to name a few. I liked this style because it was developed in Louisiana by Louisianans, for the peculiarities of Louisiana's climate yet they were rapidly being replaced by the ubiquitous air conditioned brick rectangles that constituted "good taste" in the mid-twentieth century.

I wondered if this beautiful old structure could be rehabbed and saved from ruin. My thought, when I saw it, was, *I need to talk to Andy about this house.* I wonder if we could move it to The Reserve and rehab it. It would be perfect for the two of us.

The twin villages of Nemaquah and Issaquah Pointe were just coming on line. Both have coastal themes and feature Low Country architecture. This house would be perfect there. Others have rescued and transported similar old houses to these villages, rehabbed them, and the results were spectacular.

I came back to reality.

"That's where I grew up," he said. "That house has a garçonniere. I saw you stop when we drove past it. I don't know if Kevin told you that that's where

I grew up or not or whether you could see the staircase laying down on the gallerie but that was the stairway that used to lead to it. The entry was through the front porch, right in front of the far set of French doors.

"Miz Delia and her daughter lived a little farther on but they left and the house blew down in Hurricane Betsy in 1965.

"Kevin's parents live over there," he continued, pointing past the wreck to a neat white frame house on brick pillars with well-tended flower beds and bushes.

"My aunt Claire and her friend, Terri, live across the road and my paw-paw and my maman live next door to them. They're pretty old now. Claire an' Terri take care of 'em rather than puttin' em in an old folk's home." He pointed out two other narrow white frame houses, identical to the first one except that the wood had been covered with white asbestos siding.

One of the houses had neatly trimmed boxwood hedges leading to the entrance while the other had brightly-colored flowering plants leading to its entrance. All of the houses except Andy's old house looked prosperous and well-tended.

We followed Kevin through the double carport to the side door of the house, passing a new gray Ford Galaxie with a white vinyl top and the conversion van behind which Andy had parked his Firebird. On the side of the van was a picture of Wile E. Coyote carrying a sign saying *"Yipes!!"* as he disappeared over a cliff. The Roadrunner waved "bye-bye" from the cliff from which the coyote had fallen, smiling a devilish grin. He carried a sign saying, *"Meep-meep."*

Kevin entered the small warm kitchen without knocking. It was occupied by a hippy middle-aged woman and two slender younger ones who chatted and laughed amiably as they cooked.

They stopped abruptly when they saw Kevin and me in the doorway. Andy, who was behind me and still out on the carport, climbed up the three cement steps, squeezed past us, and introduced me to his mother and sisters.

Jolie-Marie Bourgeois looked up at me in awe—my head almost touched the popcorn ceiling-- and gave me a quick smile. "You should'a tol' me you were bringing comp'ny, T'Beau," she said to Andy, an' *you"* she said, pointing to

Kevin, "should'a brought him in through the *front* door. He's a guest. He don'
wanna see all this mess, no!"

She smiled and wiped her hands on a nearby dish towel then offered her right
hand to me. "I hope you like crawfish, Ween. I bet they don' have *dat* in
Chicago." Her Cajun accent was much more pronounced than Andy's, Paul's
or Kevin's.

Jolie-Marie was an older, fleshier, female version of Andy. Or should I say,
Andy was a younger, male version of Jolie-Marie? She had the same Gypsy
dark complexion as Andy. Her wildly curly hair had been pulled straight back
and tied in a bun, leaving waves that looked like the sea on a dark, dark night.
The jet black color of her curls was threaded with silver above her forehead
and near the temples. Her violet eyes looked tired, having dark circles under
them, but otherwise, as beautiful as her son's. Although she was now thick
around the middle and had crow's feet at the corners of her eyes, she was still
a strikingly handsome woman. Andy had said she had been the belle of the
bayou at one time. It was easy to see that she had been a looker in her prime.

She wore a yellow cotton housedress and fuzzy blue house slippers. Around
her neck, nestled in her ample cleavage, was a small gold crucifix. She wore
no makeup.

Andy's sisters, Cammie and Elaine, looked nothing like Andy and Jolie-Marie.
Cammie had straight, chestnut-colored hair with blond highlights and coffee-
brown eyes.

Elaine, the younger of the two sisters, had hair the color of wet sand in some
places and butterscotch in others; large blue eyes, and chipmunk cheeks. I
could hardly resist the desire to pinch them. She looked more like Paul's or
Kevin's sister than Andy's. They ushered us through the tiny kitchen and into
the spacious living-dining room with its highly-polished pine floors.

A large crucifix made of dark wood and flanked by framed pictures of the
Sacred Heart of Jesus and the Immaculate Heart of Mary looked down
benevolently on those sitting in the room and greeted those entering through
the front door.

A large, fuzzy area rug lay in front of a taupe-colored sofa, matching loveseat,
and two armless chairs; separated by a wooden coffee table and two end tables,

made the room seem a bit crowded. Tall ceramic lamps on the end tables, a grandfather clock, a television set, and an oak bookshelf completed the room's furnishings.

A stiff crocheted doily ran the length of the top of the TV set that sat glaring at us from one corner of the room.

The set was tuned to a baseball game but the sound was muted. Family photographs and more religious images smiled down on the room from pleasantly-arranged groupings on the sage-green sheet rock walls. A knee-high rubber plant and a huge schefflera, well over six feet tall, sat near the two windows in the room.

I walked over to take a better look at the pictures. Andy accompanied me, giving a running commentary of the people and events. There was one of high school-aged Andy in a tuxedo with a blonde girl in a long pink dress, taken at his senior prom; Andy in cap and gown, receiving the valedictory awards at his high school graduation, and an unsmiling Andy in his U.S. Marine Corps dress uniform. He was a Cajun version of the All-American Boy.

Despite the fact that his beautiful locks had been shorn, I liked this one best of all because his beautiful violet eyes, with their sensuous gull-winged lashes, and his Wally Cleaver lips now became the focal points of the photo.

Kevin and Paul had started drinking Budweisers that one of Andy's sisters had brought out on a large blue plastic tray that looked as if it had once served time in some school's cafeteria, while Andy and I perused the photos. Paul had lit up a Marlboro and placed the pack on the coffee table beside a large pink ceramic ashtray.

Although there were four bottles of beer on the tray, there was only one beer mug, freshly washed and hurriedly dried.

"The mug's for you," Andy smiled. "You're comp'ny. They never would've done som'pn like that for us three bums. In fact, they wouldn'a even brought us our beers if you hadn't been with us." Andy picked up his beer and sat beside me on the loveseat. His hands caressed the bottle of beer in an unconscious attempt to disguise his nervousness.

Elaine returned and sat on the wide arm of the sofa nearest the kitchen door. She had an angelic face that was ringed by soft sandy curls and Andy's wide eyes, only in a lighter shade of blue.

After the usual questions about my height, she began asking questions about Chicago, which seemed farther away and just as foreign as Viet Nam, where Andy had spent two years of his life as a military policeman.

"Why don't you and Andy come up to visit sometime?" I said. "I'd love to show you the city."

"Not me and Paul?" Kevin smiled a marijuana-induced smile. He had indulged in his own product on the way to Belle Glade. I chose to abstain.

"You should know by now that you and Paul are always welcome, Bud," I said, smiling at him indulgently as he peered at me through half-lidded eyes. I meant it whole-heartedly. In a short time I had known him, Kevin had begun to remind me of the younger brother I never had.

"You an' Paul can go," Elaine said. "Not me, though. *Pas moi!*" She said, pointing to herself. "*Jamais!* I've heard 'bout the cold weather and the snow piled up over the cars' hoods, and the robbers and rapists and gangsters up there.

"I'll stay right here in Belle Fleur Parish where it's nice an' warm. I *don'* like cold weather. I'm gon' stay right here where the people know each other, an' you can leave your doors unlocked at night and not have to worry 'bout some nut comin' in and killin' you." She had her mother's heavy Cajun accent.

A new Pontiac Bonneville with a dark blue body and white vinyl top pulled into the driveway and parked in front of the Rover, diverting her attention from the evils of Chicago. Three or four small children ranging in age from about four to about ten, scrambled out of the rear doors almost before the driver could come to a complete stop.

A dowdy dishwater blonde woman and an even heavier, bald man followed the children, disembarking into the unrelenting heat and humidity from their air-conditioned auto and, with little ado, headed for the chilly air of the house. The man stopped a minute to admire the Rover. Halfway up the short driveway, the woman barked some unheard command to two of the younger children who were turning cartwheels on the lush green lawn, oblivious to the heat.

Through the sheer curtains of the picture window, Andy announced that they were "Tante Clotilde and Nonc Yogi," Paul's parents.

In a matter of minutes, the older newcomers had come through the carport and were entering the kitchen to kisses and greetings from Jolie-Marie and her daughters.

Paul, who had said little until their appearance, jumped up from his seat. "Fuck!" he said. "I forgot to water the plants. Y'all wanna come?"

Andy shot me a quick smile. "Want your first look at a stand of Belle Glade homegrown?" Before I could answer, he stood and said, "Let's go through the back way. I'll show you Paradise."

I thought he had done that last night but I didn't voice that sentiment. I just smiled. "Lead the way," I finally said.

"We'll meet y'all by the pond," Andy said to Paul.

Paul nodded, leaving by the front door and avoiding his parents. Kevin followed closely behind.

Nonc Yogi entered the room with a bottle of beer in one hand and glowered at Paul's and Kevin's retreating figures. He gave a bear hug to Andy, who introduced him to me.

Yogi turned to Andy. "Where they goin' in such a rush?"

Andy shrugged. "Paul remembered somp'n he had to do an' Kev went with him."

"They in such a rush Paul couldn't say hello to me or his mama?" Yogi asked, still perturbed by his son's and nephew's rudeness.

Andy hunched up his shoulders but said nothing.

Yogi shook my hand with a firm grip, still looking through the window at the two retreating figures. "Nice car," he said. "*Very nice!* How much she set you back?"

I said. "It's a loaner."

Nonc Yogi had too much face for his tiny features. He reminded me of Poppin' Fresh, the Pillsbury Dough Boy, with a wide expanse of face that held two small blue eyes, a small nose, a pelican jaw, and a wide mouth that was curved in a big smile.

Andy excused himself and me, saying that he wanted to show me his property but that we would be back in plenty of time for the boiling of the crawfish.

"I don' want you to miss this, Ween!" Nonc Yogi said with a wicked grin. We left by way of the kitchen, repeating the same story to the women.

We crossed the carport, leaving the chatter of the women behind and entered the neat backyard, which was enclosed by lantana, birds of paradise, and crepe myrtle; and carpeted by the same St. Augustine grass as the front lawn.

A neat chain link fence that had weathered to a dull gray color enclosed the rear property. At the far end, almost hidden by boxwood hedges, was a narrow metal gate topped by a metal spaniel that pointed the way to Paul's mobile home.

We entered a shady, area bordered on one side by fan palms, azaleas, and large, moss-draped live oaks that must have been at least a hundred years old, then crossed an unpainted wooden bridge with high hand rails over a narrow ravine. A narrow stream ran at a trickle about fifteen feet below.

"The vegetable gardens are in plots behind the trees on the other side of the ravine," he said, pointing off to the east.

"That little stream's an offshoot of Bayou Mal Enfant." Andy explained. "The bayou's about a thirty yards or so that way," he said, pointing straight back. "You gotta see this," he said. "There's gators in there, yeah," he warned, "so be careful."

On the other side of the bridge, we came to an open, grassy area surrounded by day lilies, camellias, azaleas, and banana plants with their flagrantly phallic magenta flowers in full bloom.

The chirping of birds and the clearness of the humid air was interrupted only by the lazy buzzing of the myriads of insects and the occasional loud "*SNAP!*" that rent the air like gunshots.

"What's that snapping sound?"

"Garfish," Andy said. "Meanest fuckers in the world. I'd prefer to meet a hungry mama gator than an alligator gar any day," he continued.

I looked around, appreciating the place. "This is beautiful," I said, my mouth agape.

Andy smiled a knowing smile. "Mos' people feel like that when we bring 'em back here," he said, offering me a joint. "Let's go down to the bayou's edge. Be careful, though, OK?"

"Let's not," I said.

"*Chick-enn!*" he said, making clucking sounds.

We walked slowly along a narrow trail passing a joint back and forth, swatting insects, and dodging palm fronds, Spanish moss, and low-hanging tree branches as we went.

When he felt it was safe, Andy took my hand. "They can't see us here," he said, squeezing it gently as we continued along the path. "Thanks for putting up with this shit," he said. "I love you all the more for doin' it."

"No problem," I said. "That's what life's like in a small town closet. I understand but it didn't seem necessary to me. Paul and Kevin assumed that we had slept together, anyway. What do you think would happen if they knew about us?"

"Kev an' Paulie wouldn' have a problem wit' it, I'm sure," he said, "an' I think my mama would be cool about it," Andy replied. "I can just picture Nonc Yogi's face. But I think my daddy would have a heart attack. No son of his would ever be a fag, especially not his only son, whom he expects to carry on the family name."

We arrived at a cleared circle among the trees. It was surrounded by plants that had bloomed earlier in the season, camellias, and azaleas, mostly. Down by the edge of the bayou, Louisiana irises competed with the water hyacinth. They were still blooming. We sat on an old cypress log to which legs had been added. It had been cut in half, sanded smooth, and topped with many clear coats of varnish, making it into a wide, comfortable bench.

Our shirts were drenched in sweat. I removed my outer shirt but left my undershirt on. Andy did likewise. I peeled the moist fabric away from my skin and flapped it up and down a few times. The moving air had a refrigerating effect and felt good against my skin.

"I should'a brought some bug repellent," he said, swatting and killing a mosquito that had decided to feast on my left bicep. His hand lingered.

"Make a muscle," he said. I did. His hand lingered and caressed my bowling ball-sized bicep. "You work out," he said. It was a statement, not a question. "I like that," he smiled.

"So do you," I caressed his bicep and kissed his full, pouty lips. "I'd feel a whole lot better about this if you had some real-world experience in falling in love," I said. "You need to know what's out there before deciding to settle down with one person. The world still hasn't slapped you around enough. You've been a little hot house flower up until now."

"I could'a had all the experience you think I need," he replied. "I was in the Marines for four years. I could've had anything I wanted in Saigon on R&R. It was all there. I *chose* not to. New Orleans is only forty-five minutes from here. I c'n drive there anytime I want. I chose not to go there an' look for sex with some meaningless stranger cuz I knew I'd meet you again. I wanted to be... *pristine* for you. I love you, I want you, an' I want to be with *you an' only you.*"

"I reached over and kissed his pouty lips again. "I love you and I want to be with you, too, but I'm not...pristine. I feel like you've been cheated in this deal."

Andy smiled. "We both can't be virgins," he said. "You did what you felt you had to do an' I did what I felt I had to do. The important thing now is that we both commit ourselves one to the other."

"So when do we tell your family about this momentous decision?"

His violet eyes darkened several shades to a royal purple as he remained speechless. Finally, he said, "I want them to get to know you first. Then we'll tell 'em, OK?"

I nodded. "Whenever you're ready."

We walked about a quarter of a mile saying little. My arm was draped over Andy's shoulder. His arm was around my waist. As we walked, he pointed out significant sites from his childhood. We enjoyed quiet moments and Andy's memories.

When we entered another clearing nearer the road, Andy dropped his arm and moved a step or two away from me. Across the roadway that ran perpendicular to the secluded path, Andy pointed out Paul's double-wide mobile home tucked away among tall pine trees but connected to Nonc Yogi's house by a brick pathway.

We crossed the road and turned onto an intersecting pathway that ran discreetly from Paul's mobile home deeper into the woods. The shield of trees and shrubs grew thicker with every step.

"Paul and Kev should be nearby," he said. "The pond's about a hundred yards back.

He smiled. "Everything on this side of the road from the end of Nonc Yogi's fence this way is mine."

"Land baron," I teased.

"What's mine is yours," he said, standing in front of me and placing both hands around my torso. "I bought land every time som'pn came available," he continued.

"A little farther on is where Miz Zah's house used to be. She's the colored lady I tol' you about. When they left, the house stayed vacant for years," he explained.

"I wanted that property and worked hard to get it. I even went to work offshore to get the down payment. They were rentin' from my great uncle, Nonc Ro-bair. "Finally, I bought it. I was jus' out of high school.

Nonc Ro-bair decided to sell everything he had when I was away in the Marines. When I came home, I bought that too. Nonc Ro-*bair* was my grandpa's brother. He never married. Never had a woman that I ever heard of. You think he might'a been gay?"

"They say it runs in families," I said.

"I bought everything he had to offer. He kept the last fourteen acres for himself. That's where we're goin' now. These acres run along the bank of Bayou Mal Enfant.

"I was really happy 'bout buyin' the land 'cuz it kept the land in the fam'ly and the money I paid helped him pay his own way in a really nice retirement home without havin' to depend on relatives to take care of him. He didn't die rich but he did die independent," Andy said.

"When he died, he left me the last few acres of his farm out here an' his little house in Skylarville.

"You mean the house you live in?"

Andy smiled and nodded. I could see the pride in his eyes.

The terrain changed visibly on Andy's side of the road. Where the deep, lush green of mid-summer vegetation had abounded on the other side of the road, on this side, the prevalent color was gray. There must have been about a hundred different shades of it, from silver-white to the clearest dove gray to the darkest gray, almost black.

It was like *The Wizard of Oz* in reverse, but where Dorothy and Toto went from black and white to full color, we went from full color to black and white, with so many tones of gray it was surreal.

The ground on the other side of the road had been hard-packed and dry. On this side, it was moist and springy. It squeaked underfoot as we entered a cypress wonderland.

The Spanish moss that draped every tree branch as if hung there by a deranged exterior decorator, ranged from silver gray to dirty white, to black, like a Spaniard's beard.

The cypress trees, togged down with it, were silver-gray in the sunshine. Even the pond water caught and reflected the tones of gray surrounding it. Only the many species of palms refused to give up their lush green color.

Several herons, stately and white, feeding in the shallow waters of Andy's pond, or posing regally for "Mr. DeMille" to take their close-ups, added to the monochromatic palette. An anole, resting halfway up the trunk of a nearby sweet gum, had changed from its usual lime green to pewter in order to blend in.

Dozens of cypress knees and their parent trees bordered the path, which had been all but obliterated by the mushiness of the boggy area we had entered. They extended a considerable distance out into the pond before finally, reluctantly, giving way to open water. AC/DC blared on a boom box in the distance. "T-Boy's nearby," he said.

"Who's T-Boy?" I wanted to know.

"Sorry. Kevin. That's his nickname. You'll hear somebody call him that before this day's over. Prob'ly his mama or one of my uncles or aunts. I usually call him Kev now but every now and then, I slip and call him T-Boy."

We rounded a bend and found Kevin sitting shirtless on a wide baby-blue blanket atop a Bermuda grass carpet, surveying the surreal scene of cypress knees and trees. Dappled sunlight mottled his skin. Behind him, away from the water, as if not wanting to get her toes wet, a giant pecan tree shaded a large part of the area. Her still-growing daughters provided shade to the rest of the area, which probably consisted of an acre or two. Nothing grew beneath their wide-spread boughs.

A few feet away from him, under Mama Tree, a huge chrome-fronted boom box with more dials and lights than I had ever seen in my life, sat atop a long wooden picnic table with matching wooden benches on both sides.

Kevin was smoking a joint that seemed as big around as my wrist. Short, golden hairs glistened on his arms and chest in the gentle sunlight that filtered through the trees. Paul was nowhere around.

Johnson grass, muscadine and scrub palm provided a dense green backdrop. He looked up as he heard our approach. "Welcome to Belle Glade, Asshole of the U.S.A.," he said to me as he proffered the joint.

I accepted, inhaling deeply. I passed it on to Andy, who did likewise.

Kevin reached into an ice chest next to his right elbow and pulled out three frosty Dixies. He gave one to each of us and kept the third for himself.

"I was hoping for ice water," I said, "but this'll do. This place is beautiful but it's like a sauna." I swigged lustily from the can.

Andy walked to the radio and turned it off then turned to me. "Did I lie when I said I'd show you Paradise?" The pride on his face was palpable.

"No, you didn't," I smiled back.

We sat on the blanket, clinked our cans together, and chugged our beers, passing the gigantic joint back and forth among us.

"Come see. I wanna show you som'pn," Andy said after resting and relaxing about twenty minutes, beckoning to me and rising from the blanket as gracefully as if he had been helped up by the hand of God. I rose somewhat less gracefully and followed him about fifty paces to Kevin's rear, to a narrow opening in a dense stand of red-stemmed muscadine vines, their clusters of burgundy grapes almost the exact shade as my dad's Range Rover.

We crossed a wide, thick plank bridge over a narrow ditch about three feet deep. Johnson grass and cattails lined both sides and covered the bottom. There was no water running through it at the moment. "Watch out for water moccasins," Andy warned.

We walked into a sugar cane field, slapping the broad, rough-textured leaves out of our way as we went. If I had been in this desolate place with anyone except André François Bourgeois, my dad's admonition would have been foremost in my mind. Paranoia would have kicked in and I would have been in "fight or flight" mode, but being with Andy, I knew that nothing would happen to me unless it happened over his dead body.

About three hundred yards in, enclosed on all sides by a three foot high chicken wire fence "to keep the rabbits out," was a stand of some of the healthiest-looking marijuana plants I had ever seen. They were just beginning to bud out. The stand covered at least a quarter of an acre. Entry and egress were accomplished by peeling back a portion of the fence, which was attached to a stocky wooden post by a wire coat hanger.

"God's little acre," Andy winked. "They're all females. We're ready to harvest now," he continued. "We don't want 'em to go to seed."

"What took y'all so long?" Paul said. "I thought y'all had decided not to come." He came from the opposite direction, down a cane row, carrying two metal buckets of water, which he poured on the base of the plants nearest him. Shirtless, his long, lean, muscular torso glistened with perspiration.

"We came up the trail," Andy said. "I had to show him the sights."

"If you had taken the dollar tour, you could'a seen the Empire State Building and the Eiffel Tower," Paul said to me, handing me an industrial-sized freezer bag full of marijuana. It was about the size of a throw pillow and just as thick, crammed to bursting with leaves and buds. "Take this back to Chicago," he said.

"I picked it jus' before y'all got here. You'll have to dry it out before you c'n smoke it but be sure to tell your Chicago friends that this is the local product. It's better than anything they get from Mexico or Colombia. We call it Bitch Weed." He gave me a sly look, seeing the questioning look on my face. "When you smoke it, you'll know why. You c'n leave it at my trailer an' pick it up on your way back to Skylarville if you want." He handed a second bag to Andy.

I shook his hand and sincerely thanked him for the gift. That would last me well into next year. "You're not worried about being raided?" I asked.

Andy shook his head. "My land stops on the other side of that plank bridge we jus' crossed. McGuiness Farms owns this land. Nobody's gon' raid Mr. McGuiness' Farms. Ray McGuiness is the mayor of Thibodaux an' one of the largest landowners around here."

"I'm jus' their poor neighbor," he threw in innocently. "I don't know *nothing* 'bout *nobody* growing *nothing* back here but sugar cane. "We do this every year. We're ready to harvest an' take down the fence, anyway," he said.

"Ray McGuiness has been tryin' to get me to sell him my acreage for years 'cuz he wants access to Bayou Mal Enfant but I'll never sell."

"Don't the people who cut the cane notice that there's this bald spot in the field every year?" I wanted to know.

"Not really," Andy said. "There's bald spots all over this field for one reason or another. It's not like they still do it by hand anymore. There's just one guy inside an air-conditioned cane cutter. They jus' operate the machines. They're high up there in the cab. They prob'ly don't even know that there *is* a bald spot. They just turn the cane cutter around and start down the next few rows."

Kevin appeared through the opening still holding his beer. Paul looked at Andy and me and laughed. "Kev has the most amazing timing. Just as I finish doin' all the work, he shows up. It never fails."

We re-crossed the plank bridge and entered again into Andy's world. We sat on the blanket Kevin had brought, guzzled our beers, and sweated like pigs.

"We grow the best stuff right here in south Louisiana," Paul said, "but it's for private consumption. We're the nation's asshole so we should be rewarded *somehow,* for it."

"Kevin said that once before," I said. "What'd you mean by that?"

"This is the Mississippi Delta. Mississippi River is the country's digestive tract," he answered. "It runs right down the center of the country an' catches all the water from east of the Rocky Mountains to just west of the Appalachians. If you flush your toilet in Chicago, sooner or later, it'll pass by here on its way to the Gulf."

Andy and Paul smiled and nodded in marijuana-induced agreement.

"Hell, I don't mind the fact that every time people up north flush their toilets or whatever, it ultimately ends up here," he continued. "If it wasn't for that northern shit, we wouldn't even be here. All of south Louisiana was built from shit washing down from up there over millions of years. That's why this place is so fertile.

"The dope we grow is comparable to anything grown anywhere and superior to mos'," he boasted. "So, who knows? You might be smokin' some of your own ca-*ca*." he smiled.

I could not provide a counter-argument for the theory, nor did I try. I allowed the effects of the homegrown to overpower me as I relished the serene sights and sounds of this verdant oasis.

The hoard of mosquitoes and other blood-suckers that had dogged us savagely from the time we entered the trail near Andy's parents' house had stayed behind, around the last bend in the trail.

I understood why when I saw the three apartment houses for purple martens, three floors of four apartments each, set on high poles around the clearing, and the birds themselves swooping and doing kamikaze-type dives, feeding on any flying insect that dared to come near.

I looked out onto the pond as Andy told of pre-adolescent days when he, Kevin, and Paul had camped out on its bank on summer nights next to huge bonfires to keep the gators at bay, telling stories of the Blue Lady, the Jelly Man, and the Rougarou, and scaring themselves silly; how they had skinny dipped, drank their first beers, and smoked their first joints here. For Kevin and Paul, their first tobacco cigarettes were smoked here, too. Also for Kevin and Paul, their first sexual encounters were consummated on blankets in the boathouse after senior prom.

As I listened, picturing an adolescent Andy, Kevin, and Paul skinny-dipping in the pond, I watched the purple martens as they scrambled for insects in some of the most spectacular dives I've ever witnessed. I became fascinated with the antics of two young mockingbirds that darted back and forth over the shining ripples, raising a hell of a ruckus, their gray, black, and white feathers blending perfectly with the area's color palette.

A few yards away, a yellow and black banana spider about as wide across as my hand, wove the first strands of its new web between two branches of a sweet gum that stood to one side of the pond.

A willow trailed its leafy fingers languidly into the quiet waters of the pond a few yards away from an old boathouse.

***

More cars had arrived at Andy's parents' house and were now parked on the beautiful St. Augustine lawn. The family members had gathered under a long, cement-floored pavilion with the same Mediterranean-blue asphalt-shingled roof as the house. It was as wide as the two-car carport but about twice as long, allowing ample space for dining and dancing. Multi-colored Christmas lights were strung from the rafters of the structure's open ceiling.

A combination laundry room on one side and powder room on the other separated the carport from the pavilion. Open on all sides except that nearest the carport, it jutted out from the rear of the carport like a spear in the side of a wounded gazelle.

The four corners and mid-section were supported by white painted wooden beams about as thick around as my wrist. Down the middle, two long wooden picnic tables, placed end to end, sat covered in newspapers being held down by strategically placed bricks, plates, glassware, rocks, and anything else that would prevent the newspapers from flying away before the eating had begun. Long wooden benches similar to those beside the picnic table near Andy's pond, stood along both sides awaiting familiar butts.

At the far end, Nonc Yogi tended a tall, red, bullet-shaped contraption that resembled a World War II bomb casing with a hot-foot. Great billows of steam erupted from the upper end as Yogi opened and closed the lid, testing the water. He had just thrown a packet of Zatarain's Crawfish Boil, about a dozen whole potatoes, and sections of corn on the cob into the water as we piled around the corner.

Yogi rose from his green-and-white nylon webbed lawn chair with a smile when he saw the four of us arrive through the spaniel gate. He offered us a Dixie and pulled four lawn chairs around the tall, red, covered cauldron he was tending. Paul walked over and kissed his father's cheek.

"I been waitin' for you, Ween," Nonc Yogi called. "Come over here by me." I did as I was told. "Did you know that crawfish scream when they hit the boiling water?" he said when I stepped beside him.

"No," I answered, in all honesty. Ganja was *really* good!

"Watch," Nonc Yogi replied with glee as he pulled a green fifty pound mesh sack near the fire and uncovered the cauldron. "Put your ear close to the water," he commanded.

I put my ear near the water and felt a shiver run down my spine as I heard, or imagined I heard, the screams of hundreds of tiny voices as the crawfish in the sack slid into the boiling brew. Then, after a few seconds, only the bubbles could be heard as the tiny screams fell silent.

Nonc Yogi smiled a Jack-o'-lantern smile. I grimaced.

"How could you eat something that screams like that before it dies?" I asked.

"Dey scream *befo'* dey die, not *after*," Nonc Yogi said pragmatically.

I returned to my seat and sipped my beer. Andy stifled a giggle from behind the beer he was drinking. Paul and Kevin looked on quietly, smiling, but saying nothing. The ganja we had smoked *was* good!

Jolie-Marie, her daughters, and John Bourgeois, Yogi's triplet brother, turned the corner of the house, followed by Paul's younger siblings and two middle-aged women, both of whom sported unfashionably close-cropped hair. They all carried newspaper bundles for the table. Eating crawfish is a messy business.

Andy introduced me to John, his father; his Aunt Claire, and Theresa Lipinski, called Terri, her "friend." While they were occupied with spreading the extra newspaper and setting up, Andy explained that Claire and Terri had met as nuns in the convent of the Sisters of St. Kilda in St. Cloud, Minnesota over forty years prior, and that they had left the convent to be together more than twenty-five years ago.

As women, their relationship was accepted, and Theresa was treated as a member of the family. Two men, he said, could never live as openly and never be accepted as the two women were. "Just when we need it the most, they hit us with the reverse double standard," Andy said jovially.

"Know what they say 'bout two women?" he continued.

I shook my head.

"They believe that two women don't have the necessary 'equipment' to fulfill each other's needs so they couldn't possibly sin against God. They also don't have any 'seed' to spill as men do, so biblically, they're okay.

"They always focus on the sexual aspects of being gay."

I saw the two women eyeing Andy and me as we talked. "They've got our number," I whispered to Andy. Terri slowly made her way around the gathering to where Andy, Kevin, Paul, and I sat. Claire, sparrow-like, followed closely behind.

"We saw you two from the kitchen window," she smiled, showing a significant gap between her two upper incisors. Like her surname, her accent was Polish.

She was a raw-boned farm girl, tall, sturdy-looking, and rather mannish in appearance. She wore no makeup on her porcelain skin. Her sandy blonde hair looked as if it had been hacked off by a weed-wacker.

She was as ordinary as a mud fence except for her smile, which seemed warm and genuine. Her eyes, the color of root beer, were kind and sincere.

Blue rayon pants covered her ample behind and a sky-blue blouse covered her ample bosom. I felt sure that somewhere in their tiny house, the matching rayon jacket hung in a closet, waiting for cooler weather. She wore white Keds over white knee-high stockings on her very large feet. She appeared to be in her mid-to late-fifties and at around six feet, she was the second-tallest person present.

Claire, following Terri around like a puppy, smiled as if listening to a private joke. She also sported unfashionably short hair. She wore a long sleeved white blouse, navy blue skirt that came to the middle of her calves, and small gold cross under her Peter Pan collar.

"Know what Claire said when she saw the two of you?" Terri inquired, smiling.

I shook my head. Andy said nothing but he suddenly become quite pale.

Terri continued. "She said, 'they look like G.I. Joe and a colored Ken.' Everybody in the kitchen agreed. It's really amazing. You two should be on a store shelf somewhere." Claire smiled, blushed furiously, but said nothing.

It didn't help that Andy was wearing camouflage pants and a snow white crew-neck Marine-style tee shirt.

"I guess that's a compliment," I said, "so thank you." They refused our lawn chairs when I offered them but Terri went back to their original places, hefted up the two heavy deck chairs on which they had been seated, and brought them over to where we sat. The woman was *very* strong.

Kevin brought beers for everyone seated within this group within a group. It was obvious to me that a clique had been formed based on presumed sexual orientation. I don't know if Paul and Kevin caught it, though.

After eating crawfish pie, crawfish etouffé, crawfish bisque, seafood gumbo, stuffed redfish, jambalaya, and more boiled crawfish than I ever knew existed, I almost felt like a member of the family. Yogi appointed himself my personal tutor on how to "suck the heads," peel the tails, and *bacler les plats* (clean your plate; eat everything). He was a very good teacher.

"You were born in Chicago, Wayne?" Claire finally said, her voice hardly above a whisper.

"No. I was born in Houma," I said.

"You were born in Houma and never et crawfish?" John Bourgeois chimed in, incredulous. He looked a lot like Yogi, his fraternal twin, but he was taller, trimmer, and the handsomer of the two. Yogi, however, was the more sociable twin.

"I've had them a few times," I replied, "but that was a long time ago. I never spent much time in Louisiana and my parents aren't originally from here so I never developed a taste for them, but now that I've learned to suck the heads, I'll have to have them more often, even if I have to have them flown up to

Chicago. That's definitely an art as well as an acquired taste. I don't want to lose it."

"Know who his ol' man and ol' lady are?" Paul asked. "Ask him his last name."

John Bourgeois hesitated.

"Ask him, Nonc Jean," Paul insisted.

"This boy's gon' pester me to death til I find out your las' neem. You're not Fats Domino's boy, are you?"

I smiled and shook my head.

"I saw the Range Rover. That's one hell of a car. Expensive! *Real* expensive! Costs way mo' than my house, my car, an' my van *combined*. Not many *white* people could afford that sucka. Who's yo' fam'ly?"

Every face in the gathering turned to me.

"Mallory," I finally said, leaving it at that.

"*Mallory?*" Jolie-Marie said before pronouncing her final determination. "That's not a Louisiana neem."

"As in *Mallory Medical Center in Kingstown*," Paul said, suddenly a little chatter-box.

The light bulb in Jolie-Marie's head finally went off. "The colored doctors?" she asked, her violet eyes twinkling. "I know your mama!"

Paul smiled and nodded vigorously. "We've heard the story a few thousand times," he said.

"Your daddy fixed up Yogi's back," John Bourgeois said. "Did a *real* good job, too. I remember when Yogi cuddn' even sit up. Now look at him!"

Yogi's wife, Clotilde, nodded and smiled through ragged teeth.

John said to me, "When T-Beau an' his sisters were kids, my wife used'ta make me drive past y'all's house every time we went to Houma. An' that was *befo'* the lane was widened an' paved. At that time, there wasn't nothin' out there but y'all's house an' lot of sugar cane. Then they built your pa-paw's house. Boy has it ever changed now! You can't even get near the place since they dug the lake an' re-channeled Bayou St. Eloi, makin' it an island."

Jolie-Marie spoke next, kind of dreamily, as she thought back decades. "I remember when ya mama and daddy first came to Louisiana," she said. "Me and John were fixin' to get married. I was workin' at Grossman's Department Store in Skylarville. They went out of business a long time ago.

"Anyway, I was workin' there and it was the custom not to allow colored people to try on clothes in the store. They had to buy what they wanted, take it home, an' try it on there. I'm 'shamed to say that now, but at the time, it was the custom.

"One day your mama came into the store with a big black poodle-dog wearing a rhinestone collar. She came through the door, looked around, an' jus' stood there, lookin' around as if to say, *"What a dump!"*

"She was wearing a high-collared pale green silk blouse, a two-piece Kelly green cashmere suit with the big shoulder pads like Joan Crawford used to wear. It had pearl buttons down the front and silk *ker-cheef* the same color as her blouse over one breast pocket clipped on with a big diamond brooch, green suede heels, an' black silk stockings. Her seams were perfect.

"She was like som'pn out of a movie magazine! She was gorgeous! We'd never seen anybody dress or move like that, 'specially not a colored lady. It was winter so she was wearing a full-length black mink coat, fur-lined leather gloves, and a little green pillbox hat with the black fishnet veil studded with little-bitty rhinestones. That was high style back then.

"The whole store stopped, I tell-ya!! *Nobody* moved." She turned toward her husband. "You 'member how there was the balcony that ran around the first floor, where Mr. Saul an' them could look down an' see what we were doin'?"

He nodded. "The mezzanine."

She nodded; seemingly surprised that he remembered the word. "Well, the whole ground floor got completely silent. The mezzanine was where Mr. Saul's office was. The family members all had their desks along the front wall of the mezzanine so they had a good view of the front door and they could see what we were doin'.

"Everybody who worked up there lined the rail lookin' at her. You could hear a pin drop," she said, continuing her story, enjoying the rapt attention she had garnered.

"Yo' mama jus' stood there lookin' around like she was deciding whether she wanted to come in or move on to a better quality store. An' at that time, there *was* no better store. Not in Skylarville, Houma, or Thibodaux, anyway. Grossman's was for the elites. Most colored people, even the teachers, didn't come in too often 'cuz they couldn't afford the prices.

"If I didn't work there and got an employee's discount, I never would'a been able to afford it. Mr. Saul was cheap. He only gave his employees a three-percent discount. "Every other store in town gave five," she said, diverging from her original story, "but it was quality stuff."

"Well, finally, your mama decided to come all the way in. Stores back then weren't like stores today," she said. "At that time, everything was behind the counters in glass cases. If you wanted somp'n, you had to ask for it an' the salesgirl would take it outta the case an' show it to you.

"I worked in sundries, close to the front door, so I ran up to her and asked if I could help her. She said wanted to see our best women's wear.

"All of the people in the store were gawkin' at her. Her an' that big black poodle-dog. I still remember his name, *'Sir.'* He was a champion!"

"Sir," as she called him, died before I was born but I've seen hundreds of photos of him. His legend lives on even to today. His registered name was *Champion Creswic Big Sur.* His call name was "Sir." He is the progenitor of all of our Creswic dogs today.

Jolie-Marie Bourgeois continued her story. "The *better* ladies' wear was on the third floor so I led her towards the elevator. Mr. Saul was comin' down the stairs as I led her to the elevator. He asked if *he* could personally help her. She smiled an' asked if everyone got this kind of service. Mr. Saul said no, but it wasn't everyday they got such a distinguished lady in there.

"She said, 'no thank you, sir, this young lady'—me—'is helping me.'"

"Saul Grossman wasn't about to insult her by tellin' her she couldn't bring the dog into the store or that she couldn't try on what she was buyin' in the store. I know Mr. Saul didn't have a prejudiced bone in his body but it was the custom an' maybe even state law, that said that bat'rooms, dressin' rooms, water fountains, and such, had to be segregated.

"That dog sat beside her when we got in the elevator like he'd been ridin' up an' down on one all of his life. When we got to the third floor, she made a hand sign for him to lay down, and then another one for him to stay *an' that dog didn't move from that spot*!

"He was layin' like the Sphinx, you know, kind'a sittin' up, on knees an' elbows with his front paws crossed like the gentleman he was, lookin' around an' payin' attention to wherever she went, but other than that, he could'a been a statue. Some of the salesgirls were tryin' to pet him or to get him to disobey her command but he wouldn't move. The most he did was to wag his tail when they'd pet him. An' you should'a smelled him!" she said. "Jean," she laughed, "that dog smelled better than *you*! He had some kind'a expensive doggie perfume on him. Smelled almos' like Chanel!

"She bought over two hundred dollars worth of merchandise that day and tried on whatever she liked before she left the store. Mr. Saul told us she could try on whatever she wanted. That kind'a ended the practice of colored people not bein' able to try on clothes in the stores aroun' here, anyway," she smiled. "If Grossman's was doin' it, it hadta be all right.

"When she was through, she made a hand sign and the dog jumped up from where he was layin', went and sat in front of where she was standin', and then moved to her left side. Jus' like a soldier. He had been layin' there for 'bout forty-five minutes.

"She snapped the leash on him, an' Mr. Saul had the boys put all of her purchases in the trunk of her big, black Packard sedan and she an' the dog drove away. Mr. Saul was smiling. I was smiling, an' most importantly, she was smiling.

"After that, whenever she came in, she always asked for me by name. When we got married," she said to her husband, "she sent us that beautiful silver service on the buffet in the dining room."

"How's she doin'?" she asked me. When I responded that my mum was well, she said, "Ask her if she remembers Jolie-Marie Bonvillain from Grossman's Department Store in Skylarville. That would'a been 'round 1945. She was a customer til after Mr. Saul died and his kids took over. Mr. Jake, Mr. Sal, an' Miz Iris ran that store into the ground!"

We stayed another two or three hours, eating and drinking, mostly. I couldn't eat another crawfish if my life depended on it. Summer days are long in Louisiana. Sundown wouldn't be until around nine o'clock. It was around seven when I began to make gestures toward leaving.

I thanked the Bourgeois for their hospitality and began saying good-bye. Andy, Paul, and Kevin also took leave. "You always welcome here, Ween. Come back anytime," Jolie-Marie said as we were about to pull away.

We piled into the two cars, stopping only briefly by Paul's mobile home to pick up our gifts.

***

"Master Wayne," said Butters, in his stiff British accent, "your friend, Mr. Bourgeois, is on the line. I'll transfer it immediately." I was fully awake now. A click or two later, Andy was connected. A soft click ensured privacy. It was seven-thirty in the morning.

"Hello, Handsome," I said, trying to get the sleep out of my voice.

"Wayne?" Andy said. There was a rushed tone to his hushed voice. "I can't talk long. I've gotta get to work. The sheriff's office has a suspect in Eck's murder. They arrested him this morning. I've gotta go," he said, almost in one breath.

"Andy, Wait," I almost demanded. "Where are you calling from?" I wanted to know.

"Home. I'm on my way to the office now. I punch in at eight. Clem, the guy who was in the office when you came in, called me and told me 'bout it. Why?"

"I thought you were calling from the office. I was going to tell you that maybe that was a bad idea."

"Get your ass over here if you want the story! I've gotta go! I love you!" He clicked off before I could say 'I love you, too.'

***

The sub-Arctic air of the Skylarville Police Department slapped me awake as I crossed the room and approached the desk. Andy was talking to an elderly, blue-haired woman whose tired face was seamed and crisscrossed with so many tiny wrinkles, it looked as if tiny seamstresses had worked on it all night.

She was complaining about the theft of a case of ramen noodles by a person or persons unknown as she inhaled the smoke from her cigarette and exhaled it, dragon-like, into Andy's face. Andy winced as he tried to avoid the noxious vapors. He looked up and smiled a dazzling smile when he saw me.

When he was finished, he called me up, his eyes still watering from the dragon lady's fumes.

"The chief's over at the Sheriff's Office," Andy said. "You can go with me. Have a seat. I'll be ready in a few minutes."

The folding chairs that lined the puke-green walls of the S.P.D. were occupied by several people who sat scattered as far from one another as they could possibly get. A dirty young man sat on the far end of the first row, nearest the interior wall. A very clean-cut, preppy type sat next to him reading *Mohammad Speaks* newspaper.

A skinny blonde woman in a pink halter top, yellow shorts that even Daisy Duke would not wear in public, and blue flip-flops, sat on the other end of the same row. She appeared to be in her late thirties or early forties. She puffed incessantly on a long brown cigarette and coughed up something which she spat into a dirty man's handkerchief when she thought no one was looking. I chose a seat on the opposite end of the second row, as from her as I could get.

An elderly woman with a small child sat in the last row. The child, about four or five years old, whined that she wanted to go home. The woman talked soothingly to her, calling her "Baby," and telling her that they would leave soon.

Andy finished with some papers on his desk, picked up an official-looking legal-size pad, and beckoned to me to follow him through a series of intersecting hallways and to a black door marked **"Police Personnel Only"** in fading stenciled letters that at one time may have been white but were now a light gray and rapidly approaching eradication.

We got into a baby-blue and white Ford Crown Vic with the S.P.D.'s logo, *"We Protect and Serve,"* and the town's coat of arms painted on the doors. It sat like an oversized, blue and white hound, with its motor running and air conditioning blasting, waiting for its master.

Andy explained that although the walk would only take about ten minutes, this conveyance saved him valuable time. As Information Officer for the S.P.D., time was of the essence.

When we passed the main branch of the Belle Fleur Community Bank, he pointed to the digital clock/thermometer, which read:

"IT'S TIME TO SAVE.
TIME: 8:30.
TEMPERATURE: 103 F."

in lighted letters that scrolled across the sign's face.

"It saves us from sweatin', too," he joked.

The Bellefleur Parish Sheriff's Office was housed on the first floor of a three-story white Art Deco building that, according to the bronze plaque near the front door, had been built during the administration of Governor Huey P. Long.

We passed through a set of metal-and-glass double doors and entered a narrow vestibule that served as a buffer between the torrid mid-summer Louisiana heat outside and the glacial interior.

Three steps later, we passed through a second set of double doors and into a wide corridor with large white terrazzo squares for flooring.

Two tall black public telephones hung appended to the walls on both sides of the hallway under twin curved staircases with brushed metal handrails. They cascaded down to the first floor in graceful waves, each pushing the other farther and downward.

An anemic Bellefleur Parish phone telephone book hung limply beside each phone from metal chains.

The sky blue walls behind each telephone sported numerous telephone numbers penciled, penned, or gouged into it.

The B.S.O. was at the end of the hallway, behind a wall of glass. We entered through wide glass doors that hissed closed behind us, sealing an air-lock with a quiet *"ssshusssh."*

"Mornin,' Andy," said an Eve Arden look-alike with auburn hair, arched eyebrows penciled in, heavy blue eye shadow, lightly rouged cheeks, and candy-apple red lips.

She wore a navy blue blouse with a wide, crisp, white sailor's collar with navy blue piping about a quarter inch in from the edges, and white buttons about the size of fifty-cent pieces down the front.

She sat on a high wooden stool working on a stack of papers at the front counter so I could not see the lower half of her ersatz sailor's outfit.

"Hi, Charlie," Andy smiled and introduced me. "This is my friend Wayne. He's a reporter from Chicago. The sheriff ready?"

"He's in the press room." She smiled and extended her hand to me. "My, you're a big one! I'd hate to have to pay your clothing bills. What brings you to our little Podunk town?" she asked. "Surely not Deputy Eck's death," she said, before I could answer.

"Not really," I said. "I was on vacation when I heard about it. I decided to check it out."

"We'd better go," Andy interrupted before she could say more.

"See ya!" Charlene smiled.

I followed Andy through oak double doors with the sign, *"Press Room"* above it on the oak lintel.

"I guess we can start, now that Deputy Bourgeois is here," said a sandy-haired, barrel-chested man who appeared to me to be in his mid-40's. "And who'd you bring with you, Deputy?" He sat at the head of the room in the center chair of five that lined a long, wide oak table painted coffee brown.

Forming a 'T' with the sheriff's table were two long, wide oak tables. Twelve chairs lined the sides of the two tables and there was one at the bottom of the "T" that sat directly in front of the Sheriff.

The front chairs were occupied by a number of others, all except two of whom were men. All carried small tape recorders and had aimed mini-microphones toward the sheriff and the chief of police, who sat immediately to the sheriff's right. I took out my tape recorder and aimed it at the duo at the head of the room, too.

Andy and I took seats toward the far end of the room, at the second of the two tables that formed the stem of the "T".

"This is…" Andy started to say before I interrupted him.

"I'm Steven Wayne Mallory of *The Chicago News Register.*"

"*Why* are you bothering yourself with such a piddly story?" the sheriff almost whined.

"Nothing better to do," I replied. Andy and several of the others in the room chuckled a time or two and then fell silent.

"Lord," the sheriff continued. "Y'all must really be hard up for news! You'd think in a big city like Chicago, they'd send you to cover a murder or two in Chicago before sendin' you down here."

"I was here on vacation when I heard about the murder and I requested permission to cover the story," I explained. "Surely you remember that Deputy Eck made national news only a few weeks ago when he…."

"Don't even remind me," the sheriff said, holding his head in his hands. "Well, let's see your press card." I stood and moved to the front of the room.

"Did you say your name is Goliath?" the sheriff commented. I ignored his attempt at humor, sliding my press card and drivers license out of my wallet and handing it first to the chief of police, who looked it over and handed them to the sheriff. This was his bailiwick but I felt it would have been rude to pass over the police chief, who was nearer to me, in favor of the sheriff.

The sheriff handed my credentials back to me and sighed. "Take a seat and we'll get started, I guess." He opened a manila folder in front of him and began to read.

"At Oh-five thirty hours this morning, a suspect was arrested in the murder of sheriff's deputy Cletus "RC" Eck. Currently, the suspect is being held in the Bellefleur Parish Jail.

"At this time, no further information is being released to the public pending further investigation."

"Why was he arrested, Sheriff? What made you arrest him?" asked a chubby, bespectacled young man who looked as if he were just out of high school, when the sheriff closed the manila folder, indicating an end to the "press conference."

"The suspect was arrested on other charges and during that arrest, the same caliber gun that was used to kill Deputy Eck was found on his person."

"But what was he doing to get him arrested in the first place, Sheriff?" the young man insisted.

"Suspicious activities," the sheriff said. "During the arrest, officers found that he was carrying a pistol that's the same caliber as the one used to shoot and kill Deputy Eck. We're waiting for ballistics. At this time, John, that's all we're prepared to say," the sheriff said, rising. With him, the chief of police, who had said nothing the entire time, rose with the sheriff. Before they left the room, I asked, "Sheriff, what exactly does that mean? 'Suspicious activities?'"

"Just what it sounds like," the sheriff said, peeved.

"Maybe I should rephrase my question, then," I said. "What suspicious activity was he perpetrating when he was arrested?" The sheriff looked at me blankly but said nothing. I continued, "In other words, what was he doing at the time of his arrest?"

The sheriff opened and closed his mouth a few times like a fish out of water, but he said nothing. He turned to the chief of police, banged the manila folder on the table in front of him, and both turned and walked out of the room without replying

"That was a big zero," someone in the room said. It was the woman's voice. There were two women present. I didn't know which of them had spoken.

***

I left *Creswic House* through the kitchen, taking Gracie with me. We passed through the swimming pool area to a small open carport where the golf carts were kept. I put the large dog on the front seat of the cart next to me and we took off toward *Bisley,* my grandmother's mansion in the Bilbury Ridge section of Creswic Estates.

Bilbury Ridge is a small, picturesque subdivision that has been designed to look like a village in the Cotswold region of England. The streets are hilly and cobbled, the signs are unobtrusive, and the bridges over the wide, winding canal are low and graceful.

All of the homes are in proportion with one another. Many are half-timbered in the Tudor tradition. All bricks in the homes are custom-made and all of the honey-colored limestone is quarried in the same quarry in Indiana. Roofs are either made of slate or layer upon layer, upon layer of special roofing material that resembles thatch.

All of the structures in Bilbury Ridge are in keeping with the architectural styles of merry old England before Victoria's interminable reign; Norman, Gothic, Tudor, Stuart, and Georgian. Low stone walls and English ivy abound.

The Bilbury Ridge Preservation Committee is one of the strictest at La Belle Terre Reserve when it comes to authenticity of design and its imprimatur must be given before any new construction can take place within its confines.

Bisley has most of the external elements of Anne Hathaway's large Tudor cottage in Stratford-on Avon, especially when it comes to her lovely gardens, but it is not an exact copy.

When my grandfather was alive, he and my grandmother divided their time between estates in England, Bermuda, and Louisiana. Their home in Louisiana was called *Vernonburg*, my grandma's maiden name. It is next door to *Creswic House* on twenty-five acres, and is the second-oldest structure in The Reserve after *Creswic House*.

My grandfather designed *Bisley* to meet the needs of two elderly empty-nesters when *Vernonburg* became too large for them. *Bisley*, however, was not built until after his death.

Vernonburg is now owned by my oldest brother, Daniel and his wife, Pippa. They have six children and it is lively and vibrant once again.

Gracie and I followed the shores of Lake Laura for over a mile, passing purple marten condominiums and bug zappers every eighteen to twenty feet. We entered the rear of Grandma's estate through an unobtrusive iron gate, and followed a shrub-lined cobblestone walkway until we came to the trellised half-moon gate in a white picket fence that surrounded her rear garden. Jacaranda and bougainvillea peeked over and through the pickets, welcoming us.

I could hear the *"I'm aware of your presence"* barks of Henry, my grandmother's silver standard poodle and best friend, long before we got to the house. Henry was on guard and took his job of protecting my grandma very seriously.

Gracie ran ahead of me. I turned the corner and was met by the strong, feisty voice of Victoria Vernonburg Mallory, who greeted me from somewhere in the back of the garden, near the high stone wall that surrounded it.

"It's about time you got around to visiting your poor old grandma," she smiled. Her proper British accent was as strong as ever.

She stood up in the far corner of the garden, digging implements in both hands, and said, "Don't step on my flowers. Stay on the path. I'll come to you." The path was a wide walkway made of bluestone and edged with rose-colored bricks set on end and at a forty-five degree angle like a series of dominos caught in the process of toppling over.

I had heard this same admonition every single time I had ever visited her. When I was a boy and she lived at *Vernonburg,* it was daily. Sometimes, several times a day.

She gingerly tiptoed through the rows of zinnias, roses, primroses, and almost every other flowering plant that could be crammed behind the picket fence.

Although they were widely varied, everything came together and was in perfect harmony, like the varied instruments of a great symphony orchestra come together when making beautiful music. Although she has a doctorate degree in chemistry, her passion is horticulture. Her flowers, shrubs, trees, and garden design have won her many gardening awards.

She arrived on the path a few seconds later and threw her arms around my mid-section, pulling me down toward her and giving me a hug and a big kiss on both cheeks.

"You never did like kissing your old grandma, did you?" she asked, not really expecting an answer.

"Let me look at you," she said, holding me at arm's length and smiling. "You look more and more like your grandfather every day. Come in! We'll have tea and scones."

I hugged her again and kissed her on the forehead, for she was a tiny woman, measuring barely five feet tall. "It's good to see you, Grandma. You're looking great. Feisty as ever, I see."

"Aren't you going to say hello to Henry?" she wanted to know.

I reached down and petted the big dog on the head. He, however, was more interested in sniffing Gracie's butt than in saying hello to me. "How old is this dog, Grandma? About fifteen?"

"He turned eight last month," she said, "and he's as sprightly now as he was when I got him." He had been a birthday present from me after her previous dog, Oliver, died.

Grandma initially suffered a deep depression over the loss of my grandfather, her life-long companion. She began spending more time in Bermuda and

England, both of which had stringent quarantine laws for dogs being imported into the country. I wanted her in Louisiana with me. In order to get her back, I decided to give her a puppy, which cannot travel to either place without spending long months in quarantine.

She had not wanted a dog in her life but she was too gracious not to accept him. After an initial rocky start, they had settled into a relationship unlike any I had ever seen. I did not know how much longer Henry could last but that decision was not mine to make. Currently, he was healthy and active, just as she was. I feared that when one went, the other would soon follow but that, also, was not my decision to make. Time would take care of itself.

***

We entered the rambling half-timbered stone and brick mansion through a round-topped oak door beneath a triple-arched stone entry, floored in gray slate. The door led directly into a large mud room. The air-conditioning felt wonderful.

Grandma placed her wide-brimmed straw hat on a peg near the door and her gardening gloves on a shelf in a cubby designed especially for them.

She then sat on a seat with a pull-down bottom similar to those in movie theaters but cushioned in a nubby scarlet fabric, and removed her gardening shoes. She placed them on the stoop outside the door and kicked into a pair of fuzzy yellow house shoes, then continued into the house.

The sights and aromas of her home were as familiar to me as those in my own home or that of my parents. Flower fragrances from the garden, antique upholstered furniture stuffed with horse hair, stained glass lamps, the aroma of beeswax on fine woods, the distinct perfume of leather furniture and leather-bound books, all gave a personalized fragrance to the substantial home that she calls *Bisley*.

Grandma led me to a small walnut-paneled drawing room off the library and rang for her butler, Fisk, who arrived as if from nowhere. "We'll have tea and scones here, Fisk," she said.

"It's good to have you back, Master Steven," Fisk smiled. He had been my grandparents' butler since they were first married. I've known Fisk all of my life. I had no idea how old he must be but he does not seem to have aged even one day in all of the years I have known him.

I smiled, nodded my head, and thanked him. He silently left the room and returned after a few minutes with a large silver tray containing a rose-colored Japanese teapot, two matching cups with no handles, and a rose-colored plate covered with a Battenberg lace doily and piled high with scones.

For the dogs, he brought a pile of freshly baked dog biscuits and two ceramic dishes filled to the brim with cool, fresh water. He placed them in one corner of the room, near the doorway and he placed our silver tray on an elegant circular cherry wood tea table with crimped edges that reminded me of the edges of homemade pies.

Grandma had aged gracefully and very well, like fine wine or pewter. Her memory, body movements, and attractiveness had not diminished over the years. Her teeth were like antique ivory. Her hair, gun-metal gray, was neatly and simply coifed, and almost the same exact color as Henry's. She was a no nonsense woman who had little time for fripperies.

She settled herself on a small settee covered in floral chintz, near a large diamond-paned bay window that overlooked her front garden. Thick room-size rugs made by hand in India, Afghanistan, and Iran softened footsteps on the heart pine floor. "I hear that you've been doing some investigating into that deputy's killing."

I wondered how she got her information. I nodded. "That's right, Grandma, but how'd you know?"

"I don't get outside The Reserve very much anymore but word gets back to me," she replied. "Since we came here from Bermuda, I've seen a lot of changes in this area. Some of them have been positive, like the end of segregation, but others have been a rehash of the same old stuff, only now, Jim Crow wears a smiley face. Sometimes, it's harder now to know who the enemy is than it was in the 1940s."

She continued. "Did you know that the young man they arrested for that murder is Rosie Coleman's grandson?" Her proper British accent lilted softly across the small room. "He didn't do it," she said. "I've known him since he was a lad. No relative of Rosie's would kill."

"Who's Rosie Coleman?" I asked, recognizing the name but not quite placing it.

"Rosie cleaned for us for years. She was the only local woman we could find who'd clean for Negroes, and she was the very best. All of the others would come to us when they needed money or when they were between jobs, promising that they would be faithful to us but as soon as a white woman called, they'd leave us high and dry, regardless of how much we paid them or what our needs were."

I had heard the story a million times over my lifetime. That's the principal reason why almost all of our servants are foreign. The vast majority are from the Bermuda, England, or the English-speaking Caribbean. A few are from Latin America, Asia, or even continental Europe but very few were American.

"Rosie came to us while *Vernonburg* was still being built," she continued. "She said she wanted to work for a Negro family because she had never known any Negroes who could afford domestic help. She had gone to your parents but they already had a full staff. They referred her to me. We already had staff that I had planned to bring in from the Islands but we still didn't have a full complement. She was a young mother at the time. Little Rosie was about twelve or thirteen when Rosie came to work for us. She died shortly after Artie was born. She was fifteen. Maybe sixteen.

"She had run away from home with some guy old enough to be her father. He took her to Jacksonville, Florida, where he abandoned her when he found out that she was pregnant and only fifteen.

"Even though Rosie was anxious about what was happening to Little Rosie, she never missed a day and she did not bring her problems to work. Artie was born in Jacksonville and Little Rosie died there. She did ask our help in bringing the baby and the body back to Louisiana and we were more than happy to help.

"Rosie's a proud woman and to ask for help meant that she really, *really* needed it. She had to care for her grandson from the time he was an infant but still, she was there every morning on time, to do a full day's work.

"She took night classes and received her high school equivalency diploma and she took the investment classes that the Reserve offers all of its employees. She worked her way up from third floor maid to house manager.

"Under her and Fisk, *Vernonburg* and *Bisley House* ran like clockwork. And when she retired, thanks to the investment and retirement planning classes, she had 'a good chunk of change,' as they say here in America."

I lowered my voice, "Grandma, shouldn't Fisk be well past retirement age?"

My grandma is not usually given to loud outbursts but this one was explosive. "Wayne," she said between guffaws, "this is Andrew Fisk, Arthur Fisk's son. Arthur is about Rosie Coleman's age. He retired three years ago. Just after your last visit."

I now remembered the legendary Rosie Coleman, who had remained faithful to the family through births, weddings, and my grandfather's death. Through hell and high water, so the saying goes. It was only old age and the onset of rheumatoid arthritis that had separated her from the family.

"When she called me a few days ago asking for advice, I knew she needed help," Grandma said. She calls a lot just to chat but rarely for advice or help so I told her I'd help in any way I could.

"I've already talked to Robby about defending Artie. He's a fine young man. About your age, I believe. Robbie, of course, is not a criminal attorney, but he has promised to find the best criminal attorney in the country.

"Rosie did not ask me for money for Artie's legal fees but I told her that I'd take care of the bill if she chooses the attorney that Robbie finds for her. I know that if she chooses a lawyer from around here, that poor boy will be sending her post cards from Angola."

She referred to the Louisiana State Prison at Angola, Louisiana, not the African country for which it was named.

"Robbie" is my third brother. One of the triplets. They're after Daniel and Jeremy. Lucas and Mariana are the other two. Then there's me, the youngest.

"If he's lucky, Grandma. If he's not so lucky, he could end up sending them from Angola's Death Row."

"You're right about that, Wayne. Louisiana is not known for liberal attitudes on any subject but when it comes to a black man accused of killing a white man, especially if that white man is a law enforcement officer, even a hated one, those conservative attitudes take on the quality of a lynch mob," Grandma said sadly.

"I went to the *'quote-quote'* press conference but the sheriff didn't say anything. The chief of police was also there. The chief didn't open his mouth except once, to yawn. All the sheriff said was that they had a suspect in the killing and that they were waiting for ballistics tests. He said the suspect was picked up for 'suspicious activities' and that he had previously threatened to kill Deputy Eck. In the course of the arrest, it was discovered that he had a pistol that was the same caliber as the one that killed Eck," I said.

"Rosie says he didn't do it and I believe her but we'll talk more about that later," she continued, "but tell me, have you found yourself a nice girl in Chicago?"

I took a deep, exasperated breath. Grandma has known about my sexual orientation for years but she has chosen to ignore it, calling it "a phase."

"No, Grandma, but I have found a nice young man from right here, whom I'm really interested in. You'll meet him tonight at dinner."

"Tonight??" she said, surprise in her voice. "This must be a very special young man for you to bring him to our weekly family gathering so soon after meeting him."

"He is," I said, somewhat starry-eyed. "I met his family yesterday. But I didn't just meet him. I met him thirteen years ago and you'll never guess where I met him!"

"So tell me," she said, now getting caught up in my own enthusiasm. I told her about our meeting thirteen years ago and how we reconnected again two days ago.

When I finished, she said, "You remind me of your dad, when he told me he had met this little girl on his first day in kindergarten and how he was going to marry her someday. And he did!! More than twenty years later. Since then, I've never doubted that there's such a thing as love at first sight.

***

Monday is Servants Day Off for most of the Great Houses in The Reserve so we tend to eat out, order in, or cook for ourselves. We gather at different houses to grill, watch movies, play cards, have drinks, or swim. Or we eat at one of The Reserve's fine restaurants.

Andy arrived a little after six wearing a light-colored sports jacket, dark slacks, highly-shined shoes, a linen dress shirt, and a silk tie. He was shaved, showered, flossed, and curried to within an inch of his life. He had drenched himself in expensive cologne. I hardly recognized him when Butters led him upstairs to my bedroom.

"I went to the front door this time," he said, smiling. "I see what you mean. That main foyer and the round room with the dome are sump'n special."

The round room to which he referred is the Rotunda, a marble-columned homage to Andrea Palladio.

If you remember my example of how Creswic House, if seen from the air, is built roughly in the shape of a large capital letter *"I,"* with the grand foyer being directly in the center of the lower cross bar, the Rotunda is immediately adjacent to the foyer, a marble atrium sitting like a giant onion behind the foyer and rising up three stories. On the first floor, it transitions the visitor from the main foyer to the Grand Gallery that traverses the length of the house from south to north, ending at the gilded double doors of the Grand Ballroom.

Three sets of black marble pilasters with gold-leafed Corinthian capitals line the east and west sides of the Rotunda on the first floor. Between them, floor to ceiling curve-topped windows provide plenty of natural light.

On the second floor, the pilasters wear Ionic capitals. Wide marble railings supported by marble balusters in the shape of gigantic chess pawns look down on the first floor from above.

On the third floor, the marble columns wear Doric capitals. The glass-enclosed, glass-ceilinged Sky Room looks down onto the floors below through floor-to-ceiling plate glass windows or outside, to La Belle Terre Reserve and beyond.

Hanging from the center of the beautiful hand-painted dome is a massive crystal chandelier handmade in Czechoslovakia, which illuminates all three floors.

"Why are you dressed like that?" I wanted to know. "You'll die in this heat and humidity. You should know that better than I do. We're grilling steaks outside tonight. My nieces and nephews want pizza so I guess they'll start up the pizza oven, too.

"Why don't you leave the jacket and tie up here? You can pick them up on your way home tomorrow morning," I hinted.

"I'd like to spend the night but I gotta work tomorrow," he said. "Plus, I gotta take care of Wallace. Another time?" he added. Nothing beats a try but a failure.

After being close for about an hour, we headed downstairs to the swimming pool area.

"It's huge!" he said. "It's bigger than the pool at Pontchartrain Beach."

"I wouldn't know," I said sourly. "Pontchartrain Beach in New Orleans was for whites only when I was growing up. Blacks went to Lincoln Beach several miles down Hayne Boulevard from the larger, fancier, better-equipped Pontchartrain Beach.

"Sorry, I forgot," he said, falling silent.

"No need to apologize," I said. "It wasn't your fault. That's why my parents built this pool. They didn't want us swimming with people they didn't know. In case you haven't figured it out, *Creswic House* was built as a reaction to the segregation around it. La Belle Terre Reserve is an extension of *Creswic House*."

"Must be nice," he smiled. "All we had was my little pond or Bayou Mal Enfant."

"But you were entitled to go to Pontchartrain Beach, to use the public library, to sit at any lunch counter, or to use any bathroom you wanted. We weren't, so my parents had to make our own little non-discriminatory world or keep us out of Louisiana as much as possible. I'm just glad my parents and grandparents had the wherewithal to do so."

"I'm jus' glad they made you," he said, kissing my hand. "Do I have to ask for this hand in marriage or do you have to ask for mine?" he smiled. "When two men marry, what's the correct protocol?"

"I don't know," I said, "but if this is a proposal, I'll marry you. We can figure out the protocol later."

My parents, whom Andy had already met, were there. He shook hands with them, made small talk, and looked around, bewildered, at all of the other Mallorys gathered there. I introduced him to all of them.

I had not seen the youngsters. As they arrived, my nieces hugged and kissed me. My older nephews hugged me and shook my hand. The younger ones still got a kiss as they arrived. I inquired about grades, boy- or girlfriends, and other activities then steered Andy to my grandmother, who arrived with Henry as if she were the Dowager Empress of China.

Wearing full make-up, she was the only other person who had overdressed for the occasion. Grandma never left her home unless she was wearing full war paint.

"Isn't he something?" I asked her as Andy blushed unabashedly.

Grandma took a few steps backward. "Yes, he is," she said, smiling. "I didn't know they grew them so handsome in the Brulé! You two make an eye-catching couple. It's just a shame that you'll never be able to give me great-grandchildren."

"You already have a whole passel of them, Grandma," I said, sweeping my hand across the yard. There were nine children from fifteen down to three months old, splashing in the pool, or playing soccer on the upper lawn, being held in arms by loving parents, or frolicking on the lower lawn with five or six standard poodles in several colors. The sight of so many beautiful, confident, happy, well-dressed chocolate children gamboling with so many beautiful standard poodles in so many colors was a sight to behold.

"But none from you. You were always my favorite," she whispered. "You were the one who went everywhere I went. You used to help me pick out plants for my garden, and even helped me plant them until your feet got so big." She pointed down to my size fourteens. "What size are they?"

I laughed but didn't answer.

"You're a very handsome young man," she said to Andy, "but you've done something unforgivable."

"What's that, M'am?" Andy furrowed his brow, wanting to know,

"Whenever my grandson comes back home for a visit, he *always* visits me at first light. Because of you, young man, he didn't visit me until this morning. That was more than seventy-two hours after he arrived," she said, half-seriously.

"You can blame that on Deputy RC Eck," Andy said. "He went and got himself killed a few days ago. Wayne went to the police department to find out about the murder. It was already past first light when we met."

"I'm told he was a very nasty piece of work," Grandma said. "Did you know him?"

"Yes M'am. I had to work with him on a daily basis. He was the Information Officer, which is like a public liaison, for the Bellefleur Parish Sheriff's Office an' I'm the Public Information Officer for the S.P.D., so our duties put us in almost daily contact."

"You can call me Grandma, Gram, or Grammy," she smiled. "That sounds so much better than *'M'am'*," she said.

Andy nodded and beamed.

I introduced him to Jeremy, Robby, and Daniel, the three brothers who were present that day: Robby and Danny live most of the time in Louisiana. Jeremy, who is currently visiting with his wife and children, lives most of the year in

England. I also told him that my other two siblings, Lucas and Mariana, live abroad; Lucas in England and Mariana in Bermuda.

Danny, the oldest, is an attorney who specialized in property law. "He's the Chief Executive Officer and the Chief Operating Officer of La Belle Terre Reserve," I explained.

"Jeremy and Lucas are also attorneys and international bankers whose sole job is to care for Mallory family financial interests worldwide, including the Mallory Family Trust. Jeremy lives here and has a beautiful farm in the Kingstown Estates section of Kingstown, near where Laurette stopped traffic.

Lucas lives most of the year in England but keeps a large townhouse in Bilbury Ridge, near where my grandmother now resides.

Robby, who now prefers to be called Robb, is the Chief Executive Officer of McGrath Fine Candy Confections, International; and Lady Esther Cosmetics, International. He lives in England most of the year.

Mariana lives in Bermuda most of the year with her lover, Helene. She is an actuary and is president and CEO of her own insurance company. "I told you it runs in families, didn't I?" I said.

I also explained that all of the Mallorys, including me, spend part of every summer in England, part in Bermuda, and part in Louisiana whenever possible.

"Do your brothers and sister all have five names, too?" Andy asked when were out of earshot. I nodded.

"Well????" he smiled.

"Well what?" I said, playing dumb.

He looked at me as if I were really dumb. "Are you gon' tell me their whole names? I think it's so cool. It sounds so...aristocratic."

I sighed a deep sigh. "Danny's whole name is Alistair William Sebastian Daniel." I paused while he took it in then I continued.

"Jeremy's is Jeremy James Ashford George, and Robb's is Rupert Augustus Edwin Roderick. They're the three who're here today with their families."

"My brother Lucas' is Lucas Philip Leopold Sylvester, and my sister is Mariana Charlotte Elizabeth Johanna. Now you know everybody's entire name. Tomorrow I'll give you a test to see how many you remember."

"Hell, I can't even remember your whole name," he said. "Let's see…" He thought hard, holding both index fingers first to his temples and then bringing them to a point just above the bridge of his nose, between the eyebrows, trying to recall. "Steven Wayne," he began. "I remember those really well 'cuz when I first met you, you were Steve and now you go by Wayne. Then there was Adelbert—who could ever forget that one, but it's the last one I can't remember."

He thought for a minute more and snapped his fingers with a loud *snap*! "*David,* he almost yelled. King David. That's who you remind me of. Well, not necessarily King David, but a king. You have that air about you. Steven Wayne Adelbert David. Right?"

I smiled, nodded, and kissed him. "Right!" I said. By the way, in Chicago, most people still call me Steve. It's only family and people I grew up with who call me Wayne.

"That must be confusing," he said. "I think I might jus' add a couple to my own name," he said, still smiling. "Whadda ya think of André François Xavier (he pronounced it in the French manner, Zhav-YAY) Etienne Bourgeois?

I forgot to tell you. I Americanize it but my actual name on my birth certificate is André François Bourgeois. Xavier is my confirmation name. It's not on my birth certificate, though, but I could add it and Etienne just to round it out. Whadda ya think? And coincidentally, *Etienne* is French for Stephen."

Laurette arrived while we were still discussing possible additional names for him. She was a tall girl, probably around five-eleven; maybe six feet, and still in riding togs, complete with helmet and riding crop. She carried herself like a queen, not like a lot of tall girls who tend to slouch, so as not to reveal their true height.

She wore a tight pink t-shirt that said: *"LA BELLE TERRE RESERVE"* in a scarlet semi-circle across her chest, and *"LIVING HERE IS A PRIVILEGE, NOT A RIGHT!"* across her flat, girlish stomach, in a semi-circle curving upward. In the space in the middle was a silhouette of an equestrian taking a fence.

I gave her a big hug and kiss. "I love your t-shirt," I said.

"I designed it myself," she smiled. "They beat it into our heads at school," she continued, so I decided to design and sell t-shirts. I've made quite a bit of money in the bargain."

I introduced her to Andy. She smiled, and extended her hand to him.

When I gave her his compliment, she kissed him on the cheek, thanked him, and said, "Welcome to the family." She then turned and whispered in my ear in a theatrical whisper, "He's gorgeous, Unkie. I'll take him if you don't want him."

"Sorry," I whispered back in the same theatrical whisper, "he's taken. Get your own."

"You go to school here?" Andy wanted to know.

Laurette nodded. "Country Day," she said casually, referring to the New Canaan Country Day School, the Reserve's most exclusive. "I've gotta talk to my dad," she said to Andy, scanning the crowd, "Excuse me."

"He's up top with Gram," I said. "Under the pergola."

She shook Andy's hand again, taking leave. "I hope I'll see you again, Andy. Welcome to the family."

"I thought all of the Mallory children went to school in England," Andy said when we were alone.

"Some do and some don't," I said. "Louisiana's a different place from what it was when I was growing up. Both England and Bermuda have really strict laws regarding the importation of animals. Laurette loves her horse and her dogs. There's no way she's going to allow them to sit in quarantine for six or so months. I don't even know what the waiting period is for horses.

"There are several other private schools here in The Reserve. There's no need to send the kids off so that they can get a quality education anymore. Teaching a Mallory, though, is a bit intimidating for the teachers."

***

We sat on the upper patio under the wisteria-draped pergola at bistro tables seating four persons each. Grandma and my brother Danny were seated at our table. Danny's wife, Pippa, was absent, having spent a long day at the medical center.

Our purple martins were doing their job of keeping the area free of insects. Those little birds are worth their weight in gold on summer days.

"So you're my baby brother's latest love," Danny said when the small-talk had ended.

"*Only* love," I corrected.

"You make it sound like he's had a million of 'em," Andy said, his Cajun accent more pronounced against the clipped tones that private schools in England had bred into Danny.

Danny continued. "No, that's not what I meant, but I've met two of his previous boyfriends. I adore my brother. He's the youngest and I want him to be happy."

Grandma, who is never at a loss for words, said, "When, in the past, has he ever said, 'I love this man,' Daniel? Haven't you noticed the difference between this young man and the others? Haven't you noticed the way they interact? How they look at each other? It's not the same and I don't believe you have anything to worry yourself about."

Danny nodded. "Yes, Grandma, there's a big difference between this young man and the others. When they're not together, they're constantly looking for each other. They're inseparable. But that's the first stage of love: Lust or mutual attraction. I just worry at how fast this is developing."

To Andy, he said. "Wayne and I have always had a special relationship. I'm the oldest and he's the youngest. I'm his big brother. The one he came to, to defend him if he needed it. To pick him up if he fell, to dust him off and send him on his way. To make sure that nothing bad ever happened to him.

"He is a great uncle to my children and all of our nieces and nephews. He's got a heart as big as Texas. He's generous to a fault. He's my oldest daughter's godfather and more importantly, he is my best friend. We call each other three or four times a week. He was my best man when I got married. In fact, he was the one who talked me out of not running away from the church at the last minute. If it hadn't been for him, I'd have been *gone*!! M.I.A.

"But personally, I don't I believe in love at first sight. I like the old type of love, where it grows slowly and then flowers. Where you get to know one another, learn to complete one another's sentences. Know the other person's likes and dislikes. To me, love that grows fast is like a weed. It is not planned or cultivated. One day it's not there and the next it's there."

We told him the story of how Andy and I met thirteen years ago and how, serendipitously, we just reconnected.

"You mind if I call you Danny?" Andy asked.

"Of course not," Danny said.

Andy continued, "I met Wayne thirteen years ago. He was fifteen years old and I was thirteen. I certainly wouldn't call that som'pn that grew up overnight. When I kissed your brother for the first time, I knew that this was the person I was destined to spend my whole life with.

"We exchanged phone numbers," I picked up where Andy left off, "and promised to stay in touch but Grampa died and I left his phone number in my pocket instead of stowing it in my wallet. One of the new maids washed my pants without checking the pockets and I couldn't call him."

"Oh, how I remember that!" Danny said. "So you're the boy from St. William's Academy?

Andy nodded. "When he didn't call me, I called him but he'd gone to Bermuda for the rest of the summer. After that, school started an' he went back to

England. I'd'a called him in England if I'd known what school he was at. I'd'a gotten the beatin' of my life," he smiled, "but it would've been worth it. I kept callin' this number every summer for years but he was never home. He was always somewhere else."

Andy took out his wallet. From it, he pulled out the scrap of paper I'd given him with our phone number in my own hand when I was fifteen. He showed it to Danny and then to Grandma. "I've had several wallets since then but the first thing I've transferred from the old wallet to the new one was this scrap of paper. It's the only thing I had to go on and it was my link with Wayne. I don't even need it anymore. I know it by heart but I keep it anyway. One day, I'll have it framed.

"We lost contact for a while but I always knew we'd meet up again. I never doubted it for a minute. What's meant to be is meant to be and it'll happen when it's time for it to happen.

"Wayne and I discussed that first kiss the first day we met and again Friday night. We both felt something beyond electric, didn't we, Wayne?"

I nodded. "I'd never kissed anyone before Andy so I didn't have anything to compare it to, but I can tell you without a shadow of a doubt that I never felt it again until I kissed him again Friday night, thirteen years later. It was like a jolt of electricity that passed between us.

"You know what people in other countries think of black people," I said to Danny. He smiled and nodded, knowing that although blacks may be denigrated in this country, we're highly valued and highly sought-after in many others.

"I was like a kid in a candy shop," I continued. "I wanted to find out what caused that jolt of electricity that I felt when I kissed Andy when we met. I've kissed a lot of men over the years on five continents trying to find that same jolt but I never did until I reconnected with Andy again Friday afternoon.

"His was the kiss by which I judged all others. I wasn't as sure as he was that I'd find him again. I just kept hoping that I would but with so many Bourgeois' in the Bellefleur-Terrebonne-Lafourche parish area, I could've spent the rest of my life dialing numbers and not got the right one. Needless to say, though, I tried. Then, one summer, I called the operator for the number and she said that it was unlisted. So I knew he was somewhere in Bellefleur Parish but how was I going to find him if his number was unlisted? That's when I stopped looking. That must've been two or three years ago.

"If Eck hadn't been killed, I wouldn't have gone to Skylarville and if I hadn't gone there, I wouldn't have met Andy again. It was serendipity."

Andy said, "It's had a lot of time to take root and grow. Absence makes the heart grow fonder, so they say, and believe you me, I'm 'bout as fond of this one as anyone could possibly be.

"We both were lookin' for the other, hoping to find the person we knew would fulfill our lives. The one we were destined to find one day and spend the rest of our lives with.

Danny smiled and shook Andy's hand. "A gay version of Longfellow's *Evangeline*," he smiled. I wish I'd been that sure of what I was getting into when I married Pippa. I was a nervous mess. I kept second-guessing myself right up until the time I said 'I do.' You remember that, Wayne?"

I nodded. "How could I forget? I practically had to hog-tie you just to keep you from going out the window. The music started and you went to pieces. 'Let's call it off. If we're really meant to be together, it can wait another six months.' You remember that?"

Danny smiled, remembering what he thought was a big mistake. "I want to wish you both the best. It's a shame you blokes can't have a ceremony. I'd be happy to be the best man—if my brother asks me."

Danny addressed himself to Grandma. "What do you think, Grandma?" Her dog Henry had sought her out and lay beside her, his head across her left foot.

"There's nothing to say, Danny. You've heard the story of how your parents met on their first day of kindergarten a million times, right?"

Danny nodded his head. "Who in this family hasn't?" he smiled.

"So what better example could you possibly have than your own parents?" These boys look at each other like your father looked at your mother, the way your grandfather looked at me, and the way I looked at him until the day he died. That says it all.

"I have no reservations about your relationship at all." She turned and pointed to the lower terrace where a small band played *Stella By Starlight* and several couples were dancing, including my parents. "Look at how your parents move. How they hold each other. They're practically copulating..."

"*Grandma*!!" I cut her off, not wanting to think such things about my parents.

"Well how did you think you got here?" she smiled coyly, playing with the string of pearls around her neck."

***

Rosie Coleman's family home in Avoca consisted of a rusting trailer in back of a large, old, dilapidated wood house set high on brick piers. It was the fraternal twin of the one in which Andy had grown up but it was in slightly better shape.

Although most of the paint had flaked off and the wood had silvered, there were still patches of mustard yellow paint in protected areas near the eaves and vestiges of white around the windows under the porch and on the few pieces of gingerbread trim that still clung to the square wooden porch columns. The property on which the house and trailer were situated comprised approximately three acres.

A huge pecan tree stood in the center of the property and shaded the trailer like a mother hen covers her chicks. Farther to the rear, a vegetable garden was well tended. Lush green lawn, smaller pecan trees and sweet gum trees, and flowering shrubs completed the yard. Across La. Hwy 1, Bayou Lafourche flowed lazily southward, toward the Gulf of Mexico.

I pulled off the road and drove onto a shell driveway that ended abruptly a few yards in. Children with dirty faces peeked out of the torn screen door of the front house. I continued around back to the trailer, waving at the children, who smiled shyly and waved back.

"Miz Coleman?" I called, knocking at the screen door of the trailer.

"Yes?" responded a pleasant voice from inside.

"I'm Wayne Mallory. I need to talk to you. Do you have a minute?"

A rotund, smiling woman came to the door. Her gnarled, arthritic hands were covered with soap suds. "You don't have to tell me who you are. I'da reco'nized you anywhere. You're the spittin' image of your grandpa," she said.

"Sorry about my hands but I was just finishing the breakfast dishes. Come on in and sit down," she continued, wiping her hands on her fresh, crisply ironed cotton apron. The pockets were in the shape of two blue bunnies. "Would you like some coffee and a sweet roll?"

"May I have the roll and the a glass of milk, instead?"

She led me into the kitchen, where she returned to the remaining dishes. "I can't begin a new job 'til the first one's finished." When the dishes were done, she brought me two lemon bars on a plate with a tall glass of milk.

For herself, she poured a cup of Luzianne coffee.

She seated herself opposite me at the table. Having finished this dishes, she could give me her undivided attention.

We talked a while about the Mallory family. I gave her an update on all members she knew and then started on the younger generation, whom she did not know. Then we talked about her family. I was interested in the family that lived in the big, dilapidated house in front of Miz Coleman's trailer.

"They're trash," Miz Rosie said bitterly. "I rented the house to that girl's mama an' she moved her daughter and grandchildren in. Since then, the house has been tore apart by those li'l monsters. I don' blame the kids, I blame the grown-ups! They're not watchin' the children and they don' care what they do. They figure it's not their property so why bother?

"If you know anything 'bout me from your grandma and your parents, you'd know that Rosie Coleman don' like trashy people. Rosie Coleman don' like dirt."

I looked around the trailer's kitchen, which opened onto a spacious living room. The home was immaculate. Everything was in its special place. I liked the smell of the pine cleaner Miz Rosie used. Her house contrasted sharply to the dirty smells and dirty children I had passed when I arrived.

"Can't you kick them out?" I asked.

"If I do, it would jus' cause hard feelings. I don' like to have people havin' hard feelins to-wards me. I've decided not to fix the house up at all and then, they'll get tired and move on. That way," she reasoned, "there'll be no hard feelins."

"That seems a little extreme to me," I commented. "That house is in what's called the Louisiana Vernacular style. It was developed right here in south Louisiana for this climate: it's made of cypress because termites don't eat cypress. It has high ceilings so that the heat rises away from the people inside, keeping them reasonably cool before air conditioning was invented; it has a wide porch to catch the breezes; a steeply-pitched roof to shed rainwater; and high brick piers to keep it dry when the waters rose.

"You have a treasure here, Miz Rosie. There used to be a lot of them all up and down the bayous but now, they're tearing them down and building ranch-style houses that could be from anywhere.

"If you let it go, it'll cost you a fortune to rehab it. Why don't you just tell them that you need to do the repairs now, ask them to move out, and then, just not invite them to return? You'd cut your losses before they get too large and you'd have to tear the house down and rebuild. That's a sturdy old house and I doubt that you could rebuild it for under $100,000. *If* you could even find enough cypress to do it with. That's hand-sawn cypress siding. And now it's against the law to harvest cypress trees.

Rosie smiled as she mulled over this idea. She nodded. "I like it. I'll tell 'em tomorra."

I took a small tape recorder from my briefcase and turned it on. "This will be helpful for me and also for your lawyer," I explained. "I want you to speak loud enough for the mike to pick up your voice and I want you to try to give it to me as chronologically as possible. That means 'in order,'" I explained.

"I may *look* ignorant but I'm not. I read a lot." She smiled sweetly, took my hand, and said, "Come with me."

I followed her to what the manufacturer intended to be a third bedroom at the very front of the trailer. Three of its four walls were loaded with books on almost every subject. They rested on wooden shelves that cantilevered out from metal stiles bolted onto the frame of the metal home. The wall facing the street was a floor to ceiling bay window curtained with a nubby cream-colored fabric. The flat, industrial-style carpeting had been replaced by thick, oatmeal-colored Berber.

A comfortable-looking white metal daybed covered with a fluffy bronze-colored satin duvet and four yellow throw pillows stood front and center in the room. Beneath it, an industrial-looking trundle bed peeked out from among the fringes.

A club chair covered with a yellow slipcover with fringed edges and its matching ottoman stood discreetly in one corner, across from the daybed. Four reading lamps, two of which were Tiffany-style stained glass table lamps and two torchères augmented the original overhead light.

I felt foolish for assuming that this woman was uneducated or *under*educated but we came to an unspoken understanding then and there.

Miz Rosie led me back to the kitchen and told me the story of her grandson, Artie, her daughter, Little Rosie's, only child. Little Rosie died shortly after Artie was born. "He never even knew her, really," she said, "so the only mama he ever knew was me.

"He was always a good boy," she said, "I raised him to be that way." She recounted story after story of how he was always willing to help people in Skylarville, where he had grown up.

"Sometimes I'd bring him to work with me," she said. "You don't remember playin' with him some'a those summers when you were a li'l boy?"

I smiled and nodded, remembering the skinny little boy a year or two younger than me but a head or three shorter, who'd occasionally come to swim in our pool or play with my siblings and me.

We were terrible snobs and wanted nothing to do with this little interloper who was thrust upon us by our grandmother and her maid, but I would never tell this to Mrs. Coleman now.

I remember that Artie was terrified of horses so, whenever he showed up, we'd find reasons to head for the stables. I never claimed to be a saint when I was growing up.

At that time, only *Creswic House, Vernonburg,* my grandparents' house about a quarter mile farther down C'est Vrai Road, and sugar cane fields for as far as the eye could see, existed there.

My parents' Number One rule concerning the swimming pool was "NO ONE SWIMS ALONE. It was Olympic in length and depth.

That meant that *someone* had to stay there and entertain the little interloper and since he and I were the closest in age, I was the "someone" elected to do so by my older siblings in a rigged election. Being the youngest is not all fun, games, and pampering!

I found that Artie wasn't a bad kid. In fact, I came to really like him. I taught him to swim when I noticed that not only was he terrified of horses and our standard poodles, but of deep water, too. Before the summer was over, I even got him up on a horse.

"Was he anywhere near Spookie's that night?" I asked.

"People 'round here calls it 'Spookie's,'" she corrected, "to rhyme with cookies. He has an alibi for where he was. He and three of his friends: O'Neal Foster (she raised the index finger of her left hand and tapped it upward with the index finger of her right hand.), "Billy Rowe," (she raised the middle finger and tapped that one upward, also.), "an' Mark Blouin (she raised her ring finger and also repeated the tap.), were drinking at a female friend's house in Thibodaux.

"Her name's Candice Faucheux." She pronounced again, slower, into the tape recorder, "*Can-DEESE FO-shay.* Don' ask me how to spell her last name," she smiled, turning to me.

"She a no good, trashy sort of girl. I keep tellin' Artie not to fool around with that sort of girls but he seems attracted to 'em like a fly to doo-doo. Pardon my French," she smiled, covering the offending orifice with her right hand.

"Candy one of those ol' high-yella girls from down the River. You know how dark-skinn-ded mens fall all over theyselves for a high-yella girl with long, silky hair. Frankly, I think she a parstitute but I caint prove it."

"Well," I said, "the important thing is that he has an alibi. Can you give me the names again, and their addresses and telephones, if you have them. The more information you give me, the better it'll be for Artie. I'll ask the sheriff if I can interview Artie but I doubt he'll allow it."

"You don' really think the sheriff's gon' let you talk to Artie, do ya?" Rosie asked rhetorically. "You from a big city newspaper. You might just ask the right questions and he might jus' have to free my boy. Then he'll have to get off his lazy ass an' go out an' find the real killer."

"Do you know any reason why the sheriff would choose Artie even though he has four witnesses who'll attest to his whereabouts?"

"The whole system 'round here's geared to getting' as many black men off'a the streets an' into prison as possible. The sheriff an' that no-good chief a' police jus' wanna pin this on somebody-*anybody*- so that it'll be over an' their quiet li'l town will go back to sleep. The real killer is out there somewhere, and I'll bet you my bottom dollar that the real killer's white, not black," she said.

"Ain't no black person gon' be hanging around Spookie's or even in downtown Skylarville at that time o' night. Ain't nothin' for a colored person to do downtown. The Skylarville police stop 'em an' arrest 'em jus' for bein' down there."

"Spookie's don' even serve Negroes inside," she continued. "They got a li'l window to serve Negroes. Negroes calls it, *The Hole*.

"If a Negro wants to buy som'pn from there, he gotta go to the back side of the buildin' an' ring a bell. Somebody inside asks what they wants an' sticks a hand out to take the money.

"A minute or two later, they brings the liquor an' closes the li'l hole. "It's been that way fo' years. Nobody goes there 'cept the really bad winos 'cuz they stays open late. Nobody with even an ounce of pride would ever go there, that's fo' sure."

"That's against the law. Has been for years. Why hasn't anybody filed discrimination charges against the place?" I wanted to know.

"Cuz they call theyselves a private club! You gotta be a member to enter," the old woman said. "Who'd ever wanna join that club but a stone racist?"

"Why do you think the killer's white?" I asked, leaving the question of discrimination alone for the minute.

"'Cuz 'round here, black people don' kill whites, that's why. Blacks kill other blacks. Whites kill other whites an' whites kill blacks, but blacks *don'* kill whites!"

"Not even when it's somebody as hated as RC Eck?" I wanted to know.

She nodded. "Eck was hated by mos' people but there was an element in the parish that really respected him. They was even talkin' bout runnin' him for sheriff against St. Amant an' then, after he's been sheriff fo' a while, runnin' him for senator against Catash."

"How do you know all this, Mrs. Coleman?"

"I'm a retired member of one of the best cloak 'n dagger organizations of all time," she smiled. "I'm a retired black housekeeper. I'll betcha I know more 'bout your family than you do."

She slowly nodded her head and smiled a knowing smile. Don' worry. It's all good. You got a good family. They looks out for their servants. They offer 'em education, teaches 'em how to save for retirement, an' looks out for 'em when they get sick or in trouble. I could also tell you some of the dirty things the Catashes an' some of the other white families did to 'em when they found out who had bought up all that land.

"Good thing your family had enough money to fight 'em an' put 'em in their place. I'll bet your parents never tol' y'all bout that, did they?"

I shook my head. "No, they never did."

"I got money, yeah." she said. "But if I hadn't gone to them savings an' inves'ment classes, I'd be on Relief now. There ain't even one other retired housekeeper in the area cuz they cain't *afford* to retire. Ain't got nothin' to retire on. They work til they bout to drop then they goes on Relief," she said, "but I got a good amount socked away thanks to your grandma an' grandpa."

I smiled, proud of my family, and thanked her. She returned to the theme at hand when I pointed to the tape.

"If you ever wanna know som'pn 'bout a certain white person or family, ask their maid," she continued. "I ain't talkin' bout them po' trash white families in the Brulé. I'm talkin' 'bout families that can at least afford to pay a maid. If they can't afford a maid, they ain't hittin' on nothin' no-way.

"Maids is like furniture in mos' rich white homes. They say things an' never realize that the maids are there; that the same person who jus' served their cake or their punch at their fancy private meetings has eyes, ears, an' a brain. We hears an' sees everything. We know who's got money problems, who's sleepin' with who, who sick, who beats up their wives…all kinds of things.

"We also have the sense to know who to tell it to, an'…if we smart," she laughed, "when to keep our mouths shut!"

"So somebody was interested in running Eck against St. Amant," I said, trying to keep her on track.

"Right on," Miz Rosie said, "an' they wuz beginnin' to collect money for that purpose. Around here, you gotta buy the office. It goes to the highest bidder jus' like when they bid on a Thanksgiving turkey at the Cath'lic church auctions. St. Amant bought it when Gaston Bordelon died. Gaston held it for over thirty years. Every four years, he had to come up wit' the cash."

"What would've happened if someone hadn't come up with the cash?"

"They'da *lost*, Wayne," Miz Rosie said. I could detect by her intonation that she was wondering if she was talking to a complete dunce or what? All of the civics lessons I'd ever had were for naught, I thought. Now I was finding out how the system *really* works.

"Who's controlling all of this?" I wanted to know. "Who're they paying to buy these offices?"

Rosie reached over and turned off my tape recorder. "Senator Noel Catash," she whispered. ""He's the senator for Bellefleur Parish so he The Man now."

"The Catashes have held the senator's position for as long as I can 'member but now he wanna run for gov'na and leave his senatorial seat to his son, 'Li'l Noly,' but Lil Noly's been in so much trouble 'round here that ain't nobody gon' vote for him."

"You know for sure?" I asked.

She nodded. "There's *a lot'a* of things I know! Senator Catash wouldn'a cared if it was Eck against St. Amant, jus' as long as the money was the same. That would'a meant mo' money for him cuz they would'a been bidding against each other, upping the price, but somehow, the Catashes found out that Eck was really after the senatorial seat an' the sheriff's job was jus' a steppin' stone. That's when the problems started."

She reached over and turned the tape recorder back on. I felt like one of the Watergate conspirators, with gaps in the tape.

"So your theory is that the…Powers-That-Be killed Eck and picked Artie as their scapegoat?"

"Koe-rect," Miz Rosie said, nodding vigorously and smiling, relieved that I was not a complete dunce. "It's a theory," she continued. "I don' know if it's right or not. I ain't Einstein but I think it's correct. There were so many people who hated Eck for so many reasons that I could be far out in left field.

"I heard that they wuz plannin' to bill him as the next Huey Long. They gonna say he's for the L'il People. The poor. Poor whites, I'm pretty sure."

"Does Artie have a criminal record? You know, arrests and convictions, arrests and no convictions, trouble with the police? Anything that would send the police to his door?"

"Yes," Miz Rosie said, lowering her eyes. "He was arrested for attempted murder an' served seven years at Angola. He still on parole. He jus' got out 'bout five months ago. This could send him right back up the river."

Anything else?"

She recounted several minor incidents and added that she did not believe that her grandson was guilty of attempted murder either, but since he only had a local lawyer appointed by the court, he agreed to a plea bargain and spent the next seven years at Angola. "When he got out," she said, "he was one bitter young man."

"How bitter?"

"He threatened to kill Eck."

My jaw dropped. When I had picked it up off the floor and set it back in place, she explained that Eck was the arresting officer and only witness to the crime."

"Who'd he attempt to murder?"

"He didn't attempt to murder nobody, Wayne," she said, "They *say* he tried to murder Eck."

My heart skipped a beat. "So, they have quite a history together, don't they? When was all of this?"

"That would'a been around Christmas, seven years ago," she recalled, holding her head back and staring at the ceiling. "Yes, I remember it well now," she said.

"It all started during a traffic stop near St. Cyril Church on the Bellefleur side of the Bellefleur-Lafourche Parish line. RC Eck stopped Artie on his way to spend the holiday with me. He accused Artie of speeding, going *thirty-eight* in a thirty-five mile zone.

"Artie told Eck that he was going the speed limit and that if he wasn't, why was it that the three cars in front of him, as well as the two cars behind him, had not been stopped.

"It was rainin' that day. Drizzlin.' Artie told Eck that it was because he was black. Eck didn't like to be argued with an' reached into the car and pulled at Artie's shirt.

"Well, nobody touches Artie," she continued. "Artie pushed the door into Eck's belly, jumped outta that car an' put a whipping on Eck's ass—excuse my

French," she laughed, covering her mouth again, "that he prob'ly remembered until the day he died. They had to take him to the hospital, but not befo' he'd cuffed Artie to the door handle of his car an' kicked him in his privates a few times.

"He'd called for back-up when he stopped Artie's car. They arrived to find a fight goin' on. They took Eck to Bellefleur General Hospital and they took Artie to jail. No doctor for where Eck had kicked him. His balls swolled up to the size of grapefruits.

"At the trial, it was Artie's word against Eck's and they believed Eck."

"I can understand them charging him with resisting arrest and assault on a police officer or any of several other things, but how'd they get attempted murder?" I wanted to know.

"Well, I don' rightly know," she replied, "but they said that after Eck was down an' Artie was kicking him, he all but smashed Eck's nose, mouth, head, and face. Artie was like a wild man, they said, and if he hadn'a slipped in the mud, he prob'ly *wudd'a* kicked Eck's brains out—what little he had, anyway."

Andy would remember the incident, I thought.

"After the trial, when they'd convicted and sentenced him, Artie looked right at Eck just befo' they took him away, and said, 'I'm gon' kill you when I get out, you son of a bitch,'" she continued. "He called that man names I won't repeat even today."

"And he did this in open court?" I asked, incredulous.

She nodded slowly and sadly. "He set hisself up for what's happenin' to him now."

***

I had time to kill so I took the long route back to The Reserve, heading north on La. Hwy. 1, to Attakapas Bayou Road, traveling twenty or so miles, and entering The Reserve through Pleasant Valley, New Bern's largest subdivision.

Although there is no valley there, it is a very pleasant place to live with its winding streets that meander up small hills and into dingles past schools, pocket parks, houses of worship, and outdoor sports facilities, all of which have been especially created to provide a pleasant driving experience for the motorist and a pleasant living experience for its residents. It is inhabited mostly by young families just starting out or empty-nesters who want to downsize their homes without sacrificing their quality of life.

Wide sidewalks under street lights designed to look like the lamp posts of Paris meander past custom designed homes set back from the sidewalk just far enough to provide privacy to the homeowner but still close enough that they can comfortably hold conversations with passers-by without shouting.

Most of the houses in Pleasant Valley have wide front porches. All are set behind low picket fences. The challenge is that no two fences can be exactly alike and no two houses could look exactly alike. This provides for a wide range of possibilities and brings out a lot of hidden creativity.

Pleasant Valley is a mixed housing community in that although the majority of the housing stock consists of single family detached homes on quarter-acre lots, there are beautiful townhouse communities such as Bay Thorne, Thorne Hill, and Larrabee Oaks, and multi-storied condominium housing. There are also a small number of rental units available there.

I had Moros y Cristianos for lunch at "El Jíbaro," a Cuban and Puerto Rican restaurant that had opened since my last visit. Its rear patio overlooked The Boardwalk and Bayou *Pain Dure*, a picturesque waterway that runs through New Bern and meets up with Bayou St. Eloi on its way to the Bayou Belle Fleur as it meanders southward to the Gulf of Mexico. Bayou *Pain Dure* is really a man-made canal but "bayou" sounds better.

The Boardwalk resembles Riverwalk in San Antonio, Texas. There was a sizeable crowd already seated when I arrived but no waiting. I had my choice of several tables on a quay that jutted out a substantial distance above the canal. I chose one at the far end of the quay, and listened to the soft Afro-Cuban jazz through hidden speakers.

The Reserve's security force was housed in a six story glass and steel building with large bronze-tinted windows directly across the canal from where I sat.

Next door to it and towering over it like a protective older sibling was Esperanza Children's Hospital, where my mother spends most of her waking hours.

It was exactly twelve o'clock when I sat down to eat and exactly one o'clock when I paid the smiling waitress and departed. I called *Creswic House* to find out if there were any messages. I imagined that there were none, for if there had been, Butters or Rosa Braithwaite would have called me at Rosie Coleman's house. I was right.

Driving across the canal over a wide, hump-backed stone bridge that separated the Reserve's security headquarters from El Jíbaro Restaurant, I entered the building, introduced myself, and asked the desk sergeant if I could have several copies of Miz Rosie's tape made.

Capt. Ronnie Gagneaux came out to greet me. Ronnie's family also lives in New Canaan. His father, Chief of Security for The Reserve, was a hard-core lawman, and his was one of the first families to move into The Reserve. Ronnie was my age and had attended a military school in Virginia.

I, of course, went to school in England so we only saw each other during our school vacations. Still, I considered him a good friend from childhood and was happy to see him again after so many years.

We caught up on what had become of our lives while one of his subordinates was making the copies. We parted with him issuing me an invitation to play a round of golf and an invitation to visit his home for dinner before I returned to Chicago.

"You should come back here to live," he said as I pocketed the tapes. "It's a great place to live but I certainly don't have to tell that to you. Your parents built this place expressly for you and your brothers and sister and you're not even taking advantage of it," he admonished.

I told him about the property I owned at Sissquaha Pointe in Sissquaha Village and about the house in which Andy had grown up, which I was considering buying, rehabbing, and moving to Sissquaha. He thought it was a wonderful idea. "Let me know if you need any help," he said, after shaking my hand and giving me a great bear hug goodbye. Now, all I have to do was talk to Andy about it, I thought.

I roamed around The Reserve, seeing all of the new additions that had taken place during my three-year absence and trying desperately not to go out of my mind as I longed for just a few more intimate minutes with Andy. I then drove to Sissquaha Village to see my own four-acre parcel of paradise.

It was as beautiful as ever. It is situated on a peninsula and juts out into Lake Colombe like a boot in the water, making it the "*pointe*" in Sissquaha Pointe. Magnolia, tupelo, river birch, chestnut, and moss-draped live oaks at the front of the property gave way to silver-hued cypress and a variety of palms nearer the water.

I could imagine sweeping green lawns leading up to the house, enlarged to accommodate our needs but still in keeping with its original character, situated about a hundred feet from the street, behind the huge live oak that dominated the left side of the property.

I would leave the front of the property unfenced but build a picket fence around the perimeter of the house to keep the dogs in and nocturnal critters out.

I waited until three-thirty before calling the Skylarville Police Department, thanking South Central Bell for the nickel phone call. Louisiana was the last state to have it.

Andy answered on the third ring. "Andy, this is Wayne," I said. "I need to talk to you. I've got something I want you to hear."

"I've got som'pn for you too. Meet me at my house 'round four," Andy replied. At exactly four o'clock, Andy was pulling into his driveway as I turned the corner onto Ligustrum St.

He parked his Firebird under his carport and I parked the Rover behind it. We entered the house together, following the same ritual of turning on the lights, stereo, and air conditioner immediately. We kissed for a long time, trying to make up for the time we had been apart.

After he showered and attended to Wallace, giving the little dog some *"me time,"* while I mixed drinks, we settled down on the living room sofa. I told Andy about my conversation with Miz Rosie. I told him about her connection to my family and about the theory she had developed as to why Artie was chosen as scapegoat.

Andy handed me a thick manila envelope. "Crime scene photos and investigator's notes," he said. "You can look at 'em later.

"I'll never forget when Eck got his ass kicked." Andy laughed.

"I didn't remember the name of the perp but I'll never forget that day. It was one of the happiest days of my life. I was hopin' the bastard would die but I knew what would happen to the person who killed him, especially since the perp was black.

"Everybody who knows Eck laughed at how he'd gotten his ass kicked by a tiny li'l guy with the heart of a tiger."

"Eck was in the hospital for two or three days and then off work for two or three weeks," Andy continued. "He could've done desk duty but he just couldn't face people laughing at him 'cuz a tiny little black guy had kicked his ass."

"Tiny?" I said.

Andy nodded. "I don't remember exactly how tall the guy was but he's tiny. I don't remember how much he weighed but maybe one-ten wet and Eck was a big brawny guy."

Andy said he didn't know anything about the buying or selling of public offices but he did not doubt that it occurred. He said Bellefleur Parish had been the private fiefdom of one or another powerful family since it was incorporated.

"I don' doubt that one or several families could get power and pass it on from generation to generation. Charging minor officials for the privilege of holding office is not unheard of in these parts," Andy said. "I know the Catashes have been doin' it for at least four generations," he continued. I jus' didn't know how it was done."

He told me about the Albarado family in Plaquemines Parish, south of New Orleans, which had held power and office for several generations as the Catashes did in Bellefleur Parish. The Albarados and the Catashes came to power during the reign of Huey P. Long, "the Kingfish."

Old Judge Lloyd Albarado was even more racist than old senator Catash. Judge Albarado didn't want black people in the parish at all, for any reason. If a black person ventured into Plaquemines Parish, he was soon harassed into leaving or arrested if he didn't move fast enough. Or he simply disappeared.

"You know how you hear stories 'bout different towns across the Nation that have signs that say, *Nigger, don't let sundown catch you here?*" he asked. "They're called Sundown Towns."

I nodded.

"Well, old Judge Albarado had signs like that printed up and put on all roadways leading into the parish. "That's not a joke! It's a fact! They didn't come down 'til the early 1970's, when the United States Department of Justice ordered federal troops to take 'em down."

"Is he the one who was excommunicated from the Catholic Church?" I asked.

Andy nodded. "Him, his family, and a bunch of others from Plaquemines, St. Bernard, and Orleans Parishes. One of the Protestant churches with similar views took them in."

"I remember seeing pictures of old Judge Albarado and his families being baptized at a local church. The picture was splashed over the pages of the national weekly magazines and on the television news shows across the country. From the picture I saw on TV, he was as dark as Senator Catash with dark, curly hair. Don't tell me he was also a *pasant-blanc*, too!

"I don't know, Cher," Andy said again, taking my hand into his, "hell, I don't even know about my own family but some black people in New Orleans' Seventh Ward claim to be his relatives. Of course, they look like they're white, as do most of the people in the Seventh Ward, from what I've been told. I saw them on TV. The one who spoke for the family was named Sylvester Albarado and the strange thing is they look whiter than the judge.

"Although the Albarado family is no longer as politically active as they once were, they still call the shots under the table and behind closed doors down there," Andy said. He reasoned that someone must be looking after the family's interests, which were considerable. "They've invested too much time and money in that parish to just let it slip away from 'em," he said.

"I suspect that they're not going to let go of that kind of power, either.

"In Lafourche Parish, the Hahn family rules the northern half and the Dufrene family rules the southern half," he continued. "I don't know how that happened."

When he finished, I told Andy about the conversation I had had with Rosie Coleman but did not play the tape for him. It was too long and there were other, more intimate things to do. We headed for the bedroom, gently ejecting an overenthusiastic Wallace from the room.

Andy liked the feel of cold sheets against his naked body so he always left the air conditioner in his bedroom on at the coldest setting. Frankly, I could've done without the jolt to my system but, his house, his rules.

Once I had gotten past the jolt, I hugged and kissed him again and again. He lay on top of me, resting his head against my chest. His right hand caressed my face and hair.

"I love hearin' your heart," he smiled up at me. "It's strong. Healthy! I can tell."

I used my left hand to keep him close to me and my right to stroke and caress his firm butt. We remained in that position for a long time, kissing and cuddling before continuing on to more intimate acts.

Fortunately, after our first odyssey, we fit together like a hand and glove. His eyes told me that all was well and that I could proceed. I looked down on his handsome face and was reminded of our first meeting, when we were teenaged schoolboys. His eyes were closed, mouth slightly open, going along with the rhythm I played out on his body. His body responded to my thrusts with thrusts of its own, telling me to go deeper, harder, and longer.

After a while, our bodies were in complete synchronization, one with the other. Our moans and groans were even timed exactly. Call and response. We were musicians. We were an orchestra of two.

He opened his eyes, smiled at me, and pulled me down on top of him. Then he kissed me and held me tight. It was one of the most erotic, loving, and delightful sessions I had ever experienced.

When we finished, we slept. It was Wallace's scratching at the door that woke us up. I looked at the clock on the nightstand in the darkened room. It was 9:45 P.M. Andy slept on. I did not want to awaken him.

I needed to use the bathroom. When I opened the bedroom door, Wallace bounded into the room and onto the bed, awakening Andy. "That was good," he said. "Excellent."

I didn't disagree.

***

"Wayne, I was thinking," Andy said, when we were dressed. "There's someone you might want to meet. I think she might be of help to you."

"She?" I asked, surprised.

He nodded. "Her name is Melodye Matherne and she's a young black reporter at the *Skylarville Daily Sentinel.* I'll give her a call.

I hadn't planned to work with any other reporter. Andy noticed the grimace on my face when he mentioned Ms. Matherne's name.

"I've always worked alone and like it that way," I explained. I knew the complications of ego, my own included, and I've always sought to avoid them. Still, I thought, Ms. Matherne is from Bellefleur Parish and it was her by-line on all of the *Sentinel's* stories covering the murder. I only saw two women at the so-called press conference and both were white.

I agreed to meet with her but I had made no promise as to whether I would share my interview with Rosie Coleman with her.

I invited Andy to dinner at *Creswic House.* "It's informal, so leave the jacket at home. Wear your jeans and a tee shirt. I want them to see your body," I smiled. I kissed him again and again, and left.

Shakespeare was right. Parting *is* such sweet sorrow.

***

I re-thought my idea of asking the sheriff's or the police chief's permission to interview Artie Coleman.

I decided the better way of doing it was just to visit him. Visiting hours were at two o'clock every day at the parish jail. I would be one of his visitors tomorrow.

Although the sheriff and police chief knew I was investigating the story, they had no reason to suspect that I knew Artie. Presently, he was not restricted from having visitors but if I showed any interest in him, he would suddenly be placed off limits.

If asked who I am or what relation I have to the prisoner, I would give them my Illinois drivers license and tell them that I am a friend. Technically, that was true. Although I had not seen Artie in more than fifteen years, we had become friends by the time we parted company. I wouldn't be lying.

I doubted that they would allow me to bring in a tape recorder. Besides, that would be a dead giveaway that I'm a reporter after a story. I have a pretty good memory except for numbers, and believed that I would have to depend on it to recall most of what Artie would say but I needed legal proof of what was said before I could print anything. No self-respecting journal would print anything based on the reporter's memory.

If they wouldn't let me visit Artie, my default method would be to get my brother Robb to visit Artie. I could go as his assistant. As a lawyer, he has a right to see his client and to bring a paralegal to take notes.

***

Skylarville, La.

I entered the newspaper office through a narrow gray door on the side of the yellow brick building and climbed up a narrow set of stairs covered by threadbare brown carpeting. At the top of the stairs, through another narrow gray door, I entered an open room about twice the size of Andy's kitchen. It contained twelve desks set close together in two's, face-to-face.

An old-fashioned manual typewriter sat atop each. The din of ten typewriters clacking away was the only sound that greeted me. This is what it must have been like during the 40's and 50's, considered to be newspapers' heyday, before the advent of television, I thought.

A large Army-issue desk with *"Betty Bourne, secretary,"* incised into the faux woodgrain finish of her plastic name plate sat empty to my left.

A plaster wall painted the same sickly green as the waiting area of the Skylarville Police Department, ran for another four or five feet and then turned southward for another six or so feet until it came to another door, the upper half of which was glass. *"Staff only"* was stenciled across the glass in heavy black sprayed-on letters.

Through the glass window in the door, I could see long tables laid out in either a "U" shape or a reverse "L" and several people scurrying about with paste and scissors, pasting the newspaper together.

Neither in the room in which I stood nor in the lay-out room beyond, were there any computers. Not even one. I wondered if I had stepped through a time warp. All this scene needed was a cigar-chomping bulldog of an editor, called *"Chief,"* to complete it.

Instead, a young man about my age rose from his desk next to the entry door to the layout room. "Can I help you?" he asked. He had a scraggly beard, a disproportionately large head covered with greasy-looking dark brown hair that looked as though it had not seen a comb for several days, and a wide split in his two front teeth. Thick-lensed glasses in colorless frames sat atop a long, sharp nose and in front of tired blue eyes, the left of which was slightly crossed.

His wrinkled J.C. Penney Oxford dress shirt was open at the neck, exposing a dirt ring around the collar and a dingy white cotton tee shirt beneath it. A few dark chest hairs peeked out above its crew neck like naughty but curious children.

His tie was a well-worn red-and-white noose around his neck. His long sleeves were rolled up to just below the elbow, exposing hairy arms, blue veins, and fish-white skin. His nameplate said *B.J. Edmonds, Managing Editor.* His smile seemed sincere.

"I'm looking for Melodye Matherne," I replied.

"You must be the Chicago reporter she's been talking about all morning. He pointed to a young woman sitting at another Army-issue desk near the center of the room, next to one of the building's support columns, and banging at her typewriter. The name plate on her desk said *M. Matherne*.

I looked at her again. I could've sworn that Andy had said she was black. This woman had shoulder-length chestnut colored hair and a "peaches-and-cream" complexion. She was very beautiful. Edmonds saw my confusion and smiled smugly.

"She's on deadline right now," he said. "Have a seat at any of the empty desks. She'll be with you shortly." He pointed to a group of desks in the back of the room that had no one's personal effects on them. I took a seat at one of them. She looked up from her typewriter and said, "Wayne?"

I nodded.

"Hi, I'm Melodye. I'll be with you in a few. I have to finish this damned re-write. Deadline's in ten minutes." She then lowered her head and went back to her story. I watched her as she typed, corrected, cursed, typed some more, smiled at me, cursed some more, and re-typed. There was nothing at all that would indicate that she had African ancestry, I thought. She was at least eleven times lighter-skinned than Andy.

When my siblings and I were younger, we called people like her "blue-veiners" or said they were members of The Blue Vein Society. We found out later that there actually was a Blue Vein Society and that their requirements were exactly that.

In Louisiana, centuries of intermingling of the races had produced Melodye Matherne and people like her. By and large, they thought of themselves as the true aristocracy among Negro society because they were black in name only in many cases.

Before The Reserve became a reality, the only way we could meet other children of similar background was through Jack and Jill, a club for upper-class Negro children, and through any of several country clubs my parents belonged to across the country. The nearest Jack and Jill branch to us was in New Orleans, sixty miles away. It had very few dark-skinned children as members.

Until the 1960's, being a member of the Negro aristocracy in south Louisiana, especially New Orleans, did not necessarily mean that one was more intelligent, better educated, had more money, or was more fortunate than the next person. The only requirements were light skin, straight or wavy hair, very few African features, and blue veins. A French or Spanish surname helped. The fewer African features one had, the more welcome he was in that world. Baton Rouge society, however, was more tolerant of darker, more African-looking people. Education and refinement were the *carte d'entrée.*

Most blue-veiners thought that because of their skin-color, they were inherently better than those of us of darker complexions. They had a sense of entitlement that I have rarely seen in people of color outside The Reserve. It was, of course, that lack of color that gave them this sense of entitlement. Many could pass for white whenever it was convenient for them to do so, such as on public transportation.

We, the Mallory brothers, pointed out to several of them that we did not have to take public transportation. They did have the advantage, however, when it came to using public facilities. When nature calls, they could find decent public restrooms or restaurants. There was no guarantee that anyone in the Mallory clan would be so fortunate, regardless of what make and model car we arrived in. That was the reason why the idea of The Reserve was conceived in the first place. It was meant to be a place where educated, cultured, people of all races, hues, nationalities, and religions could develop that same sense of entitlement that whites and "blue-veiners" had developed in this country over the course of the last two hundred years. If my siblings and I, my niece Laurette, her siblings and cousins are any indication, The Reserve has been a roaring success.

I remained at Melodye's desk while she talked to Edmonds. I noticed that her desk blotter was covered with adolescent scribblings of Andy's name in curlicue letters, hearts, flowers, hearts-and-flowers together, and in one corner, '*MLM and AFB*" was written inside a large heart she had colored in with a red correction pen. Entwining it were vines with heart-shaped leaves. Ms. Matherne had a major crush on Deputy Bourgeois and obviously, a lot of time on her hands. I wondered whether Andy was aware of it.

Melodye returned to her desk smiling. "Ready to go, Wayne?" she asked perkily.

"Let's go," I said. I started to rise. "I was looking at your desk blotter, I said hesitantly. "It's none of my business but I was wondering if you and Andy are dating."

She turned several shades of red and looked down at her now clear desk. "Oh, that," she said sheepishly. "Just a childish crush. I don't believe he even knows I exist… on a social level, anyway. Please don't mention this to him. We're just friends…I'd like it to be more than that, though," she confided. "Where do you want to eat?"

"I'll let you choose the restaurant. You're familiar with the area," I said.

Leaving the newsroom, we walked to a crowded café at the intersection of Fifth and St. Mary Streets, a half a block from *The Sentinel's* offices and directly across Fifth Street from Spookie's, where Eck was killed.

One good thing about working in a small town is that every place is close to every other place, I thought.

Fifth Street runs north and south, past Spookie's Bar and Pool Hall, past the front doors of *The Sentinel* and its adjacent parking lot. It ends about two miles away, at the intersection with Catash Blvd, near the campus of Skylar College.

Zapody's Café sits squarely in the middle of the crossbar of the *"T"* formed by the intersection of Fifth and St. Mary. Spookie's is directly across the street from Zapody's, on the southeast corner of that intersection. The bar's entrance is on St. Mary while three French doors provide access to the pool room from Fifth Street.

Zapody's had originally been a large Acadian-style family home with wide front and rear porches. The smaller shop in which we ate had originally been a cobbler's shop, which stood nearer the sidewalk and to the left of the main house.

A long wooden building to the rear of the main house had originally housed the family's horses, carriages, and servants. Accessed from an alley and closing off the entire rear of the lot, it formed the north end of a natural corral for the family's horses and space for their carriages.

With the advent of the motorcar, it became a four-car garage with servants' quarters above, and later, when the home was turned into a restaurant, it became a working chef's kitchen and storage area.

The corral became a lovely brick-paved patio with sparkling fountains and lush plantings between the main building, the smaller cobbler's shop, now turned restaurant, and the kitchens.

The two front buildings were tied together by the main building's deep front porch and narrow gangway that ran alongside and between the two buildings.

Diners had the choice of eating in the former cobbler's shop, the main house, or on the patio.

Diners sitting at window tables in the cobbler's shop, called The Cobblery, had a full length view of Fifth Street, which ran from there southward to the town limit. Sixteen side streets intersected with Fifth Street before it intersected with Catash Blvd, which ran parallel to St. Mary.

"Did Andy take you to Spookie's?" Melodye asked when we were seated at a small table in the former cobblery's large bay window. She also pronounced it to rhyme with cookies. "It's been closed since the shooting."

"No," I responded rather curtly, still miffed that this blue-veined interloper would try to steal my boyfriend and then act as innocently as if nothing had happened. I laughed to myself when I realized that Melodye had no idea of the blossoming relationship between Andy and me, and, in reality, *I* could be considered the interloper. She was there first—kind of.

A young brunette, whose name tag said "Bonnie" in cute pink letters to match her pink and white gingham dress, pink apron, and white sneakers, came immediately and took our order.

Melodye introduced her to me. I smiled and shook her hand when she offered it. "You brought a tall one today, Melodye," she said. Melodye explained that she sometimes ate here with Andy or with some of the other writers from the newspaper. Melodye ordered the blue plate special, which consisted of red beans and rice with andouille sausage, cornbread, and a cold Pepsi.

I ordered the dirty rice special with sliced turkey, wheat bread, and a cold diet Pepsi. We talked as we waited for the food to be served. Most of the talk was about Chicago and its three major newspapers. Melodye was all ears. I could see she was ready and willing to blow this one-horse town in favor of the bright lights of the big city.

I had read all of her articles on the murder of RC Eck. I thought she was a very good writer and that she was probably ready to head for a more challenging job than what *The Sentinel* had offered her up to this point. Now that her by-line was appearing on the national wires, I figured that she would be offered something very soon.

I finally broached the matter of her race. "Andy told me you were black," I finally said.

"I am," she smiled. "Selective breeding. My ancestors tried to breed all of my African features out of me and my siblings," she continued. "I'm like a pedigreed dog."

I looked up in surprise but before I could speak, she continued. "Chihuahuas don't know that they're the smallest thing out there. They see themselves as being all dog. As much 'dog' as the big ones," she smiled.

"That's me! Under this white façade, I'm all Afro-American."

I nodded. I could definitely agree with that. "I know about the 'One Drop' rule," I said. "One drop of traceable African blood and you're considered black. I guess what I don't understand is if you're that white, why continue to consider yourself black just because of some archaic and racist law?"

"It's not the color of your skin that makes you black; it's what's in the heart. I love being black even though superficially, I'm not.

"It's all skin deep," she sighed. "What bothers me is that darker-skinned blacks think that just because we're lighter skinned, we've had it so much easier than they have that we shouldn't call ourselves black. They call us house niggers, 'traitors to the race,' and all kinds of ugly, ugly things. I've never betrayed my race and I never would.

"All of my ancestors for at least six generations have chosen partners who had straighter hair and lighter skin and eyes than the previous generation. I don't doubt that at some time in the past, those things did get us easier jobs or more recognition from whites than some other darker-skinned blacks but it didn't give us a pass, either. As I see it, all of us are like dogs, waiting near the table for some crumbs to fall off. That we might be more pampered than some others doesn't make it any easier. We might get an extra crumb every now and then, but we certainly weren't allowed to sit at the table as equals.

"Look," she continued, "I'm here trying to make a living for myself. I'm not saying that I didn't get the job because of how I look. Maybe I did, but that's not my doing. I'd prefer to think that I got it because I'm a damned good writer and I speak Cajun French, but maybe I did get it because technically, they've hired a black writer, thereby fulfilling somebody's quota for Affirmative Action but I can't help that. All I know is that six-hundred and fifty dollars a month after taxes does *not* allow for many luxuries. I live from paycheck to paycheck and sometimes, one paycheck doesn't even stretch til the next one gets here. And we get paid weekly!

"A lot of people, especially my darker brothers and sisters, think that being light-skinned, or '*bright,*' as it's called around here, is a blessing but it's not. I'd much prefer to be your color and deal with the overt racism rather than the covert racism that I see day in and day out."

"What do you mean?" I wanted to know.

"When white people see you, they know that you're black and they act accordingly or they say what they think they *ought* to say. They may be thinking the worst things about you and they may hate to be near you but they don't usually say those things out loud unless they're what I call 'rabid racists.' Most of those racists have either died off or gone to ground. It's not politically correct to say those things now, right?"

"I guess I'd have to agree."

"When they see me, they assume that I'm white and they say all of those horrible things they were really thinking when they saw you and smiled in your face just a few minutes before they turned to talk to me. Sometimes they say some God-awful things about black people.

"I have to check them but by then, the thing is said and once something has been said, it can't be taken back. There are some things that 'I'm sorry' just can't cover."

She was wearing blue jeans and a pink knit top with a white collar. She raised the collar and showed me a red, black, and green Black Liberation pin and smiled.

"I always wear my pin," she said. "It sort of speaks for me like dark skin speaks for you. Sometimes, though, white people don't know what it is. When I tell them I'm black and that it's a symbol of solidarity, they immediately think I'm some kind of black radical, ready to burn their homes to the ground and line them up against a wall and shoot them.

"They don't care about how the Confederate flag affects me or what it means to me when they wear it or decorate their cars and homes with it. But let a black person show even half the enthusiasm for the Black Liberation flag as they do for the Stars and Bars and they think it's the second Mau-Mau Revolution.

"They're ready to get out the guns and start a war. But it's all I have. If I didn't wear my little pin, I'd have to start every conversation with a white person with, something like, 'Hi, my name is Melodye Matherne. I'm really black even though I don't look it.' If I don't, I could hear some really racist remarks. You might call that a pre-emptive strike," she smiled. "You can imagine how inconvenient that would be to start every conversation that way."

She stopped, took a sip of water, and continued. "The sad part is that I can't even win with that.

"A lot of black people think I'm really a white person trying to infiltrate the black community."

"Are you serious?" I wanted to know. I had never thought about her dilemma. It had never occurred to me that someone her color would get it from both sides of the racial divide. She had opened my eyes to a new type of discrimination. Sometimes one can be so blinded by the woods that he, or she, can't see the trees.

She nodded. "I cover community affairs both for blacks and Indians. I've been told many times that Mr. Dillworth sent me to infiltrate the black community and report back to him."

"Who's Mr. Dillworth?"

"The publisher of *The Sentinel*," she said. "He's a real jerk. I wouldn't say he's a racist, though. He considers himself a 'Southern Gentleman' but he's really just a jerk who's tried to clothe himself with some manners and soft speaking voice unless he's using his favorite phrase, *'heads will roll!!!'*

"I'm from the south end of the parish," she said. There are white Mathernes and black Mathernes. In most cases," she laughed, "the black Mathernes are generally whiter than the white Mathernes...."

Andy walked through the door of the café just as I thought his name. I sat with my back to the door and was completely unaware of his presence until I saw Melodye's face. In mid-sentence, she had suddenly become a gushing schoolgirl. I turned to see the object of her attention, as if I couldn't guess.

Andy, who had been scouting for an empty table, noticed us just as I turned around. He smiled a dazzling smile, waved, and came over immediately. "May I?" he asked to no one in particular as he found an empty chair at an occupied table, asked if he could borrow it, and pulled it up to our table.

After having put the chair in place, he placed both hands on my shoulders as he passed behind me. "Hey, Wayne," he said, leaving his hands on my shoulders and squeezing them gently in lieu of a handshake.

"Hey, Bud," I said, placing my right hand on top of his left hand, which was on my left shoulder. Andy ruffled my hair and sat in the chair he had brought over.

"And what am I, Deputy Bourgeois?" Melodye said, miffed at being excluded from the greeting, "a sack of potatoes?"

"Of course not, Miz Matherne," Andy said, following her fake formality, "and if you were, you'd be the prettiest sack of potatoes ever." Andy bent at the waist, a la Rhett Butler, and kissed her extended hand. Melodye turned a beautiful shade of cerise. Chivalry was still alive and well in the Deep South, I thought.

"I went to your office for the arrest reports but Clem was there instead," Melodye said, puzzled. "He said you were off today." Andy was in uniform and obviously on duty.

Andy smiled a mischievous smile. The violet eyes danced in merriment. "I had some personal business to take care of this morning," he said. "I thought I'd need the whole day but it turned out that I finished it in only a few hours so, since I didn't have anything else to do, I went back to work. You know I'm a workaholic, Miz Matherne."

I said nothing but I could have thought of some very interesting and highly erotic things we could have done. I'm always thinking with my little head when it comes to Andy.

Melodye's and my meals came at that moment. Bonnie greeted him like an old friend, took his order, and told him she would put a rush on it. "I'm hungry enough to eat an alligator," he said, looking hungrily at my plate.

"I'll give you some of mine," I said, "but when yours comes, you'll have to pay me back, OK?" Andy agreed and went to the kitchen door to get an extra plate. When he returned, I pushed half of my food onto his plate.

We ate and talked. The conversation turned to RC Eck. They shared what they had. I held back on the information I had about Artie Coleman. Melodye swore on her Associated Press Style Book that she would never reveal that Andy was the source of her information.

She would be Woodward to my Bernstein. Or was it the other way around? Andy, of course, would be "Deep Throat," an appellation he and I thought most appropriate.

***

We sat in his squad car at the intersection of St. Mary and Fourth Streets with the air conditioning running full blast. "What'd you have to do this morning that you took half a day off work?" I asked after Melodye had gone back to work. I had hardly been able to contain my curiosity during the meal.

"I drove out to Belle Glade," Andy said, "and had a long talk with Mama."

"About what?"

"Us. She already knew, or at least she suspected that there was *sump'n* between us. She told me as much before we even left the crawfish boil. I told her I'd come back today 'cuz I needed to talk to 'er.

"'Bout the only time we can talk is during the daytime during the week. She's there by herself. Any other time, there'd be my daddy an' sisters an' prob'ly some of the aunts, uncles, or cousins to interrupt. I took her to lunch at a place in The Reserve named Custards. She won't eat anything but Louisiana cuisine an' they have a great seafood selection an' then, I took her for a tour of The Reserve itself. She couldn't believe all of the development that's taken place since she used ta' make my daddy drive past y'all's house. You should'a seen her. Her mouth was open the whole time, an' the only things open wider than her mouth was her eyes! She was like Alice in Wonderland!

"We must'a talked for about three hours. Non-stop. No interruptions. It had been a long time since jus' she an' I talked honestly 'bout anything. It was one of the best days I've had with her since I came back from 'Nam."

"Well, what did you come up with?"

"I was really honest with 'er. I tol' her that I'm in love with you. She said she knew from the minute she saw us together when we were lookin' at the pictures in the living room.

"She tol' me a story her *muh-maw* tol' her when she was young. She couldn't remember it exactly, but she said it had always stuck with her. The story goes som'pn like this: *'A long, long time ago, when the world was young, the Creator made the souls of all the people who would ever live on earth but he decided to send them down to earth a few at a time.*

"At first, he sent down two and then four, and then eight or ten. From the very beginning, there were problems. They always divided themselves up an' fought against one another for even minor things an even though everything they needed was provided for 'em. All they had to do was to eat, sleep, an' procreate.

After a while the Creator decided that it would be better if the souls didn't have it so easy, so he made storms, deserts, wild animals, and true love.

He told 'em that up 'til then, he had provided everything for 'em but from then on, they needed to do some things for themselves to earn their place on the earth. He told 'em that they would have to work for a livin,' provide their own shelter, hunt for their own food, and earn what was previously given to them. They would also have to find their own mates in order to know what true love is.

"He also decided that from that time and forward, he would divide each soul in half an' send the two halves to earth at the same time. The halves would never again feel whole until they found their perfect mate, their Other Half, so to speak.

'Sometimes they found each other right away and sometimes, they never did but nothing felt right with 'em until they found their true Other Half. It wasn't until they found the exact match that they felt completely whole, completely satisfied, and completely at peace.'

"She said in the story, the assumption was that one half of the soul was male and the other half was female but, she figured, since the Creator made gay people just like he made straight people, he must've made some souls where both halves were female, 'like Terri an' Claire,' she said, or where both halves were male, 'like you an' Wayne.' That's exactly what she said," Andy smiled, 'like you an' Ween.'"

I hated to interrupt his story but I did. "Wouldn't it make more sense that if the souls were divided in half, they would be the same gender and that to give them different genders would come later?"

"You're a genius," Andy said. "I'd never thought of it like that. Makes sense to me and it further validates our existence."

He continued. "She said the souls must always find each other. They're usually not too far apart geographically but they may spend years lookin' for one another, like Evangeline and Gabriel, or you and me, but sometimes they would have to travel great distances to find one another, like Terri an' Claire. They had to go all the way to Minnesota. Terri's from Saskatchewan in Canada.

"She also told me that Nonc Ro-*bair* was gay. People 'round here thought that he was a little strange, since he never took a wife an' never kept comp'ny wit' no women, but since he never kept comp'ny with no man, either, they couldn't be sure.

"That's what I was sayin' before. If you get to be a certain age an' you're still unmarried, people begin to *'shoo-shoo'* behind your back."

I raised my eyebrows, not understanding the term. He raised his hand to cover his mouth and made soft whispering sounds behind it. "Shoo-*shoo!*" he said when he lowered his hand. "Onomatopoeia," he smiled.

I nodded, suddenly understanding. "Maybe I'm a stickler for language," I said. "He may have been *homosexual* but from what you've told me, I doubt he was gay."

"What's the difference?" Andy wanted to know, now raising his own eyebrows.

I responded. "As far as I'm concerned, *'gay'* is a lifestyle and *'homosexuality'* is a condition."

"I still don't follow," Andy said.

"To me, a person is gay," I said, "if he leads a certain lifestyle. In addition to being attracted to the same sex, he goes to certain places and does certain things. In short, if he led a certain lifestyle, he was gay. People use them interchangeably and everybody gets lumped into the category of 'gay' but I think it's unfair. Homo-sexuality is simply the condition of being attracted to one's own sex. It's genetic. Like hair, eye, or skin color. Or height, or having a propensity to certain medical conditions. There are a lot of *homosexual* men who'd love to be gay but their own temerity or the society they live in doesn't permit it. In short, they're 'in the closet.'

"You said your uncle never acted on his condition. Nobody even knew for sure that he was homosexual. If he had acted on his attraction to his own sex or visited certain places to find others that were attracted to their own sex, or if he'd lived a certain lifestyle that was indicative of his attraction to his own sex, then, I'd say he was gay. If he didn't, I'd say he was homosexual. Make sense?"

Andy nodded. "So I was homosexual til we met then I was gay and then, when we were separated from one another, I was homosexual again?"

"I think you were gay when they pulled you from the womb. You just didn't know where the gay baby bars were," I smiled, holding his hand. "As I said, I'm a stickler for language. Continue with your story."

He took over. "She said, 'sometimes the souls don't find each other til they're on their death bed, like Nonc Ro-*bair*.'"

"So how'd he find his Other Half?" I wanted to know.

"Nonc Ro-*bair* never wanted to go to church. You couldn't push, pull, or drag him in, not even on Christmas an' Easter, the two big holidays. I don' know why but he cursed priests an' nuns all his life. He always said religion was full of baloney and that the Latin Mass was a bunch of '*weedie-weedie*' that nobody understood."

"Nonc Ro-*bair*'s Other Half was Father Balaban right there at St. Christopher Church in Belle Glade.

"They knew of each other but they didn't *find* each other til Nonc Ro-*bair* started failing. He was up an' down at first, then gradually, he took to his bed an' never got up again.

"Frankly, I think Father Balaban was scared to visit Nonc Ro-*bair*. Nonc could be terrifying when he was mad 'bout som'pn. Father Balaban made one visit to Nonc's house when he first got to St. Chris an' Nonc was so terrible to him that just stayed away from Nonc after that. Nonc kept a shotgun by the door and wouldn't hesitate to use it.

"Nonc definitely stayed away from him but when he got sick, they took him to St. William's Hospital. Father Boyd was the hospital's chaplain but he couldn't speak French where Father Balaban spoke it fluently. He always visited his parishioners on Sunday afternoons.

One Sunday, he came by an' asked Nonc if he wanted him to pray for him, hear his confession, or receive communion. Nonc shot the bird at Father Balaban but Nonc's roommate wanted to, so Nonc had no choice but to let him stay.

"Father Balaban came back every day purportedly to talk to Nonc's roommate an' usually, Nonc would pretend to be asleep while Father was there. Or he'd turn his television set's volume way up to drown out their conversation.

"When Nonc's roommate an' life-long friend, left the hospital, Father still came by to visit. If he didn't come in his priest clothes, Nonc would talk to him 'bout anything but religion. Mostly, they talked about fishin'. Both of 'em loved to fish.

"When Nonc was discharged, Father Balaban got up the nerve to visit him again at his house wearing his priest clothes. He asked Nonc if he wanted him to hear his confession and offered him communion. Nonc said no, but if he came back in regular clothes, they could go fishing together. Father took him up on it.

"She said they became best buddies and they had 'bout two years together but they were the happiest of Nonc's life. He was *really* grumpy most of his life. Nobody liked to go visit him an' he seemed to prefer it that way.

"Mama used to send me over there to help him 'round the house. I'd chop wood for him, or is she had cooked som'pn she knew he'd like; I'd take him a plate. His house was always dark with this yellowish glow 'cuz he used kerosene lamps instead of electricity but he had all kinds of interesting old books an' magazines from before World War I so I'd sit in the swing on his porch and read or he'd tell me stories 'bout World War I. 'The *Great* War,' he called it. He was a doughboy. If you look on the bookshelves of my guest bedroom, I still have most of 'em. I even have his uniform.

"When he got older, he moved to the house in Skylarville, closed up the house he lived in in Belle Glade, an' rented the other house down the road to Miz Delia an' her daughter.

"On the day Nonc died, Father Balaban carried on so badly that Mama an' the other family members who came to claim the body knew *som'pn* was wrong. She said they knew som'pn more than just friendship had developed between 'em. When he calmed down, he told Mama, Terri, an' Claire the whole story.

"He said they were well past the age where their relationship was sexual but they found other ways of expressing affection. Besides, he was faithful to his vow of celibacy but he knew that Nonc Ro'*bair* was his soul mate and he didn't try to fight it.

"When Nonc wanted to move to the nursing home, Father Balaban talked him into comin' back out to Belle Glade an' practically moved in with him. He stayed with Nonc til he died.

"Nonc died holding Father Balaban's hand. Twenty-four hours later, Father Balaban was dead, too. Mama said it was from a broken heart cuz he wasn't sick at all. The coroner said it was from 'natural causes. They were both eighty-five when they died. They were born five days apart, just in different states.'"

"Were they buried together?" I asked.

"No," he said, shaking his head. "Father Balaban's family took his body back to Canada."

"She also said, 'If that's the way God made you, that's the way you gotta be. Anything else is a sin 'cuz you're not followin' His will. He knows what he's doin' an' he knows how he wants you to be." She said, 'He *don'* make mistakes.'"

"Now that's a smart woman," I said.

"She said when she saw you and me together yesterday, she noticed that I couldn't take my eyes off you for more than a few seconds. It was like I had som'pn to live for again."

He brushed away a tear from his right eye with his right index finger. His left eye was also beginning to well up. He removed a crisp white handkerchief from his right rear pocket but did not use it.

"She said she didn't remember your name but when she saw us together, she knew that you were the boy I'd been trying to find for so long.

"She cried with happiness for me an' I cried too." He wiped both eyes with his handkerchief and held it in his hand for future use.

"I tol' her that I can't live without you an' if it means that I've gotta move to Chicago to be with you, that's what I'll do," he said.

"She said she understands but she hopes it won't come to that. She doesn't wanna lose her baby boy," he smiled. He dabbed the tears from both eyes. His scleras were red and his long eyelashes were wet. Some had clumped together as the tears continued to flow.

He fished a small bottle of Visine from his front right pants pocket, held his head back, and plopped two drops into each eye. He held his eyes closed for two or three seconds and opened them. "I don't know what I'd do without this stuff," he said, smiling, as he checked himself in the unit's rear view mirror.

"Do you cry a lot?" I asked, worried.

"No," he responded, "but sometimes Clem an' I share a joint at lunch or before we go home at night."

He gave my hand a long, tight squeeze. "I've gotta go. Let's talk about this some more tonight. This is not the kind of thing we should be talkin' 'bout in a squad car on a street corner in downtown Skylarville."

"I'll see you at your house at five thirty, OK?" I reassured him. He drove me to the Rover and got out as I emerged from the passenger's door. He gave me a warm, tight embrace, holding me close a long time. "I know I've found my Other Half," he whispered.

"I know so, too," I whispered back.

***

I drove to a discount clothing store in a strip mall near the edge of town where I purchased a blue work shirt, a pair of wrap-around sunshades, a welder's cap, and some spearmint chewing gum. I was wearing jeans so I didn't have to worry about trousers.

That done, I drove to the Greyhound bus station, where I put on the newly-purchased clothing and loaded my mouth with wads of chewing gum. I then drove to the Bellefleur Parish Jail which occupied the third and fourth floors of the same white stucco Art Deco building that housed the Sheriff's Office. Andy's office was two blocks away.

A light drizzle had begun while I was in the bus station. By the time I got to the jail, the rain was coming down steadily. That shortened the line of visitors waiting in front of the jail. The female visitors reached into their purses and pulled out a wide assortment of umbrellas in every imaginable color. Most of the males left.

A recorded voice on the telephone had told me that visiting hours began at 2 P.M. daily and that visits last for thirty minutes. Detainees were allowed to have two visitors daily. If there was the third visitor for a particular detainee in one day, they would be sent away.

The recording also said visitors needed one piece of government-issued identification and that they would not be allowed to bring anything into the visiting area.

It was exactly ten minutes of two when I arrived. I left my press card and other journalistic identification in the Rover and kept only my wallet with my Illinois driver's license on me. As few of the male visitors had umbrellas, I decided to leave my dad's large black umbrella in the Rover and tough it out with my fellow he-men. The line started to move as I walked up and I took my place at its end.

They brought us inside out of the rain and allowed us to visit in groups of five. I was in the second group. The young male clerk on the other side of the bullet-proof window had a handsome face despite its severe acne-scarring. He took my license, recorded some information on a long, white sheet of paper, and told me to have a seat in the waiting area; the detainees would be out as soon as they could be rounded up.

I waited a half hour or so as those ahead of me finished up their visits and my group was called to take their places.

Artie Coleman was definitely height-challenged though he was by no means, a midget or a dwarf. He probably stood five feet tall in his stocking feet; five-two at most. Now I know why Eck was embarrassed by having been beaten up by such a tiny person. It would be like a Chihuahua beating up on a Doberman Pinscher.

He now had the body of an athletically-gifted, copper-colored Napoleon, but it was almost as if he had not grown more than an inch or two since I last saw him. He was eleven years old then. I was thirteen.

As a kid, he wore his hair shaved down to the scalp and lined all around, as was the fashion then. It was called an Ivy League haircut. We all wore it.

He now wore a large Afro to camouflage an elongated head shaped like a loaf of French baguette bread, placed horizontally on a scrawny neck. When we were kids, we made jokes about the shape of his head. Out of his earshot, of course.

He now wore a scraggly beard and mustache that made him look like *"Itchy Brother"* in the King Leonardo cartoons.

In another life, he might have been a terrific gymnast with his long fingers, very broad chest, bowling ball biceps, and ropey veins that bulged when he flexed his arms under his orange jumpsuit.

Although *"XXTRA SMALL"* was stenciled across its back in bold black letters, it fit him like a pup tent. The word *"LADIE'S"* had been blocked out in black ink by some diligent jail employee, it was still faintly visible under the room's harsh lights.

"Who here to see Artie Coleman?" he yelled, not recognizing any of the visitors.

"Me," I answered. I beckoned him to a booth at the far end of the room, away from the other detainees and their visitors.

Artie looked perplexed as he sat down in the booth before the heavy mesh screen that separated the Good Guys from the Bad Guys.

"Who you?" Artie asked, his voice loud.

"Keep your voice down," I said in a voice just above a whisper. "I'm Wayne Mallory. Your grandmother asked me to talk to you.

"You one of the Mallorys that my Gram used to work for?"

I nodded. "I'm Wayne. The one who taught you to swim, play tennis, and ride a horse.

Artie's face broke into a gold-toothed smile. *"Damn!"* he said, stretching out the word. "Whatever you been eatin,' Boy, give *me* some'a *dat*! Hey," he said, "When the Lord tol' you, *GO,* you thought he said *GROW*, huh?" He smiled at his joke. "How tall you?"

I told him. "Look, Artie," I said, "We don't have much time. Thirty minutes. I managed to get my tape recorder in so I can record our conversation. Is that OK with you?" I took out the same transistor tape recorder I had used to record the conversation with his grandmother and placed it discretely on the ledge near the mesh screen.

Artie nodded. I told him to get as close as he could and speak as loudly as he could without calling attention to what we were doing. The deputy on my side of the screen sat on a metal stool near the entry door reading a lurid men's magazine. There was no one on the other side to accompany the detainees.

We used up all of our allotted time. His story was essentially the same as his grandmother's but he provided much more detail plus the phone numbers and addresses of his witnesses. When I saw the deputy headed our way, telling visitors that their time was up, I stopped recording and slipped the machine into my pocket.

"Tell your Gram thanks for payin' for the lawyer for me," he said. "I didn't kill that fool!" He sounded like the little boy he looked to be. Artie stood up just as the deputy came up to our booth. "Thanks for coming to visit me," he said. "Come back real soon. I have to tell you some mo' shit." He placed his hand against the wire mesh grill. I did the same. That was the best we could do for a handshake. I got the distinct impression that Artie Coleman was no killer.

The rain had stopped when I finally walked out of the jail. Steam rose skyward from the sidewalks as puddles began to dry up when the heat returned. The world smelled freshly-scrubbed, cleansed of the pollen, dirt, mold, and other irritants, by the brief shower.

I arrived at Andy's house about fifteen minutes before he was due to punch out. I sat in the Rover in his driveway with the windows rolled down and Sarah Vaughn on the cassette player.

"What's up, Dude?" Kevin Blanchard said. He had arrived from the car's rear and I had not noticed him until he was at the window.

"You scared the shit out of me!" I said.

"Sorry. Mind if I get in? I'm kind'a dirty, though." He was still wearing the work clothes and boots he wore each day to the shipyard where he worked as a welder. Plastic goggles and a metal torch-lighter hung from his belt. In one arm, he cradled a yellow hard-hat with the name *K. Blanchard* written across the front in large black letters on white adhesive tape.

"Hop in," I said.

He pulled out a man-size handkerchief with a white center edged in brown plaid, and spread it on the leather passenger's seat before getting in. Inside, he pulled a joint out of a large billfold that hung from a metal chain that ran from his belt to his left rear pocket and offered it to me. We shared the joint and talked about inconsequential things for about fifteen minutes. I figured that Andy should be just punching out just about now, and that a in another fifteen or twenty minutes, he would be home.

"Let's go get some beer," I suggested. "Andy should be starting for home just about now."

"You really like him, huh?" Kevin asked.

"Yeah' I really do," I replied.

"You've been good for him, too," Kevin continued.

"What's that mean?"

"Well, since you've been comin' around, T-Beau seems happier. He can be real moody sometimes but since you've been comin' around, he laughs more, he smiles more...just *happier*. And he parties more now."

"More?" I asked, astonished. "How can that be? The man's a party animal."

"Not really," Kevin said, shaking his head. "He *used'ta* be. A long time ago. But he hasn't been all that...happy, if that's the right word... not til you came into the picture." He looked at me with sincere brown eyes. "But now he seems to enjoy life again.

"I don't know if you understand what I'm talkin' about 'cuz you've only seen him like he is now but he wasn't like that two weeks ago. It's sort of like when you have a cold. You can't smell and you can't really taste. You eat because you have to, but not because you enjoy it. You know what I mean?"

"I follow you," I said. "Go on."

Kevin continued. "Well, that's what he was like before you showed up. But now, he enjoys life again. I can tell. I'm closer to him than anybody except maybe Tante Jolie."

"His mom?" I asked. I raised an eyebrow for verification but Kevin continued on. "Somp'n happened to him a long time ago an' it just about sucked the life out'a him. Did he tell you 'bout it?"

"No," I said, shaking my head. "What happened to him?"

"I don't think it would be right for me to tell you. When he's ready, he'll tell you, I'm sure.

"Don't get me wrong. We still got together an' partied a lot, but the impression I got is that he was jus' doin' it 'cuz we wanted it, not 'cuz he really wanted to do it. He jus' turned 29 in May. I turned 27 two weeks before him an' I still feel like a 20-year old. He seemed like an ol' man until you came. Now, he's like the same old T-Beau."

"Did you do military service?" I asked.

He shook his head.

"That'll change you," I said. I started the engine to get the beer. "And then he's in law school. That's serious business. I don't know how he can work, go to school at night, and party, too."

Kevin continued. "At one time he was considerin' becoming a priest or a religious brother. Did he tell you that?

"No," I said. "He's never said a word."

"That was before he went to the Marines. I don't know what changed his mind, though. When he got out of the Marines, he got the job at the police department an' never talked about it again. Then he started law school. Seems to me like he did it to take his mind off'a whatever was botherin' him. That keeps him really busy. We hardly see him during the regular semester. He usually goes directly from work to school.

"I'm not too good with words but I see a big change in him. I jus' don' know what he's gon' do when you go back to Chicago. I guess it's like being shot into the sky in a rocket and then having to parachute back to the ground. He's gon' hit the ground hard, even with a parachute."

"That's a pretty good analogy," I said. I love the way people in south Louisiana express themselves. "So you think I had something to do with this change in him." It was a statement, not a question.

I pulled into an empty space in front of the liquor store. We left the Rover and walked across the parking lot. "I *know* you have som'pn to do with it. I just don't know how or what. It's no coincidence that he went from an A-Number-One-Grouch to Mr. Hospitality.

His brown eyes searched my face, cutting into my soul as if searching for any deceit, dishonesty, or disingenuousness.

He waited a longtime before he spoke again. Before he did, he wet his lips, "don't hurt him. He's been hurt enough already."

I took a deep breath and was about to ask how Andy had been hurt and by whom but he held up the index finger of his right hand, anticipating my question, and said, "when he's ready, he'll tell you. That's not for me to do."

I left it at that but a bond was forged between Kevin and me at that moment. An unspoken alliance never to hurt Andy Bourgeois.

"Don't tell him this but me an' Goo were planning to take him to New Orleans an' get him laid. We thought that might'a been the problem. T-Beau's a good lookin' dude an' he just turned 29 years old. He's still a virgin. Sort'a reminds me of ol' Nonc Ro'*bair*."

"Who's Goo?"

"Paul. From when we were kids. Everybody in Louisiana's got a nickname. His is Goo. We don't call him that too much anymore, but every now an' then, it slips out."

"Why 'Goo'?" I wanted to know.

"Cuz when he was in kindergarten, he'd shit himself by lunch for the first month or two. Every day, he'd go home with goo in his pants. It jus' kind'a stuck.

"He did it cuz he wanted to go home. Sister Mary Margaret finally got wise an' tol' Tante Clotilde to send an extra set of clothes for him so when he did it, she'd clean him up an' send him back to class instead of sendin' him home."

"So," I said smiling, "What's your nickname?"

"T-Boy," he said. "I guess they couldn't come up wit' nothing better."

We bought two twelve-packs and went to Skylarville's only Chinese restaurant for take-out so that no one would have to cook. When we returned, Andy had arrived and was already in the house. He opened the door before I could ring the bell. Kevin handed him the beers and left for his house next door. He said he would shower; change clothes, and come over for dinner when he finished.

"I was here earlier and I met Kevin," I said. "We went for beer and Chinese while you were out. I hope you don't mind his coming over for dinner. I didn't invite him. He just kind of invited himself," I said, as I placed the bags on the kitchen table. "I know you wanted to talk about your day with your mum."

"No problem," he said, kissing me. "Paul and Kevin are like brothers to me. They're *almost* always welcome. I couldn't stop him from coming if I wanted to."

I recounted the conversation Kevin and I had had, especially Kevin's skyrocket analogy. "Mind if I give you some advice?" I said.

"No, go ahead."

"If I were you, I'd get all of the family together and tell them the truth. Your mum already knows and if Kevin doesn't know, he's sniffing out the truth like Nonc Yogi's old hound dog."

Andy smiled. "Nonc Yogi doesn't *have* an old hound dog."

"That's beside the point. You know what I mean. These people love you and they want you to be happy. In essence, Kevin and your mom said exactly the same thing: You were miserable while I wasn't here but now that I'm here, you've come alive again. They want to see you happy and if I make you happy, that's what they want for you. I don't think that anyone would think any less of you if they knew that you were gay. They don't even seem to mind that I'm black…and this is Belle Glade, Louisiana. At one time, I could've ended up alligator bait."

"We both might," Andy smiled. "Jus' jokin,'" he added when I frowned. "You don't know some of the things they say 'bout gay men. Every stereotype you can imagine."

"So tell them what Popeye used to say." "'*I YAM WHAT I YAM AND THAT'S ALL THAT I YAM!!*' Who can't understand that?

"When you first told me that you loved me, I didn't want to get involved with anyone because I'd been hurt. I don't know that this won't be another hurt for me but I know I have to do what I have to do. I realized that I couldn't fight the inevitable. I realized that we belong together so I didn't fight it anymore. Since I've accepted the fact that we are going to be together, somehow, some way, I'm a lot more peaceful, more tranquil, about it. Haven't you noticed?"

"Yeah, I've noticed it. It jus' kind of slipped up on me," Andy said, holding my hand tightly. I changed the subject to ease the tension in the room. I told him about my visit with Artie Coleman.

Andy smiled. "I was wonderin' what happened to the fancy, designer duds you usually wear.

"They're in a bag in the car." I replied.

"Can I hear the tape?" he asked. I ran out to the car and retrieved the tape recorder and played it for Andy. "He had a plausible alibi for his whereabouts at the time of Eck's murder," I said.

"Make a copy of this for Artie's lawyer." he said. "He'll be back at home in no time."

***

I met Melodye Matherne for lunch at the local Burger King the following day. We exchanged information about the case. I gave her what I had and she gave me what she had: Nothing.

Most of our conversation was about the innocence of Artie Coleman and how I had obtained the information so fast. She assumed that Andy had provided the information about Artie's arrest and would not be dissuaded from that idea.

I had called the four friends before I met Melodye. I wanted her in on the interviews. I also shared the tapes with her, presenting her later with her own copies for the news story.

After lunch, we drove to the Mechanicsville section of Houma, where many of its black citizens were packed tight as sardines in tiny houses, mobile homes, and an assortment of flea-bag hotels.

We found O'Neal Foster's shotgun house on Louise Street fairly easily. O'Neal answered after two knocks. He was a giant of a man, almost as tall as me. Good-looking, too. The color of a chocolate bar, with a wide chest, narrow hips, a close-cropped beard, a large, neatly-trimmed mustache, a broad nose and large, sensuous lips. He and I completely filled his tiny living room.

O'Neal offered Melodye the armchair and me, a seat on the matching sofa. He went through the adjacent bedroom into the kitchen and pulled up a wooden ladderback kitchen chair for himself.

He then returned to the kitchen for beers for me and himself. It was automatically assumed that, as a man, I would drink beer. He asked Melodye, however, what she wanted to drink. The choice was beer, Seven-Up, or ice water. She chose beer. I handed her mine and asked for a Seven-Up.

The house's only air-conditioner, located in the adjacent bedroom, hummed loudly as we talked. Although it was working at full capacity, the living room in which we sat was still uncomfortably warm. Noticing that Melodye and I were beginning to perspire, O'Neal offered to bring in an oscillating electric fan. Both Melodye and I agreed that the fan might be a good idea. O'Neal set the fan atop a tall wardrobe opposite Melodye. He then settled down for the interview.

O'Neal told us much the same story that Rosie Coleman and Artie had told me. "Look Man," he addressed himself to me, "I know that Artie didn't do it. We was all wit' da nigga the night Eck was killed. Artie wasn't even in Skylarville that night. He was here in Houma. After we left Candy's house, he spent the night right there on the couch were you're sittin'."

A large brown cockroach skittered across the wall that faced me. A few minutes later, its mate and two family members did the same. O'Neal saw my gaze momentarily wander and followed it to where the cockroaches marched. He calmly picked up a can of RAID that sat on the coffee table, stood, sprayed the entire cockroach family, killing them in one or two passes of the spray.

Satisfied, O'Neal continued the conversation after depositing the RAID back on the coffee table.

Cockroaches are as endemic to Louisiana as are alligators, garfish, crawfish, and mosquitoes. They can only be kept at bay by constant heavy spraying of pesticides. In old, uninsulated houses such as O'Neal's, even that would not help.

"Everybody know that Artie kicked Eck's ass so bad that he was in the hospital for almost a month," O'Neal continued, "so Eck was out to get Artie. Artie tried to stay out of Bellefleur Parish as much as he could," he continued.

"He moved outta his aunt's house in Skylarville and to Houma to avoid runnin' into Eck. When he jus' had to go to Miz Rosie's house in Avoca, he took Old Bayou Black Road out of Houma to Bayou L'Ourse and then took the swamp road from Bayou L'Ourse to Labadieville, and from there, north to Avoca."

For whatever reason, he had skirted The Reserve rather than driving through it, even though the commercial roads, like C'est Vrai Road, Thomy Lafon Blvd., Mallory Blvd., and Los Moros Blvd. were open to the public.

"Man," O'Neal was saying, exasperated. "He took me on that trip once and it was a long haul. I thought we'd never get there! It took almost two hours instead of the usual forty-five minutes."

We found and interviewed the other two men and they told identical stories: They were all partying that afternoon at the home of Candice Faucheaux. They met around 3 pm and Artie and O'Neal left together around 11:30 PM. They drank beer, listened to music, and smoked a l'il weed. Artie, still on parole, had not participated in the pot-smoking and had not left Candice's house, even to buy beer.

Candice, however, was not home. She had not been home earlier that day when I called her from Skylarville. Still, with the recorded statements, though not under oath, the men, along with Artie Coleman, gave pretty credible evidence that Artie was nowhere near Skylarville on the night RC Eck was killed and that he was an obvious scapegoat for some darker, more sinister, motive for Eck's death.

Billy Rowe could add nothing that had not been stated and restated by the others.

There were two messages for me, Butters said, the first was from my brother Robb, who said he wanted to meet with me and Andy at *Creswic House* at 7 P.M. The lawyer who would be representing Artie was going to be there. He had heard Rosie Coleman's tape and wanted to talk to me.

The second message was from Andy. He said he would call again at 5. It was very important. He left no telephone number so I assumed that he would call from home.

I told Melodye about Robb and the new lawyer and invited her to stay for dinner. "This may be a long night," I said. "We're going to have to go over each of the tapes we recorded today plus those of Artie and Rosie Coleman."

***

Andy's call came at 5:05 PM. "The sheriff's detectives' report came in a few seconds ago," he said. I waited while he paused dramatically.

"Go ahead," I urged.

"I've read the statements of all of the witnesses. There were six in all. Three of them were visual witnesses and the other three are 'incidentals.'"

"What's an 'incidental witness'?" I wanted to know.

"Those who were on the bar side of Spookie's. The bartender, the waitress, and three patrons. None of them saw anything but all heard the shots and were on the scene within seconds. They ran from the bar to the pool hall and found Eck slumped over dead and bleeding all over their newly-covered pool table. They were more interested in trying to determine the damage to the table top than in going after the killer," he replied.

"The more important witnesses are those who actually saw som'pn. Actually, they all saw the same thing. Two of the witnesses were eating at Zapody's. They had the same table we had today, in the cobblery's front window, looking down Fifth Street. At night, only the cobblery is open for light meals, coffee, and snacks.

"The interesting part of all of those interviews was that no one reported seeing a short black man anywhere near the scene. All, including the pedestrian who was walking his dog when he heard the shots, said the person running away from the scene was a tall white man wearing a Mardi Gras mask or face paint.

"That witness, Victor Hugo Hébert, is a retired judge; well known and well-connected in the community. He was the person who came closest to the killer in that the killer ran toward him after the murder. Judge Hébert lives in that huge mansion at the corner of Cornwall and Fifth. There's a wood fence between his back yard and *The Sentinel's* parking lot."

I remembered the high unpainted cypress fence with the fronds of banana plants peeking out from above it when I arrived to visit Melodye.

The graceful pre-Civil War mansion looked like a giant pink and white layer cake topped with a tall octagonal cupola and widow's walk instead of a bridal couple.

This enormous neo-Classical Revival mansion, called *Skylark*, was symmetrical on all sides, completely surrounded by brick-floored galleries on the first floor and ginger bread balconies on the second and third. *Someone* had gotten awfully rich on slave labor, I thought.

It was the original home of the Skylar family for whom Skylarville was named.

The main façade faces Cornwall Street and is an excellent study in antebellum Creole architecture. Behind a waist-high wrought iron fence, painted black, it sits squarely in the middle of manicured lawns behind moss-draped live oaks, magnolias, and water oaks older than it by at least a century. Hot pink azaleas that bloom in the spring, and white and hot pink crepe myrtles that bloom all summer, were planted by the original owners to compliment their choice of paint color.

Andy continued. "Judge Hébert was walking his dog *up* Fifth Street when the shots were fired. He said they walk around the block every night in good weather. They walk from his back gate on Fifth toward Spookie's, on the corner of Fifth an' St. Mary, go up St. Mary to Fourth, up Fourth to Cornwall, take Cornwall back to Fifth, and to his back gate again.

"He said they had just started their round when he heard the shots. He thought they were firecrackers at first but when he looked up an' saw a man run out of Spookie's and *down* Fifth Street toward him, he knew they were gunshots. He said his dog started barkin' at the shooter.

"The shooter then noticed the judge and the dog, changed course, ran into *The Sentinel's* parking lot and jumped over the fence that separates it from the back yard next door. *The Sentinel's* lot is very well-lit, of course, since they have reporters and pressmen coming and going at all hours.

"That area used to be all residential," he continued. "Rich people used to live there, clustered around St. John Sigma Episcopal Church, two blocks away, where they all attended. Those who still live here like Judge Hébert, the Hoffmans, the Cheramis, an' a few others, still have a lot of money but as they die or move out, the houses are being repurposed and gradually, the neighborhood's becoming all commercial.

"Spookie's was originally a family-owned corner market til an A&P moved in two blocks away, at Third an' St. Mary. That was back in the '30's. The owners couldn't compete with A&P and sold the store to Luke Trosclair, the daddy of Marcel Trosclair, the guy who owns it now. White trash if there ever was any," he lamented.

I hated to interrupt him. He was on a roll, but he would have to reiterate all that he was telling me, to the rest of the group tonight, so I suggested that he come to dinner and save it until then.

Andy said the sheriff had stamped the file "CONFIDENTIAL" in bold red letters and had it hand-delivered to the Chief Authement, who had taken it out of Andy's hands as soon as it arrived.

Clenard "Clem" Robichaux, Andy's partner in crime, had shared the contents of the document when he made copies for the Chief. Clem, of course, did not know of Andy's involvement with Melodye and me, but he and Andy shared a mutual dislike of Eck and both were interested in how their nemesis had met his demise.

Andy agreed to come to dinner and bring the copies for our perusal. I could hardly wait to see him.

I told him that I had interviewed Artie and that Melodye and I had interviewed the three young men named by Artie as witnesses to his whereabouts that night.

***

Alexander Relicourt, called Xander or just Xan, of the law firm, Relicourt, Konigsberg, Simmons, Hatfield, Etzig, Marsh, & Dunn, was one of New York's brightest young criminal defense attorneys. He and my brother Robb had been best friends at Walsingham International School years ago.

The Relicourt in the firm's name, however, was Xan's father, not him. Xan was licensed to practice law in about six states. Because Louisiana's laws were based on the Napoleonic Code rather than English Common Law, Xan had spent nearly a year studying to pass the Louisiana Bar. He lived in Robb's guest house at The Reserve during that time. He and I had become good friends while doing so.

He had arrived at Bessie Coleman Airport, La Belle Terre's own, by private jet earlier today specifically to defend Artie Coleman. He figured that this would be a very simple case to wrap up. Still, my grandmother's final bill would not be cheap.

This time, the young carrot-top would stay in the Presidential Suite at The Praetorian, one of La Belle Terre's newest concierge hotels, a guest of The Reserve, for the duration of his stay in Louisiana. He and Robb arrived promptly at seven. My parents and grandmother joined us at seven-thirty. Andy, wearing Marine fatigues and a tee-shirt, had arrived at five-thirty so we could spend some private time together.

After dinner, we adjourned to the Children's Library and went right to work. Andy handed the copies he had made to each of us, including Melodye, who had sat quietly, almost sullenly, throughout dinner. When asked if something was wrong, she said no and smiled wanly. She was the first to leave. The rest of us lingered over drinks until Andy and I excused ourselves and left by the French doors in the drawing room.

I led him along a wide stone path that led toward the tennis courts but branched off toward a small round, Grecian-style gazebo that sat on a bluff overlooking a large pond. Ike and Tina, our swans, and their cygnets, nested on the shore nearby. They are ill-tempered but beautiful buggers.

I flicked a switch behind the tennis courts and an ethereal silvery-white light, meant to simulate moon glow, lit the pathway that led to the stone gazebo, which was also illuminated by discretely-placed lights near its domed ceiling and in the surrounding vegetation.

Crickets chirped and benign night creatures stirred as we approached the gleaming white structure that glistened in the moonlight. We eschewed the curved marble benches and chose to sit on the wide granite steps, holding hands, and talking about personal things.

"Melodye was acting rather strangely tonight," I said. Andy nodded but said nothing. "She started off her usual self," I continued, "but she got sullen as the evening wore on."

"Just tired, I suppose," Andy finally said.

"I don't know whether I should tell you this," I said, "since I was asked not to, but I think you should know that Melodye has a hell of a crush on you."

He nodded. "I've known for a long time," he said. "But how'd you find out? Don't tell me she tol' you 'bout it today while y'all were together."

"No, she told me yesterday when I noticed that her desk pad was covered with your name surrounded by hearts, flowers, and ivy. The whole shebang. She's got it bad."

"How do you feel about that?" Andy wanted to know.

"At first, I was jealous and then I figured that there was nothing to be jealous about. I can't control your feelings or hers, only my own, and, to be perfectly honest with you, I can't really control my own. I had no intention of falling in love with you or anyone else again, but I did, so why shouldn't she?"

We moved from the steps, where we originally sat, down to the pond and I now stood above him and slightly behind him. My leg touched Andy's back and shoulder. My hands caressed his face, relishing the roughness of his beard, which was again beginning to grow out. We stood this way for many minutes, trying to make sense of the whole series of events that had brought us together.

Away from the lights of the house, the stars shone brilliantly in the country sky. The pond, with its abundant aquatic life, especially bullfrogs and bream, provided me with a sense of tranquility that I seldom felt anymore.

There was so much we still had to discover about one another, but there would be plenty of time for that. I realized that this initial period of almost overwhelming attraction for him would not last forever, but I expected that by the time it ended, we would be so old that we would have no desire for anyone else.

I took his hand, which had been extended to me, pulled, and helped him from his seat. He stood next to me, gazing out on the pond and saying nothing, his arm draped over my shoulder. The only artificial light source was that of the gazebo on the bluff above us and the low voltage footlights that lined the walkways. The occasional skitterings of turtles or bullfrogs were the only sounds we heard. The heavy plantings of night-blooming jasmine and magnolia grandiflora released their scents into the cotton candy air, intoxicating me with their fragrance.

"You goin' tomorrow?" Andy finally said, breaking the silence.

"Going where?" I wanted to know.

"With Robb and Xan, when they confront the sheriff an' the chief."

"I wouldn't miss it for the world. Xan said he plans to sue the BPSO for the loss of Artie's job and for his false arrest.

"Do you think Melodye suspects 'bout us?" he wanted to know.

"I don't know, but neither do I care."

***

CHARLOTTESVILLE, VA.

Gentlemen:

By now, you should have named your organization if not previously named and your new recruits should be well into their training.

Consider this when looking for acceptable candidates:

1) Their backgrounds:
   a) Look first for our kind of boy. Boys of similar racial background as ours. In short, boys of White Anglo-Saxon Protestant backgrounds.
   b) Look for alienated youths. The "bad boys," the risk-takers, will be your best candidates.
      i) St. Francis of Assisi once said, *"Give me a boy before his fourteenth birthday and I will give you a Catholic forever."* That same principle applies here. Set up boys' clubs, scout groups, wilderness explorers, etc and winnow out those who would not be acceptable for our purposes.
   c) Curry those who are natural leaders; those whom the other boys naturally flock to.
   d) Boys without strong male role models are ideal.
   e) Sentimental boys are not to be ruled out but should be encouraged to become more independent in their thinking. Ridicule is a good way of getting them to give up their "namby-pamby" ways. If that doesn't work, get rid of them. They cannot be trusted. They may be gay.
   f) Set up tests to see which boys are "real men in the making" and which are just "girly-boys."

Boys interested in mechanics and carpentry, working with their hands, are what we want.

***

Rev. Charles Edward Hinkle, who had grown up in Ciminee, Tennessee, had founded his congregation, Rock of Ages Free Bible Church, in response to what he saw as a need to preserve the Southern way of life. He saw the younger White Southerners being corrupted by the south Louisiana way of life and he would have none of it.

He banded together with a small group of fellow rednecks to save the souls of the children of the oilfield workers from the corruptive influences of this strange land in which they had settled.

"Let the good times roll!" Hinkle snorted to his small congregation, "Is that a slogan for our youth? Instead, it should be, *'If it's White, it's RIGHT.'"* He got hurrahs from the congregation.

RC Eck had given lip service to these admonitions, if nothing else.

***

Melodye Matherne and I timed my visit to the Sheriff's Office so that I would arrive exactly five minutes after she arrived there on her morning rounds.

As part of her beat, Melodye's job was to collect newsworthy items from the BPSO, Skylarville Fire Department, and the SPD. She perused the arrest reports that were placed there for her and the local radio station by the Information Officer, as possible news stories.

Neither Chief Authement nor Sheriff St. Amant had mentioned anything about Artie Coleman's arrest. There was no arrest sheet for him in the pile.

Melodye had found out through me that Artie had been arrested and the reason for his arrest. St. Amant denied that Artie was the suspect who had been arrested in connection to Eck's murder when she asked him about it. In fact, the sheriff denied that Artie was even in jail. Chief Authement disavowed any knowledge of Artie's arrest.

I wanted to confront the police chief about this obvious lie and to be there when Xan and my brother arrived for an unannounced meeting with him.

Walter Dillworth, editor of *The Skylarville Sentinel*, had told Melodye to "dig a little" to see what she could find out. Melodye had dug and dug until her literary nails bled but she could find nothing substantial enough to print. My information, however, had been a treasure trove for her.

Andy, her dream lover, had been placed under a gag order by his boss. Although he was not the Information Officer for the BPSO, he had filled that position since Eck was killed.

Whenever Melodye approached him about the arrest of the murder suspect or course of the investigation, Andy pulled out a memo written of Chief Authement's official stationery, as Chief of Police for Skylarville and read the Department's official response:

> *"There is no information forthcoming at this time. Should the detectives investigating the incident turn up newsworthy evidence, Sheriff St. Amant and/or Chief Authement will issue a press release, hold a press conference, or I will pass it on to you personally."*

That was exactly what she printed.

***

"You're a little late today, Miz Matherne," Chief Authement said to Melodye as she entered the BPSO through the rear door. "Aren't you on deadline?"

Melodye nodded and smiled.

"Want a donut?" he pointed to a box of Krispy-Kremes on the counter.

"No thanks," she said, shaking her head and tossing her long chestnut-colored hair back over her shoulders. She went directly to the press desk to peruse the arrest reports.

I entered through the main entrance at the front of the building just as Melodye sat her purse, tablet, and pen down on the desk.

"Mr. Mallory," the chief smiled a reptilian smile, "to what do I owe this visit?"

"We've been trying to see you and the Sheriff but you've not been available to either Melodye or to me," I said, "so we decided to spring a little trap on you. By the way, you can thank me later for the donuts and the great Jamaican coffee you're drinking."

Melodye reappeared smiling. The chief looked like a deer caught in a car's headlights. He did not know which of us to address or which of us to accuse.

"Busted!" Andy said. He hummed the first four notes of the *Dragnet* theme. "*DUMMM DA-DUM DUM!!*" He and Clem burst out laughing but a stern look from their boss cut it short.

"So talk," Chief Authement said. "I've got nothing to hide. I've always been available to y'all but I am a busy man. You can't just come in here and expect me to be able to deal with your problem right away. I know you think this is a sleepy little southern town where there's no crime and I have a deputy named Barney who carries his one bullet in his breast pocket, and that all I have to do all day is go fishin' with Opie and play my harmonica like Andy Griffith but there's real crime here and I'm in charge of seeing that it gets cleaned up."

"Chief," Andy said.

Authement looked up as if a life preserver had been thrown. "Yes, Deputy?"

"Uhhh," Andy hesitated. "Andy Griffith plays a guitar, not a harmonica."

The chief ignored him.

"We'd like to talk to you about the arrest and subsequent incarceration of the suspect you and Sheriff St. Amant talked about in your press conference in regard to the killing of Deputy Eck," I said. "What's going on with that?"

"Oh, that?" the chief temporized. "We let him go. We had nothing we could hold him on so we released him two days ago. I thought we had put out a press release to that affect. Didn't we do that, Officer Bourgeois?"

"No, Chief. And this is the first of my hearing that we had released him," Andy said. "Why don't you give me his name and I'll call over to the jail just to be sure."

We all turned toward the front door as my older brother and Xan entered.

"*More of you-all?*" the Chief whined, seeing the two handsome, well-dressed men enter the building.

"Good morning, are you Chief of Police Authement?" Xan said. We had given him lessons on how to pronounce the chief's last name: "*ODY*-mon." After a few tries, he was saying it like a native. "I'm attorney Alexander V. Relicort of the law firm Relicort, Konigsberg, Simmons, Hatfield, Etzig, Marsh, and Dunn, and we've been hired to represent Mr. Arthur Lee Coleman, who is being detained in the Bellefleur Parish jail.

"And I'm Rupert Mallory, head of the Mallory Legal Trust," Robb said. Both he and Xan handed their business cards to Chief Authement. "We need to talk," Robb added with a note of finality. "Is there somewhere private where we can do that?"

"Andy, call Sheriff St. Amant and get him over here but *don't* tell him why I need him. Just tell him it's urgent. I'm not gon' to take on these guys plus the press alone."

Andy was already dialing.

***

Sheriff St. Amant stormed into the office like an out-of-control locomotive whose engineer had bailed out and left it running at full throttle. "What's so fucking urgent, Bubba, that *you* couldn't come over to *my* office?" he wanted to know. "Who are *you* to summon *me*?" he asked Chief Authement.

He looked around for the first time. "What the ... Who *are* all of these people?"

He looked around the room again, this time, seeing instead of just looking. He recognized both Melodye and me. "What's goin' on here?" He cocked his head at an odd angle, looking like an inquisitive sheepdog.

Chief Authement, visibly relieved, said, "Gentlemen, this is the man you need to talk to."

Xan and Robb handed him their business cards and formally introduced themselves.

That over, St. Amant said, "There's no one named Arthur Lee Coleman in the jail at the present time. There never has been anyone named Arthur Lee Coleman in my jail."

"Yes there is, Sheriff," Andy, standing near the door.

"Bourgeois, why are you even here?" St. Amant wanted to know.

"Cuz' I want him here," Authement said, pulling balls from somewhere deep within his scrotum. "He's *my* Information Officer and *I* want him here."

"Sheriff, I visited him two days ago." I said. "He told me the whole story."

"And *we* visited him yesterday." Xan said. "Well, Mr. Mallory here," he pointed to Robb, "visited. I didn't want to call attention to myself so I forfeited the opportunity to visit him personally at that time but as his attorney, I felt I needed to talk to him and go over some things with him. That was half an hour ago, Sheriff. He was there then."

Xan reached into his brief case, an ultra-expensive number made of some exotic animal's skin, with gold initials, and distributed typed copies of my interview to the sheriff, the chief of police, Andy, and Melodye. "This is a notarized copy," he said.

Both Authement and St. Amant looked at the thick document as if it were a water moccasin, poised to strike.

"There are also copies of statements from the one actual eye witness, who saw the shooter as he ran out of the building, and from witnesses who swore that Mr. Coleman was with them in Houma when the crime occurred."

Authement and St. Amant continued to stare at the document with apprehension. Authement, at least, skimmed through the pages while St. Amant merely looked at its front page.

"I want my client out of jail within the hour," Xan said in a threatening but polite tone.

"How'd y'all find out he was even there?" he asked nobody in particular. When no one of us deigned to respond, I said, "We've got our ways."

Authement looked up at St. Amant. "How you wanna handle this fiasco?" he asked in an "I-told-you-so" voice.

"It's not a fiasco," St. Amant said. "Yet."

"Well, the ball's in your court," Authement said.

"Gentlemen—and lady-- would y'all mind if Sheriff St. Amant and I had a few words privately," he continued. "Why don't y'all go out and have a seat in the officers' break room? It's much more comfortable than those metal chairs. I believe there's still some coffee and donuts. We'll be back with y'all in a few minutes." He almost sounded apologetic. He opened the door ceremoniously and we filed out. Andy stayed behind.

"You too, Officer Bourgeois," St. Amant said. *"Out."*

"I take my orders from the fat bald guy behind the desk," Andy said, not moving. He looked toward Chief Authement.

"My deputy stays," Authement said. "I want a witness to whatever new bright ideas you come up with." The door closed, leaving the rest of us in the bullpen. Behind the closed door, we could hear voices rise and fall.

Melodye used one of the phones on one of the empty desks to call her editor. It did not appear that she would be finished over here in time to write her story today. Other than that, she sat silently alone.

Fifteen or so minutes later, a gray man with a gray fringe of hair around an otherwise balding pate, entered the office through the rear door, rushed to Authement's office door, and knocked twice.

"That's Leonard Babin," Melodye said, "the district attorney, the parish's legal counsel." The door opened almost immediately and Leonard Babin bustled in.

Voices continued to rise and fall for fifteen or twenty minutes more before the door again opened and Andy exited smiling. His even, white teeth gleamed and his mustache danced as he beckoned for us to enter.

"Gentlemen and lady," St. Amant began, "The man hiding behind the flag is Leonard Babin, the Bellefleur Parish District Attorney." Babin was actually standing next to the large United States flag in the corner of Authement's office nearest the windows that faced the street.

"Leonard's kind of a ghost," St. Amant continued, "which is why I said he was behind the flag. It was my attempt at humor to lighten up this situation," he continued. "We don't usually see Leonard except in extreme situations."

"Why don't y'all introduce yourselves? Leonard, I know you already know Melodye Matherne, girl reporter, sort of like Lois Lane, only prettier." He smiled a smarmy smile. His attempts at humor had failed miserably. No one laughed, or even cracked a smile.

Xan handed a business card to Mr. Babin. My brother and I did likewise.

"I am duly impressed," Leonard Babin finally said. "Heavy hitters," he said. *"Very heavy hitters."*

"He looks like Zeppo," I whispered to my brother. Robb let out a bellow that completely destroyed the somber mood of the occasion. The others looked to us for enlightenment.

"Excuse me," Robb said, still sporting a wide grin. "My brother just told me an inappropriate joke."

In all of my life, I had never known him to lose his cool in a professional situation.

The others looked perplexed. "Please continue, Mr. Babin," he said. "I was thinking exactly the same thing," Robb whispered to me, still smiling.

Besides Bermuda, one of the places we visited on a regular basis to escape American racism was Mexico. We rented a great stone and glass mansion behind high stone walls in the Lomas Virreyes section of Mexico City, near Chapultepec Park. Lomas Virreyes was one of the oldest, wealthiest, and most elegant neighborhoods in the country. The President lives there in a lovely estate called *La Casa Rosada* (The Pink House).

When I was maybe twelve years old, my parents decided to hire chauffeurs to drive us from Mexico City to Acapulco in two limousines. Six rowdy children, two adults, and a chauffeur in one car would have taxed the nerves of a saint, especially on the narrow, winding mountain roads.

On the way, we visited the very beautiful towns of Cuernavaca and Taxco. Along the way, between the two towns, vendors standing along the highway held up hand-made textiles, handicrafts, and food, among other things. We stopped for a rest in a little settlement somewhere near Taxco. I have never known the name of it.

While my parents were looking at some silver objects and beautiful hand-crafted blouses for various relatives, I met a tawny-skinned boy who appeared to be around thirteen or fourteen years old. He had a beautiful smile and coal-black bangs that kept falling down over his dark, penetrating eyes. He was wearing the typical peasant's dress: a flimsy, woven cotton shirt and pants set that looked to me like pajamas, and wide leather huaraches with tire treads for soles.

The boy, named Miguel, beckoned to me from around the corner of an old adobe house.

When I arrived at the spot where he was standing, he raised his shirt, exposing a brown hairless chest, two darker brown nipples, the beginnings of a "love trail" of silky black hair that started just above his belly button and ended at the heavy cord sash that held up his gauzy pants; and a baby iguana no more than a week old.

I felt my first pangs of lust, looking at the boy's golden brown torso, and my first pangs of love looking at the tiny iguana baby.

The boy spoke no English but I spoke fluent Spanish. He took my hand and rubbed it on his chest from navel to nipples and back down. He then raised my tee shirt and rubbed his hand on my chest, from navel to nipples. It was obvious he had never seen a black person before but that he liked what he saw. So did I.

He then gently touched my face, beginning at the jaw line down toward my chin and back upward. Last, he touched my hair, gently at first and then, when he realized that it would not cut or prick him, with more enthusiasm.

"Que padre pelo tienes!" he whispered. "What cool hair you have!"

I believe I would have had my first kiss right then and there but my sister, Mariana, saw me standing there, back to the group, talking to the boy and wanted to find out what was going on. She ran over to where we stood enjoying the smoothness of each other's skin. His excitement was obvious beneath his flimsy pants, as was mine under my Levis.

The boy removed his hand from my chin and straightened up, all business again. He then took the baby iguana and placed him in my hand and said, *"Cincuenta pesos."* Fifty pesos, about four dollars. He held up his ten fingers and opened and closed them five times, as if I did not speak Spanish.

I was no rookie to Mexico. I knew the art of haggling and offered him twenty-five pesos. *"Veinticinco,"* I said. Miguel held firm at fifty pesos until my parents called and I started to walk away.

"Treina y cinco pesos," he said with finality. Thirty-five pesos were a little under three dollars. The game was over. I paid him with a fifty peso bill, smiled, waved to him, and walked away, taking the baby lizard away in my arms. Miguel went to get change and to find a box to house the tiny reptile.

He returned with a handful of money for change and a box large enough to accommodate a growing reptile. I waved off the change and held his hand one last time. I would have loved to have kissed those soft, sensuous lips but dared not. He smiled and shook my hand, holding it longer than customary. "Amigos," he said.

"Amigos," I repeated.

Mariana, to whom I was closest, and I hid the little lizard among the tons of baggage in the limo in which we rode. My dad, our chaperone, was none the wiser until we arrived at our villa in Acapulco.

I named the baby lizard Zeppo after one of the Marx brothers.

Leonard Babin's attempt at a smile and his unblinking golden-green eyes that appeared to rotate separately at times, looked exactly like little Zeppo's.

"We have obviously made an egregious error and we would like to rectify it immediately," Babin said, reviewing the business cards we had handed him. "We have already notified the jail that they are to ready Mr. Coleman for release and that they are then to have a deputy escort him here to be with his legal counsel. He should be here in less than twenty minutes."

Melodye scribbled furiously. I had pressed the *"RECORD"* button of my tape recorder before I set foot in the office.

"I just want it known for the record," Authement said, "that the Skylarville Police Department had nothing to do with Mr. Coleman's arrest or detention. Mr. Coleman is a resident of Lafourche Parish and he was at his home in Thibodaux when he was arrested by Thibodaux police on a warrant issued by the Bellefleur Parish Sheriff's Office. Mr. Coleman was extradited to Skylarville and has been detained in the Bellefleur Parish Jail since then. You got that, Melodye?" he said.

Melodye Matherne nodded her head as she finished writing.

"Y'all mind sittin' outside while we wait for Mr. Coleman?" Authement said. All of us, including Andy, filed out of his office and into the officers' break room while Leonard Babin, Chief Authement, and Sheriff St. Amant remained in Chief Authement's office.

Melodye used one of the telephones on one of the empty desks to call in her story. While she was busy, I approached Andy, who stood apart, leaning against another desk, looking out onto the building's parking lot.

"You okay?" I asked.

Andy nodded. "I'm fine," he said. "My ears are still ringing. You should've heard the cursing and name-calling in there," he smiled. "I'm just tryin' to get it all out of my head. They're scared to death!"

I leaned next to him and put my arm around his shoulder. "As soon as Artie gets here and we've had time to interview him—or whatever—maybe we should get some lunch. Zapody's?"

Andy nodded again. Xan came over to where we stood. "You guys make a great looking couple," he said, just as Melodye finished her phone call. She looked up to find my arm around Andy's shoulder and had overheard Xan's comment. She blanched and walked stiffly away without saying anything to anyone.

"You going after her?" I asked Andy. He stood there, contemplating whether he should or should not.

"I'll go with you," I finally said.

Melodye stood smoking a long filtered cigarette under an awning that sheltered the building's rear entrance from both the boiling sun and Louisiana's frequent rainstorms. She faced the parking lot, seemingly in her own little world.

"Is there anything you want to know, Melodye?" I asked when she turned her head upon hearing that someone had followed her out. She then turned back toward the parking lot and the street beyond, ignoring my question. She continued smoking but said nothing for a long time. "No," she finally said, rather curtly. "I guess there's nothing more to be said.

"I should've known something was wrong when I practically threw myself at you and you completely ignored me," she said to Andy. She sounded hurt and a little embarrassed.

"Melodye, ma chèrie," Andy said softly, "Most people would've gotten the hint then."

Melodye's head jerked forward apparently involuntarily. She looked at both of us for the first time. "Some people can take a hint! Not me, though! I guess I just have to be hit over the head with a club to get the idea that I'm not wanted."

She turned to me. "Congratulations. You must've had a real good laugh when you saw my desk blotter. You just waltz in here, Mr. Mallory, and the poor little country boy just swoons and submits but I've been trying to get him up to my bed for at least two years and not a goddamned thing!"

I took the first part of the statement first. "First of all, Ms. Matherne, I met Andy thirteen years ago.

"Second, No. I didn't laugh when I saw your blotter. At first I was angry that you had the audacity to want to take *my* lover away from me but then I realized that that wasn't going to happen so I felt sadness that you'd suffer when you found out that Andy's wired differently from straight males.

"I wondered if you'd be angry when you realized that I had 'waltzed in' and taken the object of your affection. I guess you are, aren't you? But because of that different wiring, there's not a whole lot you could've have achieved, even if he had tried," I continued, "so let's be friends, okay?"

She looked at me as if I had slapped her then she began to walk away, across the parking lot, headed toward her office, when a tall, lanky young man with a large Afro loped into the parking lot and directly to her. An ancient double-lensed Rolleiflex hung around his neck by a dirty plastic camera strap.

He was a handsome young man with dark brown skin, a wide face, a faint mustache, and a healthy smile. He appeared to be just barely out of his teens. He wore bell-bottom blue jeans and a navy blue tee shirt that said *Nicholls State University* on the front and *"Comeaux"* across the yoke in white iron-on letters.

He ran immediately up to Melodye and noticed her reddened eyes.

"You've been crying. What's the matter?" he said rather sympathetically, just as a shiny new black Ford Crown Victoria, roared into the lot, narrowly missing the news couple.

She wiped her eyes with a Kleenex she pulled from her bag and once again, Melodye Matherne, news reporter, was all business, telling the young man how to photograph, what to photograph, from which angle he should photograph, and whom to photograph. He bore it all with remarkable aplomb.

Artie Coleman recognized us immediately and opened the sedan's rear door before the car had fully stopped. The car screeched to a halt, leaving skid marks on the cement.

"Hey, 'Wayne,'" he shouted as the two plainclothes detectives who accompanied him attempted to rein him in. He was almost delirious with the joy of freedom and the exercise of power that had been performed on his behalf.

"Unhand me, Nigga!" he demanded as the younger of the two detectives, a burly blond football player type with dimples and a crew cut, grabbed Artie's left bicep to prevent his escape. The young lawman released the arm as if it were a bag of hot coals.

Artie's new pair of blue jeans and white cowboy shirt with blue stitching and faux pearl buttons still bore their original store creases. His tan pointy-toed shoes were unscuffed and the Kevlar vest that he wore all but swallowed his entire body from neck to knees.

Andy explained that the vest was the customary protocol when transporting prisoners.

"When they came to lock me up, I was already in bed. They brought me here wearin' my drawers and a tee shirt," Artie said, explaining the new duds. "They didn' wanna release me like that so they went over to K-Mart an' bought me all these duds. Not bad, huh?" he said to me, posing and turning around for me like a model on a catwalk.

He held me in a long embrace. "If there's ever anything...*anything* you need and you think I can help, jus' call me, Bruh! I'm at your service! That goes for your parents an' grandma, too. I'm at the service of the whole Mallory family 'cuz I know I'll never be able to pay y'all back any other way," he whispered.

"Don't worry about it, Artie." I'm just glad you're not going to be railroaded for something you didn't do," I responded.

I introduced him to Andy and Melodye. The photographer snapped away. Since I had not been introduced to him, I did not make the introduction. Artie gave me a big hug, smiled and gave his hand to Melodye and the photographer but refused to shake Andy's hand when offered.

The two detectives who had accompanied Artie shook my hand then Melodye's and told Andy that they were instructed to deliver Artie to Sheriff St. Amant, who was waiting for him in Chief Authement's office.

We marched into the building. Andy led the way, followed by the older detective, Artie, the younger detective, Melodye, the photographer, and me. Along the way, we were joined by Xan and Robbie.

Someone had redecorated the area beyond the officers' break room into a makeshift conference room. The desks had been placed along the sides of the room and the chairs had been placed in a "T" formation in the center of the room.

Three high-backed padded chairs with desks in front of them had been placed along the crossbar of the "T". Chairs with no desks were along the stem of the "T."

Authement, Babin, and St. Amant were in Authement's office when we arrived, so Xan, Robbie, and Artie took the desks in the crossbar. Andy snickered, knowing, as we did, that they had not been the intended triumvirate.

Andy went to the closed office door, knocked, and announced that Artie had arrived. When they filed out of the office, they were surprised to find that Xan, Artie, and Robbie were already seated at the desks they had intended for themselves.

"Gentlemen and Ms. Matherne," Xan said, "this is Mr. Arthur Lee Coleman, the young man whom Sheriff St. Amant denied was even detained at the Bellefleur Parish Jail.

"It was a clerical error," Leonard Babin interrupted.

"And who are these two?" I asked, pointing to the two detectives.

"They are Detective Kerry Poncelet," he said, pointing to the younger of the two, "and Detective Captain Philip Pousson." Each man nodded his head when introduced.

Artie seethed. He rose and walked back and forth from one side of the room to the other, his small but powerful chest heaving. His eyes were storm clouds. *"Whatever it was,"* he said, *"it's gonna cost y'all muh' fuckers! It's gonna cost y'all plenty!"*

"Be reasonable, Mr. Coleman," Leonard Babin said, as if placating a small but very angry child. "It was an error. You made certain statements that might be construed as threats against the life of Deputy Eck. When he was shot, it was only natural that we would seek you out."

"Y'all wanted to pin that murder on me!" he almost shouted. *Y'all wanted me to fry for som'pn I didn't do. Worst of all, y'all didn't care who really did it just as long as y'all had somebody to pin it on, and who better to pin it on than me?*

"Well, muh' fuckers, it's payback time! I'm not only gonna sue Bellefleur Parish, but I'm gonna sue y'all personally! An' trust me," he continued, a pot about to boil over, *"I want it all! I want y'all's houses an' cars an' clothes, right down to y'all's dirty, stinky drawers! Everything right down to the toilet paper an' the pictures on y'all's walls."*

"Gentlemen," Xan said when Artie had put a lid on his own pot, "the paperwork will be filed tomorrow."

"Mr. Coleman," Authement said calmly. "I assure you. The Skylarville Police Department had nothing to do with your arrest."

"Tell it to the judge!" Artie replied as he slammed the door behind him.

***

I treated Artie to lunch at Zapody's. Andy had paperwork to catch up on and Melodye refused, stating she had to finish her story for tomorrow's edition. After lunch, I chauffeured Artie to Rosie Coleman's house in Avoca.

I turned off La. Hwy. One into Mrs. Coleman's driveway and recognized the silver Rolls Royce Silver Shadow saloon car that was my grandmother's and parked next to it. Her driver sat reading a paperback novel in air-conditioned comfort while he waited for my grandmother to return.

Artie and I got out of the Rover and noticed that the larger, wooden house was now unoccupied. It appeared that Mrs. Coleman had acted upon my suggestion and that it worked. We circled around the house to the trailer behind it.

There, among the trees and flowers, I found my grandmother offering suggestions to Mrs. Coleman as to what plants and flowers she could still grow. Grandma was down on her knees testing the soil. The fine, dark earth stuck to her fingers and knees as she began to rise. I rushed to her side, offering her my arm. "On the ground again, Grandma?" I teased as I eased the elderly woman into a standing position.

She took my hand. "I want you to know that I'm perfectly capable of standing up on my own, Wayne," she smiled, "but being that you're such a gentleman, I'll allow you to help me."

She turned toward Artie. "My, my, Arthur," she smiled, "you certainly haven't grown, have you? Come, give me a hug!"

Artie smiled and came forth as Grandma brushed off her hands. "I wanna thank you for gettin' that lawyer for me?" he said, almost shyly.

"Don't mention it. I knew no grandson of Rosie's could do what they said you did. Seems like you're going to be coming into some money soon, once the lawsuits are over. I don't see how you can lose."

Rosie Coleman interjected. "This is still Louisiana, you know, Miz Victoria. Things that seem simple everywhere else have a tendency to get complicated here. Why don't we go inside? You can wash your hands and we can get outta this heat." The temperature was around ninety-eight degrees and the air was like cotton candy. There was at least ninety percent humidity.

We filed into Mrs. Coleman's trailer. Artie helped my grandmother up the steps. I helped Mrs. Coleman.

"I already told Wayne but I wanted you to know that I'm grateful for all you did for me. If I get som'pn outta this, I'll give it to you for the lawyer's fees," Artie said.

"You don't owe me a thing, Arthur," Grandma said, heading for the kitchen sink where Mrs. Coleman had already washed and dried her hands with a paper towel and stood holding a clean one for Grandma. The rest of us took seats in the trailer's living room where Miz Rosie had indicated.

"Didn't Wayne tell you that Alexander's law firm has decided to take the case pro bono?" Grandma asked. "Anything you get from this is yours."

"Ah, what's pro bono, Miz Victoria?" Artie asked meekly.

Grandma smiled. "Basically, it means free. The actual term is 'pro bono publico,' which actually means 'for the public good,' but it's been shortened to just 'pro bono.' They don't even try to imply that it's for the *public* good anymore," she smiled.

"Every large law firm that I've ever heard of takes a small percentage of its cases for free. Good public relations and all that rot," she harrumphed. "I'm sure there's a substantial tax write-off involved, too."

"I had planned to pay the attorneys for their services but they believe that this would be a good pro bono case. I'm sure they saw the public relations value of it, since it could possibly become a high profile case that would showcase their firm."

"Xan didn't tell me anything about it being a pro bono case," I said when I could finally get my words in.

"I'm sure he didn't see any reason to tell you," Grandma said. "After all, you weren't involved in the financial end of this situation, were you?

"Robbie told me, earlier today and asked me how I felt about it," she continued. "I told him that it was fine with me, just as long as they didn't let these folks down. I still expect the highest level of legal representation. Robbie feels that they'll get it so I have no problem with *not* paying."

Changing the subject, I remarked about the vacating of the old front house and the repair work that was due to begin soon. Mrs. Coleman went into her bedroom and returned with a set of blueprints and a list of proposed renovations. "When it's finished," she said, "I'm movin' into the big house, myse'f."

I needed to go over some of the information Miz Rosie had provided when she turned off my tape recorder during the first interview. I asked her if she wanted to do this now and she agreed. This time, she did not object to the little machine. She spoke candidly about what she knew and provided me with the names and phone numbers of the Catash maids.

"Jus' remember, Wayne," she said sternly, "that a dog that brings a bone also takes one. It's not a one-way street. One of 'em might jus' tell her boss that you been askin' questions of a personal nature. Things could get pretty sticky, so you watch your back."

"Wayne, you're here on vacation. Why don't you just enjoy it with your friend Andy and let the authorities find the killer?"

"Grandma, there's a killer out there running around loose," I responded. "The last time they 'found the killer,' it was Artie. Who's to say they won't pin this on some other hapless black man?

"Whoever it was, that man did us all a favor. It's like trying to find the man who shot down George Wallace. Let it go, Son."

"Grandma, that man may have done us a favor but I'll be willing to bet he didn't do it on for our benefit. There's a good reason why somebody wanted Eck dead and I aim to find out who and why. I *can't* let it go."

"Well, before you go knocking on peoples' doors, be sure to take Andy with you. He's the one with the gun and the badge." She smiled but she was very serious.

Grandma knew that I would not just let it go. I hadn't begun this quest because of Artie Coleman and I wouldn't let go of it because Artie was cleared of any charges. That was an aside.

"Don't worry, Grandma, I'll take Andy whenever possible but he has to work days and that's when I have plenty of time. By the time he gets off, a whole day is lost.

Grandma left half an hour later. Mrs. Coleman, Artie, and I walked her to her car, where her driver helped her in and closed the door behind her. Backing the limousine onto the busy highway was not an easy feat. Traffic stopped in both directions to allow the big car entry onto the roadway. People in Louisiana had a healthy respect for wealth.

Mrs. Coleman and I completed our interview a little before 5. Andy would be getting off work soon. I would be able to make the drive from Avoca to Skylarville, roughly fifteen miles, in less than fifteen minutes.

Andy had showered and changed into civvies by the time I arrived. He had heard me drive up and met me at the door with a beer and a kiss.

When we were settled in, Andy told me that the coroner had finally released Eck's body for burial. Now, the only problem was finding relatives who would take charge of it and make funeral arrangements. So far, no relatives had come forth but the Sheriff's Office was still checking the Poinsett, Mississippi area for any next-of-kin willing to take charge. Andy surmised that Eck's employee benefits package would bring someone out.

Rev. Charles Hinkle had already come forth and said that he and his congregation, to which Eck belonged, would be happy to give Eck "the kind of funeral he deserves."

"If he got what I think he deserves," Andy said, "they'd throw his ass on the back of a garbage truck and let them take him down to where they dump the rest of the trash. *That's* what he deserves."

I told Andy I planned to visit Senator Catash the following day.

"Why don't you wait til after Eck's funeral?" Andy suggested, "I'll go with you. The funeral's tomorrow morning but even though he was with the Sheriff's Office, not the SPD, Chief Authement has ordered all of us, even the black officers, to attend in our dress uniforms. This is the first time a law enforcement officer on active duty has been killed in Bellefleur Parish."

I agreed to wait for Andy.

***

Just after I walked into my bedroom suite, the phone rang. I picked up, thinking it was Andy but to my surprise, a female voice responded when I said "hello" in my sexiest voice.

"Who is this?" I wanted to know. "How'd you get this phone number?"

"This is Candy," she responded, as if I were a personal friend.

"I don't know any Candy." I responded, miffed.

"My real name is Candice Faucheaux," she said. "You left a message for me to call you a few days ago. I was out of town so I didn't get the message 'til now." Her voice was as sweet as treacle.

"I wanted to talk to you about Artie Coleman but he's already been released from jail so I guess there's nothing I need to discuss with you at this point, Miz Faucheaux. Thanks anyway, though."

"I know he's out of jail," she said. "He's sittin' right here beside me. I have some information that you may be able to use," she said, now more business-like. "We think this might be important. Can I meet you sometime tomorrow? We need to talk."

I could go while Andy was at the funeral."

***

A small hand-lettered sign told visitors to use the side door of Candice Faucheaux's small house in Houma. It was sided in green aluminum made to resemble tree bark.

I followed the sign to the carport where a new Japanese sedan sat with its windows rolled up except for a half-inch crack near the top. Her house was a double shotgun, twice the size of O'Neal Foster's house, and only about four blocks away, on Bergeron St.

Candice Faucheaux answered the door on the second knock. Miz Faucheaux was gorgeous. She was just under six feet tall, with honey-colored skin and the greenest gold-flecked eyes I had ever seen. They were almond-shaped, giving her eyes a slightly feline quality.

Her African-textured hair, like her complexion and eyes, was auburn with both honey-blond and chestnut highlights. She wore it casually pulled away from her face in a ponytail that hung to the middle of her back, tied with a thin black satin ribbon. The black knit blouse and black leotard she wore looked as if she were ready to go to a ballet rehearsal.

Her wide mouth with the pouty lower lip that reminded me of Andy's, was fixed in a wide, dimpled smile. She had a split between her two upper incisors.

Her body was that of a dancer, lithe and athletic, with feline grace and perky breasts the size of medium-sized coconuts.

I knew exactly why Artie Coleman had ignored all of his grandmother's warnings to stay away from her. She looked like she could lead a man down the road to perdition with no speed bumps or road signs to slow his descent.

"Are you Candice Faucheaux? I asked when she opened the door. She nodded and invited me in. "Call me Candy," she said, closing the door. Her voice was like rich, tupelo honey. "God, you're a beautiful man," she said. She did have a way with words, I thought, smiling.

I entered the small kitchen that was about the same size as Rosie Coleman's. Gray marbleized Formica with blue trim covered the kitchen table at which

Artie Coleman sat wearing a trim pair of jeans and a ribbed "wife-beater" undershirt that would have been too small for me even when I was twelve.

Artie rose when he saw me. "How you doin,' bruh?" he smiled. He shook my hand, then embraced me in a hearty bear hug.

"Come on in," he said. He beckoned me to follow him into the living room. Candy followed me carrying a tray with two cold Dixie beers, two frosted beer mugs, a tall glass of lemonade filled with ice cubes, and a long straw.

We towered over Artie like two adults over a small child but in this place, Artie was definitely the Alpha wolf.

We entered the modest living room via a narrow hallway that passed the open door of a tiny bedroom painted pink and accented with sheer pink curtains. Behind them, a black-out shade was pulled down to the top of a window air conditioning unit that hummed quietly and cooled the area efficiently.

A large black and white teddy bear with a red satin bow around its neck and a large brown-skinned doll dressed in a pink ruffled dress sat on the pink satin bedspread.

The living room, however, was painted baby blue with white trim and navy blue curtains, and white leather furniture. Blood-red throw pillows provided the accent color.

A large-screen Zenith console television set, a shiny metal étagère, a gas space heater under one of the room's two windows, a three-tier bookcase, and the requisite window air conditioner that spewed its cool air into the room, were the only other furnishings.

"Remember when you came to the jail an' I told you I had some more shit to tell you?" Artie said to me. I nodded. "Well, now I can tell you. I wasn' *about* to say this while I was still locked up. The guards sometimes listen in on the prisoners' and visitors' conversations."

"That's what I was afraid of," I replied.

I pulled out my tape recorder, placed it on the coffee table in front of him, and turned it on.

"Well," Artie said hesitantly, "This is really embarrassing. I wouldn't tell this to nobody else but you an' you gotta promise me that if you use it, you won't use my name. My baby here knows 'bout it but nobody else. *Nobody!*"

He hesitated a full four minutes before mustering the courage to utter the words. I turned off the recorder. It was recording nothing. "Whenever you're ready, Artie, let me know and I can start the tape again," I said, as a way of reassuring him that whatever he was about to disclose, I would not judge him. I rewound the tape from the beginning and waited.

"Tell 'im, babe," Candy urged, nudging him in the ribs.

"Ready?" I asked, clicking the recorder on.

"I met Eck once before the fight that sent him to the hospital," he said timidly. "I was about fifteen or sixteen years old. Just got my license."

"He stopped me when I was on my way into Skylarville. He brought me to his nasty-ass apartment… to have sex with me."

I tried to remain as neutral as possible lest I interrupt his disclosure but I had to direct this conversation. "Wait," I finally said. "There must've been something that occurred between being stopped for a traffic infraction and ending up at his apartment."

Artie nodded. "He pulled a gun on me an' made me…go down…on him! The nasty bastard didn't even wash!"

"Tell 'im the rest, babe," Candy said. "Tell 'im what you did!"

Artie hesitated. His back was hunched over and he avoided my eyes.

"Artie," I said, "you were the victim. You have nothing to be ashamed of. That dead bastard is the one who should've been ashamed."

"If you don't tell 'im, I will," Candy said. "It's really kind'a funny! Go on, babe! Tell 'im!"

"I threw up on him," Artie finally said in a torrent of words. Once the disclosure was out, Artie straightened up and smiled. He looked, for all the world, like a pre-teenage boy. "I ain't never tol' this to nobody but my baby, here. Not even my Gramm.' *Especially* not my Gramm. You sho' you can keep my name out'a any news stories?" he wanted to know.

I nodded. "No problem. I can always use a pseudonym. Tell me what happened. Try to do it in order."

"You know the first thing he said when he got out'a his car?"

I shook my head. I couldn't imagine.

"He smiled and said, *'new meat!'* I didn't know what the hell he was talkin' about but it didn't take me long to find out.

"He was parked in the shell parking lot on the levee side of the Shemida Temple Church. You know where I'm talking 'bout?" I nodded, picturing the white clapboard building that was a poor man's reproduction of the Taj Mahal on one side of the highway and its parking lot across the road.

"My Gramm always told me not to argue with cops but I knew I didn't have a tail light out so I got out'a my car to see. It was an old hooptie but it ran pretty good. It had jus' passed inspection so I knew he was lyin.'

"Jus' as I got to the back of the car where he was standin,' he took the butt of his service revolver an' smashed my tail light. The right one. Then he said, 'See, I told 'ya!' in that cracker accent of his! He took my driver's license and then he cuffed me an' put me in the back of his squad car. The back windows were tinted so nobody could see in.

"Instead of getting' in the front to drive me to jail like he said, he got in back with me and started rubbin' his hands on my legs an' thighs, then he unbuttoned my shirt an' started rubbin' my chest.

"He said he liked 'smooth' boys like me. He also said he could make it go away if I 'cooperated' with 'im. He uncuffed me then he took out his dick an' told me to suck it. I told him no. He asked me two or three more times an' when I refused, he *re-cuffed* my hands to a metal bar behind the front seat. I told him 'cooperate how?'

"He then put his hand on my crotch, playin' with my zipper. He said, 'you know what I mean, *boy*, don't act innocent with me!'

"Then he asked me if I'd ever been to jail before. I shook my head. I started shakin' all over, I was so nervous!

"He picked up on my nervousness an' said, 'Yeah, they're jus' *waitin'* on a pretty li'l boy like you. You know what they do to firs' timers?'

"I said no. He said, first, the jailer would give me a full body cavity search. 'He puts on some rubber gloves an' sticks his finger up your butthole to make sure you're not carryin' drugs up there, an' then, they take this long metal rod an' stick it into your dick to make sure you don't have no venereal diseases.' I cringed at the thought of anything goin' up either place but if I had'ta take one, it would be the finger up the butt! I was almost in tears jus' *thinkin'* about a long steel rod goin' up my dick." He looked over to Candy, grimacing.

When he recovered from the thought, he continued. "Then he said, 'I have a better idea. I'm gonna hav'ta take you to jail but I'll do the examination myself. That way, you won't hav'ta have that steel rod up your pecker.

"He unzipped my pants an' pulled out my dick. Then he said I was 'gifted' for such a 'li'l mouse.' He kept playin' with it but I didn't get hard 'cuz I was so nervous.

"He got down on the floor wackin' off with one hand an' playing with my wang with the other. When that didn't work, he told me to lay back. He put his hot mouth on me an' I heaved right on his head an' back!

"He got really pissed an' slapped me across the face hard, calling me every name in the book. Then he said now, he'd hav'ta go home an' change his uniform and I was gonna hav'ta go with him! He was covered with puke. It was in his hair an' under the back of his collar an' down his back. He jumped out'a the car, took off his shirt, wiped hisself down as best he could, then he hopped in the front seat, an' took off with lights an' siren on!"

Candy offered me a brownie that she had just baked. I think she did it more to lighten the mood and break the tension. Although it had occurred a long time ago, it was very hard on Artie, remembering that incident.

I had spied the brownies on their kitchen table when I entered the house. I love brownies and although my brain said I shouldn't accept one, my tongue betrayed me. My head nodded, my mouth said yes, and my hand was out and reaching for the napkin even before she offered it.

"I love brownies," I said, as a way of mitigating my uncouth behavior. She also offered me a tall glass of milk to accompany it, which I gratefully accepted. When all of us had been served and the plate stacked high with the brown demons, Artie continued his saga.

"To make a long story short, he took me to his apartment, washed off the vomit, he uncuffed me then he pushed me down on the bed, grabbed a big jar of Vaseline, pulled my pants and drawers off, greased up my ass with a big glob of grease, then he laid on top of me an' did it to me, gruntin' and snortin' like a big ol' water buffalo. He was a big ol' sweaty white boy who smelled like vomit an' BO. He nearly crushed me when he got on top of me, he was so big. That muffucker must'a weighed two hundred pounds. I weighed a hunnert an' ten.

"When he finished, he took a dirty towel and wiped my ass. He tol' me if I ever told anybody what he'd done, he'd hunt me down an' kill me. Then he let me loose. He wouldn' even take me back to the church parking lot. I hadta walk back to where he'd left my car.

"I bled for days an' I couldn't sit down without pain or use the bathroom for a few days after that.

"I didn' know what to do or where to go for help. I couldn't go to the cops! I felt dirty, used, an' embarrassed. I jus' hoped he didn't have no diseases.

"I couldn' sleep. I lost my appetite, an' I didn't have nobody I could talk to. I put gauze in my drawers to sop up the blood an' I put Vaseline on my butthole to ease the pain. Finally, I healed up an' the pain went away. It took about two weeks, though."

When he had finished his story, he added. "You promised me that you wouldn't use my name. That still goes, right?"

I nodded, my eyes too full of tears to verbally respond. When I had a sip of milk to wash down the brownie, and could talk again, I said, "You don't have to worry, Artie. I gave you my word that I won't use your name and I won't."

"He tried to arrest me again a few years later," he smiled, showing his gold incisor. "I told you 'bout the *first* time just now, when I was just a kid but I was ready for 'im that second time. I'd grown up since then. I wasn't scared of him no more."

"A buddy of mine would be interested in hearing this," I said, not mentioning Andy by name. "Would you mind if I played this tape for him?"

"Who you wanna play it for?" Artie wanted to know, now wary.

"My mate, Andy," I said.

Artie and Candy looked at each other for a long time but said nothing. Finally, Artie said, "you *gay*?"

"In England, a *mate* is a good buddy, as they say here. You'd think that by now, since it's been almost fifteen years since I last lived in England, that those expressions wouldn't just slip out every now and then but they do."

"*Riiight,*" Artie said, comforted. "I'd forgot that y'all talk funny. I never did find out what a *kipper* is."

"It's a herring. A fish. But, for the record, I *am* gay," I said.

Artie stopped for a minute. *"For real?"* he inquired. "You don't look like it and you *sho'* don't act like it. If you hadn't said nothin,' I never would'a known. But that's cool, too. After all you did for me; I don't care if you wanted to fuck donkeys!"

I had turned off the tape and was about to store it in my bag, when Artie said, "Do y'all know anything about Eck's runnin' for sheriff? I don't mean you. You jus' got here, but I heard that he was plannin' to run for sheriff of Bellefleur Parish."

"Who'd you hear that from?" I wanted to know.

"I heard it directly from him. He *tol'* he was gon' run for sheriff?"

"In fact, he said it twice when he was tryin' to arrest me that second time, when I kicked his ass. He said he was tired of niggers runnin' the parish. I still don't know what he meant by that.

"He seemed pretty sure he was gon' win the next election. He always was an arrogant som' bitch but he was worse lately."

"You saw him after that second time he arrested you?" I asked.

Artie nodded. "I tried to stay out'a Bellefleur Parish as much as possible but that ain't always possible. When I did see him, though, he left me alone for the most part. He knew what I'd do to him but one day, when I was comin' out'a the library in Skylarville, not even his jurisdiction, he was passin' by in his patrol car an' pulled over. All I could say was *'aww, shit! Here we go again!'*

"He beckoned me over to the car. He was in there playin' with hisself an' said, 'You remember my friend, here?' I ignored him. Then he said, 'Yours was the best piece of ass I ever had. When I'm sheriff, you'd better stay your skinny black ass out'a Bellefleur Parish 'cuz there won't be nothin' in the world that's gonna keep me off'a you!'

"I thought he was gon' try to arrest me again on some trumped up charge like he did the last two times but he didn't. I asked him if he was expectin' to kick St. Amant out'a the job an' he said, 'yeah. I got *som'pn* on *somebody* in Bellefleur Parish that's gon' knock the sheriff right out of Office. An' then, I'm gonna pay you back for what you did to me! You made me a laughin' stock an' I got a long, long memory. I'm gonna get you, *my pretty*!" Then he floored it.

"Did he say what he had and who he had it on?" I inquired.

"No," he said, "but whatever it is, it mus' be pretty damaging. I don't really think it's on the sheriff himself, but on whoever pulls the sheriff's strings, but they always say that when the mighty fall, all of those beneath 'em fall with them."

Candy stood, giving her long, taffy-colored legs a stretch. I switched off the recorder a second time. "Want another brownie and something to drink, Wayne?" she said. I nodded and indicated a Pepsi would be fine this time. "Baby?" she said, directing herself to Artie, who had stretched his matchsticks out in front of him and rested them on the coffee table.

"Beer for me," he said, every inch the cock of this rock. "Miller if we got any left. If not, whatever's there."

"We think that whatever he had on whoever he had it on got him killed." Artie said.

"It seems that *somebody* thought that Eck was gettin' a little too big for his britches but from what I understand, there's people in Bellefleur Parish who wanted Eck to be the new sheriff but the people who put St. Amant in office wanted *him* to stay there."

"I thought that was the purpose of elections: to decide who would hold office," I said.

"You know that politics are dirty, Wayne," Artie continued. "And Louisiana politics are dirtier than most. The world and the country worry about California and New York politics but nobody cares what goes here as long as they keep the niggers in their place.

"The Catashes run ever'thing 'round here. If somebody was even *thinkin'* of runnin' Eck, they'd hav'ta go through Senator Catash before they even tried sump'n like that and it's not too likely that he was gonna approve Eck for the job. Eck didn' have two cents to rub together. He was po' as a church mouse and he was from Mis'sippi.

"St. Amant is born and bred Cajun. I don' know how good he speaks French but he surely speaks an' understands more than Eck ever did. I can't see Catash ever even *thinkin'* about goin' with an outsider over a native. It's sort of like being Pope. They're always I-talian 'cause them I-talians stick together. Been that way for centuries."

He's probably right, I thought. "But what if they were planning to run Eck for sheriff *without* going through Catash?"

"Now that would be interesting," Artie said, pondering my assumption, stroking his three chin hairs. "That could get Eck killed fo' sho'."

"If that's the case, though, I wouldn't be a bit surprised if the other side started taking shots at someone behind Catash—or St. Amant himself," Candy said, rejoining the conversation and distributing the drinks and more brownies from a large round platter.

I have covered street gang wars in Chicago for many years. One side does something to piss off the other and in the end; there are a lot of bodies on ice in the morgue.

"Still," she continued, "I can't see anyone taking shots at St. Amant."

"Then who else is there?" Artie wanted to know.

"He would be the most likely victim if they want to retaliate but I just can't see that happening," she said. "That badge accounts for something!"

This time, it was Artie who had to concede. "Me neither," he said. "It's gon' be interesting."

"If my theory is correct, that would explain it," I said, "but they could've murdered Eck for any number of other reasons. Maybe someone didn't like that he recently stopped that march against him and made all of those people get on the ground with their heads down and their asses in the air. Some of them are old."

"That was an all-black march and the shooter was white," Candy reminded us.

"I'm just pointing out that it could've been for any of a hundred reasons, including the strip searches he subjected people to," I said.

Artie thought for a minute. "I try to tell things in order so forgive me," he said, "but there's somp'n I haven't told nobody before." He lowered his voice and held his head down in shame. "Even my baby here don' know 'bout what I'm 'bout to say." He paused a long time before continuing.

"I...had more 'encounters' with Eck than I tol' y'all about."

I waited but Candy urged him on. "So?" she said.

"That was befo' I kicked his ass that final time." He was now on a roll so I let him talk. "Eck liked me. When he put his lips on my...thing, I got hard. I might be small in size but I'm real big...down there!

"When I didn't come to Skylarville no more than I absolutely had'ta, Eck started comin' to my house lookin' for me. He'd have a warrant for my arrest.

"A fake one he'd made up hisself, then he'd flash it in front 'a my Gram' an' tell her that I was wanted for questioning, that if things went well, he'd bring me back home. If not, she could hire a lawyer to get me out'a jail.

"Then he'd cuff me, put me in the back of his unit an' take me somewhere where he could do what he wanted with me.

"Once or twice, he took me to an office in the Belle Fleur Professional Building." I closed my eyes a minute, trying to picture where he was talking about.

"I can't picture it," I finally said.

"It's right next door to Belle Fleur National Bank, squeezed in between the bank and Kaplan's Department Store."

My face lit up when I finally remembered the narrow steel and glass building to which he referred.

I now remembered it well. It was an innocuous modular glass, steel and brick number that was, as he said, squeezed in between the Arthur Kaplan Building and the bank. They fronted the side of the Bellefleur Parish Jail and the Bellefleur Parish Sheriff's Office. There were five or six floors in the building.

Kaplan's was a three-story, high-end department store that had come to the area in the early 60's. It, the bank building, and the professional building had been built around the same time and looked enough alike that most people believed that they were one. It can be assumed that the same architect designed all three.

"I don't remember what office it was, but I think it was a lawyer's office and I believe it was on the third floor."

"About how long ago was it, Artie?" I asked.

"Maybe eight or nine years ago."

"Why'd he take you there?" I wanted to know.

"He was scared somebody'd see the patrol car parked on some side road or street an' see what he was doin' to me. He said he knew the guy whose office it was, where nobody would bother us.

"He took me there, undressed me, laid me down on the couch in the waitin' room then he did whatever he wanted to do to me. Usually, he'd jus' blow me so I'd jus' close my eyes an…"

"Think of England," I said, finishing the statement for him.

"Huh?" he said, frowning. He missed my joke. "I don't know nothing about England. Never been out'a the state of Louisiana. I jus' let him do his thing. I thought of some woman doin' it to me, not some big ol' nasty redneck."

I explained that the statement about closing one's eyes and thinking of England was a well-known expression among British women, whose husbands could care less if they enjoyed the sexual connection they were forced into. He and Candy nodded their heads, not really understanding the significance of the statement but too polite to admit it.

"This went on a few times but then I moved out'a Assumption Parish and Eck didn' know where I went. He couldn't find me until that day when I kicked his ass an' he kicked mine.

"Eck was a horny bastard. He said the person whose office it was, was going to make him rich, was going to make him sheriff, and was going to make himself rich in the bargain.

"He said there was a lot of changes coming for Bellefleur Parish and that they were coming with the next election. He was really sure of that."

"Anything more specific?" I asked.

"I know that whatever evidence they had—or thought they had---on whoever they had it on, was in that office," he said, shaking his head.

I had no knowledge of which tenants were there but since they were across the street from the jail, the courthouse, and the sheriff's office, I imagined that most of the tenants would be lawyers. Andy would know for sure and if

I had time, I'd drive by there tomorrow to see which names came up on the roster in the lobby.

"OK, guys, I need your complete silence about something because if you breathe a word to anybody about this, it could get someone I love very much, fired, killed, or possibly both. Do I have your word?"

"Yeah," said Candy, "Sure."

"Brother, do you even have to ask me?" Artie said. "Your grandma just offered to pay beaucoup bucks to get a high-priced New York lawyer to get my po' black ass outta jail. If it wasn't for her, I'd still be sittin up there. You *know* you can count on me."

"Artie," I said, "Remember when they brought you in from the sheriff's office to the police station?"

Artie nodded.

"Remember I introduced you to the dark officer with the curly hair?"

Artie nodded again. "That ol' boy with the violet eyes?"

I nodded. "You wouldn't shake his hand."

"Yeah, I remember. I was mad at anybody who even *looked* like a cop."

"His name is Andy Bourgeois. He's a real good friend of mine. He's my lover, in fact. He worked as hard to get you out of jail as the rest of us did, but he did it from behind the scene, if you know what I mean.

"Andy's the SPD's information officer. He has the same position with SPD as Eck had with the BPSO. He fed me information that cleared you."

Artie broke out into a huge smile, revealing the golden incisor. "Any friend of yours is a friend of mine," he said. He then got up and stepped across Candy, extending his hand in friendship. I rose to shake his hand. He gave me a bear-hug and a soul handshake, touching our entwined hands to his heart.

"I never thought that ol' Cajun boy would wanna help me," he said.

"He's a really good guy," I said, showing no sign of my true love for Andy. "I need to bring him in on this. I'll let him hear the tape and then I'll probably need to bring him together with Candy and you."

"That's fine with me," Artie said, still smiling.

"Fine with me, too," Candy agreed. "Maybe y'all could come over for supper."

I had stuffed myself on brownies and Candy invited me to stay for supper. I declined, saying that I still had a lot of things to do and people to see. "Another time," I assured her.

I looked at my watch. It was now 4:30, the height of Houma's rush hour. Although the city is small, it is divided right down the middle by the Industrial Canal and there was no way to go from the east side of the canal where O'Neal and Candy lived, to the west side of town without having to cross the canal. To make matters worse, there were only two ways to cross it: over it via two draw bridges, or under it via the Houma Tunnel.

One would think that, with the heavy boat and barge traffic on the canal or Bayou Terrebonne, which intersects with the canal at Main Street, the tunnel would be the way to go, but traffic into the tunnel backs up sometimes for miles because of the large number of oilfield-related industries in town, all of which let their workers off about the same time.

I opted for one of the bridges, hoping that I could get across without having to wait for water traffic. The Bridge Fairy was in a good mood because the Main Street Bridge was down and I was able to cross.

Just after I crossed over, the warning lights began to flash and the gate lowered, cutting off traffic for what could be as long as 30 minutes. "Thank you, Bridge Fairy," I said sincerely. "I owe you one!"

Traffic out of Houma, toward Skylarville would still be slow but at least it wouldn't stop except for the myriad of stoplights between the canal and Houma's shopping mall on the outskirts of town. After that, I could reach speeds above a snail's pace.

***

I arrived at *Creswic House* at five and immediately called Andy. It seemed like months since I had heard his voice and; even longer since I had had a chance to kiss those lips.

"Will you have dinner with me tonight?" Andy asked before I could invite him to the same.

"I'd be delighted," I said. "I have a lot to tell you," I continued, referring to my conversation with Artie and Candy. We agreed to meet at six but instead of meeting either at his house or *Creswic House*, I suggested a new Brazilian restaurant in downtown New Canaan.

"I've never had Brazilian food," Andy said hesitantly. "You think I'd like it?"

"I guarantee it."

"I'll pick you up at *Creswic House*," he said, "and we can go from there. "Should I wear a jacket and tie?" he wanted to know.

"This is Louisiana, a substation of hell," I laughed. "It's too hot to wear that stuff." In all fairness, there are three fine dining restaurants in The Reserve, one French, one Chinese, and one Mexican, that mandated coat and tie, regardless of the weather but they kept their air-conditioning at a temperatures low enough that diners welcomed the extra layer or two, even on the hottest summer evenings.

Andy arrived a little after 6:30. I met him at the door with a big hug and a kiss.

"You make my heart skip a beat," Andy said when our lips finally parted.

"And you, mine," I said, leading him up the stairs to the second floor. When we got to my bedroom suite, he handed me a small present wrapped in white gift-wrapping paper with a silver ribbon and a small silver bow.

"What's this?" I said, perplexed.

"Open it and find out," he said with a sly grin.

I restrained my enthusiasm as I tried not to tear off the paper and ribbons but, instead, gently unwrap it.

Inside, nestled in gauzy white tissue, was a flat oblong box covered in maroon velvet. The name of Goldstein's, Skylarville's more expensive jewelry store was stenciled in fancy gold lettering on the cream-colored satin that lined the roof of the box's interior.

Judging by the size and shape of the box, my first thought was a watch or a pen and pencil set but when I opened it, I found a gold keychain with three keys.

The keychain, with its Florentine finish, had the initials "SWM & AFB" engraved in a smooth heart-shaped design in subtle bas-relief. Attached to the keychain were two regular-sized silver-toned keys and smaller one made of gold.

"What's this?" I asked, now completely perplexed.

"The two big keys are the keys to my house and car," Andy answered, "and the gold one is the key to my heart. It's been locked up for so long and you're the only one to open it."

"I can accept key to your heart but not the others," I said, kissing him yet again. I started to unclip the two silver-toned keys from the ring and return them to him. Before I could do so, Andy squeezed my fingers. "What's mine is yours," he said, his lavender eyes sincere and slightly moist.

I desisted. "But I don't have a gift for you," I said.

"Yes you do," he said, unbuttoning my shirt. He put his ear to my chest and, through my undershirt. "Yes, you do, if you're giving me your heart."

"It's yours," I replied. "Since the day we met."

The sun had not yet set but citronella candles on every table and on tiki torches at six foot intervals protected us from mosquitoes and other biting insects that would've made dining al fresco impossible.

Andy thought he could help with the list of tenants for the bank building. He thought that Artie would have to be a little more accurate because although there were not a lot of tenants in the building, there were four per floor and all of them were lawyers doing business in and around the Belleterre Parish Courthouse.

While we ate, Andy made another pronouncement. "I've decided to tell my family about us," he said calmly.

"That's wonderful!" I said. "After agonizing over it for so long, you just decided that you're going to tell your family that you're in love with another man?" When are you going to make the announcement?"

"I don't know exactly when but I was thinkin' bout doin' it Sunday if you're not busy that day. I figure that we could drive out to Belle Glade Sunday afternoon and tell 'em then."

"You're remarkably calm," I noted. "Have you been smoking some of that home-grown?"

"No," he said, shaking his head. "And to tell you the truth, I haven't even wanted any since we solidified our relationship."

"Me either. Tell me more," I said.

"There's really not a lot to tell," Andy said. "I love you and I want my family to know about it. Those who don't like the idea or can't handle it can deal with it any way they want.

"I really admire Teri an' Claire," he continued. "They did it and I figure that if they had the balls to stand up to the world and declare their love for each other, what kind of man would I be if I couldn't do the same?"

"That's a good way to look at it," I observed. "Are you going to tell Paul and Kevin first or are you going to tell everybody at the same time?"

"They've been my best friends since we were born. I think they deserve to know a little before the rest of the family," he said.

"I think they have a pretty good idea already. I'll just be happy that we don't have to play that stupid 'Game' of yours anymore." I reached over and kissed him lightly on the lips. He looked around to see who had observed the kiss. Since more than half the tables on the terrace were occupied, many of the diners had observed it. No one said anything.

Andy blushed. "I've never done anything like that in public," he said.

"Look around you," I said. "No one here is eating alone. At some tables, married couples are enjoying a night out. At others, courting or engaged couples are doing the same. And there are at least two tables where the diners are two males. Might they be gay like us or maybe they're just old friends who happen to like Brazilian food?

"Who knows?" I answered my own question, "and who cares?" The whole purpose of The Reserve is to give minorities a chance to be themselves. Not just blacks but all minorities, including sexual minorities.

"Really?" Andy said, incredulous.

I nodded.

"It didn't start out that way but it is now. Nobody's gonna say anything if we kiss in public?"

"Would you say anything if you saw a straight couple kissing?" I asked. As if on cue, the female half of a young couple near the door shrieked and stood up to give the male half of the couple a great big kiss. She held her hand before her, admiring a large diamond ring. The other couples on the terrace began to applaud their new beginning.

"Champagne for everybody!" the young man half announced in a loud voice.

"Do you know them?" Andy said.

"I shook my head. At one time, I knew everyone in The Reserve but it had grown so much and so rapidly that I no longer had that luxury.

Waiters, who had obviously been forewarned, immediately began passing out glasses of champagne to all of the tables. Chateau Lafitte-Rothschild from one of the better years was the young man's choice. When all of the tables had been served, the young man stood and said, "Ladies and gentlemen, tonight, this lovely lady has consented to become my wife. I'd like to drink a toast with all present plus some special guests..." With that segue, two older couples entered the terrace through one of the sets of French doors and joined the newly engaged couple, kissing, hugging, and congratulating them.

"Obviously the parents," Andy said.

Although the engaged couple was only a few years younger than us, neither they nor their parents were familiar to me. I was becoming a stranger in my own land.

We drank toast after toast until we decided to leave.

"That couple gave me an idea about how to tell my parents about us," Andy said when we were in the Firebird.

"You want to share it?"

Andy smiled and nodded. "That was done with such class," he said. "We could do the same thing. You think your parents are available next Sunday night about this time?"

"I can ask," was the only thing I could say. I didn't know how hard it would be, or what it would take to get my parents to drive to Belle Glade with me but I had a week to try to convince them that it was safe.

***

"Kevin?" I inquired.

"Yeah," a sleepy voice responded.

"This is Wayne. I need a favor.

"Anything. What's going on?" he wanted to know.

"I need you to go with me on a mission. Can I pick you up in about an hour? You sound like I woke you up."

"That's okay. I was 'bout to wake up anyway. What's goin' on?"

"I'll tell you when I see you. An hour? We can have breakfast together. I need to talk to you about something rather important. Between just us, okay?"

"OK. Nothin' bad, is it?"

"No, not at all. See you in about an hour. Where's Paul?" I asked. "I haven't seen him for a few days."

"He's offshore. He won't be back for fourteen days." I vaguely remembered somewhere that Paul had said he worked on an oil drilling platform and he worked fourteen days onshore and fourteen days off.

"Oh," I said, disappointed. "I wanted to talk to both of you, since you're Andy's best friends.

"It's som'pn bad, ain't it?" Kevin said, now worried.

"I assure you it's not," I replied. "In fact, it's quite the opposite. I'll see you in an hour."

I hung up the phone, showered, and dressed. Half an hour later, I was on the road to Skylarville.

I parked my new Land Rover in Andy's driveway and used the door key he had given me to enter his house.

Wallace was on guard until he recognized my scent. He accompanied me to Andy's bedroom. I opened the top drawer of his bureau, and took out his jewelry box in which he kept one of his more valued possessions, his Marine Corps ring. He seldom wore it but Andy has not gained an inch of excess poundage so I had no reason to believe that it wouldn't fit him now. Nevertheless, I kept my fingers crossed.

I slipped the ring into my pocket, returned things to exactly as I had found them, let Wallace outside to relieve himself, gave him a Milk Bone, and locked up the house.

Kevin was waiting for me beside the Rover in Andy's driveway. "Another new car," he said.

"I got tired of using my parent's vehicles," I said, "so I bought my own. I'll probably leave it down here when I return to Chicago."

"Must be nice," he smiled. He looked around. "T-Beau's not home, is he?"

"No. He gave me a set of keys and told me to use the place as my own. I had to get something."

"He gave *you* a set of keys?" Kevin inquired, incredulous. "In all the years we've lived next door to each other, he has *never, ever* given me a set of keys to his house. An' I'm his *cousin!*

"What's going on?" he continued. "T-Beau is really private sometimes an' for him to give you a set of keys to his house…

"And his car," I smiled, dangling the set of keys and key ring before me.

"An' his car?? That's his baby!! He won't even let me drive it." His eyes were wide in disbelief.

I nodded. "Hop in," I said. "I'll tell you about it over breakfast."

We smoked a joint before we arrived at The Reserve's gates some twenty minutes later and entered New Canaan via C'est Vrai Road. I pointed out *Creswic House* behind its high brick walls, across Bayou St. Eloi and turned south on Kingstown Road, into the village of Kingstown.

At the intersection of Kingstown Road and Thomy Lafon Blvd., I turned east for a block and parked the Rover in a neat, tree-shaded parking lot that ran almost the entire block, behind the businesses.

"We're here," I said. "Come on."

"Who's Thomy Lafon?" Kevin wanted to know.

"He was a free man of color during the 19th Century. He was one of America's first black philanthropists and probably America's first black millionaire. At one time, his name was a household word but now, he's largely forgotten. I'm very glad that my parents chose to name one of The Reserve's major thoroughfares after him. There's a statue of him on the corner.

On the other corner is a statue of Henriette Delisle, the founder of the first Catholic Order of black nuns in the United States, the Sisters of the Holy Family. They run St. Scholastica Academy. It's all-girls. St. Martin de Porres

High School is for boys. The Society of the Divine Word, an order of Catholic priests and brothers runs St. Martin's.

Kevin marveled at the streetscape: wide, tree-lined sidewalks, outdoor cafes, small businesses with discrete hand-made signs over their entrances, flowers, flowers, flowers everywhere, and the well-dressed people who appeared to be on their way to work. "I've never been here before. "It's beautiful," he said.

We went to THE LARGE LADY PANCAKE, WAFFLE HOUSE & CREPERIE, my favorite breakfast place since I was a kid. It was eight-thirty and the place was full. We were greeted by a smiling young woman who took my first name and told me there would be a short wait.

The huge waiting room was separated into six small, intimate vignettes designed to resemble a high-end living or family rooms.

The motif in each was *chiaroscuro*: black backgrounds with white or silver accents or the reverse. Twelve fluted Corinthian columns supported the tin ceiling painted silver, and divided the room into its six vignettes. Silver, white, or gray appointments completed the overall picture.

All of the artwork, whether painted, photographed, or sculpted, followed the light and dark theme. Scattered about on bookshelves or tabletops were black and white photographs in silver frames.

A highly-polished concert grand piano stood at the far end of the room, near a huge marble fireplace with a white marble surround.

We took seats in high-backed Queen Anne chairs made of black faux alligator hide studded with nickel nail heads. The wing chairs were separated by a black lacquer side table bearing black and white 5x7 photograph of a happy little Maltese dog in a silver frame and a tall silver-toned reading lamp.

We faced a tufted camelback sofa upholstered in heavy damask the color of old pewter. The area rug on which the whole vignette rested was a battleship gray cut pile with black and white free-form patterns. Beneath the area rug and throughout the room, black marble tiles reflected upward like obsidian mirrors.

Each area vignette sported its own variation of the chiaroscuro theme. Some customers waited in groupings of four leather club chairs facing one another and separated into pairs by a glass-topped leather travel trunk that served as a coffee table on a faux zebra-skin rug.

Others chatted across glass and chrome coffee tables while seated on plush sofas upholstered in black velvet.

Kevin marveled at the walnut-paneled walls, the tin ceiling, the carefully-tended plants, and the quality stained glass chandeliers that hung from silver chains far above.

"It can't be!! That *can't* be Wayne Mallory you've got sitting in my waiting area waiting for a table," bellowed The Large Lady himself, Julian Batiste, owner of the restaurant.

"Oh no, no, *no*!!" he told the young hostess as he bustled down the aisle of the main dining room from the kitchen. "No, you didn't…I just *know* you did *not* put Wayne Mallory, my favorite customer, in the waiting area and told him to sit and wait for a table.

"Girrrrl," he boomed to the hostess, "if you weren't my adopted daughter, I'd fire you for this…this…*sacrilege!"* he smiled. "Wayne is Reserve royalty! Would you put Prince Charles or Princess Anne in the waiting area?"

The girl shook her head no. "I didn't know," she said almost inaudibly.

Mr. Julian was a big ebony-colored man with a big, booming voice that matched everything else about him. He was dressed in a pink shirt with a pink apron, pink pants, pink soft-sole shoes, and a high pink toque.

He called himself The Large Lady, not after the palms that peeked over diner's shoulders from hidden corners throughout the restaurant, but because years ago, he had been a female impersonator--a very large female impersonator--called *Mae B. Moore, The Large Lady.* I am told that he did a fan dance that would make even Gypsy Rose Lee blush.

He had a beautiful singing voice and sang everything from grand opera to standards and torch songs. Before that, he had played defensive lineman on Grambling College's football team.

When his career in show business ended, he worked as a professional boxer, a stevedore, a roustabout, and as a general laborer, shoveling coke into the furnaces in a steel mill in Harvey, Illinois.

I was told he called himself *Mae B. Moore* because when he did his infamous ostrich fan dance, called *FANdangle*, or his *Dance of the **Six** Veils*, he always promised his audience that one day, there "may be more."

It was not until his final performance—one show only—that he revealed all. There was no more to show and the career of *Mae B. Moore* ended there but the *Large Lady* lived on in the name of his restaurant.

He turned to the other customers in the waiting area and addressed them: "I'm sorry folks but this is Wayne Mallory, the youngest son of the founders of La Belle Terre Reserve so, if I treat him a little bit differently, please forgive me but I've known this one since he was an infant. I changed his diapers, if y'all can believe that. I guess you could say I'm his fairy godmother." He smiled, fluttered his eyelids, curtsied, and looked demure.

"His parents befriended me when I was still a mere *demoiselle* of 19. Later, they loaned me the money to go to culinary school and then loaned me the money on top of what I already owed them for school, to open this business. They welcomed me into not only to The Reserve, but into their beautiful home when nobody else would even be seen talking to a big sissy like me.

"So if I put him and his handsome young friend ahead of you-all, *please* forgive me but if it wasn't for this man's parents, there would be no La Belle Terre Reserve, no New Canaan, no Kingstown, no New Berne, no jobs; no *nothing*. So again, I beg you-all to forgive me for being deferential.

"*But* so that there are no hard feelings, Mama don't like to have hard feelings, breakfast is on the house for everybody in the waiting area. How's that sound?"

People smiled and nodded assent. A few applauded their approval but no one left or appeared to resent the arrangement. I knew many of them as a child and they shook my hand and reintroduced themselves to me. They had not recognized me as an adult and, since most of them were adults when I was a child, I did not recognize them now as senior citizens.

Mr. Julian counted the eight people ahead of us and said, "Rhonda, give me their bills when they finish. Order anything you-all want, OK?" He smiled an engaging smile, took my hand, and led me into the main dining room while beckoning Kevin to follow.

He was a large man. Built like an ox but every inch a lady. He stood around six feet, six inches tall and weighed around three hundred pounds, sixty percent of which was solid muscle and forty percent was padding from too many pancakes, waffles, and crepes. He still moved like a boxer despite all attempts not to.

Mr. Julian had a huge bald head that looked like a giant *Raisinette*, and he now wore granny glasses to accommodate his failing eyesight. I had no idea of how old he was but I imagined him to be somewhere near my parents' ages. He was already an adult when I was still a child.

I introduced him to Kevin after he had seated us on a Juliet balcony a few steps above the main floor of the restaurant. He wanted to know all about my life in Chicago and begged me to return to The Reserve. "You belong here," he said. "Not in Chicago."

I gave him my condolences over the death of his longtime partner, Mr. Charlie, with whom he had operated the restaurant since the early 1960's.

"Mr. Charlie" was Charles Crochet, a local boy who was neither too proud nor too prejudiced to work for blacks. When he heard that a new pancake house had opened up in The Reserve and needed staff, he was one of the first to apply for a job. He started off as a busboy but later became Mr. Julian's lover and partner. For many years, he was the only white person living full-time in The Reserve.

The Large Lady Pancake, Waffle House & Creperie was a breakfast restaurant.

It opened at five-thirty each morning seven days a week and closed precisely at noon, when the Reserve's carillon played Schubert's "*Ave Maria*" and St. Martin de Porres Catholic Church's bells rang out for Catholics to pray the *Angelus*.

After the restaurant closed for the day and clean-up finished, Mr. Julian and Mr. Charlie would take their daily walk around their neighborhood with their "children," at least four, and as many as six, fluffy, white, Maltese dogs, all of whom were immaculately groomed and wearing his or her own color-coordinated outfit that consisted of collar, leash, and either sweater or raincoat during inclement weather.

Mr. Julian and Mr. Charlie built a beautiful pink and white Italianate Victorian style house dripping with charm and gingerbread, in the Dumbarton Woods section of Pleasant Valley and were the stars of their neighborhood.

Since Mr. Charlie's untimely death due to lung cancer, Mr. Julian said he now only had two Maltese left. As each grew old and died, he did not replace it. What a shame! The Reserve was richer for the presence of Messrs. Charlie and Julian and their yappy little "children."

After he had returned to the kitchen saying, "Wayne, don't forget, breakfast is on me," I explained to Kevin why Andy had given me the keys to both his house and car.

I also explained why I had gone into Andy's house and what I had removed. I asked his help in returning the ring and in accompanying me to the goldsmith's shop a few doors down.

"That's cool," Kevin said when I was finished talking. "I always pictured gay people to be more like Mr. Julian," he said. "I never would'a guessed that you were gay. I pretty-much knew 'bout T-Beau, though," he continued. "Not by anything he did or how he acted, but when you live with somebody, you jus' know.

"Does that mean that you're gon' be movin' down here or is T-Beau gon' be movin' to Chicago?"

"We still haven't worked that out," I replied. "I left here for just the reason why we're sitting here, getting the royal treatment while some of those other people are still waiting to be seated."

"It's not always fun to be the center of attention, especially if you're 'different,' as I was, growing up. At that time, the Reserve was a whole lot smaller. There was our house, my grandparents' house, and then later, my uncle and aunt's house across the lake. The only other buildings were the main building of the medical center and I knew everybody and everybody knew me. We got everything we wanted from our parents but in return, we had to be little saints. We were *The Romper Room Do-Bees."*

"I remember *Romper Room*," Kevin chimed in. "I remember the teacher, Miz Caroline, and that the good kids were the Do-Bees and the bad kids were the *Don't-Bees*. I used'ta wanna be a *Don't-Bee*," he smiled. "T-Beau and Goo wanted to be the *Do-Bees*."

I ruffled his hair. "It figures that you'd want to be the *Don't-Bee*," I said. Although I didn't know him well, I truly liked Kevin. "How would you feel if all eyes were trained on you from the time you got up in the morning until the time you went to bed?"

"Belle Glade ain't that much different," he said. "All small towns are like that."

"Maybe so but it was more intense here because wherever we went, there was somebody watching us. Waiting to see what we wore, what we did, or what we didn't do. There was always somebody there to say, 'I know your parents' or 'I know your parents wouldn't want you to do that,' or 'I'm gonna tell your parents.'

"Then there were those who wanted to use us to get closer to our parents. They were the worst.

"I didn't want to live like that. I knew I was gay. My parents knew I was gay and that my sister, Mariana was a lesbian. They had no problem with it and they didn't care who knew it. But it just seemed to me that The Reserve was strangling me. I didn't mind being home on vacation but the thought of staying here full-time was not at all appealing to me. I wanted the bright lights of Paris, Chicago, L.A., London, or New York.

"New Orleans was just beginning to desegregate when I left here. There were gay bars but we, I mean blacks, were welcome in some bars and right across the street, we weren't allowed to enter.

"I was an American citizen yet I was treated better outside the country than right here in my own state. That was the reason why The Reserve was built in the first place, as a haven for the Mallory kids first of all, and then, for other black professionals who didn't want to have to move north to get equality."

Kevin nodded his head. "But things have changed since then."

I agreed. "Things have changed a whole lot. That's why I'm considering moving back here. It's not like I can't leave whenever I want to visit the bright lights of other cities and New Orleans isn't like it used to be, either.

"I'll tell you one thing," Kevin said. "If you decide not to move back to Louisiana, whether you live in The Reserve or outside of it, T-Beau'll follow you but he won't be happy anywhere but right here in good-old south Louisiana. You need to consider him, too, in whatever decision you make.

"It's sort of like being pregnant and eatin' for two. Now, you're making decisions for two."

Our food arrived, served by one of the most gorgeous chocolate waitresses I've ever laid eyes on.

I told Kevin my idea about the abandoned house in which Andy had grown up. "I'd like to buy it, move it to The Reserve, rehab it, and move into it." I said. "I'll show you my lot and where I want to put it."

After a huge breakfast with everything Mr. Julian could stuff into us, we waddled down the street to the goldsmith, Ivan Johnson, who insisted that Kevin was right for me.

"But I'm not gay," Kevin protested.

***

TWO DAYS LATER

"You don't seem to be at all surprised that I'm gay," Andy said to Kevin as we sat in his cozy kitchen.

"Dude," Kevin replied. "I've known you were gay since we were little-little. We're like brothers. We've eaten together, slept together, smoked dope together, an' done just about everything else together. 'bout the only thing we haven't done together is date chicks. Think about it.

"When Goo and I discovered girls back in seventh grade, you distanced yourself from us. That's when you first started talkin' bout wantin' to be a priest. Remember? You started prayin' a lot an' goin' to Mass every day."

Andy smiled and nodded. "I thought maybe I could pray the gay away. I made novenas an' all kinds of promises to God that if he would change me, I would give my life to him as a priest or religious brother."

"That made no sense," Kevin said in devastating honesty as he went to the stove and ladled out a third plate of rabbit sauce piquant for himself. "What difference would it make to be straight if you wasn't gon' be usin' it no way? You might as well have jus' become a gay priest and saved yourself all that prayin'."

Andy smiled a wide smile. "That makes sense now but it didn't when I was thirteen. All I knew is that I was different in the worst way an' I didn't wanna be gay."

"Nobody wants to be gay," I said. "Society has told us that being gay is one of the worst possible things there is. I did almost the same thing.

"We're Anglican High Church," I said. "Church of England. Episcopalian in America," I said when I saw their faces. "High Church is just like being Catholic except for the whole Pope thing. The queen of England is the head of the church instead of the Pope.

"Anyway, I had decided to convert to Catholicism and go to Lourdes on one of my school vacations to be cured."

"Did you go?" Kevin wanted to know.

I shook my head. "I don't know why but I never did. I did go to Rome to the Vatican, though, and I talked to a really wise priest there. He told me that God doesn't make mistakes. God loves me just as I am so if the only reason I was converting was to be cured of homosexuality, I would be better off staying Anglican.

"Sounds like what Brother Anselm told me 'bout becoming a priest or brother," Andy said.

SKIN DEEP

329

"So what happened?" Kevin wanted to know.

"About what?" I inquired.

"'Bout bein' cured of gayness," he said.

I looked at Kevin in exasperation. "I'm still gay, aren't I? That priest was right. God made me the way he wanted me to be. God doesn't make mistakes. After that, I was at peace with being gay. It didn't bother me anymore. Anyone who didn't like it could go fuck themselves. I told my family and that was that. That was about the time I met Andy, I guess." I said.

"It was a little harder with me," Andy said, knowing that his cousin knew all along that he was struggling with his sexuality. "A *lot* harder! I knew that God didn't make mistakes and he made me the way he wanted me to be but I felt so alone. Who was I going to talk to about what I was feeling? You?" he said, turning to Kevin. "You and Goo were too busy chasin' girls and playing football to pay attention to me.

"I mean, I was part of the group but separated from y'all at the same time whereas before, we shared everything. So to me, the easiest way was to say that I was gonna be a priest then nobody expected me to be out chasin' girls."

Kevin washed and I dried the dishes while Andy rolled joints from his stash. When we finished the dishes, we joined Andy in the living room.

"You gon' give it to him now?" Kevin whispered to me. I nodded.

Andy had rolled over a dozen perfectly-sized joints and lined them up on his rolling tray.

I then handed him the package. I was wrapped in white iridescent paper with gold ribbon and bow.

He smiled and looked quite surprised as he carefully opened the package and found two gold wedding bands inside. They were elegant in their simplicity. I picked up the larger one and put it on the third finger of his left hand. It fit perfectly.

I knelt on one knee. "André François Xavier Bourgeois, I love you and I am asking you to spend the rest of your life with me as my spouse. Will you marry me?"

Andy smiled. "Is this for real?"

"As real as it gets and as sincere as I can be. Will you marry me?" I replied.

"You really mean it?" he asked, incredulous.

"Answer the man," Kevin said impatiently.

"Of course I'll marry you," Andy finally said. He smiled. "I was planning to ask *you* to marry *me,*" he said, "but you beat me to it."

"You knew 'bout this?" he said, turning to Kevin, who stood behind me holding Wallace.

Kevin nodded, smiling a big smile. "I even went with him to the goldsmith to have it made. I helped him decide on what kind of ring you'd like."

"How'd you know my ring size?" he asked, hugging me.

Kevin beamed. "He called me last week and asked me if I knew your ring size. I didn't but I knew how to find out. I tol' him 'bout your jewelry box... He 'borrowed'...your Marine Corps ring so he could get a size then I put it back before you even missed it." He sounded like a child who had successfully pulled off a daring Fathers Day surprise.

"If you don't like this style, the jeweler said we can change it, or if it doesn't fit, he can size it," I added.

"I like this one and it fits perfectly," he said. He took the second ring from the box and placed it on the third finger of my left hand and kissed me hard. Through the corner of my eye, I saw Kevin look away, not in disgust, for he was smiling, but seemingly to give us the privacy he felt we deserved.

"Shouldn't there be some kind of ceremony?" Kevin wanted to know.

"That's what I was thinking," I said. "If we're going to do this, why don't we have a ceremony?"

"I'm out of the closet," Andy said, "but not *that* out! What kind of ceremony are y'all talkin' about?"

"A wedding! What else?" I replied.

Andy blanched. "That could cost me my job," he said. "This has gotta stay between us an' our families."

"Nonc Jean's gon' shit when he finds out about this," Kevin said, now sobered. "An' wait til Goo finds out that G.I. Joe an' Ken are gettin' married!"

He stood to leave. "I've gotta work tomorrow," he said, looking at his watch. Andy offered him some of the joints he had rolled. Kevin took them and put them in a tooled leather pouch he sometimes wore at the end of a metal chain on his belt. He gave me a bear hug and one to his cousin. "I'm really glad you found this dude," he said.

"Ah," he said, poking his head back through the half-closed door, "Can I be your best man?"

"I'll think about it," Andy smiled.

***

When we were alone, Andy said, "Kev took it better than I thought. I wonder how Paul's gonna take it."

"You worry for nothing," I replied. "They love you and they just want you to be happy. If I'm the one who makes you happy, so be it."

We then reviewed the tape I had made at Candice Faucheaux's home. I had also picked up a copy of *The Sentinel* and called Melodye the following day around noon. I knew her deadline and tried to respect it. Still, I wanted to reach her before she took off for lunch. She answered on the first ring.

"Melodye, this is Wayne," I said. "Are you off deadline yet?"

"No," she said unenthusiastically, "I'm free. What can I do for you?"

"I read the paper. That was a dynamite story," I said. "And thanks for giving me first billing on the by-line."

"You did all the work," she said. "It was only fair."

"That's not the end of it," I said. "There's more. Are we still working together or should I work this alone?"

"Of course we're still working together. I'm a professional," she sighed. "I try to keep my private and professional lives separate."

I remembered her blotter. "Good," I finally said.

She then told me that she would be covering RC Eck's funeral for the newspaper this coming Saturday. With her coloring, there should be no problems. She felt that if she were darker, there would probably be some objection, if not from the family, which still had not come forward, then from Rev. Charles Hinkle, the pastor of Rock of Ages Free Will Church.

Most of *The Sentinel's* readers only knew Melodye through her by-line; few had reason to consider the fact that, despite outward appearances, she may not be white. She, after all, was the first person of African ancestry that *The Sentinel* had ever hired for its news staff and the paper's management wanted only to fill a quota.

There were, of course, darker skinned black people working in the press room but none in the newsroom until Melodye had been hired. She blended in perfectly.

During the rest of Wednesday, as there was nothing in particular to do, I spent the day beside the swimming pool basking in the sun with the dogs.

This is what I had planned to do with my entire vacation. Instead, I had happened onto the murder of RC Eck and fallen in love. This would be one vacation I would look back upon and tell my grandchildren about.

At 6:30, Andy arrived. We had dinner and played pool in the billiards room. We played six games. Andy won the first three in a row and I won the last three. "Pool shark," he laughed. "You suckered me into thinking that I was better than you at pool and then you put the hurt on me. I'm glad we didn't wager anything," he smiled.

"I wouldn't take your money," I said. During the games, we discussed the possibility of his meeting with Artie and Candy. I also wanted Melodye to meet them, though not necessarily at the same time that Andy met them.

I realized that my vacation was getting short and that I had done nothing but work since I arrived in Louisiana.

The following morning, I called my editor and requested an additional two week's extension of my vacation, since I was getting married and would be on my honeymoon.

Keith Carlson, my editor, was well aware of my status as swinging gay Man About Town. He was surprised to hear that I was giving up my bachelorhood and planning to settle down. He could see little value in my Louisiana story for *The Chicago News Register* but recommended that I contact some of the national magazines I sometimes wrote for.

My next call was to the airline. I cancelled the reservation for the following week. I would talk to my parents to see if I could finagle a ride back to Chicago on their private jet.

I then called Andy. I told him what I had done. He was delighted that I was staying longer than I had originally planned. This took the pressure off him as to whether he should go with me or stay in Louisiana.

In the meantime, he had gotten a tenant's list of the bank building's upper floors and he gave me the names of the tenants on each floor.

***

When I called Artie, I went floor by floor naming each tenant with him but none seemed even vaguely familiar. I then told them I wanted to introduce Melodye to them as soon as possible.

I wondered whether the tenant whose office Artie had visited had moved out of the building but then thought better of it. This was prime office space for lawyers. It was near enough to the courthouse the sheriff's office, and the jail that they could walk to all of them. It is highly unlikely that the tenant would move out once they had gotten the opportunity to move in.

Artie had made two interesting and helpful observations about the office he had visited. "It overlooked St. Philip Street," he said, "and it was higher than the jail. I used to look down out of the window and I could see the prisoners in their orange jumpsuits," he said.

The first observation was of little help because all of the offices in the front of the professional building overlooked St. Philip Street and the jail. In fact, the address of the building was 416 St. Philip St.

Artie's second observation, however, narrowed down the possibilities considerably. The professional building has six stories. The building that housed the jail and the sheriff's office has three. That would mean that he had been taken to the fourth floor of the professional building or higher up. If we could get Artie into the building to look out of the windows, maybe he could pinpoint the exact office. That, however, would be no easy feat.

***

La Belle Terre Reserve's residents are keenly aware of their vaunted positions in the world and many have been actively involved in "giving back" to the community (either the local community or the one from which they had sprung).

Many have long been engaged in philanthropic endeavors throughout the South. At home, we have been active in providing the facilities that the parish governments either *could* not, or more likely, *would* not, provide for its most needy citizens.

In additional to recreational facilities, like the local public swimming pools in Houma, Skylarville, Thibodaux, and Napoleonville, we formed the local housing and education councils for those families who had moved away from the many sugar cane plantations in the area or who had come in from the local swamps. Many of these people, mostly older folk, spoke little or no English.

Although there were a few black "planter" families in the quad-parish area, most black planters actually did the work of planting, worked the land but did not own it.

My parents and grandparents on both sides, as well as my grandmother's family, the Vernonburgs, had founded MVM Corporation (Mallory-Vernonburg-McGrath), an umbrella agency that provided housing, employment, and vocational-technical training for the underprivileged.

MVM's services were open to all low-income people regardless of race. Its vocational-technical school provided practical training that eventually allowed former sharecroppers and swampers to own their own homes. Children who showed aptitude were given scholarships to exclusive schools in the Reserve, throughout the United States, and abroad.

Through its employment program, it provided cleaning services for the public buildings within The Reserve as well as in the nearby cities and towns, including Skylarville.

The Belle Fleur Professional Building just happened to be one of the buildings serviced by MVM's daughter company, Truly Kleen Janitorial Services.

Truly Kleen was staffed mainly by developmentally disabled individuals who wanted to earn their own way in the world.

Truly Kleen was the solution to how to get Artie into the professional building's upper floors after hours: he, Candy, and I would enter the building with the office cleaners.

All I had to do now was find out who was running Truly Kleen and inform that person of my plan.

Danny told me that Mrs. Mattie Davidson, a large, elegant woman whom I had known since childhood, was the head of Truly Kleen. I called her and told her my plan. She had no opposition to the idea except that we not disturb anything in the offices. This was not anything I could guarantee but I gave her my word that I would take along my Polaroid, take pictures of anything before touching it, and that anything we touched or disturbed would be placed back in its original position.

"You know how it is," she said confidentially. "The office workers look for things to accuse the cleaning staff of taking or breaking. They sometimes deliberately leave money or candy on their desks to see if the staff will pick it up but they've been drilled in how not to yield to temptation.

"I'm proud to say that to date, my staff has passed every test the office workers have devised for them."

She explained that she did not actually accompany the workers to the sites. That was done by site supervisors and their assistants. She would notify Patricia Williams, the site supervisor for the Belle Fleur Professional Building, that we would be part of her crew whenever I needed to be there.

I told her we would like to do this as soon as I could contact Candy and Artie and that I would call her when we were ready to go.

***

Not wanting a repeat of the incident with Kevin at The Large Lady Pancake, Waffle House & Creperie, where we were given preferential treatment in seating because I was a Mallory, I decided to take Andy to dinner in Skylarville instead of in The Reserve.

I drove toward Andy's home after telling him that I had something special planned for dinner. I wanted to do something special for him in light of our recent engagement. On this occasion, I said, he could dress to the nines.

The Plantation Room was a large brick building that had originally been a combination meat market, meat processing plant, and meat storage facility. It was in a commercial strip along St. Patrick Highway, only a few blocks from Andy's house. It was one of the best fine dining restaurants in the quad-parish area (outside The Reserve, of course.)

I arrived at Andy's place at 7:15 P.M., enough time to have a pre-prandial drink, smoke a few joints, and enjoy each other's company before driving the few blocks to the restaurant.

"Welcome, Mr. G.Q.," Andy said with a wide smile when he opened the door. "You look like you've just stepped out of a high fashion men's magazine," he continued, looking me up and down. "You look…stunning." "You should've been a model, not a journalist," he continued. "You've got the height, the looks, and the build for it." He closed the door and pulled me downward toward his face and planted a big kiss on me.

I quickly returned the compliment, seeing him in his crisply starched white percale dress shirt, dark silk tie, the color of an eggplant, and wide black suspenders. The mass of curls had been carefully brushed into submission but, like naughty children, they were just waiting to cut loose. His wide violet eyes and his handsome dark complexion made me want to reiterate my lover's comments to me but I decided against it. Instead, I reciprocated the kiss. The force of the physical attraction I felt for this man at that moment impelled me to do no less.

Andy took my jacket and hung it in the closet. He then went into the bathroom and came out with two large bath towels which he placed around my neck and his own like gigantic bibs.

"I don't want you to burn holes in your clothes," he said as he pulled two rolled joints from a small wooden box on the coffee table. "I de-seeded it and, as far as I know, there shouldn't be a problem but why take chances?" he smiled.

I agreed, remembering many outfits that had been ruined by burning marijuana seeds. The precautions Andy was taking were justified.

When we finished, we removed the bib/towels, put on our jackets, and drove to the restaurant, which we entered through cut glass doors.

We were seated at the window table that I had requested. A magnum of the restaurant's best French champagne was promptly brought to the table by the sommelier, a jolly plump man with white hair, a large white mustache, and a wry sense of humor.

The modest Thursday night crowd was curious about the two exaggeratedly handsome young men who dined together near the large picture window that gave the diner the perfect uninterrupted view of Bayou Belle Terre below.

Actually there would not be much to see at night, not even the bayou's murky water as it ran slowly and silently to the Gulf of Mexico but the owners of the Plantation Room decided to illuminate the bayou's bank so occasionally, diners were able to get a glimpse of alligators who had come up onto dry land to dry off and wait for their next meal.

"Excuse me," said an elegantly dressed blue-haired matron in a matching blue "Mother-Of-The-Bride" dress made of silk organza.

We had finished our dessert and were about to leave.

"I'm Shirley Quizzenberry Poncelet and I was wondering if y'all could settle a little dispute between my husband and me." She pointed to a portly man about her age, wearing a green polyester leisure suit, eggshell rayon shirt, and a green-black-and-white striped polyester tie, seated near the center of the room under the trillion-armed brass chandelier.

"I don't know if we can," Andy smiled, "but we can try."

I was curious but I said nothing. Unless one was a bona fide celebrity, diners in Chicago would not ever think of approaching other diners for any reason.

We followed the woman to her table where we were introduced to her husband, Lawrence "Tub" Poncelet, a local gentleman farmer. I use the word "gentleman" advisedly.

"We were arguing over whether y'all were here in town filming a movie," Shirley Poncelet said in her most polite voice, a mixture of Southern redneck and Cajun. "I said that y'all are and my husband says that y'all are not. Well, who's right?"

"Your husband is, M'am," Andy smiled. "I'm just a poor Cajun boy. Thanks, though."

"See? I told ya," Tub Poncelet said. "Now tell 'em the rest of our little bet."

The now-chagrined woman confessed that she was so sure that she had recognized us as television stars that she had bet her husband that she would pay for our meal if we were actors and he would pay for it if we were not.

"So you're a local boy, huh?" she said, smiling amicably at Andy. I had seen more sincere smiles on Nile crocodiles. They were "digging" for information and their "bet" was their way of obtaining it.

"Yes, M'am," Andy said. "Born and raised in Belle Glade. I'm Deputy Andy Bourgeois. I'm the information officer for the Skylarville Police Department."

"And you, young man? I know you're not from these parts," she said, directing herself to me.

"Actually, I *am* from here. I'm from New Canaan. I'm Wayne Mallory," I said, extending my hand first to her and then to her husband.

"The colored doctors' son?" She inquired. "I'm surprised you're not havin' dinner at Terre Haute or one of the other fancy restaurants they have over there. I just love going to Terre Haute." She referred to The Reserve's most expensive and best-known restaurant. It's on the 36th floor, atop The Praetorian Hotel and has a floor that revolves slowly around, giving the diners a 360 degree view of The Reserve from as far south as New Canaan to as far north as the undeveloped land that will one day become True Hill, a village of yachts and watercraft, and west to Bayou L'Ourse, a small village outside The Reserve but our closest neighbor.

"Your family has certainly done a lot with former cane fields and swamps… and in so much in such a short time," Shirley Poncelet said. "I remember when there wasn't anything there but the ruins of the old *St. Bruno* Plantation mansion, the old sugar mill, and the sugar cane fields. I grew up no more than a half mile from there.

"The mansion burned down a long time ago. When I was a little-bitty girl. The old folks used to say the place was haunted but I believe it was mostly to keep us kids away from there. Me, I don' know.

"But I do know that it was a slave breeding farm for a long time," she continued, looking me up and down. "Some of the best-looking or strongest, best-built male slaves and some of the prettiest female slaves were bred right there at St. Bruno. They supplied handsome male house slaves and bed wenches to the best families throughout the south.

"I also remember when your fam'ly bought it. C'est Vrai Road was nothing more than a dirt trail that went from the highway to where the big house was. Then your parents and your grandparents built two mansions out there. And now there's Lake Laura, Bayou St. Eloi, new towns and villages, schools, churches, streets and highways, and all sorts of amenities that even Skylarville doesn't have. And all inhabited by black people. I wish more of 'em would have that kind of initiative." She started to say more then stopped short.

"Ahm," she said hesitantly, obviously not clearing her throat. "I noticed that it's just the two of y'all tonight. Did y'all get stood up by your young ladies?"

I could see where this was going but I didn't know how Andy wanted to play it so I allowed him to answer.

"No," he said. "We're celebrating our reunion. We haven't seen each other for thirteen years. No young ladies were invited. Just my friend and me."

"But it would've been so much more lively if y'all had had some female companionship, don't you think?" she continued tentatively, as if expecting agreement.

"No," I said flatly. "We had things just the way we wanted them," I said, still smiling but getting miffed. I raised my left hand to scratch my nose. My new gold ring caught her attention as it shone against my ebony skin. I saw her glance first at my left hand and then at Andy's.

"Y'all's wives didn' wanna come?" she inquired hopefully.

"We don't have wives," I said flatly.

The knowledge registered first on her blue-shadowed eyes behind her rimless glasses, then along the lines and creases of her heavily-mascaraed face, and last, on her thin red, seamed lips.

"*Para-magoos!!*" she finally said, taking her seat, reaching into her purse, and pulling out a beaded bag designed to hold one pack of cigarettes. From it, she pulled an extra-long lilac cigarette. "We won't take up any more of y'all's time," she said. "I lost the bet so we'll pay your check."

"No, Darlin'," Tub Poncelet said, "*You'll* pay their check."

I grabbed the remainder of the magnum and handed it to Andy. I left tips for the sommelier and the waiter, both of whom were excellent at their crafts, and handed the check to Shirley, shook her hand and then Tub's, and headed for the door.

We drove back to Andy's home for postprandial drinks, post-prandial joints, and post-prandial lovemaking, at the end of which, I felt as if I could crawl into that man and live inside him forever.

***

I didn't see Andy again until Saturday evening, after he had attended RC Eck's funeral. He told me about the unusual assortment of people who attended.

The most unusual, he said, was Eck's brother, Willard Eckland. He was called Willie by the family. He moved to California a few years ago.

"I don' know how they found him but he was the only blood relative to show up," Andy said.

Willie had brought his wife to the funeral, Andy said, and the 'wife" was most certainly a drag queen or a transvestite. He was sure of it. Andy thought most of the funeral-goers had not picked up on it but he was almost positive of it. He said Willie and his wife planned to stay in Louisiana for about a week and that he wanted me to meet them.

"Did Melodye say anything to you?" I asked.

"She talked for a little while but she's not the same. We used to be good friends. She kept her distance during both the funeral and the burial," he replied.

"Do you think she noticed what you noticed?'

"Melodye's a well-brought up country girl who went to Catholic school," he said. "I doubt it. Mrs. Ecklund is a very beautiful, ultra-feminine transvestite. I can't even imagine her as a boy," he continued.

"But you're a well-brought up country boy who went to Catholic school," I said, "and you noticed it. Or at least you suspect that that might be the case."

"I know my own," he smiled. "She wore a deep purple suit with a purple veil and a lavender scarf around her neck. I suspect that it was to hide her Adam's apple."

"Did you notice anything effeminate about Brother Willie?" I wanted to know.

"Not a thing," Andy responded, "He's very masculine. He's an actor. Rugged. He kind of looks like a modern version of the guy who played Superman on TV."

"George Reeves," I supplied.

Andy nodded. "I have a vague recollection of him but we didn't get a TV set until I was in high school. I know that in his time, he was considered to be extremely handsome but he never rocked my boat," he said.

"Willard Lee Eck sounds so corn-pone. That *can't* be his stage name?"

"No," Andy responded. His stage name is William Ecklundh. He also uses Billy, Bill, and Will Ecklundh. He said he plans to have it legally changed soon.

"He said he's had small parts in several movies and television shows—'bit parts' and 'walk-ons,' he called them--but nothing substantial. With his looks, though, I think it's only a matter of time before he hits it big."

"And when he does, I wonder what'll happen to 'Mrs.' Ecklundh. I hope she's got a pre-nup."

"It turns out the family's last name is Eckland; not Eck. Eck had dropped the *'l-a-n-d.'* That's why they couldn't find any family members. *Eck Land,*" he said. "That's the way Will pronounced it-- like Disneyland or Greenland.

"Eck was way out there most of the time. I even asked him more than once if he lived in Eck Land, a place underneath the rainbow, where everybody's white and only he's right? Now I know why he had such a strange expression on his face whenever I'd ask him where it was.

"Willard changed his last name from *Eckland* to *Eklundh*; spelling it *E-k-l-u-n-d-h*. He said he wanted it to have a more Scandinavian sound.

"We talked for a long time." Andy continued. "He told me he and Eck are just two of the eleven sons of a north Mississippi bootlegger and his wife, Norbert and Willa Mae Eckland. The brothers are scattered across the country. They don't have any contact one with the other. They don't even know where most of 'em are. There's a substantial difference in age between him and Eck. Eck was 39 and Willard is in his mid-twenties or early thirties.

"Guess what Eck's name was!" Andy continued with glee. His amethyst eyes sparkled. His beautiful teeth flashed in a clean, healthy white smile. His mustache danced in merriment.

"I couldn't even begin to guess," I said, caught up in his amusement.

"His real first name was *Norb*." Andy said in an Appalachian twang, smiling from ear to ear. "And, you know," he continued, "Norb fits him much better than RC ever did. His whole name was Norbert Cletus Eckland, Jr. I wish I'd known that while he was alive. Cletus is what his family called him."

"Nobody knew?" I asked.

"Nobody cared," Andy corrected.

"Didn't the S-O do a background check on him when he was hired?" I inquired.

"You'd think so, wouldn't you?" he said. "I guess it wasn't very thorough if they did one at all. I'll bet they saw that big, corn-fed redneck and hired him on the spot. Cajuns are generally short people. Eck was well over six feet. Six-two or six-three, maybe.

"Another thing. I believe is Willard's been in prison."

"Why? I'm sure he didn't have a sign on his forehead that said, *'I've been in prison.'*"

Andy shook his head. "He's got a lot of tattoos. Home-made. Judging by the large number of 'em, I'd say that he's spent quite a lot of time there. I'll run his record Monday when I go to work.

"He's very different from his brother, though. He seems to be a really good guy. Very likeable. The complete opposite of Eck.

Andy continued. "Every redneck between here and Murphreysboro, Tennessee must've showed up. There were more pick-ups there than at a NASCAR rally. Did you ever wonder how flies find shit?"

"Can't say I have," I replied. I couldn't help but smile at that one.

"Well, neither had I until today at that funeral, but it was just like that," Andy said. "Every fly in the state showed up for that piece of shit.

"Oh, one more thing, and this is significant," he continued. "The Chief asked me to take pictures of the attendees in case the murderer might be among them so Vern and I got camera duty.

"Eck belonged to some sort of lodge or fraternity. Before the funeral, a group of rednecks had some kind of ceremony for him. After the funeral home delivered the body and set up the casket, they went into the church, locked the doors, closed all the windows, and had a private service for him. It lasted about an hour. Then, afterward, they held the funeral for the general public.

"All of those guys were wearing some sort of ring or lapel pin. It might be Confederate in origin or it may just be associated with the white supremacy movement. I couldn't see them well so I asked one of the men to let me take a look at his ring. He just walked off.

"When I asked another one what it was, he said, 'nothing that concerns you!'

"Rev. Hinkle wore both the ring and the lapel pin. And Eck always wore the ring when he was alive. I didn't think much about it til now. It was an ugly ring: two diamonds for stars, one on a red background and the other on a blue background, separated by a white diagonal slash.

"I took a picture of it on his finger in his coffin. Before they sealed the coffin, Rev. Hinkle took the ring off Eck's finger and gave it to another man that I didn't recognize."

"Now that's strange," I said. "Do you think they were Masons or Shriners or one of those groups?"

"Definitely not Masons or Shriners," he replied. "I know them."

"Klansmen?" I asked.

"No sheets," he responded. "This is a new group. We'll have to wait until the pictures are developed but the symbol wasn't one I'm familiar with," Andy said. I'm gonna run it by the FBI. See what they come up with."

***

We met at The Wine Doggie, a lesbian-owned café-restaurant in New Bern, for lunch the following day. The Wine Doggie was situated along one of the many brick- and cobblestone-lined alleys in The Reserve known as pedways short for pedestrian walkways.

Andy could hardly wait for me to meet Samira Eklundh. I could understand why.

She was one of the most exotic-looking people, male or female, I had ever seen. Tall and slim as a rail, she had long, thick wavy hair that ranged in color from auburn to burnished gold, and skin the color of almonds, very high cheekbones, accented by a professional quality makeup job, and almond-shaped hazel eyes that reminded me of those of dancers in a Kabuki play. Her hair was braided in tight cornrows that hung down below her waist in golden-brown dreadlocks. Her exquisitely fine-boned fingers fluttered when she talked like mimosa blossoms in a gentle breeze.

I, who had traveled the world, could not place her accent. I could easily understand why Willard Ecklundh was madly in love with her. She was gorgeous.

I was not as ready as Andy to say that she was male but if she was really male, not female, she was one of the most successful cross-dressers I had ever seen. She wore a linen pantsuit and a long silk scarf that matched her outfit, around her neck so I could not see if she had an Adam's apple or not, but in mannerisms and movements, she was totally feminine. Even her voice was no give-away. It was in the contralto range, like the purr of a very contented feline.

My mum's favorite expression is, *"Women are born but Ladies are made."* Regardless of whether Samira Eklundh was born female or not, she was certainly a lady.

We had talked for over half an hour when I could contain my curiosity no longer and asked about her origins.

"My father is Somali," she said graciously, "a descendent of the Prophet Mohammad. My mother is half Dutch and half Burmese. I was born in

Curaçao and raised in Suriname until I was eleven. Then I came to America. California. I've been here since then."

"Interesting life and interesting mixtures of races and cultures," I said. "Are you an actress?"

"No, she smiled. "I'm a model? I don't have the brains to remember all of that dialog. I'd prefer to just sit and look pretty while they photograph me," she smiled and faked a yawn.

"We both are models but Will prefers acting," she said.

"Is that how you met?" Andy wanted to know.

Samira smiled and looked at Willard. He looked at her at the same time and smiled the same smile. "We met at a photo shoot in Hollywood," she continued. "We saw each other and it was love at first sight."

"There's a lot of that going around," Andy smiled, looking at me.

I could see how that would have been possible for them to have been instantly smitten with each other. William Eklundh, or Will, as he preferred to be called, was an incredibly handsome young man. He was an inch or three over six feet tall. Well built, with a chest wide enough to land a 747, that tapered down to a narrow waist, and hair as thick and black as coal. His eyes were large and green as emeralds, giving him the wide-eyed appearance of a child on Christmas morning.

His movements were as graceful as a ballet dancer's. An unruly shock of coal-black hair kept falling down over his forehead and covering one eye, giving him just a touch of mystery.

The man was damned near perfect, except for the unsightly jailhouse tattoos that covered his right forearm, right upper arm, and left bicep. It was if someone had defaced the Mona Lisa or spray painted Michelangelo's "David."

"How can you model with those tattoos, Will?" I asked frankly.

"Body paint," he replied. "For a long time, I was on the road to nowhere. I was on heroin and hadn't had my 'medicine,' as I called it, that day. I was so sick I didn't think I could make it through a photo shoot the day I met Samira but I was living on the streets and I needed money in the worst way. The only reason I went is because I figured that somebody there would have what I needed. There are a lot of junkies on movie sets.

"That day changed my life," he said. "If it hadn't been for Samira, I'd probably be dead by now."

He held up his arms, showing us the distinctive needle marks of a former heroin user, the vertical and horizontal scars of previous attempts at suicide, and the suture marks where the doctors had tried to put him back together.

"These are all thanks to my brother Cletus," he said bitterly. "May he burn in hell!

"Well, why did you come to the funeral?" I asked, curious.

"Because I wanted to make sure that asshole was *really* dead," he answered dryly. "My aunt Dilsey told me to come 'cuz she couldn't make it. I think both of us just wanted to make sure that he was really and truly dead."

He proceeded to tell us one of the most shocking and fascinating stories I had ever heard:

RC ECK'S STORY

The Eckland family lived in a miserable shack among the tall pines and red hills of Poinsett County, Mississippi.

The settlement was approximately three miles from the edge of Poinsett and had once been part of a large cotton plantation called *Frogmore*, owned by the Whitcomb family before the Civil War. The plantation ceased to exist years ago, replaced by squatters or small independent farmers rather than sharecroppers. Over the years, the name deteriorated from Frogmore to *"Froggymo."* Few people, black or white, called it *Frogmore* anymore.

Frogmore's manor house, never large or grand, was destroyed long ago by time and neglect and the site on which it stood was plowed under and turned into cotton fields. Most of the residents of Froggymo' were direct descendents of *Frogmore's* formerly enslaved and their houses are built on the site that had at one time been their cabins. Like their predecessors' homes, they were unpainted and poorly maintained shacks. The Ecklands were the only white family living on Froggymo.

Most of the equivalent whites lived in Paw-Paw in poorly-maintained shacks and rundown trailers about a mile down Petty Lane, the road that linked the two communities to the main highway.

Like Froggymo, Paw-Paw had also been part of the former *Frogmore* cotton plantation. Although some of the current residents were descendents of the plantation's original white inhabitants, most were descendents of poor, desperate whites who had always lived in these parts, or of "Okies" who moved east instead of west during the Dust Bowl era of the 1930's.

All of Froggymo's houses had the same floor plan: a deep, shady front porch that spanned the width of the house, which led directly into the living room through a center entry door. Two bedrooms flanked the small main room on both sides; one bedroom and the house's only bathroom were on the left and a second, larger bedroom was on the right.

Through an arched doorway in line with the home's front entry door, one entered the kitchen and, off it, to the right, a tiny third bedroom. A center exit door led from the kitchen to the rear yard.

In all, the houses measured approximately eight hundred square feet of covered living area and usually housed families of five or more, so all of the rooms except the bathroom, served dual purposes.

People slept wherever they could. Some of the families had added additional rooms off the kitchen. Others had screened-in their front porches and used them as sleeping porches in mild weather.

Norbert Eckland, Sr. had very little inclination to make home improvements. His only requirements when he settled there were that it be far from the eyes of the law and that there be woods nearby in which he could set up a still. Behind Froggymo, there was an extensive, densely wooded tract that ran for miles between the settlement and the town of Poinsett, suiting Norb's purposes to a tee. Norb made good money selling his swill but plowed none of it back into his home.

Only a few of Froggymo's houses had received a coat of paint in the last five decades. Most had hard-packed red dirt instead of green lawns. One or two deciduous trees flanked the fronts of most of the houses, offering shade to the weary residents. The homes had running water and electricity but few other amenities.

The one exception was the home of Alexander ("Ajax") and Dilsey Kirkwood. It was freshly painted every few years. They maintained an extensive green lawn with gardens that consisted of raised flowerbeds and a mixture of ornamental, edible, and medicinal plants. Most of Dilsey's concoctions were gleaned from plants she cultivated in her garden but a few came from the woods behind their home.

Dilsey Kirkwood and all of her ancestors as far back as she knew, were born and died at *Frogmore*. They were field workers. Black as the night, against the torrid sun under which they labored.

Dilsey moved with singular elegance as she went about her chores. She was as African as the day her ancestors were yanked from their homeland and put on a westward bound slave ship over three hundred years prior, and everyone who knew her marveled at her beauty, strength, and grace.

People who knew Dilsey Kirkwood knew that she had something to say when she opened her mouth and they were more than willing to stop and pay attention. Almost every baby that had been born in Froggymo or down Petty Lane in Paw-Paw had been delivered by Dilsey. Most of the teeth that had been extracted were extracted by Dilsey. And most of the minor hurts, bone-breaks, and pains, both physical and emotional, had been treated by Dilsey.

Dilsey had learned the art of healing from her mother, who had learned it from her mother, going back to Matangaland in West Africa.

Though small, the houses were not clustered together like eggs in a nest. Rather, they were widely separated along Clark Road by cotton fields or piney woods. They were set back from the road on a high bluff that overlooked a deep, slow-moving, smelly ditch. From Clark Road, most of the houses could only be approached by rickety bridges over cement culverts.

A series of well-worn dirt trails behind the houses, fields, or woods, running parallel to Clark Road and skirting the tree line of the wilderness behind them, was how most of the residents passed from one home to another on business errands or for pleasure.

***

"It's another boy, Willa Mae," Dilsey Kirkwood said in a tentative voice. She didn't know if Willa Mae Eckland would be pleased or not. "Number 'leven. One mo' an' you got yo'sef an even dozen," she said, trying to make light of a bad situation.

Willa Mae Eckland released a great sigh and smiled as she heard the gender of her youngest child. "Thank you, Jesus! Thank you that it's not a girl. I guess I'd better name this one Junior. Norbert Cletus Eckland Junior," she said in a half-daze, "cuz I ain't havin' no more.

"After ten, why you gonna name this one after Norb?" Dilsey wanted to know.

"Anything to get Norb off my back," she said, wearily. "He keeps askin' why none of the boys is named after him." She spoke as much to herself as to the midwife and the Deity. "I tol' him I'd name the 'N' child after him but I ain't gettin' no younger an' I don't know if I c'n make it to 'N.'" She smiled a wan, dismayed smile.

This one had been a hard pregnancy and an even harder delivery. It seemed to her and the midwife that this child was fighting tooth and nail to remain in the womb.

"This one's gon' be a pistol, Willa Mae. You sure you're up to it?"

"Prob'ly not but what choice I got?" Willa Mae replied resignedly.

"Lord he'p ya, Child," Dilsey said as she looked at the wrinkled red face, gaping maw, and tiny balled fists of this baby. To her, he looked like a very ripe tomato with a powerful set of lungs. She counted his fingers and toes and found all to be present. She examined his scrotum and found a penis and testicles right where they should be. His skin, hair, and eyes were all normal. She smiled despite her misgivings and pronounced him healthy. That was all that mattered to her at this point. Norb and Willa Mae could deal with the rest, including his ill temper.

Most babies cried for a few minutes after being hauled into the cold, cruel world from the safe, warm confines of the womb, but not this child. He made not a sound when she got him turned around, for he had been a "breach baby," and pulled him out of the womb, held him upside down by the ankles, and slapped his tiny buttocks.

At being slapped, he opened his eyes, looked around first at his assailant, then at her accomplice, and last, at the darkened room in which he was born with its tattered furniture and walls plastered in old, yellowing newspaper. After a few minutes of careful scrutiny, he snorted and let out a loud piercing scream. Dilsey at first thought the child was injured in some way. Coming into the world ass-backward always presented an additional set of risks, strangulation being primary.

This child appeared unphased by his backwards entry into the world but he was having nothing to do with his surroundings or his companions.

Dilsey Kirkwood's ebony face grew concerned as precious time passed and the child would not be pacified as she washed and swaddled him in his cheap yellow receiving blanket. He refused to suckle or to open his eyes for more than a few seconds at a time, as if to confirm that this was no nightmare; that he really was where he was, and with whom he had landed. Each new peek at his environment appeared to cause him new levels of distress.

Dilsey concluded that he was probably sensitive to light so she bound his eyes with gauze and told Willa Mae to leave them bound for three days. The child immediately settled down and began to suckle as any normal baby would. On the third day, she removed the bandages and although the dudgeon had subsided, the child's scowl had not. He wore it for the rest of his life.

Dilsey Kirkwood had delivered all of the Eckland children except Jesse, the oldest. Each presented his own set of problems but this child was by far, the worst. After she had swaddled him in the thin receiving blanket, she took him into the next room to meet his father and five of his nine siblings. She knew exactly what Willa Mae was talking about. Girl children among the under classes in rural Mississippi led very hard lives.

The Eckland children had come as regularly as spring rain. The older four had been spaced thirteen months apart on average and the younger ones had come at approximately three-year intervals.

"Stair steps," the people had said. Stair steps they were, indeed. Most were as plain and unremarkable as mud fences. They were as pale as milk and had dry, straw-colored hair and sad eyes the color of tree bark.

Only Jesse, Charlie, and now little Cletus, were different. Jesse had coal-black hair and sapphire-blue eyes, Charlie had carrot-red hair and jade-green eyes, and little Cletus had sand-colored hair and eyes the color of a summer sky.

Dilsey Kirkwood had welcomed each one except Jesse into the world. And what a pitiful world it was: cardboard soles in their shoes, threadbare clothing, usually hand-me-downs or donations collected from one of the local white churches, a tarpaper shack not fit for human habitation, cold in winter and hot in the summer. Windy all of the time.

They were slated for dirty hands and faces and enough dirt behind their ears to grow corn, as well as endless toil in the nearby cotton fields or the alternative, lying, cheating, gambling, or fucking their way through life.

The Ecklands' only daughter, Gertie Jo, had died within a week of being born. Dilsey had surmised that the youngster had seen the environment and knew that she could not survive there for long so she gave up the ghost as soon as she could. Young Norbert Cletus Eckland, Jr. had come eleven months later to fill her space in the lineup.

"I need som'pn to keep me from havin' more young'ens," Willa Mae confided to Dilsey two weeks after Cletus was born. "I ain't even healed up from Junior yet an' Norb's all over me. Even when I'm sleepin'.'"

"I c'n give you som'pn to take the fight outta' Norb or som'pn to keep you from gettin' knocked up again. Which one you want?" Dilsey inquired in a low voice.

"I *want* som'pn that'll take the fight outta' Norb so maybe he won't be climbin' all over me like an ol' ruttin' goat," Willa Mae replied, "but if I give him som'pn that takes away his manhood, he'd kill me, an' if he found out that you gived it to me, he'd kill you, too," she smiled. "You better jus' give me som'pn to keep me from getting' knocked again."

"I got just the thing fo' you," Dilsey replied. She returned the next morning with a Mason jar full of a foul-looking brownish-greenish liquid. "Take this ever' morning," Dilsey had said, "an' you won't get knocked up."

When the first three-year cycle passed and she did not become pregnant, Willa Mae breathed easier. When a second three-year cycle passed without the telltale signs of pregnancy appearing, she put away the baby things and Norb Junior, now called "li'l Cletus," seemed to be the last of a long, seemingly endless line of siblings.

Willa Mae also stopped drinking the potion Dilsey gave her, thinking that the heavy bleeding that lasted for almost a month straight, was the onset of menopause.

"You ought'a keep drinkin' it for a few mo' years," Dilsey warned. "Sometimes the body fools ya into thinkin' that it's finished kickin' out babies but it ain't. Sometimes there's one mo' li'l soul that needs to come into the world an' it'll do whatever it needs to do to git here."

Willa Mae continued to accept the potion Dilsey religiously delivered to her but rather than hurt Dilsey's feelings by refusing it, she poured it down the hole in the outhouse, washed out the Mason jar, and returned it to Dilsey the following morning when she appeared at the door with yet another jarful.

Shortly before Cletus' seventh birthday, she began feeling the familiar "little fish" in her belly again. Disappointed and angry at herself for not following Dilsey's advice, she calmly gathered together all of the baby clothes and furnishings she had stored away for her grandchildren.

She recalled Dilsey's words, *"Sometimes there's one mo' li'l soul that needs to come into the world an' it'll do whatever it needs to do to git here."*

This one certainly had done whatever it needed to do to get here, she thought. She had not had a regular menstrual cycle since Cletus was born. She had gone for over four years without menstruating at all. In year five, she had two short periods six months apart.

In Cletus' sixth year, her cycle started up again, just like an unused motorcycle. Like it had never shut itself off and just like she was a young woman in her twenties again. It came as regular as rain, every twenty-eight days. Even the public health nurse, who visited her and the children monthly to ensure their proper health and nutrition, had no explanation for this turn of events.

From that first flutter, Willa Mae knew that this child was different from the slack-mouthed, lank-haired, whey-faced, snot-nosed brood she and Norbert had so far foisted upon the welfare rolls of Poinsett County. *This one*, she thought, *is my Golden Child. Boy or girl. This one is going to be named after* **me**. *This one is gonna* **be** *Somebody. I'm gonna see to it!*

This one would be different from the others because, among other reasons, it had a different daddy. This was the one secret Willa Mae had kept from everyone, including her best friend, Dilsey Kirkwood. The sire of this child was a passing Bible salesman named Willard Travis Billups.

Bill Billups was tall and movie star handsome with a winning smile, a full head of luxurious chestnut brown hair, dimples, a gigantic penis, and a gift of gab that could charm the birds from the trees and the panties off of Willa Mae Eckland.

True to Willa Mae's premonition, this child was indeed different. This final pregnancy was easier. The fetus was not as restless as its siblings had been. When she sang to it, it appeared to respond to her music by gently keeping time.

By her seventh month, she had hardly any weight-gain. Her shoes still fit and she thanked God for the lack of morning sickness, aversion to certain foods, and mood swings that had accompanied the births of the other children.

Once a week, Dilsey brought her a different herbal concoction which she drank hungrily. Dilsey said it would keep Willa Mae stronger and make the child healthy, strong, and smart.

With her other pregnancies, Willa Mae had promptly thrown it up and the fetuses inside her reacted so violently toward her after she drank it that she told Dilsey not to waste her time making it.

Cletus was the most vengeful of all toward her, and he was still the most violent and vengeful of her children. Cletus could hold a grudge longer than anyone she knew. Any insult or slight, no matter how insignificant or unintentional, was a matter of personal honor to Cletus and it had to be avenged. When he was two, he took a strong dislike for anything beautiful. He would regularly snap the heads off of all of the colorful flowers Willa Mae and Dilsey had planted around the front and sides of the house.

At four, he snapped the necks of the family cat's litter of kittens. Nine in all. At seven, he broke into a neighbor's pigeon coop, killed the four pigeons there, and ate them raw. At ten, he set a neighbor's house afire.

Cletus became sexually active at an early age. Whenever he wanted to be alone, he took a walk into the woods or behind one of the many sheds, abandoned buildings, or woodpiles and masturbated. In almost every instance, a cat was somewhere nearby, a silent witness to his misdeeds.

When he walked about at night, dogs barked, signaling his passing and telling him not to trespass on their master's land but cats only observed and often accompanied him on his nightly sojourns—from a distance, of course. Cletus was deathly afraid of the cats because of their sharp claws and pointed little fangs. He also hated the hissing sound they made when cornered.

While he liked their eyes, which he said, looked like expensive jewels, he also believed they could look into his soul and see the wickedness and guilt within.

He believed the cats' eyes were witnesses to his perfidy and he determined he would kill every cat he could find and gouge out its all-seeing eyes. He would then put them in a secret place where they could never stare at him again.

One day, when he was eleven years old, Willa Mae saw him enter the woods with a croaker sack full of something alive so she followed him into the piney woods to his "secret place."

She watched as her son removed his ragged clothing when he arrived at a natural clearing along the path deep in the woods. She hid behind a holly bush some twenty feet from the clearing and peered at her youngest son and was horrified at what she saw: Her son sat down on a mat of pine needles in the middle of the shallow, hand-dug graves of approximately twenty neighborhood cats.

Over each grave was a rude cross made of sticks he had lashed together with twine and on the head of each of the crosses, where Jesus' head would have been, were the eyeless, decomposing heads of their occupants.

Flies buzzed all around, adding a dramatic, sickening, and surreal sound to the scene while maggots crawled from the eyes, mouths, and bloody necks of the decapitated heads.

Unseen by her son, she turned away from the gruesome scene and vomited into the mat of rust-colored pine needles and dead holly leaves beneath her feet.

For almost an hour she watched her son, fair-haired, blue-eyed, and chubby as a cherub in a Renaissance painting, as he played god, wearing only his dirty cotton Fruit of the Loom briefs. When he finally opened the sack, the head of a black and white cat popped out. The cat attempted to run away when released from the sack but it only had the use of its two front legs. The animal's lower body had been disabled and dragged behind it like a wet mop.

Cletus grabbed the animal's tail and pulled it toward him. The cat hissed its fury and bared its fangs and front claws, still feisty and ready to fight off its attacker. In a practiced move, Cletus deftly avoided both, grabbed the cat by the scruff of its neck with his left hand and with the right, grabbed its head from behind.

With one swift, fluid motion, he flicked his wrist and spun the cat's body around like an aircraft's propeller. By the second rotation, the cat's head was attached to its body by only a few strips of bloody skin.

Willa Mae could see the lack of expression on her son's face as he completed his ungodly act.

He then cut the remaining strips of skin that connected the cat's head to its body and threw the body into a previously-dug grave.

Cletus filled in the grave with the business end of an old rusted shovel he had found somewhere in his sojourns and turned his attention to the animal's head.

He pulled a rusted teaspoon from his blue jeans pocket and scooped out the animal's eyes, which hung from two slimy strings that were at one time the optic nerves. He bent his head as far back as it would go, opened his mouth like a hungry baby bird would, stuck out his tongue as if to receive any drippings, and hung one of the eyes above it for a few seconds before deciding not to drop it into his waiting maw.

Instead, he went to a hollow in the trunk of an old sweetgum tree and pulled from it her pilfered jewelry box from which he extracted his only treasure, a round, tall, sky blue, jar that had once contained Alka-Seltzer tablets. He then opened the slender bottle and dropped the eyes into it, one by one, and recapped it with his grimy, bloody hands.

Still oblivious to her presence, Cletus retrieved the jar, cleaned it, scraped off the label and filled it with a preserving liquid, probably rubbing alcohol or maybe some of his father's "white lightning," and something that appeared to her logical mind to be tiny eggs.

Cletus held the jar up to the sunlight filtering through the trees in beams that looked like heavenly rays sent by a demonic deity just for him. He turned it around and around, observing it from different angles. When he finished, he replaced the jar in the jewelry box and replaced the jewelry box into the hollow of the sweetgum.

He then dressed and retraced his steps down the path toward home. When he had passed the spot where she was hiding, Willa Mae entered the clearing, which she now dubbed The First Circle of Hell, and went to the hollow in the sweetgum, removed the jewelry box, and removed the Alka-Seltzer jar, whose top Cletus had tightly closed.

She held the jar up to the light filtering through the trees and nearly fainted at what she beheld: the things she thought were tiny eggs were actually the eyes of each of the dead cats whose graves she stood among.

Replacing her son's "treasure," she leaned against the trunk of the sweet gum, trying to make sense of what she had seen, heard, and smelled for the past hour. Her head hurt and her stomach was tied in knots as she stood pondering her next step. While she was there, as still as one of the wooden crosses her son had made for his victims, a vixen and three half-grown kits arrived to feast upon the head of the dead cats on their crosses.

Her stomach roiled again as she observed them devouring the newest cat's ears and pulling at the remainder of the meat, tendons, and bones where the head had been severed from the body.

Had she not previously regurgitated the contents of her stomach, she would have done so at that moment. The vixen and her young noticed her for the first time as the muffled sounds of her innards became evident. They stopped, looked to where she stood, leaning against the tree trunk with tears in her eyes for her misguided son and his bleak future, as well as for her family.

She knew her youngest son was deeply disturbed but she had no idea how to deal with it. Maybe Dilsey knew. Dilsey knew everything. But did she want even Dilsey, her best-and only-friend, to know that Cletus had arrived at this point of...whatever this was? Madness, maybe? Surely Dilsey had the answers but did Willa Mae want to ask the questions?

Later that night, she told Norb about what she had observed.

"Let him be," Norb had said. "Ain't a thing wrong wit' that boy!" He attributed the boy's actions to "playfulness." Willa Mae was at wit's end with Cletus and wanted him hospitalized because of his cruelty not only to animals but to his family members, but Norb slapped her and pointed his dirty, crooked finger in her face. "No son o'mine, *'specially not one named after me, is crazy, y'hear?"* he screamed, *"an' you ain't puttin' him away in no crazy-house!"*

Willa Mae knew that if Cletus wasn't insane, he was very, very close to it and there was something terribly, terribly...*"not right"* with him. The boy appeared to have no conscience. No sense of right and wrong, and no fear of consequences.

Willa Mae hoped that this last child would be different, though: kind, loving, forgiving, and intelligent. All of the things Cletus was not, but as every child had been worse than its predecessor, she held out little hope for this next one. In her mind, she could imagine this one being born with horns, a tail, and cloven hoofs.

Still, Willa Mae prayed that this child would not be a girl. A girl child, especially with Cletus as her next-older brother, would have a hard, hard row to hoe.

When the child was born male, Willa Mae let out a huge sigh of relief and said a silent prayer of thanksgiving. She named him Willard Martin Eckland.

Willa Mae noticed that Cletus, young as he was, was a misanthrope. He hated *everybody* but he seemed to hate females most of all. He especially hated the two women closest to him, his mother and Dilsey Kirkwood.

Cletus even hated Alvinia Todd, his first grade teacher. She had been an institution at the local white elementary school for generations. She had taught most of her co-workers, the school's principal, and all of the other Eckland children. Though she had found all of them, except Jesse, to be mentally deficient and unruly, they, at least, were manageable.

Cletus, on the other hand, was the brightest since his brother, Byron, but a holy terror to his classmates; especially the girls.

Other parents, especially those of the girls, complained constantly of things Cletus had done to their children but they confined those complaints to poor Mrs. Todd because everybody knew the Ecklands as the poorest and laziest family, black or white, in Poinsett County. They also knew equally well that to complain directly to Norb or Willa Mae would be like complaining to brick walls.

Early on, Cletus took a special dislike for those children who dressed better or whose families had even a little more than he. That was everybody in his school.

The other children, however, were not totally blameless in this matter. Cletus and his siblings were called stupid, shiftless, lazy, and the epithets that hurt most, "white trash," "*po'* white trash," and "white niggers."

The children had heard their parents use these epithets, took them to school, and used them against Cletus and his brothers, their only weapons against the Ecklands' arsenal of physical abuse.

This, in turn, spurred the Eckland children to be even meaner and more ornery toward their classmates, which, in turn, caused the classmates to exclude and denigrate the Eckland children even more.

Jesse James Eckland, Norb and Willa Mae's oldest son, was named for his maternal grandfather, Jesse James Dayleader.

The Dayleaders were from Leonardo, Kentucky, just across the state line and nine miles from Eckland, West Virginia.

Norb's father, Dove Eckland, and Willa Mae's mother, Polly Dayleader, were brother and sister, making Norb and Willa Mae first cousins. Few people in

Mississippi knew this. All of the residents of Eckland, West Virginia and Leonardo, Kentucky, however, knew but none cared. Unions between close relatives were common among this extended family.

Leonardo, Kentucky, population fifty, is populated mostly with descendents of Sarah Actright-Cortland and Spencer Eckland, the Adam and Eve that spawned the Eckland clan.

Jesse James Eckland, the oldest of Norb and Willa Mae's children, was tall, handsome, and an excellent student, and had found some notoriety as a basketball player in high school. He entered the Army upon graduation. He voluntarily surrendered contact with all of his family members except Willa Mae.

Every Mothers Day, Christmas, and June 24 (Willa Mae's birthday), an expensive present would arrive from some exotic place with a card inviting *her* to come live with him and his family.

Her favorite gift was robe from Japan made of heavy black silk. It had a wide sash, called an obi, made of white silk and the black silk piping along the seams. When she was alone, she would lock the doors, take it down from the top shelf of her wardrobe, unwrap it, and envelope herself in its cool, smooth comfort. It was the most luxurious thing she owned.

Norb was not mentioned in the invitations and on Christmas, Fathers Day, and September 29 (Norb's birthday); nothing arrived from Jesse for him.

Byron Mark, eleven months younger than Jesse, basked in his older brother's glory as a star basketball player so he, too, escaped the bad reputation his younger brothers earned for the family. He married a girl from Tupelo and they moved to Odessa, Texas in search of riches in the oilfields.

Charles Robert Eckland was about as smart as a stale turnip and began the legacy of the "stupid, lazy Eckland boys."

Like his father, he turned out to be a drunkard, a jailbird, and a wife-beater. Movie star handsome and well-hung (as were Norb and all of his sons), he populated the countryside from Memphis to Cincinnati with handsome little half-wits.

Dudley Keith Eckland, called "Dud," thirteen months younger than Charles Robert, had a deviated septum and could breathe through his nose only with great difficulty so he depended on his mouth as an alternative. Even slower than Charles Robert, breathing through his open mouth, and with red-rimmed, watery eyes due to severe allergies, Dudley became the poster child of *"Ecklandism,"* as the locals termed the combination of maladies.

The other Eckland boys, Enoch, Floyd, George, Hiram, Irwin, and Jack, reinforced the theory. They were handsome but dull as well-used cutlery.

To the locals, they were just plain stupid; the end product of all of the previous generations of inbreeding when the Ecklands lived in the mountains of West Virginia and Kentucky before migrating to northern Mississippi after Jesse was born.

One local saying was that the only time the Ecklands changed residences and moved on was when there were no more girl children being born into the family with which the males could cohabit. With eleven boys, the local residents could hardly wait for this generation of Ecklands to move on to greener, more fertile, pastures.

There was probably some truth to the story as the Eckland family had an abnormally high number of double and triple first or second cousins who had interbred and produced offspring.

Eckland, West Virginia, a small community way up in the mountains was one hundred percent family. Leonardo, Kentucky was about ninety percent. Outsiders were not welcome to settle there and most quickly moved on after they received such a chilly "welcome" from the town's residents. Only the town's teachers and parsons were welcomed, being outsiders.

The West Virginia Ecklands had married and intermarried since 1720, when they settled there. They are all descendents of Sarah and Spencer Eckland and Spencer and Mary Eckland, who had spawned twelve sons and five daughters, and six sons and three daughters, respectively.

The first American Ecklands were indentured servants to Phillip and Cora Drummond, who had purchased them to work on their indigo plantation in 1713.

Sarah Actright-Cortland was lady's maid to Cora Drummond. She was a bright and sprightly raven-haired lass of thirteen when she was indentured.

Her mother was Molly Brightship, a bawdy, apple-cheeked strumpet who primarily worked as a serving wench in a pub near Brighton, England, thereby foregoing the need to wear the striped hood that all English prostitutes wore at that time while offering her "services" to any gentlemen with a two-pence in his pocket, a smile on his face, and a penis that needed attention.

Sarah Actright-Cortland's biological father was the randy and handsome youngest son of the Third Earl of Baldringham who had spent a fortnight at the inn at which her mother, Molly Brightship, worked and engaged Molly's ministrations every night of his stay there.

When she found out that she was *with child*, Molly Brightship hurriedly bed and wed the local blacksmith's son, Robert Actright-Cortland, who also happened to be the village idiot.

One would think that the faulty genetic material that was later to infect the Eckland children was introduced into the bloodline here, but apparently not, as the only one of Molly Brightship Actright-Cortland's children to come to America was Sarah, whose father was the randy son of the Third Earl of Baldringham, not the village idiot.

Both the Brightships and the Actright-Cortlands were tow-heads or strawberry blonds with milk-white skin, and pale blue or gray eyes. They were so pale that even their freckles had freckles, so when Sarah was born with flashing emerald green eyes and raven hair, stupid as Bobby Actright-Cortland was, he figured out (admittedly with some help from family and friends) that he had been cuckolded.

Since he had married Molly Brightship in a church wedding, Robert was forced to accept the girl as his daughter, though anyone seeing her keen intelligence, sprightly personality, flashing green eyes, and raven-dark hair among her dull-witted tow-headed half-siblings, knew immediately that she was not Bobby's biological daughter. Hence, indentured servitude in America was the only likely solution to the Actright-Cortlands' sticky and obvious dilemma. Sarah carried the knowledge of her true origin with her to the New World and passed it on to her offspring.

Spencer Eckland's family origins were completely unknown, as Spencer was abandoned on the streets of Cardiff, Wales as a newborn and taken to one of the many orphanages there. The staff in the orphanage where Spencer was raised thought he was the result of a botched, late-term abortion or that he was a premature natural birth and that he would die within a few hours of being rescued.

The tiny infant, however, thrived and lived to adulthood. He was sickly, lazy, unambitious, unintelligent, and suffered respiratory complications all his life but he was a pleasant sight for the eyes and he had his way with every woman—and more than a few men—who captured his fancy. He was short of stature, bandy-legged, barrel-chested, stupid, ill-tempered, and dissolute, but hung like the horses he tended.

It was impossible for anyone who knew them to believe that Sarah, delicate as fine porcelain, would ever want to marry the slovenly, stupid stable boy regardless of his handsome face, his way with words, and his enormous member. He had never advanced even as high as groom during the seven years of his indenture, nor had he had any desire to do so.

Cora Drummond pleaded and begged her maid not to marry the ill-tempered bastard but Sarah, a gentle, determined girl, persisted. When all else failed, Cora cried and took to her bed.

The wedding took place the day after Spencer's indenture ended. Sarah's indenture was set to end four months later but as a wedding present, the Drummonds signed her manumission papers early.

Spencer, in wooing Sarah, had listened patiently to her dreams of setting up a little seamstress' shop in Williamsburg, Philadelphia, or Boston, where wealthy society ladies would visit her shop to have their fine gowns made or to purchase fine lace.

Sarah had developed a fine stitch that was the envy of all of the other seamstresses in the area. She was also a skilled lace-maker. That skill alone, which she learned from Michelle LeBlanc, a French Huguenot lass who was also indentured on the Drummond plantation, could earn her a healthy income and a place in colonial American society.

Spencer, she dreamed, would get a job in a livery stable and eventually own an inn. They would then enjoy respectable and prosperous lives of their own.

Once the marriage was consecrated, and even before it was consummated, and even before the ink on Sarah's manumission papers was dry, Spencer announced that he had decided to seek his fortune west of the Appalachians where new territories were being opened for settlement.

Sarah, as his wife, was obligated to follow him wherever he took her. On their wedding night, Sarah conceived the first of her seventeen children.

Thus the legend began.

The family settled in a lush, green valley in the mountains. There were several streams nearby for fresh water, the fishing was good, and game was plentiful. Most of all, it was far away from other people.

Their nearest white neighbor was a four-day walk away. Their nearest Native American neighbors, a friendly family group of the Pamawauskusett tribe, which Spencer found inconvenient to pronounce and quickly changed it to *Pammawunkys,* who had garnered the same reputation for sloth among their clan as the Ecklands later garnered among theirs, lived four hours walk away via treacherous mountain trails that the Native Americans had used for centuries. This suited Spencer just fine. He promptly built a small cabin and set up his still.

After a few months, Spencer traded a rusty old rifle, three bottles of home-made liquor, and two hunting knives for one of the low-functioning daughters of the tribal leader, ostensibly to keep Sarah company and help her with their growing family but he informally married her, gave her the Christian name, Mary, and completed the triad that later produced RC Eck.

The Eckland family stayed in their mountain valley for more than two and a half centuries, far removed from civilization. The longer they stayed away from civilization, the meaner they got. Few strangers ventured that far back into the mountains and few Ecklands ventured down out of the mountains, toward civilization. If they did, it was mostly in search of female companionship.

From time to time, an Eckland male would venture as far as the little town of Hollister, beyond the Cumberland Gap, find a girl he were interested in, court her, and if she showed no interest, kidnap and deflower her, then take her back up into the mountains with him.

Although this rarely happened in the more than two hundred years that the Ecklands had inhabited their mountain valley, whenever it did happen, it never failed to raise the tempers of the townspeople, who vowed they would return with their precious sister, daughter, or cousin.

They gathered their hunting dogs, all of the able-bodied men in the area, cleaned their rifles, pistols, shotguns, and pitchforks, and headed into the mountains in pursuit of the unwilling victim and her swain.

The Ecklands garnered the same legendary status as Big Foot. They were seldom seen, they had a horrible odor, and they were almost completely unschooled and unfit for polite society. Few townspeople knew them by name but most recognized them by their noxious odor long before they arrived.

Many of the local residents did not even believe that they existed but they were called the Mountain Ghosts or the Shaggy Men by those did. Parents in the area sometimes told their miscreant children that if they continued to misbehave, the Shaggy Men would come and take them away.

The Ecklands' valley was so remote that they completely missed both the Revolutionary War and the Civil War. In fact, they didn't even find out that they were now residents of *West* Virginia instead of Virginia, until two years after the Civil War. To this day, however, they will swear that they were loyal sons of the South and that they had fought under Bobby Lee and his brave boys.

By 1900, the lush green valley that Spencer, Sarah, Mary, and their children had settled had become a slag heap. The animals had run off and the trees were all dead.

In 1885, a fast talking Irishman named Kevin Keppley had convinced the clan's leader, Zeb Eckland, and his wife, Ruthenia "Ruthie" Eames Eckland, that they should allow the Tedesco Mining Company to mine for coal in the valley. Kevin Keppley convinced them that their new mining techniques would leave the land unscarred and "as pristine as the day ol' Spencer Eckland first set foot on it."

Ruthie Eckland had always had dreams of riches, fine clothes, and fancy carriages. She also had dreams of living in a big city far, far away from Eckland, West Virginia. She and Zeb left the valley and headed for New York City, never to be heard from again.

All of the Eckland descendents were equal partners in the riches the checks from the mining company paid them. Most remained in the valley, building a new church, a new school, a new town hall, and handsome wooden or brick homes for themselves but before long, the stench and the detritus from the mine had covered the entire valley with a black veil that tainted everything in it.

The forests were soon denuded. Rains and snow washed away the topsoil, leaving nothing to stop the rain from rolling down into the valley and causing mudslides. Tedesco Mining Co. built a railroad spur to haul away the coal and brought in miners from elsewhere to work the mine. Those miners brought their families, tipping the balance of Ecklands versus Outlanders in favor of the Outlanders for many years.

Many of the Ecklands, using the proceeds from the initial contract with Tedesco, moved away from the town of Eckland, West Virginia and settled en masse, in Leonardo, Kentucky, a few miles away as the crow flies.

Only the hardiest, the poorest, and the ornery-est remained in West Virginia. Those who did worked in the Tedesco mine until it pulled out of the area in 1909.

Other mining companies came and went, each leaving the valley and its occupants just a little worse off than its predecessor. By 1935, the mine had played out, leaving the valley raped, scarred, and unrecognizable. With the last trainload of coal, those Outlanders who had tipped the scales in their favor left the awful, foul-smelling valley for greener pastures, and returned it to the remaining Ecklands.

***

Will continued his saga of the Eckland family for over three hours. Andy's hand gravitated to mine like a shark to chum as I taped the entire conversation.

We sat at a café table under one of the pink and white striped umbrellas of The Wine Doggie and sipped Spanish Amontillado and "tapas" in the Spanish tradition, while he talked.

The awning, equipped with misters and small oscillating ceiling fans, provided some relief from the unrelenting heat, humidity, and bugs but not as much as I would have liked.

"Cletus was simply awful to me," he continued. He had not completely lost his Mississippi accent. "If it hadn't been for Aunt Dilsey and Uncle Ajax, I'd prob'ly be daid by now.

"*Probably*," Samira coached, "and *dead*, not daid."

"I'd *probably* be *dead* by now," Will said, correcting himself before continuing his saga:

Cletus sensed that this new child was special to Willa Mae and decided to get rid of it. Cletus hated both goodness and beauty and his baby brother was amply endowed with both.

Cletus also saw the love that Willa Mae lavished on Will and how Will responded in kind. That alone was reason enough for Cletus to kill the child. He knew that would devastate Willa Mae.

Will told us how Willa Mae had once found Cletus trying to smother him with a bed pillow when Will was three months old.

Willa Mae had left the room in which the infant was sleeping. When she returned a few minutes later, Cletus was holding a pillow over the infant's face. The child had turned blue when Willa Mae pulled the pillow away.

Cletus, with large, teary eyes, told his mother that he was playing a game with his baby brother and that his intention was not to harm the child, but to keep him entertained while she went about her chores. She comforted the wailing infant and then turned her wrath on Cletus, whom she did not believe for a second.

Cletus was black and blue for days.

"Som'pn ain't right 'bout Cletus," Willa Mae would shake her head sadly and say to anyone willing to listen. She wished she could take Cletus to a professional but the closest psychiatrist was in Oxford, at the university, too far for their old truck to travel safely. Besides, Norb would never agree to it.

There was plenty of time but no money to take Cletus anywhere. Norb, by that time, was spending most of his time in the woods tending his still and the rest of it either visiting various nefarious individuals on both sides of the Tennessee-Mississippi line, trying to sell his product, drinking what he couldn't sell, or sleeping off its effects. Besides, Norb didn't believe in psychiatrists.

"Ain't nobody gonna touch my boy's head 'cept his barber," Norb said when Willa Mae suggested it. "Ain't nothin' wrong wit' that boy that a good likkin' can't cure." Despite the constant *"likkins,"* Cletus wasn't cured. If anything, he became worse and more vicious.

Willa Mae had long ago stopped trying to lavish any affection on the ill-tempered Cletus and Norb had none to give. The more Willa Mae tried, the harder Cletus resisted. Trying to hug or kiss Cletus was like trying to hug a cactus or kiss a cobra. Maybe, if she had continued trying instead of giving up, he would have been merely despicable instead of truly odious. Willa Mae provided him with clean clothes, nourishing food, and a bed but nothing more.

When Cletus' first attempt at fratricide failed, he decided to initiate a reign of terror against the Golden Child whenever possible. Cletus became a sort of grimy domestic terrorist, striking hard and fast whenever the child was left unprotected.

Willa Mae, for her part, had vowed never to leave her Golden Child unguarded again.

She continued her vigil until one day, when, as she sat on her favorite wooden rocker on the high front porch reading movie magazines and sipping sweet tea, she began bleeding from all of her orifices, went into severe convulsions and died an agonizing death.

Coincidentally, this was two days after Norb had purchased a pound of rat poison, and the day after it vanished from the shed in which Norb had put it for safekeeping.

Cletus was fourteen and Will was three. The only witness to her death was Cletus, who just stood there watching as his mother convulsed and bled to death. He wore an enigmatic smile when Dilsey found him standing over her lifeless body. He wore the same expression when the police questioned him and at Willa Mae's funeral.

On the day Willa Mae died, the forces of Good and Evil went to war and for a long time, Evil won every battle, and was set to win the war when the winds of war changed direction.

With no one to protect him and Norb not giving a tinker's dam about his children, Cletus ran roughshod over his younger brother until Dilsey and Ajax took him into their home.

When none of the relatives would take custody of Will, Dilsey rummaged through Willa Mae's papers until she found Jesse's phone number in California. She called Jesse and his wife and told them about Willa Mae's recent passing. She also told them about the poor parenting Norb was providing for all three of the sons who remained under his roof, but especially how poorly little Willie was faring.

Jesse flew to Memphis, visited his mother's grave, collected Willie, and flew out the same day.

Dilsey and Ajax took on the responsibility of providing food and clean clothes for Cletus and Jack, sixteen; the only other brother remaining at home, as Norb sank deeper and deeper into alcoholism and apathy.

Jack Eckland was not quite as mean and rotten as Cletus but he was no saint, either. He had used Cletus as his personal scum bag for years but Jack quickly learned that he could attract more flies with honey than with vinegar so, instead of forcing the hormonal Cletus into sex, he used seduction and bribery. If everything else failed, however, he was still stronger than Cletus and could force him to submit.

Jack was a bear of a boy, Cletus was a bull of a boy, and Willie was a little lamb. He was no match for either of them. Both brothers, especially the overly-hormonal Cletus, had his way with the moppet until first the Kirkwoods, then their oldest brother Jesse, intervened.

Norb was an ill-mannered, foul-mouthed, unwashed, oversexed, uncouth man who could care less as to who would satisfy his sexual needs now that Willa Mae was no longer his scum-catcher, and Cletus was the miniature version of his father.

Sometimes Norb would visit a local bar and pick up some lonely barfly, take her behind the bar, and sate his never-ending lust, but more often, he chose one of his sons, just as his father, Dove; his grandfather, Jubal, and every other Eckland male had done when female companionship was unavailable.

"Your mama ain't here no more, boys," he said two nights after Willa Mae's funeral. "That means that one of y'all has gotta step up to the plate." He stroked himself through his dirty threadbare khakis in a lascivious way that left little doubt as to what he meant.

Each boy pointed to the other. Norb chose Jack that first night. "You're the oldest, Jackie, so tonight s'up to you." He pulled the unwilling boy into his bedroom, pulled the thin curtain that separated the bedroom from the main room, and turned off the light after pawing at the hapless teenager and tearing off his clothes. Cletus tiptoed to the doorway hoping for a free show.

"I ain't gonna do what you want me to do, Daddy," Jack said bravely.

"Oh yes, you will," Norb bellowed, "or I'll break your goddamned neck!"

Cletus heard the thuds of his father's fists against his brother's body.

"Come on, get in bed NOW!" Norb ordered.

"No, Daddy. I ain't gonna do that," the steadfast boy said. "Coach said it ain't right to do what you want me to do an' Rev. Grimes said it's a sin." Logic and religion went out the window when Jack wanted to satisfy his own lust with either of his brothers but when it was his turn to belly up to the bar, he found them very convenient escape routes.

Jack was on of the boys' baseball team at school. He was not the brightest bulb in the chandelier but at sixteen, he was over six feet tall, beautifully built with bowling ball biceps, well-developed pectoral muscles, a ripped abdomen, and tree-trunk legs. The local girls loved him despite his surname.

"Fuck Coach and fuck Rev. Grimes! Git in this bed, I said!"

All was quiet for about five minutes. Cletus, still listening at the closed curtain, was almost crushed by the weight of his brother's body as Jack came crashing through.

Jack, in his boxers, ran out of the room, through the front door, and into the night. He landed on the Kirkwoods' doorstep crying, naked, bruised, and bleeding from the half-mile run through the woods.

Norb, naked, came into the main room to the couch where Cletus lay rolled into a tight little ball and pretending to be asleep. He grabbed the boy around his neck, pulled him out of bed, and marched him into the bedroom where the act was quickly and quietly consummated.

Dove Eckland had used brute force on the pre-pubescent Norbert and Norbert's siblings.

Jubal Eckland had used the same method on his sons, of whom Dove was the oldest.

It went all the way back to Spencer Eckland.

Jesse, the oldest son, quietly acquiesced until he joined the Army. After he left home, he never directed another word to Norb again. After Jesse left, Norb turned his attentions to his other sons, starting with Byron and especially Charlie, his favorite, and working his way down.

Although Willa Mae was aware of what was going on, she said nothing, afraid for her own life. She had vowed, however, that if Norb attempted to do the same with Willie, she would intervene with an old hunting knife she had gotten from her own father years ago.

Three years after Jesse took Willie to live with him and his wife, Norb regained custody of little Willie when Jesse, still in the Army with less than a year before retirement, was killed in an automobile accident near Malibu.

Saddled with four children of her own, Betty Jean Eckland returned Willie to Norb's drunken care.

Like a spider awaiting a fly, seventeen year old Cletus waited anxiously for the day when Willie would arrive.

Cletus had never had the luxury of his own room or his own bed. From the time he was too large to sleep in his crib, he shared a fold-out couch in the shack's main room with Jack, Irwin, and Hiram.

Hiram and Irwin slept at the cushioned end of the couch and he and Jack slept at the foot, like sardines in a can. The older boys slept on two cots in the kitchen, which they folded up and pushed into a corner during the daytime.

Willie was Cletus' choice for consolation before he was taken to California by Jesse. Willie remembered and dreaded the day when he would have to return to Mississippi and Cletus' open pants.

Cletus was now seventeen, well over six feet tall, and strong as an ox. Finally admitting what Willa Mae had said all along, that Cletus "ain't quite right in the head," Norb was just a little bit afraid of Cletus and seldom bothered him for sexual services without offering to pay for them. Like a vulture, he, too, eagerly waited Willie's return.

In the meantime, he had found a drunken slattern named Agnes McGuffey at the local redneck bar in Paw-Paw, a few miles down the road from the Eckland homestead, and spent most of his time with her. Although she hated Norb's slovenliness, she loved his enormous member.

Cletus also found another, more willing sexual partner, Dilsey and Ajax's oldest daughter, Mary Grace.

Mary Grace was a year older than Willie.

Mary Grace was the pride and joy of Dilsey and Ajax Kirkwood. She had been a healthy, normal baby, meeting all of her milestones until she was six months old.

One day, Dilsey was hanging up the family's laundry in the back yard. She had bathed, fed, and changed the infant's diaper and put her down for a nap in her bassinette near a window in the family's small front room.

Dilsey told Willa Mae that she heard the child begin to fret as if she awoke early from her nap. Normally, the naps lasted two to three hours. The fretting stage of waking up gave Dilsey about fifteen additional minutes before the child was fully awake, so she continued with her chores.

She said she noticed that the infant's cries went from whimpers to panic in the matter of a few seconds. She dropped her laundry and ran toward the back door of the house but before she could open it, the child quietened. She could hear the sounds of the child gurgling contentedly, as if being fed or held. She assumed that the child had gone back to sleep and didn't continue to the living room to check on her, ignoring her "mother's intuition."

"I felt it in my bones that som'pn wasn't right, even when I thought she had went back to sleep," she told Willa Mae. "I felt like som'pn evil was 'round my baby. I blame myse'f for not goin' in an' checkin' on her." After about ten minutes, the child began crying again, but this time, they were frantic, as if she were in pain.

"A mother knows when her child's cries is normal and when they the result of stress, hunger, or pain," Dilsey said. "I knew my baby was in pain.

"I ran into the house and slammed the back screen door," she continued. "Suddenly, she got quiet ag'in. Cut off in mid scream. Like somebody had turned off a light or snuffed out a candle.

"There wasn't supposed to be nobody in the house 'cept the baby," she continued, "but jus' as my foot hit the kitchen flo', I heard the door in the front room bang shut.

"I *know* I locked the front screen do' but when I got to the front room, first thing I noticed was that it was swingin' back and forth, an', out of the corner of my eye, I saw somebody jump off the porch and head for the woods.

"It looked like Cletus, Willa Mae. I don' wanna think that Cletus would hurt my baby. She never did nothin' to nobody, but I swear to God that it looked like Cletus.

"At first, I thought he had took my baby so I checked the bassinette right off. Mary Grace was still there but she waddn' movin'. She was jus' starin' at the ceiling like she was hypnotized or som'pn."

She opened the small grocery bag she had held in her hand and pulled out a pair of very dirty, smelly boys' underpants. "I found these in the corner, behind the do'," she said.

"All Mama could say was 'call the police, Dilsey. Maybe they c'n do som'pn wit' him 'cuz I sho' cain't." Will said, pausing to take a drink of his wine, a California varietal.

The waitress came around again. We ordered dinner and moved to a table inside. Will continued his story.

"Aunt Dilsey also noticed that the baby's diaper had been removed. One of the big safety pins she used to fasten the baby's diaper was stuck into her thigh and the baby never even whimpered.

"When she got no response from the baby, she called Uncle Ajax at work and told him what she had seen and the child's strange behavior. Where Mary Grace had been a healthy, lively, responsive infant, she was now eerily silent, staring only at the ceiling.

"Aunt Dilsey and Uncle Ajax took the baby to Dr. Prentiss in Poinsett. When he couldn't get a response, he had the child transported to the Children's Hospital in Memphis.

"The doctors there said someone had shook the baby, probably to quieten her. Her little brain had been turned into jelly by whoever shook her. They also found that she had molasses smeared around her mouth and on her private parts. They said she hadn't been raped but somebody had tried to put som'pn in her-- probably a finger.

"The sheriff's deputies questioned both Cletus and Jack. Both of them had cut school that day and neither could give a satisfactory explanation as to where they were but they were young white boys an' this was Poinsett, Mississippi. The cops there weren't gonna believe that no white boy, even an Eckland, would do that to a black baby.

"During the entire interrogation by the Poinsett County Sheriff's Office, Cletus wore the same stupid expression on his face that he wore during the interrogation when Mama died.

"Although Mary Grace survived the episode, her brain had been turned into jelly while her body continued to mature naturally. She never got past the level of a three or four-year old, mentally.

"Cletus gave the Kirkwoods' home a wide berth for years, even though there was not enough evidence to prove that he had caused Mary Grace's condition. I doubt it was guilt that made him avoid them like the plague," Will smiled. "In all probability he was scared that if Uncle Ajax got a-hold of him, he'd kill him. Uncle Ajax wasn't a big man but not one to be messed with, especially when it came to his family."

Cletus lurked in the woods around the homes in the area for any opportunities that might come his way. In a place and time when no one had air conditioned homes, things went missing on a regular basis.

Whether it was food left unguarded in one family's kitchen, a pie left to cool on another family's back porch, a wallet here, a valued family ring there, scraps thrown away after dinner, or a mentally delayed girl left to play on her back yard swing, Cletus took advantage of every opportunity like the scavenger he was.

Cletus knew that the deeply religious Kirkwoods went to Bible class at New Pilgrim Holiness Temple a mile or so from the Eckland homestead, every Tuesday night and to prayer meeting every Wednesday night from six to eight o'clock. They always took Mary Grace with them but after a few minutes, the girl became restless. Her parents then allowed her to roam about the building or on the church grounds, which consisted of five or more acres, including an unused parsonage, the church proper, and the cemetery. Mary Grace loved the cemetery, where her beloved grandma was buried, and would frequently visit her grandma's grave.

Cletus found that he could coax the mentally challenged child out of the graveyard and into the woods and entice her to put her mouth on his penis if he either paid her a shiny new coin or if he coated his penis with honey or molasses.

As Cletus rarely had any money at all, least of all, shiny new coins, he rarely visited Mary Grace Kirkwood without taking along a tin of molasses or a jar of honey; whichever he could steal from neighboring houses.

Will recounted that the Kirkwoods gladly took him and reluctantly took Jack into their home as Norb became less and less responsible and began spending most of his nights at Agnes McGuffey's house but they would have nothing to do with Cletus.

"If you take one'a my boys, you gotta take 'em all," Norb said to Dilsey. "You cain't show fav'rites." Dilsey decided to leave all of them with Norb.

Seeing that his plan had backfired and he was now saddled with all three boys, Norb pleaded with the Kirkwoods to reconsider and appealed to their humanity. "My poor motherless sons," he always started out his sentences. He worked out a deal in which he would "allow" Willie to remain with the Kirkwoods if they agreed to also provide room and board for Jack.

Cletus was on his own. He would spend his nights alone in his family's home or wherever he chose—except with the Kirkwoods or at Agnes McGuffey's house. Although they were unaware of it, Cletus spent most nights battling mosquitoes on the Kirkwoods' back porch with their dog, Toby.

When part of the roof of the Ecklands' rapidly deteriorating houses fell in during a windstorm, Cletus begged the Kirkwoods to let him to move in with them, as Agnes McGuffey would not allow him to stay in her home and Norb had neither the money nor the inclination to fix the roof.

Cletus was big, dirty, smelly, surly, ungrateful, mean, and a sexual threat to both Agnes' nine-year old daughter, Connie, and to Mary Grace Kirkwood.

The Kirkwoods turned him down but after they spied Cletus fighting with Toby, for the table scraps they fed him each night, and after Norb's appeal to their Christian charity that his "poor little motherless son" was roaming around their back yard waiting for them to feed the dog, and how the boy had spent many nights sleeping alone in the fallen-down wreck that had been his boyhood home with no food, water, electricity, or protection against the weather, the Kirkwoods, prayed over the matter and, against their better judgment, took pity on the cursed boy and allowed him to move in with them.

Tall for his age, massive, extraordinarily good-looking, and wearing patched overalls that came well above his ankles, shirts that did not button across his massive chest, a drawstring belt salvaged from the Ecklands' front room's Venetian blinds, and a pair of dirty "clodhoppers" with "more hole than sole,"

Cletus personified the "Li'l Abner" look. He also brought with him one jar of honey, and one tin of black-strap molasses "just in case the opportunity arose."

Mary Grace slept on an Army cot in her parents' bedroom next to Ajax and Dilsey's bed. Willie slept behind a locked door in the second bedroom, while Jack and Cletus were given the sofa bed in the living room at night. Because of the conflict between them, one, usually Cletus, slept sitting in an armchair on the other side of the room.

Still, Ajax had a "talk" with Cletus, explaining to him that if he even looked cross-eyed at Mary Grace or at Willie, he would snap Cletus's neck as a cook would snap a young carrot.

One afternoon a few days after his nineteenth birthday, Jack stuffed his meager belongings into a duffle bag, said goodbye to the Kirkwoods, then walked the mile to the main highway headed north, stuck out his thumb, and disappeared into the night when an old black pickup truck gave him a ride a few minutes later. All of his brothers had taken the same way out of Poinsett over the years.

Norb was told of Jack's departure when he stopped by a few days later to see how his sons were faring and to pay the Kirkwoods for their room and board. He took Cletus back to their former home where, although the kitchen's roof had fallen in, the bedroom was intact and the bed was still there, and then to the local Dairy Queen for a hot dog and a strawberry malt, his payment for a job well done.

Cletus remained with the Kirkwoods the entire summer but the Kirkwoods were finally pushed to their limit in September, when school started, and Cletus refused to board the bus in front of their house. Cletus was a bully and knew that none of the children at school would dare call him a white nigger or a nigger-lover to his face, but he did not want to be seen boarding the bus on Clark Road. He did not want to explain to his friends, boys who feared, rather than respected, him, why he was living with a black family.

Ajax told him that he could either board the bus at the front of Clark Road as Willie, did, or he could leave. The boy packed his meager belongings, trudged two miles to Agnes McGuffey's home in a heavy downpour, and told Norb that the niggers had kicked him out of their house *"for no reason a'tall."* Even Norb, in his drunken stupor, found that one hard to believe.

Agnes McGuffey allowed him to spend the night at her house but made it clear to both father and son that it was for one night only. She gave father and son her bed while she spent the night in her daughter, Connie's bedroom behind a locked and bolted door.

That night, the boy quietly paid homage to Norb one last time before taking off.

The next day, after the boy had taken off for parts unknown, Agnes burned the sheets Norb and Cletus had used.

***

Cletus hitchhiked to Memphis where he spent a few days walking the streets, taking in the sights and looking for a job. He had no money and, no local address or telephone number where prospective employers could call or write him to inform him of their decision.

He was young and proud but youth and pride do not put food in anyone's stomach or a pillow under anyone's head. He made his way to Crosstown. where a variety of lifestyles are accommodated. When those of a "happier" lifestyle approached him for a date, Cletus was quick to point out, "I ain't no faggot! I don' do that!"

It was part of Cletus' plan to start afresh. His natural proclivities were undefined. Although Cletus had a healthy interest in the opposite sex, girls his age had a healthy initial response to Cletus but they quickly dropped him when they smelled him or found out his cruel, thoughtless, and selfish nature.

Cletus was misogynistic. His only interest in females was for sloppy sex. His interest was not to satisfy anyone except himself.

The girls in his school would not approach him or Jack due to peer pressure. All had known both brothers since kindergarten and would no more be seen in public with them than they would be seen in public on a date with a Negro. It just wasn't done! Dating an Eckland was as low as a white girl could go.

Cletus sat in the back of the classroom when he attended classes at all. He made noises aimed at disrupting the teacher or he stroked his penis to full erection, causing admiration among the boys and disgust (and secret delight) among the girls.

Cletus loved boxing because it was the one sport where he was an individual, not a team member, and it offered him the opportunity to pound his opponent senseless. In fact, it was because of his natural aggression that he was dismissed from the team: He did not know when to stop. Neither the bell nor the coach's whistle could deter Cletus from continuing to pound his opponent once he got "in the zone."

Cletus soon developed the reputation for being *"crazy"* as a result of his aggressiveness. If it could be controlled, his boxing coach believed he could become the "great white hope," the latest in a long line, but that would be years and miles from Poinsett's public high school.

Now, in Memphis, alone for the first time in his life with few prospects, Cletus resorted to stealing the things he needed or doing "eat and runs" in the local restaurants but that did not last long. When all else failed, he revisited selling his only saleable asset, his body, to anyone who would pay for the pleasure, give him a place to sleep, or buy him dinner. With his physical endowments, including but not limited to a nearly perfect body and a huge cock, Cletus quickly became the toast of the town among a certain segment of gay society.

Dann Vacarro, a retired banker, who owned a grand neo-Classical style mansion in Normantowne Commons, Memphis' newest and most exclusive gated golf course community, was a short, swarthy, hirsute man with large brown eyes and even larger dark bags beneath them.

Vacarro had followed all of the rules as he aged: he suffered from male pattern baldness, he had spread in the right places, and he was now suffering through a mid-life crisis. The crisis was that at sixty-six years old, he had found himself alone, unloved, and unlovable. He had never been very nice to anyone and now, in his later years, he had many acquaintances but few friends.

Vacarro considered himself among Memphis' gay elite. He drove a new, white Cadillac, he lived in the most exclusive neighborhood, and he looked down his prodigious nose at those less fortunate than he.

Although he was seldom seen at the Normantowne Commons clubhouse, whose membership came with the purchase of a lot in the Normantown Commons community, Vacarro spent much of his time at Club Aristos, an exclusive gays-only club that only took in new members when an old member died, moved, or relinquished his membership.

Most of the members were middle-aged or older, Protestant, and extremely wealthy. All were white. Most were married and living lives of quiet desperation. Many were from the Mid-South's leading families and had known one another since childhood.

Vacarro, being of Italian ancestry and Catholic, was not part of that group. He had been blackballed the first three times he applied. It was not until Vacarro came to the aid of a club member who found himself in a sticky situation involving a dead boy in his bed that was he accepted as a member.

Vacarro and the other "aristocrats" looked down upon the larger gay community and never participated in anything it sponsored. They preferred to socialize among themselves, attend the opera and symphony, dine at their own restaurant or the Mid-South's finest restaurants, and take wine-tasting tours in California, or vacation on the Cote d'Azure, Acapulco, Haiti, the Dominican Republic, Thailand, or other foreign ports where their peccadilloes went unseen and unreported.

Of course, all of the members "went slumming" in Memphis from time to time, often bringing their "finds" back to Club Aristos, which occupied the top three floors of a seven-story former department store that had gone out of business some years prior, spending anywhere from a few minutes to the entire night, and then, before sunrise, dumping them back on the streets from which they had plucked them.

Most of the members of Club Aristos were involved in sham marriages. Many had children and grandchildren whom they loved. Most had been forced to marry by their families under the threat of being disinherited.

Several were members of the clergy, who railed against homosexuality on Sunday mornings and enthusiastically participated in it the other six days of the week. Vacarro found this hypocritical and criticized one member who is a television evangelist unmercifully about his *"do as I say, not as I do"* policy.

Vacarro loved *things* more than people. He acquired things not for their intrinsic beauty or even because he wanted them, but either to show that he had the wherewithal to purchase them or to keep others from acquiring them.

He had done this when he purchased the lot on which he built his current home. When he heard that Normantowne Commons was being touted as the most exclusive community in the state, he purchased a lot overlooking The Belfry, as the tenth hole was called. It was a shortish par four of 363 yards with a view to die for.

He knew that an acquaintance and his wife wanted to purchase it for their home so naturally, he had to have it.

That lot was considered by the builders to be the premier lot in the community so Vacarro had to have it at any cost. On it, he built a fabulous neo-Classical style mansion with ten thousand square feet under roof and an additional eight thousand feet in outdoor living areas. The swimming pool was an exact replica in miniature of San Simeon's Neptune Pool.

The house itself, lacked for nothing. Its marble-encased, glass-roofed solarium was featured in the local newspapers and magazines for months. Vacarro reveled in the notoriety.

Purchasing a lot in Normantowne Commons included a club membership and, although he had no interest in playing golf because he suffered from hyperhydrosis, he didn't dance with women (and the homophobic club would not allow him to dance with men even if he wanted to), he didn't play tennis, and he either hated or was hated by most of the other club members, he went forward with the purchase just so he could boast that he lived in Normantowne Commons and, therefore, was a club member. In the three years that he had lived in Normantowne, he had rarely visited the clubhouse—unless he wanted to impress some poor hustler.

Vacarro wined and dined Cletus, regaling him with expensive gifts, the likes of which Cletus had never seen. Vacarro cleaned the boy up, took him to lunches and brunches at the club, and invited Cletus to move in with him.

When Cletus accepted the offer, Vacarro told everyone Cletus was his nephew, come to live with him from Oxford, Mississippi. That sounded a lot less "country" than Poinsett.

Cletus had been on the streets for about two months when Vacarro met him standing outside one of the city's seedier gay bars. Due to his age and lack of funds, he was not allowed inside. Several of the members recognized Cletus from previous rendezvous, but said nothing.

In fact, Cletus had eaten at the Ariston Restaurant at Club Aristos several times with various members and he had spent several nights as guest of some of those members. Memphis is not that large a town and everyone knows everyone else's business so if Vacarro wanted the members to believe that Cletus was his nephew, so it was.

Vacarro took Cletus to the city's best haberdashers and tailors, spending money on the boy like a drunken sailor. Back at Vacarro's home, he gave Cletus diction lessons, etiquette lessons, and hygiene lessons in an effort to turn a sow's ear into a silk purse.

Vacarro even reserved an elegant penthouse suite on *The Cajun Queen,* a restored paddle-wheeler that plied the Mississippi River between New Orleans and St. Louis and took Cletus to New Orleans on a two-week "honeymoon" cruise.

Cletus traded in his "high-water" pants, his threadbare shirts that no longer fit, and his tight "flappers," the nearly soleless clodhoppers he had worn in Poinsett, for the high-priced, quality merchandise with which he was being showered. For Cletus, every day was like Christmas.

Vacarro paraded Cletus around like a new puppy. Cletus tasted chutney, bouillabaisse, foie gras, etouffé, paella, espresso, andouille, and frogs' legs, among other things, for the first time in his life. He also tasted avocado, lime, and macadamia nuts for the first time. It was a new and different world for him and his cock was his *ticket d'entrée.*

Vacarro took Cletus to a general practitioner for a full check-up, to the dentist to have his cavities filled and his teeth cleaned, to a manicurist for a pedicure to remove the encrusted dirt and hardened skin from his feet, and to his hair stylist to have his hair cut, conditioned, lightened, and styled. The boy shone like a new penny.

In their daily "living sessions," as Vacarro called them, Vacarro taught Cletus the proper way to use a napkin, knife, and fork; to eat sushi, and gave him the first toothbrush he didn't have to share with anyone else. Up to the time he left home, he shared a toothbrush with his two remaining brothers, Jack and Willie, if he used one at all. When he left home, grabbing a toothbrush was the farthest thing from his mind.

Vacarro and his friends flattered Cletus, telling him how handsome he was, how strong he was, what a perfect body he had, and how much he looked like "a young Elvis."

Initially, their arrangement worked out for both of them. Cletus needed a place to live and Vacarro had something that made him the envy of all who knew him. The frog had been changed into a prince.

"Clete, you've got to bathe or shower *daily,"* Vacarro said. "I have all of the hot water you could ever want. All you have to do is turn on the tap."

No one had ever instructed him in personal hygiene. No one had answered any of the questions all growing teenage boys have. He and Jack were not close enough for Cletus to ask Jack about the questions he had. Besides, Jack didn't know any more about sex and hygiene than Cletus did.

Norb certainly hadn't told Cletus anything evenly remotely resembling "the facts of life" and Cletus would never have approached Norb with his questions. In all probability, no one had instructed Norb in the facts, either. If someone had, Norb had definitely not absorbed the lesson.

"You're certainly not going to sleep on my expensive sheets if you're not clean," Vacarro said, exasperated, when Cletus showed an aversion to soap and water.

He handed Cletus a clean but well-worn blanket, an old pillow, and an old but clean sheet. "Here, use these and you can sleep on the floor near Princess," he said. Princess, of course, had her own little canopy bed with velvet pillow in which she slept. It was a tiny replica of Vacarro's gigantic bed.

Vacarro's bed was the size of a Rose Parade float. It sat three steps above the rest of the room in a specially-created alcove on a carpeted dais. Its headboard was made of mustard-colored tufted velvet at the center of which was a large gold-leaf fleur-de-lis on a gold and white enamel escutcheon.

The bed itself had a full tester supported by hand-carved rosewood posts half the diameter of telephone posts, that rose three-quarters of the way up Vacarro's eighteen foot-high coffered ceilings.

On top was the camelback wrought iron canopy for which the bed was named, draped in alternating layers of gold and ecru silk, like a circus tent. At the center of the tester was a gold-leaf sunburst about the size of a serving platter from which the rouched layers of silk emanated. Fringes and tassels hung from every corner. The bed could have been ordered by the Sun King himself.

Cletus had never even dreamed that anyone anywhere slept in anything so grand.

Vacarro, a perfectionist, rapidly grew weary of spending the better part of an hour every day urging Cletus into the shower only to find that the boy had let the water in the shower run for ten or fifteen minutes while he masturbated all over Vacarro's heated Carrara marble floors.

Cletus was mean, selfish, ungrateful, and slovenly. He gave nothing but his temper tantrums grew worse by the day as he demanded more than Vacarro was willing to give and thinking himself so deeply ensconced in the Vacarro's heart and household that Vacarro would not dare throw him out. Vacarro's patience finally wore out.

One day, after Cletus had had a particularly violent temper tantrum, Vacarro went to the closet in his family room and took from the top shelf, a tall white box from The Collegiate Shop, one of Memphis' leading haberdasheries that catered to upper-class young men.

"Clete," as Vacarro called him, was asleep in the solarium after having spent himself in an hour-long tantrum, during which he had kicked and broken a valuable Ming dynasty urn.

Vacarro allowed the boy to sleep peacefully for another hour before awakening him and announcing that they were going out for the evening and that "Clete" should shower and dress.

Cletus always loved evenings out because they afforded him new and unusual experiences.

"Where we goin' tonight?" he wanted to know. "To the opera?"

Vacarro shook his head and smiled. "Guess again," he said coyly.

"The symphony? You promised you'd take me there. I wanna see your private box."

Vacarro again shook his head and continued smiling. "Not this time," he said. "Guess again."

After a few more wrong guesses, Vacarro said, "We're going somewhere very special. It's a surprise. Go now and get ready," he urged. "Hurry up."

After Cletus undressed, he posed like a Greek statue and allowed himself to be worshipped by the older man, who appeared to have forgiven him his trespasses.

The boy smiled as he entered the bathroom and closed the door.

Vacarro, always anxious to avoid a scene, called the gatehouse and requested that two of the guards be sent to escort Cletus off the premises when he finished showering.

The boy took a "Victory Bath," washing only his underarms, chest, pubic area, and crack of his ass. He sprayed the rest of his body with the Old Spice Vacarro had purchased for him. "What should I wear?" he asked himself, opening the double doors to the smaller of the two walk-in closets that Vacarro had designated as Cletus'.

"Don't look in there," Vacarro said, still smiling and now standing next to the large white box he had taken from the family room's closet. "I have everything you need to wear right here."

The doorbell rang. "Get dressed. I'll answer the door," Vacarro said, leaving the room on tippy-toes. Cletus beamed as he tore off the lid of the box and pawed through the layers of white tissue paper in which the "new" togs were wrapped.

Vacarro returned to the bedroom he and Cletus shared. He was accompanied by two beefy uniformed guards just as Cletus, with a huge white terrycloth towel around his waist, finished pulling out the clothes he was supposed to wear that evening.

His smile faded when he realized that they were the same clothes and shoes he had worn when he left Poinsett, but they had been washed, darned, patched, or in some other way, repaired. His old shoes had been re-soled and they had been polished to a high shine, probably their first since they were purchased.

"Get dressed and let's go, Son," the older of the two guards said.

Cletus looked up for the first time and noticed the guards. "What's goin' on, Uncle Dann?" he asked, perplexed.

Vacarro did not answer. The older guard again spoke, this time, louder. "Get dressed, Son. Let's go!"

"Where?" Cletus wanted to know.

"For starters, to the front gate," the older man said. "After that, it's up to you. Mr. Vacarro has requested that we accompany you off the premises. It seems as though your presence is no longer wanted here."

The light bulb in Cletus' head lit up as he came upon the realization that he was being dumped. "Did y'all know that I'm a minor and that I'm not really his nephew, like he told y'all?" Cletus said to the younger of the two guards, who appeared to be more in awe of the luxurious surroundings than in what was going on around him.

"Tell it to the Marines," the younger man said.

"For real," Cletus continued. "He told me to say that I'm his nephew in case some of the nosy busybodies should ask. I'm still seventeen an' in this state, that's against the law," he spouted.

"Tell that to the Marines, too. In this state, the age of consent is seventeen," the younger man said.

"Did I say seventeen? Cletus said. "I meant to say I'm....*fifteen*. Yeah, I'm big for my age but I'm only fifteen. Arrest *him*, not *me*."

"We're not arresting anybody. We're just here to see you off the premises. If you want to make a complaint against him, you'd have to go to the Shelby County Sheriff's Office but you'd better be sure you're really fifteen years old because making a false police report is taken very seriously down there. Now get dressed and let's go," the man said.

Cletus dressed without further protest. When he reached for a gold chain and cross Vacarro had purchased for him, Vacarro snatched it away. "You take only what you arrived with," Vacarro said, speaking for the first time since the guards had arrived.

"Can I have cab fare back to town?" Cletus asked.

"You just kicked over an expensive Ming dynasty urn, you baboon. It's irreplaceable. Are you gonna pay me for that?" Vacarro sneered. "If you think I'm going to give you one cent more, you're crazier than my Aunt Hattie's cat! Not on your life. *Now get out of here, you trashy bastard!*" he screamed, his voice going up in range to that of an operatic soprano.

Cletus left with the two guards. The older guard took pity on Cletus and, for the price of a blow job, drove the boy the six miles to mid-town Memphis. Soon Cletus was back on the streets, sleeping in the same park where Vacarro had found him.

Cletus contacted Scott Ping, Vacarro's closest friend, who took Cletus in when the boy told him that, for no reason, Vacarro had thrown him out.

Ping, a retired oral surgeon, was as much of a perfectionist as Vacarro. He called Vacarro to get the real story. Vacarro told him what had happened, ending the conversation with, "you're welcome to him." Cletus stayed there for a month before "the real Cletus" emerged.

One by one, Cletus contacted and was taken in by all of Vacarro's associates and kicked out when they found out that his beauty was only skin deep and that he was mean, selfish, ungrateful, vindictive, and slovenly. Sooner or later, Cletus always ended up back in the same park.

After a few months on the streets, selling himself to whoever had the price of a meal, or a warm bed for the night, it was *"been there; done that one"* where Cletus was concerned. His true nature was now well known and he had burned all of his bridges.

After a while, his enormous, unwashed member could only attract flies. His poor diet and lack of hygiene had taken a toll on his once-magnificent body. Where he had once been robust and "the picture of health," his skin was now desiccated and droopy. His eyes, once clear and bright, were tired, lifeless, and wary. His teeth had yellowed, with a large brown spot appearing on one of the upper incisors. His hair was dry and brittle and he needed a shave.

If the weather was cold and he had had no luck selling his body, he sheltered in the Greyhound Bus station. If it was warm, he sheltered among the supports of one of the overpasses that led to the Mississippi River Bridge.

Cletus had collected a few personal items, a sleeping bag, a duffle bag, a sliver of a mirror, a toothbrush, toothpaste, a comb, a few changes of clothes, and some other toilet items, and hid them under the overpass' supports.

He considered this his "spot" and drove away all interlopers. He made no friends and considered himself a lone wolf, on the prowl only for his own benefit. What he pilfered was for his own benefit. He usually brought his prizes back to his lair where he appraised their value to his survival and either kept or discarded them if they were not useful or edible.

Although he considered himself safe and hidden away from the prying eyes of others, one lonely, moonless night, Cletus was attacked and beaten by a group of the regular, less well-endowed street hustlers and left bleeding from the nose, mouth, and face with two broken ribs.

They remembered and resented how Cletus had sneered at them when he was "riding high" with Vacarro and his rich friends.

Cletus ducked out of the hospital and hitchhiked back to Normantowne Commons once more, found the same guard whom he had fellated for a ride into town when Vacarro kicked him out, and fellated him again for entry and a ride to Vacarro's home.

Dirty, disheveled, and injured, Cletus put on his most contrite, "little boy lost" face and rang Vacarro's doorbell. He started by saying he was sorry for having been so undesirable and unreasonable. He promised to become a different person if Vacarro would give him a second chance.

Vacarro accepted the bedraggled boy back into his home again, and called one of his neighbors, a doctor, who cared for Cletus' wounds. Vacarro paid Cletus' hospital bill, nursed him back to health, and brought out the clothes he had previously purchased for Cletus. They had been stored in the same tall white box in which Cletus' old clothes had been stored.

"Can I call my family in Poinsett to let 'em know that I'm OK?" he asked when he was better. Vacarro consented and dialed Agnes McGuffey's number for Cletus. When Agnes refused to accept the charges, Cletus gave Vacarro the number for his "aunt and uncle," the Kirkwoods.

When Dilsey Kirkwood answered the phone and accepted the charges, Vacarro passed the receiver to Cletus.

"Hello? Aunt Dilsey?" Cletus inquired in a louder-than-necessary voice. Dilsey was taken aback because although she had always insisted that Cletus "put a handle" on her name, he had persisted in calling her and Ajax by their given names. This sudden politeness was unnatural and disturbing to Dilsey.

"Cletus?" she inquired skeptically. "You alright? You ain't in no trouble, are ya? Where y'at?" The questions came rapid-fire.

'I'm alright. I'm livin' near Memphis," the boy continued in a too-loud voice. "An' I ain't in trouble. How *you* doin'?" he inquired. He looked up at Vacarro, raised his eyebrows, as if requesting to be left alone for a private conversation. Vacarro withdrew to the kitchen, leaving Cletus and his "aunt" to speak privately.

When Vacarro as out of sight and earshot, Cletus lowered his voice almost to a whisper. "I jus' wanted y'all to know that I'm livin' in a mansion bigger'n Elvis' with real limestone columns out front an' heated marble floors. I got six bedrooms an' *nine* bathrooms, an' a big-ass swimmin' pool. I got a maid an' new clothes, an' ever'thang.

"I don' need you niggers for *nothin'* no more," he said nastily. Dilsey could just imagine his face as he spewed the venom.

"How many bathrooms you say you got, Cletus?" she asked.

"Nine," he reiterated.

"Since when you like to bathe, Cletus? I don' know why you got so many bathrooms. We only got one an' I don' remember you ever usin' the bathtub," she smiled. "An' you *cain't* shit so much that you need nine bathrooms!"

The boy said nothing, but his ears turned red and became hot as he tried to think of a snappy retort.

Before he could fill the silence, she said, "I'm *so* happy things is workin' out fo' you, Cletus. You wanna speak to Willie? He standin' right here." Her honeyed voice hit him like a slap in the face, disarming him.

"What I gotta say to him? I hate you an' I hate Ajax, an' most of all, *I hate him!*" Cletus whispered, exasperated that he could not get a rise from Dilsey.

"I got shoes that cost mo' than your whole damned house," the boy continued to brag, spewing his venom one last time.

"Well that sho' is nice, Cletus. I'm glad fo' ya. Glad you landed on yo' feet. Have a good life an' don't forget to say your prayers." She hung up the phone before he could tell her about the silk boxers he now sported or his trip to New Orleans on *The Cajun Queen.*

He stood in Vacarro's luxurious family room for a long time with the receiver still pressed to his ear, listening to the drone of the disconnected telephone number.

Cletus promised Vacarro that he would bathe daily and become the model friend and lover. Happy beyond belief, Vacarro invited him to sleep again in his huge bed.

Although Cletus appeared to be comfortable with the new arrangement and happy to be back, he was inwardly repulsed by the effeminate man's advances but dared not rebuff them for fear of ending up on the streets again.

Vacarro reminded Cletus of one of a pouter pigeon he had seen once at the Mississippi State Fair. Vacarro fancied himself a male version of Mae West, whom he adored.

In Poinsett, men were men and women were women. There were no impersonators and no "in-betweens." No sane man wanted to be a woman.

Cletus had never known a man who used make-up and eye shadow, or who slept in a silk negligee and it disgusted him when Vacarro did them but he said nothing. Those things were womanly things and Cletus hated women. Although he hated Vacarro, he needed him, so he pretended to enjoy Vacarro's exaggerated effeminacy, his non-stop chain smoking, and even his high-pitched, yammering voice that grated on Cletus' nerves like fingernails scraped across a blackboard.

About the only thing Cletus genuinely liked about Vacarro was his silver Persian cat, Princess Margaret, who was almost a feline clone of her master. Princess Margaret sported one eye as blue as sapphires and the other, gold and as clear as the yolk of an egg or the fiery brilliance of the sun, and as deep as a well. Cletus believed that the souls of all humans rested in the eyes of cats.

Cletus' fascination with fires went back almost to his infancy. He would set fires just to watch the colors, especially the blues and golds. They gave Cletus a warm feeling in his groin. He could not explain it and probably, neither could Dr. Freud, but they were wildly erotic to the young boy and while watching a fire, he would invariably get a stiff, hard, uncontrollable erection that needed to be dealt with then and there. Although he was usually the first in the crowd to arrive, he was always the first to leave; usually with his hands in his pockets to control his erection.

Cletus felt that he had to possess those colors and anything that bore them was fair game as far as he was concerned.

When Dann Vacarro introduced him to Princess Margaret and her eyes met his, he was in love. The deep blue and the impossibly gold gold of her eyes set him off on a sexcapade that lasted a week. Dann Vacarro, thinking he was Cletus' erotic stimulus, took the newly-arrived Cletus to Memphis' finest jewelry store and purchased a Florentine cross made of eighteen carat gold on a matching gold chain.

Cletus had never seen anything as beautiful and elegant as Princess Margaret. Nothing even remotely resembling Princess Margaret existed in Poinsett, even among the richest families--and certainly not in Froggymo'.

If Princess Margaret had showed up in Froggymo', somebody would've shot her, skinned her, and cooked her up for supper, but here; she was perfumed, powdered, pampered and spoiled rotten.

Vacarro had purchased the tiny kitten not because he loved, or even liked, cats, but because he wanted a living, breathing design element in his new home.

His first stop after he had purchased the tiny kitten was not to the veterinarian, but to his "lady-friend," part-time beard, and interior designer, Hillary Lovejoy's office. "Look, Hill," he beamed, placing the tiny bundle of fur in Hillary's liver-spotted hands.

"She looks just like a miniature snow leopard! *This* is the color scheme I want for the rest of the rooms in my new place. I want a pure white interior with black and silver accents throughout. The only exception is my bedroom, and we've already gone over what I want there."

Hillary nodded and stroked the kitten's soft, luxurious fur, holding her close before placing her on a table in the center of the room, pulling out a 35mm camera she kept in a large drawer nearby, and photographing her from every angle; capturing her snow white fur, tinged with just the right amount of black and silver shading, and her large black-rimmed ice blue and fiery gold eyes.

The kitten's life with Vacarro was in no way unpleasant but nevertheless, lonely. After he had shown her to all of his friends and after the woman from the Society column had written her article about how Hillary Marcott had exactly matched the interior of Vacarro's home to the coloring of his beloved pet, he had no further use for her.

He fed her and occasionally, he would pet her but when she scratched his expensive, custom-designed furniture, instead of buying her a scratching post he had her de-clawed.

When she vocalized too loudly for his sensitive ears, he had her vocal cords removed. When she shed her long white fur all over the house, instead of brushing and combing her out, he had "kitty pajamas" made for her, and when she went into heat, he had her spayed.

Vacarro rarely paid her any attention but Cletus spent most of his time playing with her or carrying her around, or grooming her. Vacarro noticed that whenever Cletus played with the cat, he became extremely horny and commented on it to the boy. "I don't know if it's me you love or that cat! You always have an erection when you finish playing with her." Cletus, of course, denied it but whenever he had time alone with the cat and away from Vacarro's all-seeing eyes, it was she who was the object of his affection.

Princess Margaret wore a large heart-shaped gold locket on a black velvet collar around her neck. The locket opened to reveal tiny pictures of Vacarro on one half and of Princess Margaret on the other. Its exterior was studded with a large emerald-cut rhinestone. Vacarro told everyone it was a half-carat diamond.

Cletus never doubted the stone was a diamond for he knew that Vacarro loved diamonds. From the floor safe in the larger of his two walk-in closets, Vacarro showed Cletus his diamond collection: hundreds of loose stones in black velvet pouches, diamond rings, tiaras, brooches, lockets, cuff links, and chokers similar to the one Princess Margaret wore.

Vacarro also showed the boy stacks and stacks of gold coins he had hoarded against the day when the inevitable race war breaks out in this country and paper money would become worthless.

Vacarro's prize piece was his mother's wedding ring, which he had inherited when the old woman, one of Memphis' premier dowagers, died many years ago. Most of the jewelry Vacarro showed the goggle-eyed boy was inherited from her or his father.

Cletus knew where the gold and jewelry were kept and he had returned to Vacarro to get some of it. He needed a stake to leave Memphis and head to the west Texas oilfields. There were two other jewels, not just Vacarro's diamonds that he also wanted to collect before his departure.

Cletus' plan was to endure Vacarro's unceasing ministrations until the weather turned warm, then, in the spring or summer, while Vacarro followed his morning ritual of showering and putting on his "face," Cletus would enter the closet where the jewelry was kept, open Vacarro's safe, take some of the bags of loose diamonds, as many gold coins as he could, and a few select pieces of jewelry, then disappear when they went to breakfast, which they did most mornings.

Cletus planned to sell part of the loot on the street and take a bus to Odessa, Texas before Vacarro even realized that some of his prizes were missing. In Odessa or somewhere nearby, he would hock or sell the rest.

The plan almost worked. One Sunday morning, eight months after he appeared on Vacarro's doorstep, Cletus pretended to doze in post-coital exhaustion while the fastidious Vacarro tip-toed to the luxurious ensuite bathroom to "freshen up."

As soon as Cletus heard the bathroom's double doors close and the shower jets start up, he jumped out of bed, dressed, took from his pocket a small brown paper grocery bag, and headed for the large closet where Vacarro's jewels were safely stored.

He opened the doors to the gigantic walk-in closet that seemed larger than his family's house in Poinsett. The overhead chandelier the recessed pot lights and four matching wall sconces automatically turned on. When he closed the doors behind him, they turned off. He switched on the wall switch and turned the rheostat setting to "low," allowing him enough light to work by but not enough to be seen from the other side.

His mistake was leaving Princess Margaret, who adored him, outside the closet doors. Wherever Cletus was, the princess was sure to be nearby.

The safe was in the closet's floor, covered by a thick piece of blond shag carpet. Cletus quickly peeled back the carpeting, quietly opened the wooden door hiding the safe and punched in Vacarro's code, which he had memorized from the innumerable times Vacarro had opened it in his presence.

Each of the five numbers caused a sharp, very audible "beep" when 'pressed, plus there were the two entry asterisks that needed to be pressed before the five number combination. Failing to press them before pressing the combination, would cause the safe's lock not to engage. Three failures would set off an alarm.

Cletus had observed, remembered, and now, recalled the exact steps needed to open Vacarro's safe.

The safe quietly unlocked in a gentle exhalation of its breath; sounding a lot like Dann Vacarro's orgasm. Cletus didn't regard this violation of Vacarro's sanctum sanctorum as a theft, robbery, or burglary, but as pay for his sexual services to Dann Vacarro.

He dipped his hand into the wide square maw of the substantial safe, pulling out black, leather-bound wood boxes with Plexiglass fronts. The first contained gold coins. The second, loose diamonds in their velvet pouches. The third, Mother Vacarro's platinum, diamond, and gold hoard, and the final one, Vacarro's expensive watches: Cartier, Vacheron Constantin, Petek-Philippe, Baume & Mercier, Rolex, etc. All of the most expensive Swiss brands were represented. The boy felt like Aladdin, having just discovered the treasures of Ali Baba and the forty thieves. He was in hog heaven as he started dumping the contents of the boxes into his paper sack.

As an insult to Vacarro, he decided to leave a gold men's wedding band, probably from Vacarro's father, as Vacarro, an only child, had never married, He had just stuffed the last piece into the sack, a magnificent Piaget men's wristwatch, with a tiger's eye face and whose bezel and band were encrusted with pavé diamonds, returned the boxes to the safe, and was picking up the dozen or so loose diamonds that had spilled onto the floor, into the deep shag of the white carpet, when the closet's double doors opened.

Cletus had tarried too long, dazzled by more wealth than he had ever seen in his life.

Vacarro had walked into the closet to choose an outfit to wear to Sunday morning brunch at the Aristos Club. When he found Cletus on his knees in the corner and his safe open, he knew that Cletus was not there saying his prayers.

Like a deer caught in a car's headlights, Cletus could not move, could not think, and could not come up with a fast excuse. "I was jus' lookin' at some of your pieces," he stammered, trying to manage a smile as he gently removed the Piaget and returned it to the safe.

Vacarro knew exactly what Cletus was doing.

Vacarro was wearing a thick snow white terrycloth bathrobe with a large silver "V" embroidered on a navy blue escutcheon just above his heart; a large white bath towel on his head like a turban, and the pink rubber flip-flops that he always wore in the shower.

He flew into the closet like a giant harpy eagle in pink flip-flops, spreading his claw-like talons downward and around Cletus' neck.

"Steal from me? Steal from me? You bastard! After all I've given you?"
Vacarro screamed. *"How dare you???"*

Although he was effeminate and feigned weakness, Vacarro was still a man--
and a very strong one at that. Most people immediately noticed Vacarro's
hands, which were stubby but strong, thick, and most un-ladylike.

Thick, sausage-like fingers protruded from wide, thick palms like the
teats from a cow's udder. Moreover, Vacarro had fingernails that extended
downward over the tips of his fingers as if they had melted and solidified that
way. They were a Vacarro family trait.

His were the hands of a peasant but soft as clouds, for Vacarro had never done
a lick of hard work in his life. It was the softness of Vacarro's hands that belied
their strength.

Vacarro had never liked his hands, which he inherited from the generations
of Sicilian peasants who comprised his ancestry on both sides of his family
tree clear back to the island's earliest inhabitants. Living under Mt. Aetna,
his ancestors were already established farmers in 79 A.D. when Mt. Vesuvius
erupted on the mainland, burying Pompeii and Herculaneum.

They had survived all of Mt. Aetna's eruptions, too, always returning to her
base to continue the only way of life they knew. For that reason, Vacarro never
wore rings or anything that would call attention to his hands.

*"You little peasant!! I taught you to use a napkin. I taught you to use a
toothbrush and you're gonna steal from me??? You ungrateful little nothing!!"*
Vacarro raged, tightening his grip on the boy's throat with each statement of
fact. *"You white trash bastard!! Hillbilly redneck piece of shit!!"* The epithets
gushed out of Vacarro's maw like the pyroclastic flow from Vesuvius.

He held the hapless boy by the throat in a vise-like grip, cutting off his air
supply with sausage-sized fingers. No air went in and none left Cletus' lungs.
His brain began to cloud up as he lost and regained consciousness. Every color
of the rainbow paraded itself behind his eyelids. Vacarro would not release his
throat and Cletus saw scarlet begin fading to black.

Vacarro had lost all sense of reason. He had gone completely mad as he
continued to hold the boy on the deep shag carpeting on the floor of the closet,

noticing but not caring that the boy was going limp and his color and strength were fading. His heavy white robe had come open, revealing a very hairy, very unfeminine torso. Vacarro had nothing on under the robe; for he had showered and returned to the bedroom to dress for the day's activities. His abnormally small penis and scrotum had retreated as far as they could into his body to protect themselves from damage.

When he did not find Cletus in bed where he had left him, Vacarro assumed that the boy had gone outside to the patio to enjoy a post-coital smoke when heard Princess Margaret scratching at the closet door. Princess Margaret wanted to be wherever Cletus was.

In a last ditch attempt to save his miserable life, Cletus' primitive brain kicked in, the part of the brain that was all about survival. Cletus found an extra reserve of adrenalin and managed to extract his left hand from under Vacarro's leg, grab Vacarro's scrotum, and squeeze as hard as he could.

In pain, Vacarro released the boy's throat just as Cletus' miserable life was about to end once and for all. The boy gasped for air as Vacarro fell back, helpless, as Cletus continued to squeeze Vacarro's family jewels. Vacarro released his hold and the boy exploded, panting, coughing, and sucking in air like a vacuum cleaner.

He released Vacarro's testicles only after Vacarro had agreed not to press theft and assault charges against him. For a long while, they both lay on the floor of the walk-in closet hurting and nursing their points of sorrow.

Vacarro recovered first and sat panting. Spit drooled from the sides of his mouth. Tears filled his eyes. The long trail of hair that he used to cover his balding pate hung limply in front of his face, covering his left eye and giving him the look of a wild-eyed Veronica Lake. *"Get out!!"* he spat. *"Get out of my house!! Now!!! Before I fully recover and take a stick to you!!"*

The boy slowly sat up, still grasping his throat and trying to clear it. Trying to regain his voice. He could not fully speak yet but he managed to hack out, *"I'll go but I'm **not** giving back the clothes you gave me."*

Cletus had not expected the vehemence of the attack from one who gave the impression of being a weak, helpless, woman trapped in a man's body.

There were precious few parts of Cletus' body that were not screaming in pain but he managed to get up from the floor and stumble into the bedroom. Vacarro was right behind him, like a hound behind a raccoon. He grabbed the boy's backpack and removed the paper grocery bag from it. He was incredulous as he saw his treasures, his glittering friends, stuffed in it like stuffing in dumplings.

Cletus opened the double doors to "his" closet's on the opposite side of the room and began stuffing clothing into a tattered green Army backpack from which Vacarro had removed the jewels. This was the only constant in his life. He had taken it with him when he left the Kirkwoods' home what seemed like ages ago.

"You're *not* taking those clothes," Vacarro said. "I bought them and they're staying right here!" he said, snatching clothing out of Cletus' hands as fast as the boy could stuff them into the backpack.

"Fuck you, you crazy bitch!" Cletus finally was able to shout. "You're not gonna kick me out onto the streets in rags this time."

"You'll take what you had when you came here." Vacarro was still screaming. He returned to his own closet, taking his hoard with him. When he had secured the jewels in a lockable cabinet on one side of an onyx-topped center island, he pulled open a drawer that contained a neatly folded brown paper bag with the Piggly-Wiggly Food Stores logo on it. From it, he removed the clothing Cletus had on when he arrived, again washed and ironed: one tattered and faded blue cotton shirt, one pair of blue jeans, also tattered and torn, one brown plastic belt with a faux-alligator design, and one pair of red and white striped boxer shorts.

When he returned to Cletus's closet, he threw them at the boy and grabbed the boy's backpack to see what else he had taken. Cletus held onto one of the straps with his left hand and drew back with his right hand, as if poised to punch the shit out of Vacarro if he did not release the other strap.

No longer fueled by adrenaline, Vacarro released the strap, backed out of the closet, and to the huge bed they had recently shared. He reached for the bedside phone to call for security. "I'll let the police handle this little matter," Vacarro muttered.

"I don't care who you call. These clothes are mine an' I'm takin' 'em," Cletus yelled from the closet. He walked into the bedroom and jerked a linen summer shirt from Vacarro's hands and stuffed it back into the bag.

By the time he had finished packing, Vacarro was hysterically screaming into the handset. Cletus knew he had exactly four minutes before the security team stormed through the front doors. He rapidly stuffed underwear and socks into the backpack and picked up Princess Margaret for a good-bye kiss.

"Oh, no you're not," Vacarro yelled, thinking that Cletus had planned to take her along, too. Cletus put the cat down after saying good-bye and kissing her on the nose. *When I get rich, I'll get me a cat just like that one*, he said to himself.

With two minutes left before the storm troopers came barging into the room, he kissed Princess Margaret for the last time, opened the patio doors, and bound out into the sunlight, across the patio and pool deck, and onto the fairway past some early golfers.

"Stop him!! Stop him!! He's a thief!!" Vacarro yelled to the players. They ignored Vacarro's pleas. Instead, they stood watching a short, dark, hirsute man standing on the edge of his patio wearing nothing but an open bath robe and his exposing his tiny ding-dong to any who cared to look at it.

They could see that he was frantically yelling something but they were too far away to hear what he had to say and far more entranced by the tiny ding-dong than by anything its owner had to say.

Although it was not yet noon, the alligators in the long, narrow fairway that Vacarro's property overlooked, had come up from their murky lairs to get some sun and start their day. There were about six that Cletus could count. Probably a bull and his harem.

Theirs was the only part of the property that had not been altered by the builders of the complex. The cypress, oak, and hackberry trees, along with about thirty varieties of palms, and other shrub and scrub grasses had been set aside by the State of Tennessee as a nature preserve for the different species of passing water fowl that wanted to stop there to rest and recreate. Some, like the possums, raccoons, and gators, were year-round residents. Others had to be forcibly removed for the damage they caused to the lake area and to the surrounding homes.

The lake was long and narrow. Dann Vacarro lived near the eastern end of it. It ran about a half mile due west but it also divided the complex into northern and southern halves. Most residents never gave it a thought as they had cars and drove around it to the complex's main entrance. The only time they actually paid attention to it was in the spring, when the forsythia began to bloom, then the crocuses, when they awoke, and when the female alligators made huge nests, laid their eggs, and went on guard. The females attacked anything that came near their nests so residents and caretakers alike were told to stay away.

Cletus had planned his big escape for just after the nesting season. The female gators were still on guard to ensure that nothing happened to their youngsters but Cletus figured that it was better to leave then rather than earlier, when the females were guarding their nests.

Most never saw Cletus coming but the few who did, beat a hasty retreat back into the safety of the muddy waters of the lake as Cletus made his way to his own private entrance, a culvert put there so that any wildlife trapped within the compound after the walls went up, had an exit to the outside world.

Cletus had found the culvert quite by accident while walking with Dann Vacarro one perfect spring day. He said nothing then but returned when he could get out alone to do some exploration.

He found that the local snakes, some venomous, liked to meet there to beat the summer heat during the day and to hold their snake orgies during spring breeding season. Ever since he was a child and his older brothers put snakes in places he was likely to visit, like his bed or the outhouse, Cletus greatly feared snakes and their bites. Whenever he saw one, regardless of whether it was venomous or beneficial, he killed it.

He found a large, thick club to kill any denizens of the tunnel should he encounter them inside, and left it near the base of the surrounding wall, hidden away in the vegetation, near the ligustrums that had been planted to soften the sight of the wall and make it seem less like a concentration camp and more like the luxury village it was supposed to be.

When he had ensured that there were no critters inside the culvert, including spiders, he decided to stay there until nightfall. In late spring/early summer, the sun didn't set until around eight o'clock. He had a long time to wait but he had been preparing over the last several days.

Under the pretext of taking walks, Cletus had managed to abscond from Vacarro's home with things he would need. He always urged Vacarro to accompany him on his "walks" but he knew that Vacarro didn't like to sweat and that he would decline the invitation.

If he went on his own, without inviting Vacarro, Vacarro would have become suspicious and accuse him of seeing other men. There were several other unmarried older men living in the Normantown complex but Dann Vacarro avoided them like the plague. To Vacarro's knowledge, none was gay but Vacarro always maintained his distance from them, preferring to associate with married couples, all of whom found him funny and charming, and very useful.

Vacarro had acquired skills in so many different areas from sewing to repairing outboard motors.

The man was a regular one-man Heloise both to the husbands and wives. Over the years, the couples had come to accept him and his young "nephews."

Cletus was just one of several over the years but as Vacarro only adopted a certain physical type of individual, his "nephews" could easily have been brothers or cousins.

If his neighbors needed an extra hand at anything from poker to bridge, to watching *Jeopardy*, Vacarro was usually available and always pleasant. If they wanted to know the latest gossip about anything or anyone in the subdivision or in Memphis, they called Dann Vacarro.

Cletus never went anywhere without the Swiss Army knife Vacarro had bought him and he had managed to leave a flashlight, a small miners lantern, canned food and soda pop, toilet paper, and an empty backpack for the "souvenirs" he had planned to take from Dann Vacarro's home in remuneration for his many sexual services.

Cletus spent the day listening to the police sirens and hearing police radios as they searched the area for him. Some stood so close to him, just on the other side of the ligustrums, that he could have reached out his hand and tripped them.

When the search was called off, the sirens had ceased, and night had finally come, he waited until almost midnight, when the "prowlers" came out to play, before he exited his haven and walked eastward, away from the main guard house. There, in the dark, he stood on the shoulder of the road that led into Memphis, and stuck out his thumb.

He was there for no more than five minutes when he was picked up by an itinerant preacher in a shiny dark green Lincoln Town Car with a white vinyl top, whose rear seat was filled with moving boxes, clothes, and other personal items.

"Hoo-wee!! You a big 'un ain't ya?" the driver said.

"Ajax??" Cletus queried. "Is that you, Ajax?"

"Ajax who?" the driver wanted to know.

"You look just like a guy I know back home. I thought you was him," Cletus said, relieved that it wasn't Alex "Ajax" Kirkwood.

Cletus mustered up his best smile, threw his backpack on the front passenger side floor, and jumped in. He settled into the leather seat, adjusted the seat back as far as it would go, and cupped his hand over his groin, his moneymaker.

He would need a place to spend the night and this little man's home, motel room, or car seemed better than any alternatives he could come up with, as he had none.

"I'm The Right Rev. Charles E. Hinkle," the man continued, smiling and extending his right hand to Cletus in an awkward handshake.

The dashboard lights tinted the man's face a demonic green color. When he smiled, the lower half of his teeth was also tinted the same sickly green while the upper half was in shadow. Cletus got a creepy vibe from this man. In his mind, Cletus reckoned that he outweighed the man by at least fifty pounds so he ignored the warning signs.

"You one o' them queer boys?" Hinkle asked.

"Hell no!" Cletus responded, trying to muster up some righteous indignation. "Sorry, Reverend, I meant *no, sir.*" Cletus was now confused by the signals Hinkle was sending out.

"Your mama taught you well," Hinkle laughed.

If you only knew, Cletus thought, but he said nothing.

"Two things I cain't stomach is queers an' niggers. Queers are an abomination to God an' niggers are just an abomination," Hinkle said. "Period!"

"Why'd you ask me that, Sir?" Cletus wanted to know. He waited for the man to answer and studied his green-tinted face while doing so. Cletus was not stupid. He had survived on the streets and in men's arms by knowing how to "read" them.

This man, no bigger than a sock puppet, with baseball mitts for hands, pipe-cleaner arms, a torso that appeared to be no bigger around than the tube at the end of a roll of toilet paper, and a green-and-black tinted face from the dashboard lights, was proving harder to figure out than most.

"The first thing you did when you got settled was to put your hand on your *'Johnson,'* Son. That's usually a sign of a queer," the man said.

"I got 'bout a hunnert different ways of tellin' who's a queer an' who ain't," the man said. Cletus decided to be quiet and allow the man to talk. Sooner or later, the truth would come out but, queer or not, he needed a place to spend the night.

Normantown Commons, was no more than six miles from the Memphis city limits. It had just started to rain. It was too dark and too wet to walk to Memphis when he could ride.

They talked for the remainder of the trip. Cletus had decided that his best bet was to head for west Texas and look for his older brothers. He had not a clue as to where they might be but last time he had heard from any of them, they were working in the oilfields around Odessa, so he'd start his search there.

"Where you stayin' tonight, Son?" the preacher wanted to know, now more relaxed.

"I don' know, Reverend," Cletus replied in his most respectful voice, humping up his shoulders and bowing his head, hoping to inveigle an invitation to stay with the preacher, or for the preacher to provide him with enough money to get a room for the night. Without sex, however, he doubted that either would occur. "Under a bridge, I guess."

"You can't stay under a bridge on a night like this. I got a four-room suite reserved at the Howard Hotel," the preacher said. "You can stay with me, I reckon." He thought for a second. "I ain't gonna wake up an' find my throat slit an' my wallet gone, am I?"

"No, Sir, I promise you I ain't gonna kill ya or steal from ya," Cletus smiled. "I don't steal, Sir." Cletus lowered his collar and showed his neck where Vacarro had tried to strangle him. "An' the only person I wanna kill is my damned daddy. He put this here mark on my throat. The som'-bitch tried to choke me when I tried to protect my mama from a beatin.'"

"I didn't think you would," Hinkle said, placing his mitt of a hand on Cletus' knee and softly rubbing the fabric of his well-worn jeans up to Cletus' "Johnson" and back down again. "I didn't think you would," he repeated. "You're a good boy. I c'n tell. And like I said, you're a *big* 'un." He gave the now fully-aroused "Mr. Johnson" a squeeze.

They checked into the reverend's "suite" at the Howard Motel in West Memphis, Arkansas a sleazy "mom and pop" motor court that had definitely seen better days. "The Peabody was fully booked for a convention," the reverend apologized, "so this'll hav'ta do."

Cletus stood at the entrance to the tiny room after the preacher had changed his single bed room for two queen-sized beds. The beige walls matched the beige bedspreads, and they matched the tattered and torn beige curtains over the oversized window that looked onto the rutted cement parking lot and onto an identical building on the other side of it, that completed the complex.

They were in Building "A." That was Building "C." The connecting building between them, forming a large "U," was Building "B."

Cletus got a chance to get a better look at the preacher. He looked amazingly like Ajax. So much so that Cletus was about to ask him if he was colored until he remembered what the preacher had said about not being able to stomach niggers and queers. This man was a conundrum. He said one thing but clearly meant and did something else.

He was not as small as Cletus had originally thought. Cletus estimated that the man stood about five-feet, seven inches tall, shorter than the average man but not by much. Ajax might have been a little taller but not by much.

He had lank, sand-colored hair that was thinning rapidly on both sides of his head with a patch of long hair at the widow's peak just like Ajax's. Cletus could not decide whether his eyes were blue or gray, pale as they were.

The reverend's two most distinguishing features were an oversized nose that flowed out of the center of his face like Gabriel's trumpet, and his very flat ass. The man looked as if he had been whacked with a thick telephone directory so many times that whatever ass he might have started life with had been flattened to nothing.

His hairless torso looked to Cletus like it was as big around than the cardboard tube at the end of a roll of toilet paper. His arms and legs, virtually hairless, were pipe cleaner thin, white as writing paper, and almost completely devoid of muscle tone.

His smile was dead and unsettling, reminiscent of the maw of a great white shark. Scary. Cletus began to wonder if he would be the one to have his throat slit in the middle of the night and decided to sleep "with one eye open." He had learned the trick while sleeping under the bridge, where one had to be aware of any slight movement around him.

Cletus had managed to relieve Dann Vacarro of a few gold coins and a few pieces of jewelry, which he had hidden in his backpack while Vacarro was calling Security on his bedroom telephone.

Most importantly, Vacarro had neglected to collect Cletus' house key. The boy supposed that Vacarro would simply change the locks, as he had often threatened he would, should they part company. Cletus slipped the key back into his backpack and made plans for revenge.

Where Vacarro had been meticulously neat and clean, almost to the point of obsession, the preacher was the exact opposite. When he removed his rumpled gabardine suit from its garment bag, Cletus noticed that it was dirty and threadbare at the elbows and knees and frayed along the seams.

When he loosened the rumpled red polyester necktie he wore and opened the collar of his rumpled white shirt, Cletus noticed a wide dirt ring around the collar and large sweat rings under the armpits. The man's tiny teeth were yellowed, possibly from smoking, but Cletus neither saw nor smelled cigarettes or their tell-tale smoke.

Next to the strapping teenager, the preacher looked like an oversized rag doll. His fish-white body was almost hairless except for a few straggly ginger hairs in the center of his chicken chest and under his arms. He had a bit of a paunch just above his belt-line that looked to Cletus like he had swallowed a volleyball.

When the reverend removed his trousers and stood before Cletus in his baggy plaid boxers, he reminded Cletus of a small child.

Cletus first smiled at the sight of the little man standing before him with a sizeable erection, and then giggled aloud. The reverend, puzzled by this sudden burst of joviality, said nothing.

When they had finished their "abominable act," they prayed for forgiveness and then they dined on cheeseburgers at a nearby McDonalds. After that, they watched a bit of television before turning off the lights and going to sleep.

The next morning, the reverend awoke early, took a fast shower while Cletus still snored softly in the neighboring bed. That finished, he then stretched and yawned, scratching at his fully-erect cock that peeked out from the opening of his clean pair of boxers, and lay face-up on top of the covers of the bed nearest the door, waiting for the amazing teenager to awaken.

When Cletus awoke, he said nothing, thinking that since the reverend had already told him he hated queers, he was not about to initiate sex a second time lest the preacher think the worst of him.

He noticed, however, that although the reverend said one thing, his cock was saying something very different. The boy was unsure how to play this one, so he waited for the reverend to make the first move.

He followed the preacher's lead. He too got up, showered, and returned to the bedroom dressed only in a pair of tighty-whities. Like a cat, he stretched, and displayed himself atop the covers of the bed nearest the bathroom door. They were like two wolves meeting for the first time, neither fully trusting the other.

The only thing between them was a built-in nightstand, an attached double-headed lamp, and a Gideon's Bible. Cletus lay looking at the preacher and the preacher lay looking at him, each smiling a Cheshire cat's grin, for about ten minutes. When he tired of the smiling game and the preacher's cock had retreated into the opening of his underpants, Cletus clicked on the television set.

The reverend suggested that Cletus move over to his bed for the duration of the movie Cletus had chosen; a "shoot-'em-up Western with Clint Eastwood as its star.

Cletus moved over to the reverend's bed, remote control still in his hand.

"You cold?" the preacher inquired.

"A bit."

"Why don't we cover up with this blanket? The reverend suggested, pulling out a synthetic wool blanket that had been at the foot of his bed.

Cletus didn't object as the reverend's hands "accidentally" groped his crotch while pulling up the covers. "Let's see that big thing," the reverend said, his hand already under Cletus' waistband.

By the time the second victim had bit the dust, the reverend had removed Cletus' underpants and was going down on his now-throbbing cock. He never said a word. And neither did Cletus.

When it was over and Cletus had been relieved of his load, the reverend said, "now we gotta' pray for forgiveness for the sin we just committed. He got down on his knees still covered in the blue blanket. After the prayer, the reverend read the entire book of Second Corinthians from the Gideon's Bible, dressed, turned off the television set, and took Cletus to breakfast at the nearby Waffle House restaurant.

They followed the same routine the next morning. First they had sex, and then they prayed for forgiveness, the reverend read a long passage or two from the Bible, and then the reverend blew him again before breakfast, lunch, or dinner. The Bible-reading took the longest, about an hour each time, but the sex was quick, only about fifteen minutes each time. Cletus was always horny, if nothing else.

Cletus got very little sleep that first week but between "sin sessions," as the reverend called them, he found out that the reverend had been in the Poinsett-Oxford-Tupelo area searching for his long-lost brother.

"I know a lot of people in Poinsett County but I never heard of nobody named Hinkle," Cletus offered. Maybe he's over in Tishomingo County."

The reverend said he had given up the search and that he was now headed to south Louisiana to start a new church.

"I hear they're heathens down there," he told the boy. "Where you headed?" Cletus said he had some business to settle in Memphis, selling off the few things he had lifted from Vacarro's safe, and then he would head for west Texas to look for his brothers. That they both had planned to search for their estranged brothers had united them in a strange kind of bond.

They talked about their lives. Both lied a great deal about their true origins. Cletus failed to mention that he had poisoned his mother, raped his brother, had sex with his father, and shaken Mary Grace Kirkwood until her brain was mush. Nor did he mention how he had tempted the older Mary Grace to fellate him by offering her molasses or shiny coins, among other things.

The reverend told the boy that he had been born and raised on a tobacco farm near Mt. Airy, North Carolina, where the great evangelist, Billy Curry, lived.

Billy Curry was the spiritual advisor to four presidents and preached in a huge church made almost entirely of glass. "That's what I want one day," Hinkle admitted. He also said Billy Curry had preached to thousands all over the world in person and over the TV. He had founded Curry College near Mt.

Airy as well as Billy Curry Academy, a private high school, where parents of spoiled rich kids paid beaucoup bucks for Curry to straighten them out.

He said he had attended Rev. Curry's church as a child and accepted Jesus Christ as his Lord and Savior at one of Rev. Curry's big tent revivals but he had later switched to a smaller, even more conservative congregation. He also said he had been severely tempted by both God and the devil and that he had always failed the tests.

For many years, Hinkle said he was conflicted. His cock just didn't get hard for a woman. He prayed over it, asking God why this was so and why he had been called to the ministry with this impediment in front of him to block his way.

"You know what the Lord said?" Hinkle asked.

Cletus, now drained and dropping off to sleep, shook his head.

"The Lord told me in a voice plain as day, *'To tempt you, my son. I was also tempted thusly.'* I wasn't sure what that meant so I wrote to Rev. Curry and bared my soul to him. I told him all about the spiritual struggle I was having," he said.

Cletus now sat in rapt attention. "What happened?" the boy wanted to know.

"Rev. Curry sent me bus fare to visit him. When I got there, he took me into his big study where we discussed my letter. We talked about two hours. I think he really only wanted to be sure he wasn't bein' set up. Finally, he told me, 'give the devil his due.'

"I wanted *everything* Billy Curry had. I wanted to *be* Billy Curry.

"I later married Billy Curry's only daughter, Althea, but they call her Cherry.

"Rev. Curry didn't like it one bit but he performed the wedding himself.

"My wife's name is Althea Curry Hinkle'. Rev. Billy Curry is my father-in-law."

What the reverend failed to mention was that he had been defrocked after he was trapped in a very compromising position during a police sting at a well-known male cruising area near Curb City, North Carolina, a hop, skip, and a jump from the Rev. Curry's mountain lair.

Had he not skimmed off the top of the collection plates during the years he was Billy Curry's deacon, he would have been tossed out into the world penniless as the day he entered it.

As a minister of an independent church, he had no one to whom he had to report and any collection monies he received were all his. Hinkle was nobody's fool. He knew that although people *say* they want to love their neighbor, in reality, no one wants to love everybody and if he wanted to get ahead in the religion game, he would have to establish an object of hatred to rail against.

His idea was to move to Catholic south Louisiana, where no one had heard of him or the scandal that ensued after the police raid, and preach to the oilfield workers, who were far from home, lonely, and thought like he did.

He knew that the best way to rally support and a congregation was to give them something or someone to hate. He would rail against niggers, queers, the Pope, whom he called The Great Satan, and Satan's Church, the Roman Catholic Church. Those four targets were sure to attract members to his church.

Cletus and the Right Reverend Hinkle stayed together three days, fucking, praying, and reading the Bible; then they parted.

"If it don't work out in Texas, look me up in Skylarville, Louisiana. That's alligator country, boy. I'll be there. You're welcome to hook up with me," the reverend told him. "I can use a fine, strong boy like you to fill my nights." He gave Cletus five hundred dollars and bid him farewell.

Cletus remained in Memphis another week selling off the baubles he had managed to grab from Dann Vacarro's hoard. Before he left, he had one more job to do. Two more jewels to collect.

Three days after he had seen the Rev. Hinkle off, he returned to Dann Vacarro's home on a Tuesday, the day Vacarro met his friend Hilary for lunch in Memphis. He never missed.

Cletus set out early, hoping to get a ride with someone going to work in the Memphis suburbs or with a trucker looking for a little early morning delight.

He stood on the side of the road looking like a young traveler, carrying his backpack to reinforce that image. Within ten minutes, he was in an eastbound semi with a hairy old trucker who said his name was Fitch.

Fitch made it clear what he wanted so when they stopped at the first rest stop they came to, Cletus made an fifty more dollars and continued on toward Vacarro's luxurious mansion.

He jumped down from the cab of Fitch's semi a half mile beyond the gates of Vacarro's private, gated community. He walked back to the compound, found his secret entrance into the compound, a culvert just wide enough to accommodate his body. He threw his backpack over the high stucco wall, where it landed between the wall and the perfectly manicured ligustrums that hid the culvert he used to come and go without the storm troopers' knowledge.

It was now 9:30 a.m. Most of the residents who still worked would already have left. Those whose leisure was a rousing game of golf would not have arrived. Vacarro would be getting out of the shower and primping for his luncheon date. His clothes would have been selected the night prior, and hung up in the larger of the two walk-in closets to "air out."

It would take him at least another hour to shave, manicure, and perfume himself to perfection.

Cletus had all the time in the world. He lay down under the ligustrums, using his backpack as a pillow, and studied both the heavy, waxy leaves of the woody plant, and the shadow patterns caused by the rising sun as it began to appear out of the east. In a few minutes, drivers heading east, like Fitch, would be blinded by its radiance. In his hiding place, though, it would cause nothing more than interesting shadows on the stucco-covered brick wall.

From his vantage point, he could not see Vacarro's house but he would definitely see Vacarro as he floated by in his land yacht, completely unaware that Norbert Cletus Eckland, Jr. was back and that he was there to acquire the two jewels he wanted above all others.

Like clockwork, Vacarro passed by in his Cadillac Sedan de Ville at 10:45. There were many white Cadillac Sedans de Ville in the neighborhood but Cletus knew Vacarro's because only Dann Vacarro's Sedan de Ville carried a sticker on the driver's side bumper that said, *"I (heart) White Trash"* with a picture of the top of a garbage can leaning inward toward the caption and a crumpled-up white garbage bag being thrown in by a white female's manicured hand.

Cletus hated that sticker and had sworn he would eventually peel it off but the opportunity never arose. Cletus knew that Vacarro had had the sticker and ninety-nine others printed up especially to irk him. Vacarro constantly called him white trash and constantly berated poor whites as being the "sorriest bastards on this planet." He always said if a white man couldn't make it in the United States, where every playing field was tilted in his favor, he should be put in an oven like the Nazis did with the Jews of Europe and they should be destroyed.

To emphasize his belief, he had the bumper stickers printed and distributed to about thirty of them to his friends, saying that 'white trash' were only good for one thing: sex. He kept the rest of the stickers in his file cabinet as replacements in case the original one were ever removed by someone offended by its presence.

When the Caddy's tail lights rounded the gentle curve that led to the guard house and gates at the exit to the subdivision, Cletus retrieved the house key from his backpack and put his plan into action, taking off, at a fast jog, across the golf course toward the rear of Vacarro's home.

Vacarro never armed the house's alarm system because Princess Margaret always found ways to set it off. He said he paid the community's hefty homeowner's association fees for personal protection so there was really no need for such a noisy alarm system, anyway.

Cletus arrived at the home's "servants' entrance" behind the garage in no time, dodging the logy alligators near the pond, still trying to revv up their internal engines by soaking up as many of the sun's rays as they could.

He inserted the key into the door's fancy lock, hoping that Vacarro had not decided to arm the home's internal burglary alarm. He slowly turned the knob and pushed open the door a tiny bit. *So far, so good.* He opened the door a half inch or so, knowing that if the alarm had not sounded by that point, it would not, and he had the run of the place for at least four hours.

He bounded up the short flight of stairs from the mud room and entered the kitchen through a Dutch door near where Princess Margaret's stainless steel food and water dishes gleamed in the early morning sun.

Princess looked up from her food and waited curiously at the seldom-used Dutch door. Cletus picked up a box of dry cat food and rattled its contents, her signal that she was about to receive a treat. She immediately recognized him and ran toward him, remembering him as the only one in the household who had showed her even a modicum of attention.

From a set of kitchen knives of various sizes set into an oak wood block on the granite countertop, he chose a large butcher knife, laid it on the counter beside the sink. From a nearby drawer, he took a melon baller and laid it next to the knife. He rattled the box of dry cat food once again. When Princess Margaret arrived at the spot where he was standing, he bent toward her, extending a treat and whispering sweet words to her. Her sweet lover had returned.

Princess Margaret preened and rubbed her cobby body against his legs and purred a loud song of happiness at their reunion. Her raspy pink tongue licked his hand. Cletus loved the feel of feline tongues against his skin but he feared them. He took her into the family room and sat in a leather lounge chair petting her and feeding her kibble treats.

Cletus fed her the treats and kisses as she purred so loudly she drowned out the ticking of the tall grandfather clock near the entryway. When he had no more treats to give her, she licked his hand, whether out of greed or gratitude, Cletus did not know. He loved the feeling and it was soon transferred to his groin.

The time had come. Cletus removed his shoes, socks, and clothing, exhibiting a prodigious erection, as always, when cats licked his hands. He then gave Princess Margaret a last kiss and, held her over the sink with his left hand. With his right, he took up the butcher knife and swiftly slit her throat. Blood squirted in all directions as the cat, still alive but mortally wounded, attempted to claw at him with the non-existent front claws Dann Vacarro had had removed so many years prior.

The final treat she had swallowed flew through the new opening in her throat and fell, bloody, onto the countertop.

Cletus worked fast. He pulled a meat cleaver from the wood block that housed the knife set and chopped off Princess Margaret's head just below the scruff of her neck, by which he held her. He felt the last beat of her heart and her last breath as the blood, which had pulsed out of her now lifeless body, oozed into the hand-hammered copper farm sink.

Although Cletus dearly loved the feline, he felt no remorse in having taken her life. He reckoned that she was better off dead than living unloved in Dann Vacarro's mausoleum. Besides, he had come back to get something and he had no plan to leave without the treasure he sought, her eyes.

The sapphire and the sunshine marbles he had admired for so long would now be his to add to his long-abandoned collection. Cletus dropped the cat's body onto the kitchen's marble-tiled floor, picked up the melon baller, and scooped out Princess Margaret's eyes, first the topaz, then the sapphire, and dropped them into a special concoction he had made to preserve them.

Since he did not have access to formaldehyde, he had concocted a potion of equal parts white rum and rubbing alcohol, and sealed them each in its own little glass bottle.

He washed the blood from his hands, walked back into the family room where his clothes were neatly folded on the couch, and dropped the bottles into the front pockets of his jeans; then headed for the master bedroom with the cat's eyeless head and her jeweled collar in tow, dripping blood to mark the path.

Cletus opened the wide double doors and headed first for the bed, where he made a nest of the two sham pillows and reverently set Princess Margaret's head, now a bloody mess, in the middle of it, facing the entryway. He placed her collar next to the severed head and let out an unearthly laugh as he ejaculated over both and Dann Vacarro's precious sham pillows.

He then returned to the large closet, hoping Vacarro had not changed that combination but the safe's door would not budge when he tried the old combination. He had not expected Vacarro to be so negligent but he thought he had to give it a try.

When Cletus returned to the kitchen now fully clothed, he washed the blood from the melon baller, the sink, countertop, and floor, and then wiped away any fingerprints from the knives and any surfaces he may have touched: doorknobs, etc. He left the house the same way he had entered.

When he got to the pond, he tossed the alligators their own treat, the rest of Princess Margaret's lifeless body.

He returned to his ligustrum sanctuary where he retrieved his backpack, threw it across the wall, and slid out from under the wall of his own special exit.

*** To be continued in Skin Deeper – Vol. 2, the back stories ***

CPSIA information can be obtained
at www.ICGtesting.com
Printed in the USA
JSHW060727211222
35249JS00001B/9

9 781664 130517